MORE PRAISE FOR THE SENSATIONAL
NOVELS OF JO GOODMAN

ALWAYS IN MY DREAMS

"Jo Goodman keeps you turning the pages. Her delightful sense of humor, pacing and scintillating knack for mystery combine for one great read!"

—*Romantic Times*

"A delightful reading experience. This book is lovely . . . very highly recommended."

—*The Midwest Book Review*

FOREVER IN MY HEART
(winner of the 1994 National Readers' Choice Award)

"Put this historical on your summer reading list—it is great!"
—*Rendezvous*

"Jo Goodman tells a warm, enjoyable and highly satisfying story."

—*Romantic Times*

ROGUE'S MISTRESS

"The spicy passion and the added humor enhance the excellent storyline."

—*Rendezvous*

WITH ALL HER HEART

"Will you look at me, Miss Shaw?" Grey's fingertips touched her chin. With no real urging on his part, she turned to face him.

"You may call me Berkeley," she said, raising her eyes to his. "I don't mind."

"I thought some formality was in order now. I'm trying very hard not to take advantage of you."

"I don't mind."

Grey blinked, not certain he'd heard her correctly. "Perhaps you don't know what I mean when I say 'take advantage of.' "

"I think I do."

He merely stared at her, and this time she did not look away. "Yes," she whispered, as his head lowered toward her. "Yes."

Grey's mouth came down on hers. Her lips were soft, pliant. They moved under his tentatively at first, then more eagerly. Her hands lay flat on his chest. Her fingers slowly curved in the fabric of his shirt, and she raised herself up a little, pulling herself closer to him. Their mouths parted briefly, and it was Berkeley who strained forward to press her lips to his.

Grey's hands slid around her waist. He held her against him, his fingers threaded at the small of her back. Their slow descent to the bed started with an almost infinitesimal shift in weight and balance. Berkeley's fingers eased around Grey's shoulders as she was lowered under him.

The kiss deepened. Grey swept her mouth, teasing again, tasting. Her response was no mere imitation of what was done to her, but somehow richer. She seduced where he teased, savored where he tasted. She drew him in more deeply and made what was an entirely new experience for her exactly the same for him.

Grey broke the kiss, his breathing ragged. He cupped Berkeley's face and searched her features. Light from the room's single lamp flickered across her skin as he raised himself higher. Her eyes were wide, her lips faintly bruised and damp. "You *know* where this is going, don't you?"

Berkeley was held too tightly simply to nod her answer. She had to say it aloud. "Yes," she whispered. "I know." *I've always known . . .*

Books by Jo Goodman

THE CAPTAIN'S LADY
(previously published as PASSION'S BRIDE)
CRYSTAL PASSION
SEASWEPT ABANDON
VELVET NIGHT
VIOLET FIRE
SCARLET LIES
TEMPTING TORMENT
MIDNIGHT PRINCESS
PASSION'S SWEET REVENGE
SWEET FIRE
WILD SWEET ECSTASY
ROGUE'S MISTRESS
FOREVER IN MY HEART
ALWAYS IN MY DREAMS
ONLY IN MY ARMS
MY STEADFAST HEART
MY RECKLESS HEART
WITH ALL MY HEART

Published by Zebra Books

WITH ALL MY HEART

Jo Goodman

ZEBRA BOOKS

Kensington Publishing Corp.
P.O. Box Jackson Heights
New York, NY 10022

ISBN 0-8217-6145-8

Zebra Books
Kensington Publishing Corp.

http://www.zebrabooks.com

ZEBRA BOOKS are published by

Kensington Publishing Corp.
850 Third Avenue
New York, NY 10022

First Printing: April, 1999
10 9 8 7 6 5 4 3 2 1

Printed in the United States of America

This one's for some very special people
And some of them may not even know why.
Tough, I'm thanking them anyway.

Barb Jones, Sandi Heck, Becky and Margie,
That dear, dear woman Linda Meiseles,
Maggie on the bulletin board,
Detra and Rita and Cherrie,
eRobin (not a misspelling),
Carla and Elena and Lynsey,
Gina Marie and Teresa Phillips.

Prologue

Charleston, April 1845

"I didn't think you'd come."

Garret Denison looked at his brother a long time before deciding to join him. "I had to see for myself that you'd really be here. I still don't believe it."

Graham shrugged. He nudged out the chair beside him with the toe of one dusty boot. "Sit," he ordered quietly. "You're calling attention to us."

A brief ironic laugh came from Garret as he took the chair and sat. "Drink?" He eyed the thin film of dust covering his brother's clothes. Graham's usual careful attention to tailoring was not in evidence tonight. His jacket was rumpled, and the cuff of the right sleeve was frayed. Silver threads in his vest were snagged. From what Garret could see of the trousers, they hung loosely around Graham's waist and thighs. His brother had definitely fallen on hard times. These clothes didn't appear as if they were made for him. "You look as if you could use one," Garret suggested in a soft, pleasant drawl.

"Bourbon."

Garret held up his hand and caught the attention of the woman who was wending her way between the benches and tables and groping hands of the regulars. "Bourbon," he said. "Two." Except for a brief nod she barely acknowledged his order. She was slapping at the meaty fist that had caught the hem of her skirt. Garret watched a moment, then turned his attention back to his brother. "Not your usual sort of place."

"It serves my purpose."

Garret felt the full force of his brother's flinty stare. God, but those blue-gray eyes of his were piercing. To be on the receiving end of that stare was to stand accused, even when no formal charge had been made. Garret didn't flinch. Censure from his older brother might have caused him to do so in the past, but tonight, with Graham so clearly out of his element, perhaps even out of his mind, Garret let the look pass without reacting. "Tell me about your purpose, Graham. I'll try to keep an open mind."

Graham considered that was unlikely. He caught the movement of the barmaid out of the corner of his eye and waited until the drinks arrived at their table before he began. He had chosen Gilpin's tavern in Charleston harbor because it was precisely the sort of place he'd made a practice of avoiding. He was unknown here. Even though his name and likeness had been front-page fodder for every large city newspaper these last three months, Gilpin's was a place not far from his own home where he could disappear with relative ease.

His ill-fitting clothing, the scuffed boots, the dark sable hair badly in need of cutting, lent him the safety of anonymity among the crowd that frequented Gilpin's. These men were not necessarily rough or threatening; they were by and large down on their luck and apathetic as only hopeless men can be. Graham did not expect trouble this evening. The odds were against him being recognized and even greater that anyone would be moved to do something about it.

Graham had taken some pains to shed his disreputable, slightly dangerous image. Studying Garret's choice of clothing, he wished his brother had been as thoughtful. "You might have made some attempt to fit in," he said.

Garret fingered his dark mustache, then smoothed the edges as he considered Graham's words. "I didn't know what this place was until I got here. Anyway, you're supposing I don't want to be noticed. Frankly, I wouldn't care if the entire patronage of this tavern recognized me and turned on you. If I've a mind to, or you give me cause, I'll stand up tonight and point the finger at you myself, Graham. You're a traitor. You've betrayed friends and family. You've betrayed the South." Garret picked up his drink. He held the glass up to the flickering lanternlight and examined it for fingerprints left by the previous tippler. Satisfied that it had been wiped off, if not washed, he raised it to his lips and took a large swallow.

Graham permitted himself a thin smile as he watched a flush wash over Garret's handsome features. It was a shame about the mustache. It hid the beads of perspiration that Graham suspected were dotting his brother's upper lip. Graham almost laughed outright when Garret raked back his dark hair with one perfectly manicured hand and attempted nonchalance. "Not the smooth stuff you're used to," Graham said softly.

"I don't see you drinking it."

Graham lifted his glass but not long enough to consider its cleanliness. He saluted Garret, his mouth curving in a vaguely twisted smile, his eyes ironic. "To your health and good fortune, little brother." Then he belted back most of the bourbon in a single swallow.

Garret laughed in genuine amusement as Graham made a small choking sound and his eyes actually watered. "Serves you right," he said.

Reaching into his jacket pocket, Graham pulled out a handkerchief and wiped his eyes. "Granddaddy makes better swill in that contraption he hides in the woods." He shoved the handkerchief out of sight again and finished his drink. "God," he said feelingly, looking around the poorly lighted tavern. "I hope I'm never so numb I don't know bad bourbon when I taste it." He raised his glass and motioned to the barmaid. He

raised one finger—looked at his brother, who expressed horror
at first, then took up the challenge—then raised two.

"As long as we know it'll kill us," Garret said, shrugging.
It didn't appear anyone else in the tavern was cognizant of that
fact. Poor bastards. Garret settled his lean frame comfortably
in the high-backed wooden chair, stretching his legs diagonally
under the table and folding his arms across his chest. It was
only as an afterthought that he noticed his posture was a mirror
image of Graham's.

Eleven months separated the birth of the brothers. Except
for that distinction it was often remarked they could have been
twins. They were of a similar height, both being an inch over
six feet. They shared the same richly colored hair with the
texture and sheen of sable and even darker brows and lashes.
Their features were well-defined with the kind of bone structure
that lent itself to sculpture during the Renaissance. The mustache that Garret had grown when he was away at school
was an obvious distinguishing feature now. There were other
differences though, some subtle, some not, that kept those of
close acquaintance from mistaking the brothers.

Graham's aristocratic features were not softened by his eyes
as Garret's were. Garret's eyes had but one hue, a deep oceanic
blue that drew notice like the inexorable pull of a tidal undertow.
Graham's flinty, blue-gray stare kept others at a distance, even
when his congenial manner, or rakish appeal beckoned them in.
Graham Denison cultivated acquaintances, not friends. Garret's
admirers *were* his friends.

"Did you tell anyone you were meeting me?" Graham asked.

Garret shook his head. "I kept it to myself," he said. "Not
because you asked me to, but because I didn't want to bring your
shame on me. Grandmother might have understood. Father,
perhaps, though I doubt it. But no one else, Graham. Granddaddy's disowned you. Mother, if she comes out of her room
at all, won't allow anyone to mention your name. You're dead
to them. What the hell did you think you were doing?"

Graham didn't answer immediately. "Alys?"

"You shouldn't bring her up, Graham. You're dead to her, too. You really don't have the right."

"She was my fiancée. I think that gives me some rights."

"In the past tense. We both know she broke off with you before this sad bit of business was ever brought to light. Alys is very happy with the choice she's made."

Graham's features gave no indication what he thought of that. "When's the wedding?"

"June." Garret offered a slight smile. "Mother says it's just what we need at Beau Rivage to put this other affair behind us."

"That would be me."

Garret nodded. "No one ever accused you of being slow off the mark." He took a short swallow of his drink and noticed that familiarity with the bourbon did not improve its taste. "I think you'd better get to the point of this meeting, unless you're trying to be caught out."

Graham shifted in his seat. He brushed a thin layer of dust from his jacket sleeve. It was the sort of fastidious, practiced gesture he would have made to remove an errant thread from a crisply pressed jacket. His manner would have affected boredom. That pretense didn't suit his dress or condition now. He smiled without humor. Old habits . . . "I have no desire to feel the rope around my neck," he said quietly. He eyed his brother. "That's what I could expect, isn't it? If I turned myself in?"

Garret's response was blunt. "If someone didn't shoot you on your way to the hangman. But you knew the risks when you decided to come back here. Why, Graham? Why leave Boston at all? Your exploits were lauded in the Northern papers. I cannot rightly remember all the names they called you. Liberator. Deliverer. Southern Savior. Rescuer of Black Slaves." He paused, his expression considering. "Always thought that last description a bit redundant. Black Slave. It's not really possible to be a white one, is it? We're not bred for it the way they are."

Graham did not respond. Garret was so obvious in his attempt to get a rise out of him that Graham could dismiss it. Not that

Garret didn't believe what he was saying. Graham knew he surely did. It was the predominant way of thinking at Beau Rivage, indeed throughout the slave states.

"And what is that name the freed slaves gave you?" He waited a moment for Graham to answer. When his brother remained unmoved by this overture, Garret filled in the silence. "Falconer. I believe that's the name I've read. Yes, I believe it is."

"You may be right," Graham said.

"I'm sure I am. Tell me, Graham. Bitsy. Henry. Old Jake. Evie. Little Winston." He named the slaves that came easily to his mind. He was sure there were others missing from Beau Rivage that could have been added. "Did you help them all out through the Underground?"

"Yes." He saw his brother's surprise and he guessed at the source of it immediately. "You didn't think I'd admit it, did you?"

"Your arrogance continues to exceed your intelligence," Garret said calmly.

"You've always underestimated me."

"Only your backbone, Graham. And maybe your commitment. I didn't think you cared about anything. Certainly you never showed family the same devotion you showed these slaves." With a certain amount of assurance, he added thoughtfully, "How you must hate all of us." He didn't pause long enough to give his brother a chance to confirm or deny it. "Of course the slaves you helped escape from Beau Rivage represent only a fraction of your work. If the papers can be believed, then you had a hand in the escapes of more than two hundred runaways—from all over the South."

"My exploits were exaggerated," Graham said, affecting modesty. "A hundred perhaps. One hundred fifty would be my highest estimate."

A muscle worked rhythmically in Garret's lean cheek. His blue eyes did not hold the same warmth for his brother that he extended to friends. "You think this is amusing, don't you? You're laughing at all of us at Beau Rivage."

"You're wrong, Garret. I don't expect you to believe me, but you're wrong."

With some effort Garret kept a leash on his temper. It wasn't as if Graham had won anything through his behavior, he reminded himself. Noble as his actions might be considered among Northern abolitionists and a few sympathizers in the South, he had alienated everyone else. In the Carolinas, and especially in Charleston, Graham's notoriety as Falconer, the most sought-after conductor on the Underground Railroad, made him a marked man.

Garret couldn't be completely sorry about what had come to pass, and he didn't insult them both by pretending. Graham had effectively removed himself from the position of heir to Beau Rivage. He had done it in a spectacular manner and had been far more successful with this single debacle than Garret had been with a dozen smaller, insistent attempts to oust him from the family business and fortunes.

Still, there was the matter of Denison family honor. Garret couldn't ignore that. "But you haven't come to apologize for the difficulty and embarrassment you've caused us," he said.

Graham knew his brother placed Alys among those he had hurt through his behavior. "No, I haven't. But I would like you to take a message to Grandmother." He saw Garret's lip curl slightly and realized there was almost no chance his brother would deliver the message. Graham said it anyway because it had to be said. For his own peace of mind, *he* had to say it. "Tell her I acted on my convictions," he said. "Like all the Denisons before me"—he eyed his younger brother pointedly—"or after."

"You dare," Garret said under his breath.

Without waiting for his brother to expound on his anger, Graham went on. "I wanted you to hear it from me that I don't have the earring."

Garret sat up now and leaned forward. He swore softly. "It's gone?"

"You mean you didn't know?"

"I don't believe this. Are you telling me you sold it? That's reprehensible, Graham, even for you."

"Actually I was going to tell you I lost it. Otherwise, I might have sold it. I'll need money eventually to stake myself somewhere."

"So you came for money from me?"

"No, I wasn't going to ask. But if you're offering . . ."

"Go to hell." Garret belted back his drink, glanced at Graham's empty glass and waved for two more.

Graham accepted the bourbon when it came but didn't raise his glass. He was aware that the last swallow hadn't settled very well in his stomach. He sported no mustache to hide the beads of perspiration on his upper lip, and he carried no razor to scrape the fuzz from his tongue. His eyes wandered slowly about the tavern. No other patrons seemed to be similarly affected by the spirits Gilpin passed off as bourbon. But then maybe, Graham reflected, their drinks were gin or watered whiskey. Removing his handkerchief, he touched it to his brow.

Garret didn't ask Graham if he was feeling all right. He didn't care. "I hope you puke all over yourself," he said in disgust. His brother was flushed and pale at the same time. Garret didn't wonder how that was possible. He cut to the core of his anger. "What the hell were you thinking, taking Mother's earring. You know damn well she prizes it. And she means it to be mine."

Graham stuffed the handkerchief under the cuff of his sleeve, where it would be readily available. "That's your point, isn't it? That I took something that belongs to you."

"Exactly. The family's had to tolerate your gambling and whoring and drinking—"

"Careful, Garret, you'll turn my head with your pretty compliments."

Garret offered only a look of disgust in reply. "You wasted a Harvard education."

"Do you mean to say they didn't teach you gambling, whoring, and drinking at William and Mary?" Graham asked blandly. He raised his glass and eyed his brother consideringly over the rim. "I'd say you're the one who hasn't made good use of his education."

Garret ignored the barb. "Now I can add thief to your list of pastimes."

"Thief? Because of the earring, you mean? Hardly, Garret. It was given to me."

That set Garret back. "I don't believe that for a moment. Mother would never—"

"Mother didn't. Grandmother did."

"She wouldn't. It wasn't hers to give."

Graham shrugged. He didn't care if he was believed or not. Garret could check his story easily enough and discover he was telling the truth. The earring in question belonged to their mother, just as Garret had pointed out. Its value to Evaline Randolph Denison was purely sentimental. She never wore the earring since the mate had been lost years ago. From time to time she spoke of having the pearl stud and dangling gold drop made into a pendant so she could wear it around her neck, but she never did anything about it. She seemed satisfied to keep the earring in her jewelry chest and take it out occasionally to admire. The earring and its lost twin had been fashioned exclusively for her sixteenth birthday and debut ball. The gold drop had been engraved in a delicate flourish with her initials. This was part of her attachment to the piece, knowing that it was one of a kind.

Evaline valued its uniqueness but the earring always invoked a misty-eyed reminiscence of the cotillion that was held in her honor. There was a certain intrinsic value in having this opportunity to remind them all how she had been sought after and fought over. Graham wondered if he would have heard the story so often if his mother hadn't lost the earring's mate that very first night they were presented to her. She would have worn them then and familiarity might have softened her memories. The fact that her parents, who had made a present of them to her, had died a short time later only added to the poignancy of the recollections.

Graham wiped his brow again, then the back of his neck.

"Grandmother thought I should have it." She had said it was time Evaline stopped dwelling on the past, but Graham didn't mention this. "I went to her for money, and the earring's what she gave me."

"But you didn't sell it."

"I didn't have the chance." Not that he would have anyway. *And damn her,* he thought not unkindly, *Grandmother had known that.* "Mother's going to have to be told. I'm surprised she hasn't missed it already."

"Mother's retired to her room this last month. Perhaps she has missed it." He regarded Graham frankly. "Or perhaps she can't bear what's become of her son."

Graham shook his head. "Mother takes to her room if her egg is overcooked. I won't accept that I'm the cause."

"Nothing unusual in that." He sipped his bourbon and noticed that Graham was no longer nursing his. "Drink up. I don't know why you're looking out of sorts. Seems to me that you're devil-may-care now, and I'm left to make your apologies."

"I suppose you should be used to it." Graham thought the words didn't sound quite right. He heard them as if he were standing in a tunnel.

"Are you all right?" Garret asked. He removed Graham's drink out of his reach. "I think you've had enough." He grinned. "Who would have thought I could drink you under the table?"

"Perhaps they taught you something at William and Mary after all." Graham's own grin was decidedly lopsided. He was quite pleased that he had gotten the sentence out. It was a bonus that it made sense. He squinted and made a study of his brother's features. Three bourbons had not noticeably affected Garret.

"There's ... one ... other ... thing," Graham said with great effort. He looked around the tavern to see if anyone was taking an interest in his conversation. In the time he had been at the table with Garret a few men had come and gone, but the majority of the crowd was unchanged. A pair of bull-necked men stood at one end of the bar trading stories and buying each other drinks. The trio at the table in the corner were still playing cards. They only looked up when they needed to catch the barmaid's eye. A few men sat alone, but they were the exception. Gilpin's was a place for camaraderie. There was a boisterous shout followed by some hearty laughter. Someone called to Gilpin himself to settle a wager.

Graham's head swiveled around, and his eyes returned to Garret. His brother was watching him closely. Was he waiting for him to say something? Graham wondered. *Had* he been saying something?

"You said there was one more thing," Garret prompted.

Now Graham remembered. "That's right." The two words came out as one. "One more thing." Graham's drawl was more evident now. "I figure I was betrayed on my last run on the Railroad. Shot at, too. Almost killed. You wouldn't know anythin' about that, would you?"

"I do believe you're making an accusation."

Graham's head throbbed when he nodded. His vision was blurry now; his limbs felt weighted. Every minute that passed brought on some aching awareness to a new part of his body. "Believe I am," he said softly.

"Tell me where you lost the earring, Graham."

The change in subject was difficult for Graham to follow. "Don't know ex . . . eggsact . . . Don't know."

"You must have some idea."

"Boston, I reckon." He could hardly hold his head up now. His shoulders slumped.

Garret swore softly as Graham's head thumped on the table. "Boston," he said in disgust. "I'll be sure to tell Mother you lost her earring to the Yankees." Grasping a handful of Graham's thick hair, Garret lifted his brother's head a few inches off the table. He was out cold. He let go and Graham's forehead thumped hard again. Garret raised his hand and motioned to the trio of card players in the corner. They tossed down their cards and joined him immediately.

"Get him out of here," Garret said quietly. There was no chance that he would be overheard. No one, save for the men who were waiting for his signal, were particularly concerned with anything they witnessed. Graham Denison certainly wasn't the first patron at Gilpin's to slide into a stupor. The only question in the mind of some of the regulars was if Graham had passed out before his head hit the table or if the blow knocked him out. It might have been worth a wager if they thought Graham was going to be around to set the matter straight.

Garret indicated to the men that they should get moving. "We'll settle outside. I want your assurances he's not coming back to Charleston." He looked at each man squarely. "Ever."

He came awake with a start. Sitting up reminded him how much pain he was in. He lay down again and closed one eye. Someone had already managed to close the other one for him. He explored the swelling gingerly. Even the lightest pressure from his fingertips made him groan.

He let his hand fall back to his side and flexed his fingers. They didn't feel bruised or broken. Hadn't he put up a fight at all? Then he wondered who he would have fought. Names and faces eluded him now.

Taking inventory of other body parts revealed a rather extensive list of injuries. In addition to the swollen right eye there was a lump on his forehead, dried blood under a possibly broken nose, a split lower lip, and ringing in his ears. And he had found all that before he got as far as his neck. Below his Adam's apple he discovered he had two ribs that were bruised or cracked, a dislocated collarbone, and swollen testicles.

Whoever it had been had worked him over good. The why of it wouldn't come to him.

He considered his legs next. They were sore but had largely been spared. His left thigh had received a few kicks, probably misplaced, he decided, when his attacker had aimed for his groin, but other than that he believed he could walk unaided. Where he might go was an unknown to him.

He applied himself to the problem of where he was. There

were voices, footsteps, overhead. He was lying on the floor, but there were hammocks strung up in the room. They swayed as if a breeze were circulating around the four walls. There was no breeze, though. The air was close, stifling. The hammocks continued to swing.

It was natural, he supposed, that he hadn't noticed the room was rocking at the outset. It wasn't that he had been entirely unaware of it, but that he had misunderstood the cause. From the very first roll he had assumed there was a problem with his balance, something connected to the ringing in his ears. Now, as he watched the hammocks continue to swing, he realized there was too much rhythm in the motion. The room and its contents weren't spinning, merely swaying.

He was on board a ship. He couldn't imagine where.

With body parts accounted for and his immediate surroundings identified, he put himself to the task of making some sense of it all.

That was when he realized he didn't know his name.

Chapter One

Boston, May 1850

"This is cold." Berkeley Shaw's fingers unfolded almost convulsively. She felt as if she were shivering, yet except for the involuntary movement of her hand, she was entirely still. "I don't see how I can help you." Then, to be perfectly clear, she added softly, "Any of you." She was conscious of being the center of attention, of the five pairs of eyes leveled on her slightly bowed head. With some effort she raised her chin and allowed her glance to sweep the gathering before coming to rest on the only familiar face. She said nothing, but her eyes pleaded.

Anderson Shaw was immediately sympathetic. He supported the underside of his wife's extended hand in his own before he removed the object lying in the heart of her open palm.

The first thing he noticed was that it was not cold at all. One dark brow rose faintly in Berkeley's direction. For the space of a heartbeat solicitousness was replaced by censure. His disappointment in her effort went unnoticed by the others, but he knew Berkeley would register it as a tangible force. Even as he thought it, she swayed ever so slightly on her feet. For now it satisfied him.

Anderson let his eyes fall deliberately on the earring he now held and examined it in detail. It was as exquisite as he had been led to believe. A lustrous pearl stud was set in a golden crown. A raindrop of pure gold, delicately engraved with the letters ER, dangled from the stud. He knew he held a fortune in his palm. What he didn't know was if it was priceless.

"ER?" he asked as he returned the earring to its owner.

Decker Thorne's fingers folded over the earring. He placed it in his vest pocket without looking at it. A moment later his hand raked his thick, dark hair, and his attention shifted slowly, with a measure of real reluctance, from Berkeley Shaw to her husband. "Elizabeth Regina," he explained.

Anderson whistled softly, appreciatively. "That would make this . . ." He paused, searching his memory for the years in which Elizabeth ruled England. "What? Two hundred? Three hundred years old?"

"A little more than three hundred," Decker confirmed. His watchful blue eyes settled on Mrs. Shaw again and he waited to see if she would respond. There was no disappointment when Berkeley remained silent. It was exactly what he expected. He glanced sideways at his wife, and his expression spoke eloquently: *I told you so.*

Jonna Remington Thorne pretended not to notice. It was not in her nature to give in so easily, least of all to her husband when he was looking vaguely superior. Decker had taken the less difficult approach to this interview with Anderson and Berkeley Shaw. He had been cynical from the moment she had suggested it. She was the one who had held out some hope and who risked the most keenly felt disappointment.

No, she amended, that wasn't entirely true. Her gaze strayed to her sister-in-law. Mercedes Thorne had reached out to lay her hand over her husband's forearm, comforting Colin and in turn, being comforted. Jonna knew Mercedes had risked hoping as well. Colin, like Decker, had steeled himself against it. Perhaps it *was* time to give up.

The problem was, she wasn't certain how one went about surrendering. She had been the head of the Remington Shipping empire since she was fifteen. She was thirty now. The second half of her life had been devoted to running the Remington line, the first half to learning how. It was not an exaggeration to say that none of it could have come about without Colin and Decker Thorne. Colin had saved her life when she was a babe in arms. Years later Decker had saved her heart.

"Perhaps if you held it again, Mrs. Shaw," Jonna said. "You hardly gave yourself any time at all with it."

Berkeley shook her head. She wished herself anywhere but where she was. In any circumstances she would have been intimidated by her surroundings. In these circumstances, with so much pressure to perform in exactly the right manner, she was very nearly paralyzed.

It was not that anyone had been unkind to her. Quite the contrary. Jonna Thorne had received her graciously into the Beacon Hill home, showing her and Anderson into the large formal parlor herself. She made the introductions smoothly and warmly, though for Berkeley the moments passed in something of a blur. She remembered the nod in her direction from Jonna's husband. The man seemed to stand lightly on his feet, as if he were not weighted by the literal and figurative gravity of this meeting. He had a quietly amused expression that was both disarming and distancing. When he took her hand Berkeley understood the look in his eyes immediately. She had faced it, felt it, before. He was not judging her; he had already made up his mind.

Still, Decker Thorne was marginally less intimidating than his brother. It was outside Berkeley Shaw's experience to make the acquaintance of an earl. Jonna had introduced her brother-in-law as Lord Fielding, the Earl of Rosefield. Berkeley had not missed Jonna's sly, secretive smile as she performed the introduction, as if his title and lofty position were something of an amusement to her. It did not amuse Berkeley. She made what she thought was an adequate, if not particularly graceful, curtsy, and managed to murmur a greeting. Anderson would

take her to task later for her backwardness. Hadn't they practiced these social niceties for just this occasion? It didn't matter.
Berkeley was not prepared for the opaque, nearly black eyes
that seared her with a single glance. When the corners of His
Lordship's mouth lifted, only an edge of a smile was produced.
Colin Thorne extended Berkeley the same skeptical consideration as his brother.

The Countess of Rosefield, even with her beautifully solemn
gray eyes and grave smile, was infinitely more welcoming and
warm than her husband. But then an iceberg would have also
met those conditions, Berkeley thought. In fairness to Mercedes
Thorne, Berkeley acknowledged that the countess was permitting herself to hope in a way that her husband was not. Her
judgment was not fixed yet, but held in reserve.

Mercedes added her urging to Jonna's request. "Yes, Mrs.
Shaw. Won't you hold the earring once more? I've heard this
sort of thing is not always accomplished so quickly."

"Where have you heard that?" Colin asked. He added a
shade mockingly, "Gypsies?"

Another woman might have blushed at Colin's tone. That
he thought such an idea was foolish was clearly implied by it.
No color washed Mercedes's cheeks. Predictably it was her
chin that came up and she stared back at her husband fearlessly.
"Yes, as a matter of fact, that is precisely where I heard it. I
consulted a fortune-teller at the Weybourne fair."

"Can I assume you had the good sense to leave our children
outside the Gypsy's tent?"

"And risk that they would wander away while I was occupied? Certainly not. The girls were quite old enough not to be
afraid and Nicholas was entranced."

Colin's dark eyes were raised heavenward a moment. "Dear
God," he said under his breath. "Why am I hearing this for
the first time now?"

"Because of the way you're reacting, I suspect," she said
in crisp accents. "I can't say that I like you thinking I behaved
foolishly. As for why the children never mentioned it, I imagine
their silence is the truest measure of how little they were affected

by their encounter. I never suggested it should be a secret. They saw and heard dozens of things at the fair, and I recall they regaled you for hours about most of them. Some of them twice.''

Colin was slightly mollified by this. He remembered their stories well enough. Still, it was peculiar that Elizabeth or Emma hadn't mentioned a fortune-teller. Perhaps they had known as well as their mother how he would view that escapade. Nicholas, though, he would talk to. In the future, on matters of Gypsies and fortune-telling, he would have an ally in his five-year-old son.

Not certain that she had made her point, Mercedes went on. ''It really was most innocent, Colin. The opportunity presented itself shortly after Jonna had written us about the Shaws. I thought: *What could be the harm?* So I asked the Gypsy if the kind of thing Jonna had written about was possible. And she assured me it was. The handling of objects to gain some knowledge about the history of them is an acceptable practice.''

''Acceptable to whom?'' Colin said. ''Of course the Gypsy would say that. She probably would have loved to get her hands on the earrings. Thank God Decker was in possession of both of them. We'd surely be missing at least one now, and a roving band of Gypsies would be the richer for it.''

Although Mercedes did not require Jonna's defense, she was compelled to offer one anyway. ''I'm certain you're making too much of it, Colin. Mercedes would not have offered the earring to be handled by just anyone. Why this Gypsy might not have had a talent for handling at all. She was a fortune-teller. That was her gift.''

''Jonna,'' Decker said dryly, ''you don't believe in fortune-tellers.''

''Well, no, I don't. But I don't know that Mercedes doesn't, and it seems to me that she shouldn't be taken to task for making inquiries that serve both her husband *and* you.''

Decker had an urge to roll his eyes now. He looked at Colin instead. ''Jonna's right,'' he said. ''If anyone's to be taken to task, she is. This bit of nonsense today was her idea. I've mostly kept silent about it because I know it's partly responsible for you being here now. I can't regret my wife's interference when it prompts you and Mercedes to visit us almost six months earlier than you had planned. Still, I think we could have done without this little drama today.''

Anderson Shaw had had enough. He saw that both Jonna and Mercedes were prepared to take offense, but he had no care for their feelings now. It was Berkeley who required his protection. She was not watching the Thornes as they sparred, but Anderson knew she was alert to every word. The fey look in her large green eyes gave her an otherworldly expression, but her mind was fixed in the moment. He watched her head bow slightly. Tendrils of pale hair brushed her cheek. The back of her long, slender neck was exposed. He took a step closer to his wife and placed one hand at the small of her back.

Berkeley looked up, startled, and found herself staring directly into Colin Thorne's dark, implacable eyes. She willed herself not to tremble. He would think she was afraid of him, and that wasn't it at all. The man with his hand at her back frightened her much more than the Right Honorable Earl of Rosefield ever could.

At thirty-nine, Anderson Shaw was one year older than Colin Thorne and five years older than Decker. Any advantage he had in age was negligible. These men he faced were used to command and did not extend respect merely as a courtesy but rather because it was earned. Anderson knew he had given them no reason to extend it to him. Yet. Even though he understood the women were a more sympathetic audience, he was careful not to look away from the brothers as he spoke.

''I cannot think that you intentionally mean to insult my wife,'' he said. He spoke in clear, deliberately modulated tones. The rhythm of his speech was even, and there was no accent to immediately identify him with any particular part of the country. His manner was formal and learned and perfectly suited to his distinguished carriage and solemn air. ''Men with less breeding than you would not invite us into their home, then proceed to make disparaging remarks about Mrs. Shaw's gift. She did not go in search of this invitation. Indeed, it was

Mrs. Thorne who found us, and I had to apply myself quite diligently to convincing my wife that coming here was a proper thing to do. This is a trying experience for her, not at all pleasant, and far from attempting to take away any part of your considerable fortunes with empty promises, she has stated quite clearly that she doesn't believe she can help you. I'm sure the countess paid her Gypsy fortune-teller and received no better consultation than that. We, on the other hand, have traveled from Baltimore, at some expense to ourselves, and have not asked for anything."

Anderson Shaw generally thought himself a tall man. Now, drawing himself up to his full height, he still had to raise his head a notch to stare down Colin and Decker Thorne. His left hand continued to rest at his wife's back, and when he spared a glance for her his eyes were warm and admiring. Without speaking directly to her he conveyed his support.

No one observed the knuckle digging hard into her spine.

It did not take a preternatural gift to see that Jonna and Mercedes were mortified. Any rudeness on their part had been strictly unintentional, but they could not say the same for their husbands. It was clear they thought some apology was in order. The only question was who would be first off the mark to make it.

Decker, his faint smile deepening as Jonna glared at him, snapped to attention first. "I regret offending you, Mrs. Shaw. I assure you I meant to upbraid my wife. It seems I cannot do that without casting doubt on what she refers to as your gift." He looked at Colin then, daring him to make a better show of contrition than he had.

Lord Fielding didn't even try. "Likewise," he said dryly.

It was not so much the knuckle pressing her spine that prompted Berkeley to speak up, but the fact that Mercedes looked as if she might simply clobber His Lordship in front of them. "Perhaps it would not hurt to try again," she said softly. "I think I understand now how much it means to all of you."

She couldn't know that, Colin thought. This young woman, in spite of her otherworldly charm, elfin beauty, and fathomless green eyes, couldn't possibly know what it meant to any of them, least of all him. Yet Colin acknowledged that neither he nor Decker was usually so lacking in good manners as they had been today. It was some indication of the intense emotion they shared, a measure of the desperation they felt. Is that what Berkeley Shaw sensed? When even their wives thought he and Decker had abandoned hope, had this woman realized it was only that they were terrified to risk it again?

Berkeley Shaw held out her hand, palm up. She did not withdraw it when Decker hesitated but waited with such a patient air that no one in the room doubted she could remain in that exact pose for hours. Decker looked to Colin and glimpsed the almost imperceptible nod that was lost on the others. He reached in his vest pocket, removed the earring, and placed it carefully across Berkeley's palm.

She reacted immediately. Her fingers, which had only started to close around the earring, unfolded spasmodically and remained extended and splayed. "Not this one," she said, looking between Decker and Colin. "This is the one you made to test me, to see if I would know the difference between an heirloom and a copy. I told you, this is cold. I can tell you nothing of your missing brother from this piece."

Decker's quietly amused expression vanished. It was a rare moment for the others to see him unsettled. His lapse, however brief, was proof enough for Jonna that Berkeley Shaw had spoken the truth. Her disappointment was palpable. "Oh, Decker," she said quietly. "You did, didn't you?"

"Not exactly," he said.

"But—"

Colin interrupted. "I had the copy made in England before Mercedes and I left. She is only finding out about it now. I told Decker what I had done when we arrived. No one else knew." He didn't add that he understood Jonna and Mercedes would not have approved. That point was made tacitly by his secretiveness on the matter. Colin's attention was drawn to Berkeley again, and his dark eyes narrowed as he regarded her steadily. "No one could have known," he said finally. And now there was a thread of hope in his voice.

Sunlight glinted off the gold drop dangling from Berkeley's fingertips. It drew Jonna's eyes. "May I?" she asked.

"I have no need of it," Berkeley said. She let the earring fall into Jonna's open palm and watched her study it.

"It's remarkable," Jonna whispered, awed. All the more remarkable because Colin had commissioned the copy from memory. It was Decker who was in possession of both earrings. "This is quite perfect. I shouldn't be able to tell the difference. How can you?" She gave over the earring to Mercedes, who regarded it with the same eye for detail.

Mercedes looked up at her husband. "Well, Colin? How do you know this is the copy and that you haven't confused it with one of the originals?"

When Colin didn't answer immediately it was Berkeley Shaw who interceded. "I believe your husband's silence is quite purposeful. He doesn't want me to know how he distinguishes the pieces. Perhaps he and Captain Thorne are planning another test."

"I certainly hope not," Mercedes said crisply. "That you've passed this one is quite sufficient in my eyes and should be in his. Isn't that right, Colin?"

The Earl of Rosefield almost smiled at his wife's attempt to bully him into agreement. "We'll see," is what he said.

Mercedes wasn't satisfied, but neither would she argue it out in front of others. What she did not do was return the fake to her brother-in-law. There would be no more substitutions if she could help it, and therefore, no more insulting tests. "Decker? Do you have the originals for Mrs. Shaw?"

Decker's quiet amusement returned when he realized Mercedes was not going to give him back the copy. He knew he confounded her by not asking for it. "Perhaps Mrs. Shaw would give her opinion of this piece," he said. Turning around briefly, Decker lifted a black-lacquered box from the mantelpiece. He felt Jonna's curious eyes following his movement. She knew the box normally held a few cigars for guests to enjoy after dinner. What she didn't suspect until he opened the lid was that he had removed the cigars earlier. Now the exquisitely crafted pair of heirloom earrings lay on a bed of black velvet.

Decker allowed everyone to see the contents of the box, but he didn't release it to Berkeley. Instead, he gave it to Colin. The Earl of Rosefield looked at the pair inside and after a long moment chose a single earring to give their guest. "I would be very interested to hear what this piece tells you about my brother," he said. Colin placed the earring in Berkeley's hand, and this time he folded her fingers around it, holding it in place.

Almost immediately Berkeley swayed on her feet. Colin felt a peculiar heat rising from her fist, and his first instinct was to release her. His grip had already loosened when he realized that she required his support. He tightened his fingers.

Anderson Shaw's hand slipped from Berkeley's back to her elbow. "I know what my wife needs now," he said stiffly. "You may let her go."

Colin had no clear idea why he was reluctant to remove his hand. Certainly he had no liking for the steady heat emanating from Berkeley's skin. He told himself his hesitation was because she held the earring and, therefore, all it represented. It was a connection to his past, his family's history, and his brother. Berkeley Shaw was a stranger, and it followed that she might have little respect for any part of what the earring meant to Colin and Decker Thorne.

Anderson Shaw, however, was insistent. When Berkeley swayed toward him he used the opportunity gently to wrest her from Colin's hold.

"Does she need to sit down?" Mercedes asked. "Colin, please push a chair behind her before she collapses."

"No," Anderson said. "No, it's quite all right. This will pass quickly." Even as he said the words he felt his wife steady herself. She blinked several times, her long lashes fluttering; then they lifted and fully erased the hint of shadow beneath her eyes. In contrast to the heat that ran just below the surface of her skin, her face was pale and her lips nearly colorless.

"I'm fine," she said. There was no particular insistence in

her tone, so the others were surprised when Anderson let her go. "Thank you," she told her husband. "I do believe I'd like to sit down."

The immediacy with which she was offered a chair by all of them was almost laughable. Berkeley accepted the one Anderson arranged for her. Once she was seated Jonna and Mercedes followed suit, occupying the cream-brocade settee. Still holding the black-lacquered box, Colin hooked one hip on the high arm of the settee and settled for this half-standing, half-sitting posture beside his wife. Decker leaned against the green-veined marble mantelpiece, his trim, athletic frame seemingly without tension.

Anderson Shaw remained standing, taking a position slightly behind Berkeley's chair, with his hands resting on the polished cherry backrail. "Go on, my dear," he urged gently. "You've learned something, haven't you? Tell His Lordship what you can about this earring."

Berkeley swiveled on the chair. She sought out her husband's warmly colored eyes as if for reassurance. Her own eyes, impossibly large in her small heart-shaped face, implored him. Must she? she asked him without words. His reply was there in the faint nod of his head. Yes, she must.

Berkeley unfolded her fingers and stared at the earring. It was virtually identical to the previous one she held. It only *felt* different. "There are so many emotions here," she said on a thread of sound. "So much pain. I can't . . ." She turned the earring over carefully and held it in place with the fingertips of her other hand. "Yes, this is better. It's difficult to distinguish . . ." She looked up suddenly at Colin, and for once the implacability of his dark eyes had no impact on her. "I can hardly say with any certainty that you've handled this earring, yet I feel your presence strongly in it. You must have been very young when you surrendered it." She paused over her own word choice. "Yes, surrender. That has the right feel. You gave it willingly, I think, but you gave up something of yourself. You meant it to be a link that would identify its owner to you in later years."

Berkeley heard the sharp intake of breath that came from
Mercedes Thorne. She closed her eyes briefly and calmed her
thinking again. "The age of this piece makes it hard to know
what is long past and what is recent past. I may confuse the
two from time to time." She regarded Colin once more. "Your
brother is very much alive. He held on to this piece for a long
time, I would say. It was lucky for him, or at least he associated
it with being lucky. Perhaps he regarded it as a talisman of
sorts. I doubt it was ever out of his possession for long. He
must feel now as if something has been torn from him." She
hesitated, shaking her head. "No, that's not quite right. It would
be more like not being able to draw a full breath."

Jonna could not help the wide-eyed look she shot her husband. Decker did not return her gaze though. His full attention
was riveted on Berkeley Shaw.

At the periphery of her vision Berkeley was aware of Jonna's
darting glance, the surprise in her violet-colored eyes. Berkeley's own features remained schooled, as if nothing untoward
had happened. "I believe your brother is a careful man," she
continued. "He certainly was with this piece, but there is something else in his nature. It is harder to describe accurately. A
certain recklessness, I think. A carelessness that he uses as a
shield when he cares very deeply." Her pale lips formed an
apologetic smile. "I don't know if that makes any sense . . ."
She shrugged. "It's what I *feel.*"

"It makes sense," Jonna said dryly, with a touch of irony.
She had stopped looking at Decker and was now eyeing Colin
with something akin to disapproval. "Please, tell us what else
you can."

"I'm afraid this has me confused," Berkeley said. "One of
you may know what it means. I think this earring may have
been part of a larger collection at one time. I don't mean as
part of the queen's jewels. It wasn't that long ago. The other
jewelry in the collection kept changing. Yes, I'm certain of
that. Only this remained as a constant." She frowned as an
explanation occurred to her, and her finely arched brows came

together. Berkeley drew in her lower lip, worrying it gently as she considered how she might put it forth.

Anderson touched his wife's shoulder lightly. "It does no good to hold it back, dearest. Say what's on your mind. Leave it to them to sort out. No one has asked you only to tell them pleasantries."

Berkeley nodded. Anderson was right, of course, and if she wasn't mistaken, the Earl of Rosefield, though he remained silent and impassive, seemed to be willing her to offer up her explanation. "I'm very much afraid, Your Lordship, that your brother may have been a thief." Berkeley sat back suddenly as Jonna Thorne leaped to her feet.

Jonna advanced on her husband, who was no longer leaning so casually against the mantel. "You knew Colin was going to give Mrs. Shaw *your* earring, didn't you?"

Decker didn't deny it. "We had to be sure, Jonna."

"Well, I hope this has satisfied you," she said flatly. Her violet eyes blazed for a moment, then she took a deep breath and exhaled slowly. "I know you and Colin have doubts. Do you think I didn't share them? I thoroughly researched the Shaws' successes before I ever wrote to Mercedes about them. And I made inquiries through friends before I ever invited the Shaws to Boston. I didn't arrange this on a whim, Decker. I would have hoped that you and Colin could have trusted me more."

"I have every trust in you," Decker told her. He searched her upturned face before his eyes came to rest steadily on hers. "Colin and I believe you did all that was in your power to do. It never occurred to us that you would be anything less than meticulous in your research. But what my brother and I arranged here had to be done. We had to be certain they weren't frauds."

Jonna said nothing for a moment; then she nodded faintly. "Yes, of course, you're right. You had to be certain." Her hand touched his forearm, and her slender fingers tightened briefly. There was assurance in the gesture, encouragement and support. Jonna let her hand fall. She turned to Colin and pointed to the box. "May I?" she asked.

He held it out to her. His hand was shaking.

Jonna did not miss the stricken look in Colin's eyes. That he had let his guard drop in front of the Shaws for even a moment spoke to the powerful effect of Berkeley's revelations. Jonna brushed his hand with hers as she took the box. She lowered her eyes to the place she had vacated beside Mercedes and indicated that Colin should sit there. He required no further urging.

Jonna went to stand in front of Berkeley Shaw. She lifted the lid on the box and revealed the identical twin of the earring Colin had given Berkeley. Removing it, she held it in her hand until Berkeley put back the one in her possession. "No more trickery, Mrs. Shaw. This is the earring that Graham Denison left behind five years ago. The other that caused you so much discomfort belongs to my husband. Everything you sensed about it—and him—was true. I didn't anticipate their plan because Colin gave you the earring. It is Decker's sleight of hand that bears watching. Not only was Captain Thorne a thief, he was an exceptional one."

Berkeley Shaw had not expected Jonna Thorne to admit her husband's criminal past, certainly not with this odd mixture of exasperation and pride. "Then it is perfectly understandable that the captain would be suspicious of us," Berkeley said. "He knows better than any of you how important it is to gain the confidence of the victims. From his point of view it may look like that's what Mr. Shaw and I are doing."

Jonna was visibly taken back by that statement. "What do you mean?"

"Mrs. Thorne," Berkeley said patiently. "My husband and I are not the first people one usually calls for in a case such as this. I imagine a lot of effort, time, and expense has gone into looking for Graham Denison. And yet you have nothing. No one has been able to find him. Not only that, but I am aware that none of you is certain that Mr. Denison is really the missing brother. He was merely last in possession of the earring, isn't that so?"

"That's right," Jonna said.

"Well, then, I take that as proof that the four of you have exhausted every other resource for finding Mr. Denison. That makes you desperate, and that, Mrs. Thorne, makes you vulnerable. I'm not terribly insulted by the attempts to test me. At least not as insulted as my husband is on my behalf. Truly, I would have been more surprised if nothing had been done to make me prove my mettle. My particular talent is not at all the usual thing and lies outside the experience of most people."

Anderson stroked Berkeley's shoulder. She was generally not so outspoken. This speech and her quiet vehemence surprised him. They hadn't discussed this beforehand and any deviation from their normal interviews caused him concern. "Perhaps you should take the earring," he prodded gently. "As you said, these people want to know what you can tell them."

Berkeley took the earring from Jonna's hand. She did not know what to expect when she held it. She was even less sure what they expected. Her fingers made a fist, and she secured the gold and pearl earring against her heart.

Almost immediately her ears roared with the rush of blood. Berkeley knew she gasped although the sound was lost to her. She laid her free hand over her fist to keep from throwing the earring across the room. The words came without any conscious thought on her part: *They came for the baby first.* Had she said them aloud? Had anyone heard her? Yes, Colin Thorne must have. The Earl of Rosefield was staring directly at her, and for once there was no shield to hide his stunned expression.

"They came for the baby first," Berkeley repeated. "He's very small. Still in arms. Of course they would want him. It's a terrible place they're taking him from. Not evil. But terrible just the same. There is fear here. And hurt. It's dangerous and hard."

Mercedes had moved to the very edge of the settee. Her hands had tightened in her lap. As if she still wasn't close enough, she leaned forward, her gray eyes hinting of both anxiety and awe. "She's talking about Cunnington's Workhouse," she whispered. "How can she know about it?"

Similarly amazed by Berkeley Shaw's revelations, no one answered Mercedes. No one had an answer.

Words continued to rush out of Berkeley. Her attention remained focused on Colin. "You want the baby gone from this place but you're sad as well. They don't want Decker. They don't want you. The couple takes your infant brother, and you know you may never see him again. The earring, you think. You will place this family heirloom in his blankets. You will find this brother later, when you are older, and you will know him because of the earring. You will never forget what it looks like. Its image is graven in your mind."

Berkeley closed her eyes a moment. The roar in her ears was steady, but softer now. She could almost hear her own voice. Had she shouted? She tried to loosen her grip on the earring, but her white-knuckled fingers wouldn't open. The gold post on the pearl dug into the very center of her palm. "I can't make out what happened then. There are so few clues . . . I think the earring must have been found and put away. No one touches it for a long time . . . years . . . and then he finds it and . . ." Berkeley's voice trailed off. "So much anger. Betrayal. He thinks of revenge often. He thinks of hurting people." There was panic in her voice now, and her eyes clouded. "There is danger again. Great risks. He is not as he seems. There is someone else. Please, take it. I cannot . . . please . . ."

Jonna started to reach for Berkeley's hand, but Decker stopped her. "Let her finish—if she can."

Anderson Shaw nodded. "Your husband's right. She won't pick it up again if you take it now. Let her finish."

Jonna had no liking for their decision, but she let it rest. "If she asks again . . ." She didn't have to complete her thought. Her intention was clear.

Berkeley was aware of conversation around her but not the content or the outcome. What she knew with certainty was that she still held the earring. The next wave of heat from it was accompanied by a wave of nausea. The room started to spin. "He comes to you." The words were spoken suddenly, forcefully, as though she were compelled to say them, even against her will. Berkeley was no longer addressing Colin. Her body had shifted slightly. She looked past Jonna Thorne's shoulder to where Decker stood at the fireplace. "He comes here, to you. He is in pain. He thinks he may die." Berkeley frowned as the emotions she felt leaped forward in time. "It's yours again. You hold the earring; you think it's yours." Her voice diminished to a whisper. "You only realize the truth after he's gone. You try to catch him . . . you can't. He disappears . . . he—"

Berkeley cried out, startled and in pain. She shot to her feet and flung her arms outward. The earring made an arc of gold light as it was hurled toward the window. It skittered across the glass like a water strider skimming a pond before it dropped to the fringed perimeter of the carpet. As though they expected it to move under its own power, everyone save Berkeley stared at it. Berkeley stared at the droplet of blood in the heart of her palm.

They would notice her again, she thought, when she fainted.

Berkeley's lashes fluttered open. Her brow wrinkled and her mouth curled to one side. She made a halfhearted attempt to push away the smelling salts that were being waved under her nose.

"She's coming around nicely, Mercedes," Jonna said. "I think you can put the salts away."

Mercedes corked the bottle and set it on the stand beside the settee. She saw Berkeley's eyes wander about the room. "Your husband has gone with Colin and Decker to the library. It was Jonna's idea to banish them, and I quite agreed. Men are invariably not at their best around a woman suffering from the vapors."

Berkeley's reaction was somewhat defensive. "I don't have the vapors. I've never fainted before." She struggled to sit up, but Mercedes laid a gentle, but firm hand on her shoulder and held her in place. "I really should like to go now."

Jonna pulled a chair up to the settee and sat. "It's been a trying experience," she said. There was no condescension in her tone. "I can't say I would want to go through what you did. May I?"

Berkeley was unsure what she was being asked to give permission to, but she nodded anyway. Her right hand was immediately taken by Jonna, and the palm was turned up.

"Do you have a handkerchief, Mercedes?" Jonna asked. "I seem to always misplace mine."

Mercedes gave hers over and watched as Jonna wiped away the droplet of dried blood at the center of Berkeley's palm. Almost immediately another crimson drop bubbled to the surface. "Let her make a fist around it," Mercedes suggested. "It will stop the bleeding."

Jonna folded Berkeley's fingers around the handkerchief and held them in place. "There. That's better, isn't it? You wouldn't want to ruin your gown."

Berkeley didn't care at all about the state of her gown. She didn't say so though for fear of offending the other women. They were both so fashionably turned out that she couldn't imagine they would understand or appreciate her lack of concern. Anderson had chosen the leaf green silk gown she wore now. He said he had a particular fondness for this dress because it made her own eyes seem impossibly green. To Berkeley's way of thinking the gown was merely a uniform, and she wore it because it was what was required for the occasion. "How did I cut myself?" she asked.

Jonna's dark brows lifted in surprise. "You don't know?"

Mercedes smiled. "I believe if Mrs. Shaw knew, she wouldn't have asked, Jonna." Mercedes turned her attention back to Berkeley. "I think the earring's post punctured your hand. You were holding it very tightly. I shouldn't wonder that your fingers will be stiff."

Berkeley flexed her fingers around the handkerchief. Mercedes Thorne had accurately described the state of her hand. "I didn't damage it, did I?"

"Oh no, not even when you threw it."

"I *threw* it?"

"Yes, you did. Quite forcefully, too. I take it that's never happened before."

"Never," Berkeley said. The quick, negative shake of her head lent veracity to her denial. "Who would invite me to handle their priceless valuables if I had a reputation for throwing them?" She hesitated, her eyes darting pleadingly between Jonna and Mercedes. "You won't say anything . . . I mean, it would damage my reputa—"

"You have no reason to fear on that account," Jonna said quietly.

Berkeley heard Mercedes murmur her agreement, and she finally relaxed. "Was I at all helpful?" she asked. She saw the women exchange cautionary glances. Berkeley sighed. "I suppose not. I'm sorry. As you know from your research, I am not always entirely successful. I wish it could have been different for both of you and your husbands."

"It's not that you weren't successful," Mercedes said. "It's just that you told us mostly what we already knew. It confirmed your incredible gift but didn't give us much hope that we could find Graham Denison."

Jonna tucked a loose tendril of glossy black hair behind her ear. Her widely spaced, beautifully colored violet eyes were solemn. "Thirty years ago Colin, Decker, and Greydon were orphaned when their parents were murdered. The details of that aren't important now." She cast a look sideways at Mercedes, assuring her that what she said was true. "My husband was four, Colin eight, and Greydon, as you understood from holding the earring, was but an infant. No family could be found to take them, so they were placed in a London workhouse for foundlings and orphans. You described it as a hard, terrible place, and it was. Greydon was the first to be taken, just as you said. Colin believes that the couple who adopted him planned to pass him off as their own child. He could be christened with any name today."

Mercedes brushed the back of Berkeley's hand. "He could be named Graham Denison."

"Is it true then?" Berkeley asked. "Did I confirm that Greydon and Graham are one and the same?"

Shaking her head slowly, her eyes regretful, Mercedes withdrew her hand and laid it in her own lap. "No, you didn't confirm it. You didn't hold out any hope. Quite the opposite, in fact. Just before you fainted you told us Graham Denison was dead."

Berkeley's luminous eyes widened. "I said that?" she asked incredulously. "Are you certain there was no misunderstanding?"

"There was no mistaking your words," Jonna said. "We can only hope that *you're* mistaken." She hesitated, then rushed forward with her thoughts before she reconsidered them. "My husband was separated from Colin not long after Greydon was taken. He was raised by two actors who claimed they were missionaries when they went to the workhouse. In reality they were thieves, and they raised Decker to fend for himself on the streets. The earring that was in his possession was very much his talisman, just as you sensed.

"Colin spent most of his life searching for his brothers. He was on the point of believing nothing would come of it when Decker appeared. Perhaps you won't find it at all odd that it was the earring that brought them together. That was almost ten years ago."

Jonna looked to Mercedes for some assurance that she was doing the right thing by revealing these details. Mercedes's faint nod was all she needed to continue. "My husband left England for Boston shortly after that. At Colin's suggestion he came to work for Remington Shipping. He met Graham Denison in the course of his duties for the Remington line. They discovered they had some shared interests and formed an alliance of sorts, but they—"

Berkeley interrupted. Her skin was flushed suddenly, and this time the heat went all the way to her cheeks. In spite of the window that had been opened for her comfort, she was uncomfortably warm. "May I have something to drink?"

Mercedes rose gracefully to her feet. "Of course. I should have thought of it myself. Do you want spirits, tea, or—"

"Tea, please."

Mercedes reached for the tasseled bellpull just inside the door and rang for a servant. A young Negress appeared almost immediately, and Mercedes sent her out again for a tray of tea and cakes. "It will only be a few minutes," she said as she returned to Berkeley's side.

"Thank you," Berkeley said. Her eyes strayed to Jonna's. "Forgive me. You were saying something about your husband's common interests with Mr. Denison. Do those interests involve the abolitionist movement?"

Not for the world would Jonna admit to that. She lied without hesitation. "My husband is not involved in that cause, though there is some sympathy for it. Mr. Denison, as you seem to know, had earned the name Falconer for his part in liberating slaves." Jonna did not mind sharing this last information. It was printed in papers from Augusta to Atlanta, and Graham Denison was either a hero or a villain. Whether he received accolades or epithets depended on geography. North of Mason-Dixon he typically was lauded. South of that demarcation, he was a pariah. Still, what the papers had printed as fact, wasn't the entire story, and Jonna kept these secret truths to herself.

"My husband and Graham became friends but not complete confidants. I don't think it is in either of their natures to be forthcoming with their pasts. We know that Graham has a family in South Carolina. A younger brother . . . his parents and grandparents. Remington Shipping had done business with the Denisons for years. Their plantation is outside Charleston. They call it Beau Rivage." She intercepted Berkeley's inquiring look. "It means Beautiful Shore."

Berkeley nodded and hoped her cheeks weren't flushed with her embarrassment. She felt impossibly young and ignorant in the presence of these women. It was a wonder they had any patience for her. As they had pointed out, she hadn't revealed any new knowledge to them. She had only told them what they already knew. She wondered if they understood that *that* was her very special talent.

The arrival of the tea kept her from blurting out that admission. She was allowed to sit up as Mercedes poured from the silver service. Berkeley examined her palm and found the bleeding had stopped. She traded the soiled handkerchief for a cup of warm tea. "Captain Thorne didn't know that Mr. Denison was in possession of the earring?" she asked.

Jonna shook her head. "Not until Graham had left Boston. We found the earring here among some clothes that were meant to be laundered."

"It seems odd that he didn't ask after it."

"We always thought so, but then perhaps he didn't have the same attachment to it that Decker and Colin do. It is the only explanation that really satisfies any of us." She sighed and raised her own cup slowly to her lips. "In spite of that we began a search for him. Decker took out the Remington flagship *Huntress* and chased down the ship Graham was on." Only a small measure of the enormous disappointment she had experienced on that occasion was revealed now. "He was no longer aboard when we caught the *Siren*. He had disembarked in Philadelphia. It surprised us. *Siren* was on her way to China. Graham had signed on for the voyage. He had seemed excited about the prospect, then he disappeared." Jonna took a large swallow of her tea then set the cup and saucer down. "It's been a little more than five years, Mrs. Shaw. We've never heard from him, and we've never been able to find him. I find myself quite prepared to believe Graham Denison is dead."

Mercedes gasped softly. "You don't mean that, Jonna."

"I do," she said. "God forbid, I don't wish it. He saved my life, Mercedes. I owe him so much, but it's as if he's fallen off the face of the earth. I can't credit his consciously making such a complete break with his past."

"There may be a reason," Mercedes insisted. "If he were engaged in the Underground again, for instance, secrecy would be a necessity."

"There would have been word by now," Jonna said. "A

hint. He knew he would be cut off from the Denisons, but there was no reason to do the same with his friends.''

Mercedes persisted with gentle reasoning. ''You only mean that you don't understand his purpose.''

Berkeley realized her cup was rattling ever so slightly against the saucer. She willed her hands to be steady, hoping her voice would follow. ''You mustn't accept anything I said while holding the earring as an absolute,'' she told Jonna.

''You had already thrown the earring,'' Jonna said. ''Your hands were over your ears and you were on the point of collapsing when you told us Graham Denison was dead.''

''And that's the last thing I said?'' Berkeley asked. She knew immediately that she had been wrong to hope it was. Jonna and Mercedes exchanged a look again, and it was clear they were wondering what they could or should tell her. ''Please, I have no recollection of what happened in those last moments. Can you not say anything?''

''Your husband requested our silence,'' Mercedes answered. Her questioning gaze was her admission that she didn't completely agree with his reasoning. ''He said it would cause you further upset.''

Berkeley could not still her trembling hands this time. ''Then I must have mentioned San Francisco.''

''Yes,'' Jonna said. ''You did. I didn't hear you. Mr. Shaw had caught you in your fall by that time, but your lips were moving around the words. He told us what you said.''

''And my exact words?''

'' 'You can find him in San Francisco.' '' Jonna looked to Mercedes for confirmation.

''That's right,'' Mercedes agreed.

''It doesn't make sense,'' Berkeley objected. ''I told you that Graham Denison was dead *and* you could find him in San Francisco?''

''It made sense enough to our husbands,'' Jonna said. ''They're with Mr. Shaw right now arranging for your passage and enough funds to support your investigation for six months.''

Berkeley reached over the high arm of the settee and placed

her cup and saucer on the end table. She stood quickly and was immediately light-headed. She swayed on her feet before she reached for the brocade arm to steady herself. With the ease of a wraith, Berkeley passed the arms that were outstretched to help her. With a light, silent tread she hurried toward the parlor's pocket doors. Pushing them open she barged directly into her husband's chest.

Anderson's arms secured her with the strength of iron bars. "What is this?" he said, his manner patiently jovial. "Why, you're out of breath, Berkeley. Has something frightened you?" He looked over the crown of his wife's pale hair to where Jonna and Mercedes stood. Neither woman was entirely successful in schooling her features. "I see," he said slowly. "I take it they told you."

Berkeley drew back as much as she was able and raised her face. "I begged them, Anderson. It really isn't their fault."

Mercedes and Jonna looked away guiltily, caught their husbands' disapproving glances, and looked to opposite sides of the parlor.

"Why am I not surprised?" Decker said, advancing on Jonna. He carried the lacquered box under his arm.

Jonna gave him a sour look that deepened the dimple at the corner of her mouth. That made him grin at her.

Colin escorted Anderson and Berkeley back into the room. Mrs. Shaw was every bit as upset as her husband had predicted she would be. He had warned them privately that Berkeley would want no part of going to San Francisco. Seeing the proof of it now eased the last of Colin's concerns. He couldn't be sorry that Mercedes and Jonna hadn't kept the information to themselves.

"It's all been arranged," Colin told Mercedes. "In three days Mr. and Mrs. Shaw will travel on one of the Remington packet ships for San Francisco. We will receive regular reports of their progress from the Remington clipper masters who dock there. We've agreed upon an amount that will keep them in comfort, even at prices in San Francisco, for six months. If there is a satisfactory conclusion to the investigation, then there will be an additional reward.''

Berkeley felt her husband's large hands tighten on her waist. She couldn't help herself. She had to know the terms from the Thornes. ''In what way will this business be satisfactorily concluded?'' she asked.

It was Decker who answered. ''Proof that Graham Denison is dead or that my brother Greydon is alive. It may be that one outcome will make the other impossible.'' He paused. ''Or it may not.''

Berkeley simply stared at him. He could not know the consequence of what he had just said.

Decker opened the black-lacquered case and held it out for Berkeley to see. Three earrings lay on the bed of velvet now. ''You've handled all of them,'' he said. ''Choose again. This time carry Greydon's earring.''

Berkeley drew a sharp breath. ''You can't be serious. You'd trust us to take your family's heirloom to San Francisco?''

Decker's blue eyes narrowed as he considered her thoughtfully. ''I trust you to make the right decision, Mrs. Shaw. This is the final test.''

Chapter Two

August 1850

San Francisco was rising out of the ashes. Grey Janeway stood just outside his canvas tent and watched the construction going on across Portsmouth Square. One of the workers, a man on a scaffold two stories above the square, saw him and shouted a good morning. Grey raised the cup that was holding his shaving cream in a half salute. Acknowledged, the man returned to work on the intricately carved sea goddess that embellished the front of the Phoenix like a ship's figurehead.

Grey brushed lather on his face, then applied himself to removing it with a newly sharpened razor. Using a cracked hand mirror, he concentrated on not cutting his own throat while the symphony of construction offered its peculiar musical accompaniment. Long planks of lumber slammed together as they were unloaded from a wagon. Hammers pounded out the percussion. The steady breeze off the bay whistled through the boards. Copper, brass, and lead fittings reverberated as they were struck and molded by the pipe fitters.

It was not only in Portsmouth Square that the construction

had reached a fever pitch. It was happening all over as the city raised new storefronts, gaming halls, warehouses, and homes. Montgomery Street. Pine. Washington and Kearny. Grey Janeway was grateful he liked the sound of all the activity because there was no getting away from it. That lack of an escape route was one of the reasons he had put up his tent right on the square, directly across from where his new gambling house and hotel was being erected.

His suite of rooms in the Phoenix had been finished more than a week ago, but Grey elected to wait until the entire structure was completed before he moved in. The mirrors he'd ordered from London still hadn't arrived, and he was expecting a shipment of draperies and linens from Boston. He was luckier than other owners, he realized, because his orders were late. He hadn't been a quarter done rebuilding after the May 4 fire when most of San Francisco, including the shell of his new establishment, was leveled by another fire on June 14.

On both occasions the rubble was cleared away as soon as the embers cooled, and the gaming houses, the lifeblood of Portsmouth Square, rose again like the bird of ancient myth. It was after the second fire that Grey decided his gambling palace was better described by the name Phoenix than Pacific Queen.

So he changed it. In San Francisco there was always the tantalizing possibility of something better coming your way. The great fires had a way of eliminating all evidence of the city's previous mistakes. Personal ones as well. Reconstructing a life here could be accomplished with almost as much ease as putting up a new building. No one remodeled or improved. They re-created.

There was no other place better suited to Grey Janeway than San Francisco.

Grey picked up the towel lying on the stool at his feet and wiped remnants of lather from his face. He examined his chin for nicks, found none, and tossed the towel aside. The mirror he placed more gently on the stool.

Someone yelled to him, and Grey scanned the square to

identify the source of the shout. He saw George Pettigrew standing outside the El Dorado, waving miners inside with promises of riches beyond their imaginings. Of course they would have to part with a small fortune if they were ever to reap any riches. George didn't explain that outright, but the miners weren't naive. They knew what to expect inside the El Dorado's rough-hewn walls and behind the muslin curtains. The gaming was run fairly most of the time, and the women were as comely as any in the city. For fifty dollars in gold dust a miner could be shown to one of the small interior rooms that were set off from the main gaming hall. A thin muslin curtain would drop back in place to provide a modicum of privacy for the miner and his lady of the evening. The fact that the encounter lasted about fifteen minutes, and the lady would service a dozen more men before the night was through, really didn't matter. For a quarter of an hour the pan-handlers were able to forget their losses at the table, their sweethearts in Ohio, and their played-out mines.

Grey nodded in George's direction. "Get them while you can, George," he shouted. "When the Phoenix is done they won't step inside the El Dorado."

"That's a fact," George agreed good-naturedly. His teeth flashed whitely in his dark face as he smiled broadly. "Then I come work for you. People can't refuse Ol' George."

"That's a fact," Grey called back. "You come and see me in two weeks."

"Yes, sir. I surely will." He eyed a group of miners beginning to shuffle off to another gaming house and corralled them in. "Right this way, gentlemen. Don't mind sayin' the El Dorado will be happy to let you leave with more gold dust in your pockets than when you came. Just step in—"

Smiling, Grey turned away and opened the flap to his tent. When he had staked this small lot for his tent the other gambling-house owners just shook their heads at his folly. They elected to rebuild fast and add amenities as they became available. At risk was losing customers to the rival gaming hells.

There was nothing wrong with their strategy, Grey thought,

but he wanted something that stood a chance of surviving the next inferno. That required more time than the usual three weeks it took to rebuild the city. He also believed there was more than enough gold dust to be scattered around, and that it would still be there when the Phoenix was ready. Proof of it could be found after every fire, when hundreds of tiny gold nuggets appeared under the charred foundations of the gambling houses. The intense heat from the fires fused the dust that miners dropped at the tables while they played. It filtered through the floorboards, and it was seldom recovered except after a fire.

Grey had considered that problem when he started reconstruction on the Phoenix. Carpets under the gaming tables were the answer. The gold dust could be beaten out and recovered. He was expecting his carpets from the Orient any day, along with the mirrors and draperies. He still remained hopeful that he would receive them because his cargo was being carried by Remington clippers.

The bay was littered with ships now. Prior to the discovery of gold two years ago, Yerba Buena Cove was not on the route of most shipping lines. Hudson's Bay Company had given up years earlier after trying to establish commercial trade there. In spite of the accessibility of its natural harbor, there was nothing to draw profitable enterprise or a population. The settlement was tents, shanties, adobe huts, and a Franciscan Mission two and one-half miles southwest of the cove. The few hundred citizens were managed by the Alcalde in those days and they were more aligned with Mexico than the United States. It wasn't until 1847, six months after the American flag was raised in the Plaza, that Yerba Buena Cove was renamed San Francisco, the Plaza was renamed Portsmouth Square, and the nameless thoroughfare along the waterfront was christened Montgomery Street.

The irreverent denizens wondered that God had taken six days to create the world when this city by the bay happened overnight. In a town where a significant fraction of the inhabitants went by nicknames and aliases, the fact that Yerba Buena

Cove was now San Francisco seemed fitting and proper. Like most of her citizens, the city herself had a past.

The pace of life in the town was still slow back then. The occasional whaling vessel called at the harbor; there were merchants from the Far East at other times. All of that changed with the discovery of gold in the Sacramento Valley. It didn't take long for the bay to become overcrowded with abandoned ships as entire crews left their decks for the promise of a rich strike. Shipping lines made money bringing the forty-niners to the goldfields, but they could lose it when sailors jumped ship and no experienced crew could be found to return the clipper home.

Grey Janeway was counting on the Remington line to make the deliveries that were promised. As far as Grey knew none of their ships had been abandoned in the harbor. They lost a few of the crew on every call to San Francisco but never every man on board. It cost a lot to ship goods with them. There was a high price for their reliability, but it was no more than the market would bear. The profits to merchants were enormous if they could unload their wares in San Francisco. Where else in the country would someone pay one dollar for an apple or three hundred for a barrel of tea? Washbowls cost five dollars, shovels brought fifteen or twenty, and a good pair of boots required a miner to part with one hundred. Laudanum sold by the drop and a quart of whiskey couldn't be had for less than thirty dollars. Where a loaf of bread might sell in New York for four cents, it cost seventy-five on the Barbary Coast.

Grey shrugged into his shirt, tucked it in, and pulled up his suspenders. He raked his thick hair back with his fingertips, then slipped into his jacket. He noticed that the sun was already beating hard against the roof of the tent. In another hour or so the interior would be unbearably hot in spite of the winds churning up from north and east.

He nudged the pile of blankets covering the canvas floor. Five pink toes were revealed. "You told me not to let you sleep," he said. The toes curled and stretched, but there was no appreciable movement elsewhere. "You'll have a headache, remember? That's what you said."

"Hmmm."

"Don't you have to go to work?"

"I only just went to sleep."

"I don't think that will matter to Howard. He'll want you back at the Palace before the noon crowd tries to get away from him."

Ivory Edwards rolled over. She pushed the blankets down to the level of her breasts. A view of her naked shoulders was as much as she was going to allow Grey Janeway. As far as she was concerned, this was a new day, and he hadn't paid for anything else. Muted sunlight glanced off her fair skin. Her deliciously full mouth was pulled thoughtfully to one side. "What do you think of Ivory DuPree?" she said.

"Who's Ivory DuPree?" Grey asked absentmindedly. He straightened the cuffs of his jacket and brushed a piece of lint from the sleeve.

"*I* am," Ivory said somewhat indignantly. "Do you think it sounds better than Edwards?" She repeated her name first one way then the other. When she saw Grey wasn't paying her the least attention she sat up and kicked out at him. She connected solidly with his booted shin.

"Ow!" He dropped the lid of the trunk he was searching, barely getting his hand out in time. "What was that for?"

Satisfied, Ivory withdrew her weapon under the blankets again. "For taking me for granted," she said emphatically.

"I took you for a hundred dollars last night," he reminded her. "That means I don't have to pay attention to you today." He sat on the trunk lid, raised his right leg, and rubbed his injured shin. He felt the outline of the weapon he kept there. "It's less complicated. Now, what's this about your name?"

Ivory was too established in the working life to let Grey's comment sting her heart or her pride. He rarely requested her services, and from what she knew, he rarely requested them from anyone else. There were still forty men for every woman in San Francisco. She would have known if he had been regularly going somewhere else for his carnal pleasures. "Edwards or DuPree?" she asked. "I'm thinking of changing it. DuPree has a certain ... *je ne sais quoi* ..." She giggled when she saw one of his dark eyebrows arch dramatically. "You didn't think I knew any French, did you?"

"You're a source of constant surprises, Ivory." It was not usual for his flinty, blue-gray eyes to be touched by his smile. They were now. He held out his hand to her, and Ivory rocketed into his lap, blankets snapping around her like a clipper's sails caught in an updraft. He kissed her lightly on the cheek. "DuPree is a good choice. Were you thinking of an accent?"

"But of course," she said deeply, imitating as best she could the throaty accents of two or three Frenchmen she'd met. "Foreign girls get more." Ivory looked to Grey for approval.

"Not bad." He set her off his lap suddenly as something teased his memory. He concentrated to retrieve it but it proved as elusive as all the others that had ever come to him over the last five years. Was it the accent? he wondered. The woman? Or both of them together that prompted the sensation that this was a familiar scene? There was a mild throbbing in his head now, and Grey realized Ivory was looking at him oddly. He stood and laid a hand lightly on her bare shoulder. "Use DuPree. It has such an abundance of *je ne sais quoi* I won't be able to afford you."

Ivory was genuinely pleased by the possibility. Her cheeks flushed becomingly. In spite of current living conditions, Grey Janeway had amassed a fortune, even by San Francisco standards. If he couldn't afford her, she'd be a high-priced whore indeed. "You going to the wharf?" she asked, as he removed his hand. Ivory wished he had allowed it to linger there a bit longer. It wasn't often that she was touched with any sort of affection. His fingertips on her shoulder had felt a little like that. She was sorry to have the moment pass.

Grey nodded. "I'm expecting things to be delivered any day. I want to make certain *I* get them."

Ivory knew it was always possible that someone would try to take Grey's orders by bribing the cargo master. "That's some fancy palace you're building, Mr. Janeway. I've heard about the mirrors. Folks say you plan to put them right above the beds.''

"Folks say that, do they?''

He sounded amused, Ivory thought. He was very handsome when he offered up that small, half smile of his. The problem was, he didn't make the sacrifice often. Her short, glossy black curls bounced as she nodded. "That's what I hear. It will be as splendid as any bawdy house back East.''

"It would be *more* splendid,'' he said dryly. "If that was my intention.''

"You mean the mirrors aren't going to hang above the beds?''

He almost laughed outright at her disappointment. "Why don't you wait and see?''

"Does that mean you'll be needing some girls like me, Mr. Janeway?''

This time Grey tapped Ivory on the tip of her upturned nose. It was a pretty face, he thought. With the exception of her well-shaped mouth, her features were not refined or exotic. She was just plainly pretty, but that was still worth something in San Francisco. "I believe I will, Ivory,'' he said. "But don't tell your friends. I intend being very particular about who works for me. And there will be certain conditions. You may not like them.'' She looked as if she was going to ask him to explain them now, so Grey shook his head before she opened her mouth. "Later, perhaps. I have to be going.''

He ducked out of the tent into the bright morning sunshine.

The bay wharf hadn't been enlarged in spite of the demands placed upon it since the gold strike. In the past it could accommodate a vessel or two for unloading, but now it wasn't possible for a ship to get that close. Scows and rowboats were used to bring cargo in from where the clippers anchored farther out in the bay. It was probably possible, Grey mused, to walk to an incoming ship on the bows and beams of all the abandoned ones. He doubted such an undertaking would even require getting one's feet wet.

A few enterprising souls saw the potential in the ghost ships. They turned them into gaming dens and brothels and hostelries and did a fair business until the underbellies rotted out. The June fire had claimed almost half the hulks. Bright orange and yellow flames leaped from mast to mast like a hellish Jack Frost, icing the bowsprits and taffrails with an eerie, glowing light. The capricious wind carried the fire so one ship might become a torch and its neighbor might be largely spared. The bay waters reflected the scene, magnifying the destruction, not diminishing it.

It wasn't a sight Grey thought he was likely to forget. Unless, of course, someone kicked him in the head and chest a dozen or so times. That might put it out of his mind. Tipping the brim of his hat back a notch, Grey smiled thinly at his own black humor.

He casually leaned sideways against a pyramid of empty barrels and lit a cheroot. He savored the flavor of the tobacco and exhaled slowly, his eyes wandering the wharf through a blue-gray wreath of smoke.

There was considerable traffic crowding the small wharf, but Grey kept coming back to the boy. The only thing more rare than a woman in San Francisco was a child. Male or female, it didn't matter. Shooting stars were more frequently sighted than children. The influx of harlots and mining-camp followers hadn't produced many burgeoning bellies. The abortionists were kept busy while figures were kept slim and profitable.

The boy looked old enough to take offense to being called one. He might accept the vague "young man" distinction, Grey thought, but he wouldn't like it. He was of a scrappy appearance: denim trousers belted by a frayed length of rope; a faded flannel shirt with shoulder seams that hung several inches below his shoulders; and a popular slouch hat that covered far more than just the top of his head. Most of the boy's face was hidden in shadow, but there was a hairless chin that jutted forward from time to time, leading the way as the boy paced the length of the wharf.

At least Grey thought he was trying to pace. It was the sort of activity that could not be accomplished easily on the crowded dock. Flicking ash from the tip of his cheroot, Grey watched the boy dodge carts and hurdle a cask that rolled in his way. He avoided obstacles like the fishmonger's wagon, a dray sagging with its load of lumber, and a stack of crates that kept shifting location because the owner couldn't decide where to unload them. The boy agilely skirted the pyramid of barrels that Grey was leaning against and neatly stepped over a tabby cat basking in the sunshine. At the end of the wharf the boy paused long enough to scan the horizon, then he did an about-face and started his worried journey back again.

His shoulders were hunched and his eyes downcast as he passed in front of Grey. He kept his hands in his pockets. Occasionally he paused to kick a stone into the bay. Once he stopped long enough to pet the tabby. The cat followed him after that.

Shaking his head at the sight, Grey flicked what was left of his cheroot into the bay. The tip of it arced brightly before it fell in the water. Grey unbuttoned his jacket, reached inside, and withdrew a small telescope. He extended the length of it and held it up to his right eye. Adjusting the sight, Grey also scanned the horizon, but with a lot more power than the boy had had. Seeing nothing like a Remington clipper, Grey folded the scope but didn't put it away. Out of the corner of his eye he noticed the young scrapper was watching him. Grey turned his head in that direction, but the boy ducked his head immediately and moved on, almost tripping over the cat, which was wending in and out of his legs.

Noticing the youngster slowed as he made his next pass in front of him, Grey considered offering the telescope to him to use. He thought better of it when he realized he would probably have to chase the boy all the way up Montgomery Street to get it back. Grey wasn't of a mind to expend that much energy this morning.

He tapped the scope lightly against his leg as he waited. He could afford to be patient. The man he had hired as foreman for the Phoenix construction was doing a good job. Grey almost regretted pitching his tent across the square to keep an eye on the progress. Donnel Kincaid's attention to detail and his firm approach to managing the laborers gave Grey more time to devote to his other enterprises and oversee some things personally.

A movement on the horizon caught Grey's eye. He raised the scope again and held it in place until the object in the distance was fully in focus. The clipper's white sails were fully extended. Men lined her yardarms waiting to take them in as she came toward the harbor and prepared to drop anchor. Grey straightened, lowering the scope, and caught sight again of the boy watching him. He spoke just loud enough for his voice to carry to the youngster. "She's flying an American flag," he said. "And the purple-and-gold banner of the Remington line. Could be it's what you're waiting for."

The boy hurried on without giving any indication that he'd heard Grey. Grey watched him go and saw trouble coming right at him.

The Sydney Ducks were the primary reason Grey was at the wharf himself this morning. The Ducks were a loosely organized gang of felons who had tickets-of-leave from the English penal colony in Australia. They had served their time in Van Dieman's Land and the tickets-of-leave gave them opportunity to get out from Down Under—as long as they didn't try to return to England.

It was hard to know what manner of crime they had committed to receive transportation as their punishment. Grey knew firsthand that some had offenses no more serious than stealing food to feed their families. There were others, though, who had learned how to use a shiv before they knew the proper use of a fork and spoon. Highwaymen and murderers, forgers and sneaksmen, the Sydney Ducks had someone of experience in every aspect of the roughest criminal trade.

In response to the gold strike, the Ducks began arriving in

just enough numbers to cause problems. Feared and shunned at the outset, the Sydney Ducks capitalized on it, turning it into their strength. They organized, set up shanties and tents near one another, and moved about town in pairs or groups, but never alone. There were exceptions, but in the main the Ducks didn't fare well in the goldfields. Mining didn't come naturally to men who had been felling pine as punishment on Van Dieman's Land. They tended to look for something less physical, or at least some trade that required them only to use their fists.

The Sydney Ducks specialized in extortion and theft, and when these couldn't be accomplished with finesse, they fell back on brawling.

A pair of Ducks were patrolling the wharf now, waiting to see what cargo would be unloaded today, and how their fortunes might be increased by permitting the rightful owner to collect it. They had seen the Remington ship and knew they had time before she put down her anchor. They were at loose ends till then. That's when they decided to have fun with the boy.

The first thing they did was close ranks as the boy tried to slip between them. When he attempted to skirt them, they parted. The dance frustrated the boy and amused the men. Above the general commotion of traffic on the wharf, Grey could hear them laughing.

He looked around to see if anyone else noticed what was going on. He sighed. Where a number of people on the dock had been interested in the boy's antics for the better part of a half hour, they were now studiously avoiding looking in his direction. In general, because of their rarity, children were afforded the protection of the community. Grey once heard of a miner who paid fifty dollars in gold dust simply to hold a baby in his arms. Traffic halted on Pacific Street, in the heart of the roughest quarter of town, to permit a wayward toddler to cross the street without harm. This boy, however, wasn't an entirely defenseless child, and Grey imagined that's what the others were telling themselves. No one wanted trouble with the Sydney Ducks.

Confronting two of them was the same as having to face all

of them. Two now. Four tomorrow. The entire population of Sydney Town the day after.

The trouble might start with an irksome loss of inventory. If you were a merchant, you might discover broken windows in your storefront. If you were a miner, your claim could be taken over. There might be a fire of unknown origin or a crippling injury from a fall. Or, if they weren't of a singular mind to create accidents, you might just get a shiv poked in your side and yanked across your belly so you were gutted like a fish. It was a hard way to die but a good lesson to your friends.

As Grey watched, the Ducks took up position on either side of the boy and lifted him by his upper arms. His feet dangled several inches above the dock, and when he kicked at the bullies one of his shoes flew off. It sailed in the air, spinning end over end before it landed squarely in the fishmonger's cart.

Even without witnessing the look that passed between the Ducks, Grey knew what was going to happen next. They hoisted the hapless lad a full sixteen inches off the dock and carried him like a trophy in the direction of the fish wagon. The boy realized what was going to happen as well, and he renewed his struggles. He was unexpectedly silent throughout the ordeal, squirming and wriggling like a hooked worm and with just about as much sound. Somehow his hat had been pushed even lower on his face, and now it covered his eyes completely. If they changed direction suddenly and dropped him in the bay instead of the cart, the boy wouldn't know it until he heard the splash.

There was some laughter on the wharf now, a chuckle here and there as the merchants and dockworkers realized the Ducks weren't intending any real harm. There was relief in the low rumble. A few men coughed behind their hands or cleared their throats, trying to disguise their amusement. No one really wanted to encourage the Ducks. There was no telling when their playfulness would turn vicious and who their next victim might be.

Grey's small smile wasn't prompted by relief. Although he

wasn't particularly proud of it, he was being genuinely entertained at the boy's expense. He could just make out the boy's mouth opening and snapping shut again as his ankles were grabbed. The Ducks began swinging him by his arms and legs, back and forth, higher and higher, until they started their count.

One . . . two . . . threeeee. . . . Grey's gunmetal glance narrowed as the boy was sent flying. At its apex the boy's lean frame reached a height of about ten feet before he dropped like a stone, headfirst, into the fish cart. Fish flopped over the sides of the wagon and landed on the wharf. The monger scrambled to save his catch, getting down on his hands and knees to pick up the fish and toss them back. The boy came up, gasping for air, and got slapped in the face with a mackerel for his effort. The Ducks thought this was funny in the extreme. They laughed hard and loud until one of the fish came spinning tail over dorsal in their direction.

The bigger of the two Ducks made a better target. The fish struck him in the center of his chest and he actually had to take a step backward to keep his balance. His mate saw the humor in the situation but not the fish that eventually whacked him in the side of his head.

The boy was on his feet now, standing in the middle of the wagon, knee deep in fish, hefting them like knives and hurling them like darts. His arsenal was extensive, and the Ducks weren't of a mind to take the attack until he ran out of ammunition. With a great roar of *Kill the bugger!* they mounted a frontal assault, charging the wagon so the boy was shaken off-balance.

Grey took a step forward as the boy toppled and the Ducks scrambled onto the cart. With a casualness that belied any urgency he felt, Grey tucked his scope into his jacket and removed the blade from his boot. He concealed it in his sleeve and began walking toward the wagon. He stopped when the boy, owing to superb reflexes or dumb luck, managed to writhe free of eighty pounds of fish covering his torso and vault himself over the side of the cart. The Ducks came up holding fishtails but no boy, and their angry stomping soon mired them to mid-calf in slippery, stinking fish.

Grey shook his head at their adult-sized temper tantrum. He supposed the fun was definitely at an end. They were glaring at him now, not because they'd seen him smile—because he hadn't—but because the boy was running at him full tilt as if seeking his protection.

He sidestepped the boy, grabbed him by the collar of his flannel shirt, and put him at his back. "Stay right there," he ordered. The child was breathing hard. Grey supposed he couldn't catch his breath to answer, but he felt the brim of the boy's hat rub up and down against his spine. He took the motion as agreement.

The Ducks had freed themselves of scales, gills, and fins and were advancing on Grey. Behind them the fishmonger salvaged what he could of his load and hurried to lead his horse and wagon out of the way.

"Gentlemen," Grey drawled. His voice was like honey over velvet. "Can I assist you in some way?"

They knew him. Grey Janeway was not someone they would purposely set out to bother, but neither could they back down. "G'day, Mr. Janeway," the brawnier of the two men said. "Name's Bobby Burns. My mate here's Jolly."

Grey greeted them formally. "Mr. Burns. Mr. Jolly." He could feel the boy trying to peek around his arm to get a closer look at them. He pushed the lad back in place. "You want . . . ?" He purposely let his sentence trail off. Let them state exactly what they came for.

Uncomfortable, Bobby Burns shifted his considerable bulk from one foot to the other. "Aww, Mr. Janeway," he said almost apologetically. "You know we come for the boy."

"What boy?" Grey asked coolly.

"The one hidin' behind your back like he was a joey and you were a bloody roo."

"I'd have him in my front pocket then, wouldn't I?"

Burns wasn't sure what to say to that. "It was just an expression."

"A bad one." Grey looked at Jolly. He was fingering the scar that went from one corner of his mouth and disappeared into his reddish blond side whiskers. "Do you have an expression, Mr. Jolly?"

The Duck shook his head. Nothing came to his mind.

Grey continued, unruffled and pleasant. "I'm expecting a delivery this morning, and the boy, the one who's *not* attached himself to me like a barnacle to a ship's hull, is helping me collect it."

"He works for you?" Bobby Burns asked.

"He works for me."

"You didn't say anything when we grabbed him."

"That's because I didn't mind. He'd been running up and down the wharf long enough. He's a bit of a dervish, you understand, but eager to please."

The Ducks nodded in unison.

"So I didn't care that you took him in hand, but now that everyone's gone fishing, I think it's over." He pointed past Jolly's shoulder. "Our ship's preparing to drop anchor soon. Do you really want to argue about the boy?"

"Didn't know he worked for you, Mr. Janeway," Bobby said.

"Now you do," Grey said quietly. He pinned them both back with his flint-colored eyes and waited.

They shifted again, exchanged glances, then Jolly spoke up. "We have a ship to meet, Mr. Janeway. Pleasure talking to you."

"Surely was," Bobby Burns added.

Grey watched them go. When their backs were turned and he was certain their attention was on the incoming clipper, Grey let the knife concealed in his sleeve drop to his hand. He bent and slipped it back into his boot.

"You would have used that?" the boy asked huskily.

"If I had to," Grey said with complete indifference. He turned and eyed the boy critically. His shoulders were hunched again, and he was staring at the ground. Grey started to raise the brim of the boy's hat to get a better look at his face, but the child flinched as if he were about to be struck and grabbed the hat, jamming it on even tighter.

"How old are you?"

"Fourteen." The reply was sullen and reluctantly offered.

"You're alone?"

The response this time was a nod.

"Orphan?" Grey didn't waste any more words in asking the questions than the boy did answering them.

"Yes, sir."

"What's your business with that ship?"

"I'm leaving on it."

Grey almost laughed at that. "You have money?" The absence of a reply this time told Grey all he needed to know. His hand snaked out, and he grabbed the boy's chin and raised it. "They'll pitch you overboard if they find you stowed away. You're too scrawny to be any use to them but as fish bait. And how were you planning to get to the ship? You'll need money if you expect one of the scows to take you. They'll smell the desperation on you and ask for something you can't—or shouldn't—be willing to give." Grey's fingers tightened. He gave the chin a little shake and bent his head closer. His voice was still soft, hypnotically so, and deep with intensity. He stared at the large green eyes raised fearfully in his direction. "And if they realize you're a woman, you'll be flat on your back instead of bent over the bow."

Tears flooded her eyes.

"For God's sake," Grey said. "Don't cry here."

Her attempt to blink them back was only marginally successful. Several dripped over the rim of her lower lashes. She wrestled her chin free and wiped them away quickly. Glancing around, she looked to see if anyone had noticed.

"Everyone else is occupied with the ship," Grey said.

"I thought you didn't want them to see me cry."

"*I* don't want to see you cry." He observed that she flinched almost imperceptibly. God, he thought, spare him from overly sensitive females. In spite of the way he seemed to be able to lash her with mere words, Grey noticed that she continued to stare at him. "What's your name?"

"Berkeley Shaw."

"How old are you?"

"Twenty-two."

Grey was mildly surprised and not entirely convinced. He knew she was older than the fourteen-year-old boy she'd pretended to be, but he wouldn't have put eight years on her. "Is there someone I should be turning you over to?"

She frowned. "What do you mean?"

"A husband? Brother? Father?" He paused. "A pimp?"

"No!"

"None of them?"

"No," she said more softly. "None of them."

Grey found himself disconcerted by her slightly awed, wide-eyed regard. "Why are you staring at me?"

"Those men, they called you Mr. Janeway."

"That's right."

"Is that your name?"

He was more amused than frustrated. "Do you have a better one?"

Actually, Berkeley Shaw thought she might. She refrained from saying it because coincidence loomed so large that she couldn't accept what her eyes were seeing. The man who stepped forward to protect her from the Sydney Ducks couldn't be Graham Denison. "Will you help me get to the clipper?" she asked.

The change in subject didn't bother Grey. In a way it was a relief. "What's your business there?"

"I have a letter I need to deliver."

Grey felt his confusion mount. "Then you don't want to leave."

For entirely different reasons, Berkeley was confused as well. She continued to search his face. There were similarities, to be sure, with the artist's sketch she'd seen from a Boston newspaper. Jonna Thorne had given Anderson one of the accounts that had been written about Graham Denison, alias Falconer.

The article was five years old now, and Jonna had warned them the sketch was no better than an adequate likeness. It didn't capture either his intensity, she had told them, or the self-indulgent pose he sometimes affected. At best, the sketch would serve to eliminate impostors.

"You're staring again," Grey said.

Berkeley blinked. "I'm sorry." The details of the sketch, the ones that she could remember, faded from her mind's eye. She wished now that she had pressed Anderson harder to allow her to study it. He had assured her it wasn't important, and now that it might be, Anderson and the clipping were gone. "Have I been rude?" she asked earnestly. "I haven't meant to be."

Grey waved her concern aside. "Answer my question."

She tried to remember what it might have been. "You mean about leaving?"

"That's the one."

It really hadn't been a question the way he had put it to her, but Berkeley didn't think he wanted to hear that. "I'm staying," she said.

"Then you lied about wanting to go?"

"I've changed my mind." She added quickly, "But I still have a letter to take to the ship. Will you help me?"

Grey knew he should say no. He already had proof that she was trouble, and he didn't need any reason beyond that to refuse her. Besides the fact that she lied to him and had shown the good sense of a jackaroo, she was possessed of a pair of eyes that were so deep and green and compelling that no exact likeness with any natural thing was possible. They had more facets than an exquisitely cut emerald, and they were darker than a spring leaf. Even a forest pool had a bottom; Berkeley Shaw's eyes did not.

It didn't seem to matter at all that she smelled like fish.

"You're staring," she told him.

So he was. He didn't apologize for it.

"Will you help me?" she asked again.

"Yes."

She showed him a shy smile and ducked her head, embarrassed that he was still staring at her. "Thank you," Berkeley said.

Grey felt as if he'd signed a pact with one of the devil's cleverer minions. Whatever they had just bargained for, it wasn't his soul. He didn't have one to give. "Back away," he said.

Berkeley's head came up. Not sure she had heard correctly, she merely regarded him curiously.

"Downwind," he said. When she still didn't move he pointed to his nose. "You smell like fish."

"Oh." She took a few steps sideways and to the rear of him. "Is this better?" she asked.

He nodded. "Come along. And for God's sake, don't talk so others can hear you."

Careful not to get underfoot as she followed him, Berkeley maintained what she hoped was an unoffensive distance. The tabby that had been run off by the Sydney Ducks found her again and was not at all put off by her fish perfume. The cat curled in and out of Berkeley's legs and pawed playfully at her one bare foot.

Grey stopped when he reached the scow he had rented. "Wait here," he told Berkeley as he jumped aboard. It was when he landed that he turned and saw she was holding the cat. It was a bundle of purring, brindled fur in her arms, and she was allowing it to lick her face. "Get rid of it," he said.

Berkeley put the cat down and shooed it away. It scrambled away a distance of four feet before it paused, turned, and began to stalk her bare foot again.

Grey shook his head in disgust. "It wouldn't do that if you wouldn't wriggle your toes. Where's your shoe?"

"I'm not sure." She looked around the wharf for some evidence of it just as the tabby pounced on her foot. A shiver went up her spine as the damp, slightly rough edge of the cat's tongue licked the underside of her toes.

Grey saw the feline's little pink tongue flick once, then he saw Berkeley's unembarrassed, sybaritic response. God help him, he thought, when her eyes closed and a breathless sigh of pleasure escaped her parted lips. She wasn't merely trouble; she was dangerous. "Do you have your letter?"

"Hmmm?" Berkeley's wistful smile disappeared as she opened her eyes and found her rescuer scowling at her. "I'll try to get rid of her again," she promised quickly.

"Forget the cat; give me your letter."

"Oh, but I want to go out to the ship myself," she said. "I should speak to the captain personally."

Grey couldn't imagine what she thought she had to say to the clipper's master or why she thought she would be allowed to say it. "I'm not going to the ship," he said. "And neither are you. Now, do you want the skipper of this scow to deliver your letter or not?"

In answer, Berkeley turned away and reached inside her flannel shirt. From under the loose bindings that covered her breasts, she pulled the last letter Anderson had written. She stared at the folded and sealed paper and wondered if she should send it at all. She knew the contents by heart: *Mrs. Shaw and I regret to inform you that no significant progress has been made in locating either Mr. Denison or Mr. Thorne. Our most promising lead has not (in the vernacular of these environs) panned out. We extend our best regards and continue to pray that we will have something more encouraging to report next month.*

Anderson had composed it on the ship, before they had gone as far as Panama. He had intended writing all six of the progress reports the Thornes had requested during the voyage—just to get them out of the way—but other things had distracted him. He had sent off the first one himself a month after their arrival. This was the second. If there were more, Berkeley didn't know about them. She would have to try her hand at composing one, but this letter gave her another month to think about it. She couldn't hope to copy Anderson's bold scrawl even if she could duplicate the tone of his missives. The next letter would have her signature. It remained to be seen if she would have the encouraging report Anderson promised they were praying for.

"I'm waiting," Grey said with more patience than he felt. "Or are you writing it now?"

When Berkeley turned back she was holding out the letter. "May I at least give it to the skipper?" she asked.

He realized with some small shock that she didn't trust him. Apparently she was afraid he'd read it. Having enough of that nonsense, Grey took the letter out of her hand. He glanced at the name above the waxy seal. *Mr. and Mrs. Decker Thorne.* "There's no address."

"I know," she said.

"The captain of the clipper will know what to do with this?"

"You said it was a Remington clipper."

Grey nodded.

"Then he'll know," Berkeley explained.

When she didn't offer anything more, Grey simply shook his head and sighed. "Wait here while I talk to the skipper."

Berkeley obeyed, more or less. She picked up the cat and moved a few yards down the wharf so her angled view allowed her to see both Grey and the scow captain. She watched Grey hand over the letter and some coins. The two men talked a bit longer, then Grey shook the skipper's hand and headed back to the wharf. If he noticed that she had moved, he didn't mention it as he stepped up onto the dock.

The scow's crew lifted the ropes, keeping them dockside and the large, square-ended, flat-bottomed boat was pushed away from the wharf with slender poles. Berkeley stood long enough to watch it negotiate the passage between two listing, abandoned hulks, then she sat down on the edge of the wharf.

Grey looked down at her. The hat brim hid her hair and head completely from his view. Her legs were swinging lazily over the water. She looked every inch the urchin boy she had pretended to be. "Your letter's been delivered," he said.

"Yes, thank you." Holding on to her hat with one hand and the cat with the other, she looked up at him. Her expression held no trace of guile. "I didn't realize it would cost so much to have it taken out to the clipper."

"How long have you been in San Francisco?"

"A week or so shy of two months."

"And you've been masquerading as a boy for all of it?"

"Not all," she corrected. "Just most."

"God," he said feelingly, looking away from those fathomless green eyes. "You need a keeper."

"I know," she said simply. She paused, uncertain now. "I don't suppose you would—"

"Hell, no." He cut her off before she reeled him in. No rod, he thought. No hook. No line. But she *was* fishing. "You told me you were going to get rid of the cat."

She continued to stroke the tabby as if she hadn't heard him. "What are they bringing you from the ship?"

"I don't know." He hunkered down beside her. "It depends where it's been."

"You should get upwind," she said.

At first he didn't understand, then he realized she was referring to her fish odor. "It's all right. I'm used to it now."

"It's why I can't get rid of the cat," she said.

That was true enough, Grey thought, but it didn't explain why he was still hanging around. He took out his telescope again and peered through it. "She's the Remington *Rachael*," he told her. "That doesn't help me know her last port of call. Would you like to see?"

Berkeley was immediately wary. "Really? You mean you'd let me?"

A small crease formed between Grey's dark brows. "I asked, didn't I?"

"Yes, but ... I mean ..." She put the tabby in his lap and took the scope. "Thank you." Berkeley put the glass up to her eye quickly, before he could catch sight of the tears forming there. He couldn't conceive that what he had done was any great kindness. To Berkeley it was the first act of sharing she'd witnessed in a profoundly selfish city.

"You might have to adjust it." He reached over and showed her how to turn the sight.

"Oh, yes. I see. Why the ship's almost as close as my hand."

He found himself smiling at her amazement. "How old are you?" he asked again.

Berkeley realized how stupidly childlike she must have sounded. "About thirty minutes older than the last time you asked me, Mr. Janeway." She told him she needed a keeper, but he hadn't understood. She'd been sheltered in a peculiar fashion most of her life, but that didn't make her young.

Grey didn't press her. She was a curious mixture of candor and innocence. "What can you see?" he asked.

"The scow's pulling alongside the *Rachael*. The clipper crew is reaching out to her with poles."

"Grappling irons," he corrected. "To keep the scow in place while they load her." He scratched the tabby behind her ears and she stretched complacently in his lap. "Can you see anything else? Rolls of carpet, perhaps? Crates that look as if they'd be large enough to hold mirrors?"

"That's what you're waiting for?" She could only imagine the scope of his wealth if he was waiting on treasures like carpets and mirrors.

"If *Rachael*'s been to the Orient, then she could have my carpets. The mirrors will be there if she's called on London. And if she's been home to New England, I could also have the draperies and linens I ordered." Grey stood again as he heard the close approach of a wagon. "Sam!" He lifted one hand, partly in greeting, partly to stop the driver's advance. "I didn't know if I'd be seeing you after all."

Sam Hartford tipped his hat upward with his index finger and wiped his brow. A fringe of salt-and-pepper hair was pressed damply to his forehead. The fine creases at the corners of his eyes deepened as he squinted in the sunshine. "Had to unload the lumber first," he said. "Got it all stacked when I heard there was a Remington ship in the bay. Knew you said you wanted the wagon here if one came in." Sam pulled his hat back in place and pointed to the tabby dozing contentedly in Grey's arms. "Never figured you for liking cats, Mr. Janeway. You pick up that stray today?"

Grey's eyes slid away from Sam and returned to Berkeley.

Sitting there with the scope still trained on the clipper, her legs swinging in fits and starts, she seemed oblivious to his exchange with his driver. ''Two strays, Sam. And they picked me.''

Beneath the shadowed brim of her hat, Berkeley Shaw smiled.

Chapter Three

The work on the Phoenix fell into a lull when the men saw the approaching wagon. "By God," one of them called, surveying the height, width, and depth of the crates on the flat bed. "He's brought the mirrors with him!" That announcement was followed by whistles and a smattering of applause from the workers on the scaffold.

"Why are they so excited about the mirrors?" Berkeley whispered. She was sitting in the back of the wagon, just behind the driver's bench, and she had to get up on her knees to make herself heard by Grey and Sam Hartford.

Grey ignored her, but Sam answered. He glanced over his shoulder and looked down at the upturned face. "Because they think they know where they're goin', lad." He winked as if Berkeley should understand that. When he received only a blank look, he added, "Above the beds, don't you know?"

Under the brim of her hat, Berkeley's eyebrows lifted. She sank slowly back to the bed of the wagon as Sam reined in the team in front of the Phoenix.

"Heard enough?" Grey asked her a moment later. He had

waited until Sam was out of earshot attending the horses before he posed the question.

Berkeley's eyes scanned the building in front of her. Unlike the other structures on Portsmouth Square, this one was brick, not wood, and it stood a story higher than everything around it. Reflected sunlight on the rows of windows made them wink at her. Men on scaffolds were putting finishing touches on the trim, and one man, directly center of the building, was staining the naked breasts of a ship's figurehead.

"And seen enough," Berkeley said. "I think I made a mistake." She struggled to a crouching position in the crowded wagon, scooped up the cat, and started to climb over the side.

Grey grabbed her by the collar and hauled her back in. Berkeley lost her balance, fell solidly on her bottom, and caught her hip on the sharp corner of one of the crates. "Be careful," he said tightly. "You'll break one of the mirrors."

Tears sprang belatedly to Berkeley's eyes. She ducked her head to keep them from sight and hoped her sniffle was lost as the horses whinnied and snorted.

"Are you crying?" Grey asked as he dropped down from the wagon.

She shook her head and avoided his hand when he reached her chin. The cat tried to escape as she hugged it protectively.

Grey withdrew his hand and studied her bent head. "You're squeezing the cat," he said. She loosened her grip, and the tabby jumped right at his chest. It wasn't at all what he wanted but the cat didn't seem to realize that. She curled in his arms as soon as they went around her. Stroking the cat's back, Grey turned away from Berkeley. "Sam, get someone else to tend the horses. In fact, this little fellow can do it while you run some errands for me."

Sam finished tying off the reins. "What about the mirrors, Mr. Janeway?"

"Mr. Kincaid will get some of the workers to unload them." He motioned to Donnel Kincaid as the foreman walked out of the building. "The mirrors, Donnel."

"Aye, so I heard. All the way at the back of the third floor,

I was, and the news rumbled up like a Frisco shaker.'' He wiped his ruddy brow with his forearm and looked at the crates approvingly. "All of a piece, too."

"We think so," Grey said. "Sam and I only opened two of the crates at the wharf."

Berkeley, thinking she had been ignored long enough that an escape might be possible, began to slink over the side of the wagon.

Donnel thrust his large hands in his pockets, rocked back on his heels, and indicated her with a forward thrust of his square-cut jaw. "Where'd you find the bairn?" he asked Grey.

At first Berkeley thought he was talking about the cat, then she realized he meant her and that he'd called her a baby. She lifted her face long enough for Grey to see her flash of irritation before she accepted his hand and jumped to the ground.

"Sam will show you what needs to be done with the horses," Grey told her. To Donnel he said, "I wouldn't call him a bairn again. He took on two of the Ducks this morning and came close to coming out ahead."

Donnel whistled softly. A crease appeared between his fiery brows as he watched Berkeley dog Sam's footsteps. There was something . . . He shook off the thought, turned back to Grey, and was momentarily startled by being on the receiving end of his employer's watchful, flinty gaze. Donnel looked over his shoulder, wondering if he had intercepted a look meant for someone behind him, but there was no one there. "I'll take care of the mirrors, Mr. Janeway," he said. "Is there anything else you'll be wantin'?"

"That's all, Donnel."

The foreman thought he saw a hint of amusement in Grey Janeway's face now. He wiped his brow again, this time with a rag he had in his back pocket. It was the heat, he told himself, that accounted for his imagination.

Grey walked to the post where the lead horse was tethered. Berkeley paid him no attention as she wiped down the mare's damp flanks. Sam was standing over her, watching her work with a critical eye. "Sam," Grey said, "I need you to find

Ivory Edwards . . ." He paused, shaking his head, something like a smile edging his mouth as he remembered what Ivory had told him that morning. "She may be calling herself Ivory DuPree today. She's at Howard's place."

"The Palace," Sam offered. "I know who you mean."

"Good. Tell her that I need a couple of gowns from her. Her smallest ones. Something she's outgrown and couldn't bring herself to part with. And for God's sake, try not to insult her when you ask for them."

Sam's weathered face was deeply creased as he considered his problem. He scratched his brow with his fingertips. "Don't reckon I know how—"

"Well, think about it," Grey said. "Something will occur to you. Tell her I'll pay for them, whatever they cost to replace. That should soothe her a little. If it doesn't . . . duck."

"Duck," Sam repeated woefully.

"While you're there you may as well ask her where she buys her dresses, and if the seamstress has talent for making suitable gowns for a lady."

Sam frowned. "I don't think I should put it quite that way."

"Not unless you're very good at ducking," Grey said. The tabby stretched in his arms and turned over to have her belly rubbed. His mind otherwise occupied, Grey obliged without thinking. "Shoes. Bonnets. Stockings. Petticoats. Drawers. A nightshift." He stopped as Berkeley tugged on his sleeve. "What is it?"

She stepped between him and Sam and mouthed the words. One of Grey's brows arched and he looked at her consideringly, his eyes falling to the level of her loosely bound breasts. "And a corset, Sam. Ask Ivory if she has a corset."

Satisfied, Berkeley ducked out of the way again to tend to the horses.

Sam had his hat off now, and he was scratching his bald spot at the back. "You sure I'm the man to send, Mr. Janeway? Seems there's one or two others"—he looked pointedly at Berkeley's back—"around here that know something about a lady's undergarments. I'm no expert. Let the boy go. Miss Edwards wouldn't throw things at him.''

"Miss DuPree. And Ivory wouldn't let him in."

"On account he's so young?" Sam asked.

"On account he smells like fish."

Sam had to give in to this superior reasoning. Sure enough, the boy did smell like fish.

Grey went on. "Before you go, find someone to strike the tent across the square and bring my things here."

"You moving in, Mr. Janeway?" Sam Hartford was clearly surprised. "Beggin' your pardon, but you said you were going to wait until the building was finished."

"And I've changed my mind," Grey said. As owner of the Phoenix, Grey felt it was a sufficient explanation.

"But the furniture's not arrived and there's no—"

Grey almost laughed. "I've lived in a tent these past ten weeks. I think I can manage the hardships of sleeping indoors."

"Yes, sir."

When Sam didn't move, Grey said, "That's all, Sam. You can go. Oh, here, take this." He reached inside his jacket, withdrew some scrip from a silver money clip, and handed it to Sam. "Give this to Ivory. She knows this is good as gold in hand. I'll pay up later. And Sam, send Ivory my regards."

Grey watched Sam Hartford step down from the wooden sidewalk and head out across Portsmouth Square. "Leave the horses," Grey told Berkeley. "One of the workers will finish with them after the mirrors are unloaded."

That was when Berkeley realized that he had only ordered her to tend the animals because it would keep her busy and within his sights. She snapped open the cloth she'd been using and laid it over the hitching post. "I'm not going in there with you," she said.

"Really?" Grey said. He was undisturbed by this announcement, but curious. "I thought your request for a corset was an indication you agreed."

"My request? You thought I was asking for that for myself?"

"Weren't you?"

"I was simply pointing out that your list of clothing was lacking an important item. A lady's wardrobe would be incomplete without one."

"But not *your* wardrobe?"

"I didn't know you were talking about *my* wardrobe."

Grey watched, fascinated, as Berkeley's features became more animated. The green eyes flashed, and her chin came up. Her eyebrows disappeared under the band of her hat, and her mouth puckered in a pretty show of exasperation as she blew away a stray tendril of hair. "Don't you think you need more suitable clothes?"

"More suitable how?" she demanded. "That's what I'm asking myself, Mr. Janeway. I'm comfortable in these, even if they do smell like fish." She sniffed the air. "And horse sweat."

Grey was peripherally aware of two things: Berkeley's rising voice and the odd stares she was eliciting from his workers. Bending his head slightly, and leveling her with his gunmetal glance, he spoke in tones that were both quiet and intense. "If you weren't going to come in, Miss Shaw, then why come at all?"

"I didn't know you meant for me to be your whore, Mr. Janeway."

Grey's head jerked back and he stood up straight. A muscle worked in his cheek. Berkeley Shaw might as well have been the town crier for all the restraint she showed. Grey estimated that fully a third of the traffic on the *other* side of Portsmouth Square stopped to stare. By this evening it would have circulated among his associates, acquaintances, and enemies that Grey Janeway was a sodomite. "You really leave me no choice," he said.

Before Berkeley knew what he was about he had thrust the cat in her hands and was palming the top of her head. Grey wasn't conferring a blessing, though. He yanked off her hat and let a cascade of her poorly pinned hair fall around her shoulders and down her back. It lifted like a banner in the breeze and collected all the brightness of the sunshine in its corn silk length.

Grey simply stood there, stunned. He had hoped to find proof that she was a woman under her battered felt hat, but this silky fall of pale gold and platinum far exceeded his expectations. Crumbling the hat in his fist, Grey wrapped his free hand under her billowing hair and around her neck and herded her off the sidewalk.

Berkeley looked up as she was thrust toward the large red doors that marked the Phoenix's entrance. "What's that?" she asked, halting in her tracks two stories under the scaffold.

Grey nudged her, but she wouldn't be moved, at least not without some injury to herself. He followed her eyes upward and saw that she was looking through a space in the planks. "That's Rhea. Neptune's mother."

"It looks as if it belongs on the bow of a ship."

"It did. It's a figurehead." He gave her a push, and she moved this time. "But it belongs to the Phoenix now."

Berkeley entered the vast hall of the gaming house, heard the doors close behind her, and wriggled out from under Grey's grasp. She let the cat go and watched it dart off in search of prey among the stacked crates, discarded lumber, and furniture draped in yards of muslin. Running almost the entire length of the hall was a beautifully carved mahogany bar. Berkeley realized it had been recently installed because it wasn't covered by the same film of sawdust that lay over the floor. The brass foot rail was polished to a shine that was apparent even in the dimly lighted hall.

The muslin sheets outlined the shape of the protected furniture. Berkeley recognized gaming tables by their recessed tops or their peculiar kidney-bean design which allowed a dealer to stand on one side and pass cards easily to players seated in an arc on the other side. There looked to be enough chairs to accommodate a hundred gamblers and enough space at the open tables to take a crowd of two hundred more. Standing side to sideways, fifty men could put one foot on the rail and one elbow on the bar and comfortably knock back drinks for hours without fear of collapsing in the crush.

Berkeley pointed to the unfinished wall behind the bar. "The mirrors go there?" she asked.

Grey nodded. "Most of them."

"But none of them are going above the beds."

"That's right." He returned Berkeley's hat to her as she considered this.

"You just let people think that."

He shrugged and pointed toward the wide staircase at the back of the hall. "It's good for business. Come on. I'll show you where you can get out of those clothes."

"If it's all the same to you, I'll wash myself in them." When he looked at her oddly she explained, "I've done it before. In the bay. It's not so bad."

Grey glanced at the steps. There were a lot of them. The staircase curved to lend an air of elegance and drama. It had been his idea. Now he regretted it. The thought of carrying Berkeley Shaw up all those steps was not appealing, not when she was bound to squirm and kick and holler and likely to knock them both back to Kingdom Come.

He was working out the problem when two laborers came in hauling a crated mirror between them. "See those men," he said in an aside to Berkeley. "They can lift three times that weight between them. You won't present much of a challenge, and we can always put you in a crate if you do. Now, the stairs are that way. Can you manage them on your own, or do I ask Mike and Shawn to help you?"

Mike Winston and Shawn Kelly were grinning at each other as they gently set down their load. They looked on eagerly, waiting for Grey Janeway's guest to make her decision.

Berkeley jammed her hat on her head and marched off.

"Thanks, fellas," Grey called to them as he followed her. "I appreciate the help." Out of their line of sight one corner of his mouth lifted in a faint smile. Mike and Shawn had been eager to do a lot more. He caught up with Berkeley. "Can I anticipate more of these battles?"

"I expect so, Mr. Janeway."

He sighed. The tabby charged up the stairs beside him and

wound her way between Berkeley's feet. Grey had to catch her to keep her from tumbling. He felt her stiffen. "Miss Shaw, do you really think I have an interest in making you my whore?"

Berkeley squeezed out of his light grasp. "Don't you?"

"No."

"Someone else's whore, then?"

"No."

Without looking back, Grey took a few more steps. He heard Berkeley's light tread behind him.

"This is a brothel, isn't it?" she asked.

"No, it's a gambling hall and hostelry, not a whorehouse. I'm a businessman, Miss Shaw. Not a pimp. And if that's what you thought, why did you come? I didn't force you into the wagon at the wharf. You and the cat jumped in."

At the top of the stairs he turned right and headed down the hall. Berkeley had to quicken her step to keep up. "I thought you meant to help me," she said quietly. "I didn't mean that you should get nothing for it. I thought I might find work with you."

"What sort of work?"

"I don't know exactly," she said slowly, feeling her own inadequacies keenly. "But something. I'm not without a talent, you know."

Grey's tone was dry. "We'll discuss that later." He stopped in front of one of the large oak doors. The handle turned without inserting a key. "No locks yet, I'm afraid," he said. "Next week, Donnel tells me. Or the week after." He opened the door and gestured her inside.

Except for an enormous walnut desk and a pine crate turned on its end to serve as a chair, the room was empty. French doors were centered in the opposite wall and could open onto the balcony that overlooked Portsmouth Square. When she stepped farther into the room Berkeley could see part of the scaffold she had noticed earlier. She pressed the side of her face against the glass and watched the workman smooth linseed oil into the wooden goddess's hair. At least he had finished polishing her breasts.

Stepping away from the glass, her cheeks washed with a faint rose color, Berkeley walked to the fireplace. Imported marble tiles made up the lintel and jambs. The mantel was a single piece of polished walnut that blended seamlessly where it met the inlaid panels that completely covered the wall. A pair of brass sconces that still required their globes to be safely functional, flanked the mantelpiece. Above the walnut wainscoting that trimmed the rest of the room, a flocked wallpaper in two shades of blue had been chosen to keep the quarters from being too dark or close.

Berkeley pointed to the door set in the wall on her right. It was open a crack. "May I?" she asked.

"Of course. Look anywhere you like."

She supposed that if he had already furnished his apartments, he would not be so quick to extend an invitation, or at least he would feel compelled to follow her around. Berkeley knew she didn't present an appearance worth trusting. It wasn't only the fish odor that clung to her, but weeks of sleeping in alleys and scraping meals from refuse piles behind the eateries. If she had had the luxury of washing in the bay a hundred times a night, it couldn't have removed the desperate edge that poverty had given her. She wouldn't whore for Grey Janeway, but she wouldn't think twice about stealing from him.

Berkeley slowly circled the adjoining room. It would be a small library when it was finished. The shelves were in place, though lacking even a single book. Beyond that was what Berkeley suspected would be the bedroom. A bench had been built below the bay window that filled almost the entire wall, and there was also a door that led to the hallway. A dressing room completed the suite. It was narrow by the standards set by the previous rooms but still big enough to hold a massive armoire and a dressing table. The armoire was empty, and the table held no personal items.

Berkeley walked back into the bedroom. Grey was waiting for her, casually leaning in the doorway that led from the library. "Is it what you expected?"

She hadn't given a thought to expectations. There was no

denying it was a grand place, but then she would have been satisfied with a dry floor and roof that didn't leak. She didn't answer his question because she couldn't. "Is this where I'll be staying?"

Still watching her closely, Grey shook his head. "No."

Berkeley looked down at the floor to conceal her disappointment. Why had he brought her here if he didn't mean to give her shelter?

"You'll have a room down the hall."

Her head bobbed up. Her eyes were mirrors for her gratitude and her relief. "Do you mean it?"

To be on the receiving end of so much appreciation was a bit daunting. Grey's answer was clipped. "I just said so, didn't I?" He regretted his tone when he saw Berkeley flinch, but he didn't apologize. She didn't seem to be able to understand the enormous responsibility that she presented and that he didn't necessarily welcome it. Until this morning at the wharf, he'd made a point to avoid commitments that weren't totally related to business.

The tabby chose that moment to sprint into the bedroom. Her attention was immediately caught by the shaft of sunlight coming in through the window. She pawed at a dust mote that appeared to be suspended in the beam. Shaking his head, Grey watched the cat's antics for a moment. This was the Sydney Ducks' real revenge, he decided. His brief encounter with them had left him in charge of a lunatic cat and a singularly curious young woman. The Ducks could be very pleased with their morning's work. Without much effort they had managed to disrupt his life completely.

Berkeley reached for the cat as if she were a lifeline, but the tabby wanted no part of her. She leaped onto the window seat and settled in the sunlight. Berkeley stood up slowly, suddenly adrift.

Grey felt her uncertainty keenly. Until that moment he hadn't been entirely sure that she was alone. Now he knew.

Berkeley made a visible effort to shrug off her self-pity. There was nothing to be gained, and she doubted Grey would be moved by it. She didn't want him to feel sorry for her anyway. She could hardly prove her independence if she somehow became his responsibility.

"Mr. Janeway?" The call came from another room.

Grey turned toward the parlor. "In here."

Shawn Kelly appeared carrying an armload of books. "From your tent, sir. Where should I put them?" He looked around, became aware he was standing in Grey's small library, and offered, "What about on one of these shelves, Mr. Janeway?"

"That would be fine, Shawn. Don't bother to sort them."

"Oh, I wouldn't know how," Shawn said. "Never learned to read more than enough to get by." He pushed the books onto one of the shelves. "You'd better show us where you want the rest of your things. No sense moving more than once."

It was then Berkeley became aware of the approach of heavy footsteps in the hallway. She followed Grey back into the parlor in time to see a parade of workmen enter with canvas, poles, cots, trunks, blankets, cooking utensils, a pitcher, a basin, and a chair. Just when she thought no one else could fit into the room, two men hoisting a large wooden washtub on their shoulders walked in. Grey raised his hand, pointed in the direction of the dressing room, and the sea of men parted soundlessly. Berkeley jumped out of the way as they squeezed themselves and the washtub through.

"The canvas and poles have to go to the storage room," Grey told the men. "I'm not setting up a tent here. Cooking supplies to the kitchen. Leave the chair here; everything else in the bedroom."

Moving into a shadowed corner of the parlor, Berkeley watched the workmen move with choreographed simplicity. There was not even the slightest misstep as the belongings were distributed to their proper place in a matter of minutes. The men who had not gone to the kitchen and the storage room congregated back in the parlor. Grey struck a careless, casual pose that was becoming familiar to her as he hitched one hip on the edge of his desk and stretched a leg out to the side.

"Can I have a few volunteers to heat water and carry it back up here?'' he asked. "I'll need buckets of it, I'm afraid. The Phoenix's first guest will require a considerable amount of scrubbing before she's fit to take a room.''

Berkeley realized the shadows in her corner weren't nearly deep enough as the men turned in unison toward her. Cheeks aflame with humiliation, Berkeley tried to make herself invisible by staring at her feet and closing her eyes. She thought some of the men must have given Grey a silent indication they would help because no one volunteered aloud.

"Good," Grey said. "You can go. Oh, and if at any time you see Sam loitering in the hall downstairs, send him up." Grey waited until the men shuffled out and the door was closed before he addressed Berkeley. "You can come out now."

She didn't move.

"Or not," he said, shrugging as if it were of no importance. When she remained exactly as she was for longer than a minute Grey's patience came to an end. "I'm not going to apologize each time I trample your tender feelings. I expect I'll be doing it quite often."

Berkeley dragged the rumpled hat from her head and clutched it between her hands. More of her pale hair fell forward across her shoulders. She lifted her face a few degrees but still did not look at Grey. "I won't get used to it," she said softly. "I won't let myself."

"My God," Grey said under his breath. "How the hell have you managed to survive on your own?"

"By disguising myself as a boy." Now she looked at him straight on. "And you took that defense away from me when you lifted this hat off my head. All of your workers know the truth and most of the men in Portsmouth Square. If I can't hide what I am any longer, then I don't see that I should be expected to hide what I feel. You may ignore my tender feelings, but I won't let you pretend I haven't any."

Berkeley missed Grey's faint smile because she glanced away too quickly. He noticed that these flashes of temerity seemed to have the capacity to surprise her. She was staring at the floor again as if waiting to be set in her place, not realizing she had set him firmly in his.

Grey pushed out the chair the workers left behind. It scraped against the floor, drawing her attention. "Sit down, Miss Shaw."

"I'm fine," she said. "Really, I—"

"Did you think I was inviting you to have a seat?" he asked. "I wasn't. It was an order." He held up one hand, staving off her protest. "Consider your argument said, heard, and ignored. Have a seat, Miss Shaw."

With the momentum she achieved by pushing herself out of the corner, Berkeley managed to cross the room. She pulled the chair back a few feet so she wasn't directly beneath his gaze and sat down. "Is it your intention to interrogate me?" she asked.

"It is my intention that you should stop cowering in that corner." He stood, skirted the edge of the desk, and sat on the pine crate. "Let's agree to hold further discussion until the water arrives." Without giving her another glance he began leafing through a stack of papers, sorting and filing them away in one of the drawers. While she looked on silently, Grey made an occasional note on something he read or scribbled an addition to a list he was compiling.

Almost an hour elapsed before workmen appeared at Grey's suite. Berkeley was asleep in the stiff ladderback chair she occupied, her head cocked sideways at an awkward angle and her hands lying palm up in her lap. The abused hat that she had twisted and tugged while she held her tongue lay on the floor at her feet.

Grey rose from behind the desk quietly and went to the door. He met the bucket brigade in the hallway. He gave them instructions on preparing the bathtub and motioned them to use the door leading directly into the bedroom. They accomplished their task with a surprising amount of efficiency for men who had never been in service in their lives. Grey thought their eagerness to please had a lot less to do with him than it did with Berkeley's cascade of corn silk hair and the fey appeal of her leaf green eyes.

He dismissed the men, then went to Berkeley and tapped her lightly on the shoulder. She didn't stir. Grey bent and slipped one arm behind her back and another under her knees. Her head lolled comfortably against his chest. He looked down at her sleeping features and felt a small resentment for the trust she had extended him.

Grey carried her through the library and bedroom and into the dressing room. The tub had been lined with a sheet to protect her from the rough slats and filled three-quarters of the way with hot water. Two more rinsing buckets stood by. Towels, soap, and washcloths lay on top of the trunk lid. There was nothing left to be done.

"Miss Shaw?"

"Hmmm?"

"Your bath is ready."

Berkeley's only response was to offer an abrupt little snore and burrow against him.

Grey saw the cat wander into the doorway and stare at him curiously. "This could happen to you," he told the tabby. "So learn from it." He lowered Berkeley over the tub until he was in a position to drop her. Then he did.

The tabby meowed loudly, back arched, as Berkeley came up spitting and flinging water. The cat ran away. Berkeley had nowhere to go. She pushed the damp curtain of hair out of her eyes, then tried to lift herself out of the tub. She was held in place by the hand on her shoulder. "Do you mean to drown me?" she demanded, sinking back under the weight of Grey's palm.

"It has a certain appeal," he admitted. He straightened. "You can take off your clothes and put them on the floor. Call me when you're done, and I'll get them out of here." He took her silence as assent and went to the trunk. The bar of soap he pitched in her direction landed heavily in the water when she missed it. While Berkeley groped for it Grey tossed the washcloth and laid the towels beside the tub. He opened the trunk lid, rooted among the contents, and came away with another sheet. With no explanation he left the dressing room.

Berkeley felt her mouth sag a little as she stared after him. Did he really expect her to strip at his command? Wash, just because he'd thrown soap at her? The only thing worse would be if he tried to scrub her down himself. Berkeley began to heave herself out of the tub just as Grey walked back into the room. This time he was carrying a hammer, rope, and, between his teeth, two nails. He gave her a quelling look and she lowered herself into the water while he began to rig a curtain that would separate the tub from the rest of the dressing room.

"What are you doing?" she asked.

"It's for your privacy."

"I don't understand. You can just as easily shut the door on your way out."

"I could," he said. "If I intended to go out. Stay where you are. There's no need to scatter water to every part of the room. I intend to talk to you, and we can't have a conversation if there's a closed door between us. I thought this would be an acceptable compromise."

"It's not."

"It's the best I can do."

"A compromise would be for you to allow me to bathe alone and engage in conversation later."

"Yes, but that wouldn't be acceptable to me." Ignoring her bewildered expression, Grey finished attaching the rope and tied two corners of the sheet to it. The curtain partitioned off the area of the room where Berkeley sat in the tub. "No one will be bringing more hot water," he told her. "You'd do well to get out of those clothes now."

"I don't think I can."

Grey had to strain to hear her. Berkeley's voice was barely audible. "I'll strip them off you myself," he said. Grey realized that her modesty, if that's what it was, was unexpected. It hadn't occurred to him that she would offer so much resistance over such a trifle. Hadn't she told him that she would have been willing to bathe in the bay? And she had already been walking around San Francisco for weeks wearing trousers. That behavior, even though it had probably been born of necessity, didn't impress Grey as modest. "I mean it, Miss Shaw." He paused. "Your alternative is to leave. And the cat goes with you."

There was a long silence; then Grey heard her sigh. That breathy little sound was followed by some wet piece of clothing slapping against the floor. Satisfied, Grey sat on the trunk and waited. One piece followed another. Occasionally there was a soft grunt as an article proved difficult to get out of. "Finished?" he asked her when he thought she had lowered herself into the water again. There was no answer. "If you're nodding, Miss Shaw, I can't hear you."

"Yes," she said. "I'm finished."

"Then I'm going to take your clothes."

Berkeley went under the water to the level of her nose. It was an unnecessary precaution. Grey didn't come around the curtain; he merely reached under it. She watched what was left of her belongings disappear. Except for the earring she was clutching in her palm, she had nothing.

Grey wasn't gone long, but Berkeley didn't doubt she would never see those clothes again. She imagined they were burning in the same stove that had been used to heat her water.

"I don't hear anything," Grey said. "Have you finished washing?"

"I haven't begun."

"Do you require help?"

Berkeley sat up and examined the earring in her hand. She placed it carefully over the side of the tub and took up the washcloth and soap. "No," she said, resigned. "I don't require help."

"Good. I don't know anything about being a lady's maid."

Berkeley let the comment pass. She applied herself to her bath, permitting herself to experience some pleasure in the fact that she would finally be clean.

Grey sat on the trunk again and stretched out his legs in front of him. "Where are you from, Miss Shaw?"

"Baltimore." It was the last place she lived, so there was truth in that. Anderson had always taught her not to stray far from the truth. Lies were easily found out. "I was born in Charleston." She didn't mention that she had spent her first six years growing up there. "What about you, Mr. Janeway? Where are you from?"

"All over." He crossed his arms in front of him. "How did you get to San Francisco?"

"I came on a Remington clipper in June. We crossed at Panama, and another packet brought us here."

"We?"

"I meant me and the other passengers."

"I don't believe for a moment that you traveled here unescorted. Who brought you?"

Berkeley's hand faltered. The soap slipped out from under the cloth, and she had to make a grab to recover it before it floated away. "My father," she said.

"Where is he now?"

"I . . . I don't know."

"You don't?"

"No," she said. "I don't. You really don't have the right to do this, Mr. Janeway. Or are you going to tell me I can go if I don't answer your questions?"

"I was thinking about it," he said dryly.

Berkeley began soaping her hair. She raised a little lather and scrubbed hard at her scalp. "He deserted me, Mr. Janeway," she said. "Is that what you wanted to know?"

"Was he a miner?"

"He thought he could be. It was all he talked about, getting to San Francisco to try his hand at a claim. He bought a parcel of land before we left Baltimore."

Grey had heard of men coming to the Sierra Nevada foothills thinking they already had a stake in an active mine. If the parcel existed, it was played out. Most men discovered the same parcel had been sold three or four times over if they could find it at all. "Did you go with him to find the claim?"

"Yes." Berkeley closed her eyes. She did not want to think

about it. She certainly did not want to talk about it. Reaching over the side of the tub, Berkeley managed to pull one of the rinsing buckets toward her. It was more of a struggle to lift and pour, but she was enormously satisfied when she could ignore Grey's offer to help and do the thing herself.

"How long has he been missing?" Grey asked when the splashing quieted.

"A month."

"You left the mining camp to try to find him yourself?"

"Not immediately. I waited for him as he told me to do, but it wasn't safe. There were other miners. They came around too often. I think some of them suspected I wasn't my father's son."

So she had been masquerading as a boy even then. Berkeley's father had a lot to answer for. Grey had seen firsthand how gold fever could scramble a man's common sense and reasoning ability. "Why didn't you stay in Baltimore?"

"There was no one there. My mother died when I was sixteen. That's when I mar—" She stopped, realizing what she had been about to say.

"Yes?" Grey asked. "That's when you what?"

"When I made the decision to take care of my father."

"I thought we already established that you need a keeper, Miss Shaw. I can hardly credit you were the one looking after your father."

"You may believe me or not, Mr. Janeway. I won't try to persuade you."

Grey unfolded his arms and leaned forward. "Why did your father come back to the city?" he asked.

"Supplies," she said. Again, there was some truth in that. Anderson had also been interested in whoring and had minced no words in telling her. "I think he had some idea that he might go to the land office and recover his money. Not that it really matters. He left me behind, and I haven't heard from him." She hesitated. "I suspect he's dead."

Grey suspected precisely the same thing. "What now, Miss Shaw?"

"What do you mean?"

"How will you manage? You were eager to get on the Remington ship this morning, but you seemed almost as satisfied to pass on your letter. How important is it to you to leave San Francisco?"

"There is nothing more important," she said. "But as you pointed out, I need money."

"And your letter was about getting money?"

"Not at all. There's no one who's going to send me funds." That was entirely the truth. She could not imagine that any one of the Thornes would be moved to send her money. The passage of time would have had them questioning what they had seen in their own parlor. How much could they really trust her? they would be wondering. Their doubts had probably begun the moment she and Anderson had disappeared. The correspondence from San Francisco could only alleviate a few fears. Berkeley picked up the earring and laid it across her palm. She stared at it a moment before her fingers closed around it.

Decker Thorne had challenged her to make the right choice during his final test. Berkeley wasn't certain she had. The Thornes weren't likely to come to her aid.

"Are you finished, Miss Shaw?"

There was an edge of impatience in his voice that let Berkeley know it wasn't the first time Grey Janeway had asked the question. "I only need to dry now," she said. She raised herself out of the water and toweled off her hair, careful not to lose the earring. "Has Mr. Hartford returned with clothes for me?"

"No," Grey said. He extended his arm around the edge of the curtain and held out his own hunter green dressing gown. "You can put this on until he arrives."

Berkeley finished drying quickly, stepped out of the tub, and took the satin dressing gown. She knew it was going to be yards too big for her, but she didn't care. The material only caressed her skin. The sleeves slipped fluidly down her arms, and when she belted the gown at the waist it was as if she had wrapped herself in a cool waterfall.

Berkeley dropped the earring into the pocket of the robe and stepped around the curtain. Her arms were folded protectively under her breasts, and she didn't quite know where to look. She could feel Grey Janeway's eyes moving over her, and she willed herself not to blush or stammer. He made her feel young in a way she never had been.

"May I have a comb?" she asked.

Seeing her now, Grey wondered that she had been successful so long in her street-urchin masquerade. Berkeley Shaw was still a bit of a thing—the crown of her head would fit neatly under his chin—but there was no denying that she was female. Her face was heart-shaped, her generous mouth sweetly curved, and there was a provocative slant to the fathomless green eyes. Her eyebrows, arched in a delicate curve, were a few shades darker than her gold-and-platinum hair, but her lashes were darker yet and shaded eyes that were already a deep mystery to him.

Her neck was a slender stem. He could make out the pulse beating at the base of her throat. She held her narrow shoulders straight now as her arms fell to her sides. He could see that she was trying not to tug on the overlong sleeves of his gown, trying not to show that she was bothered by his scrutiny. She had pulled the robe tightly across her chest. In her effort not to expose any of her fair skin, she had emphasized the swell of her breasts. The nipples were hard beneath the fabric, their thrust plainly visible.

Her waist was tiny and higher than he would have thought given her earlier attire. She had worn the trousers low, and the flannel shirt hadn't revealed the slender line of her body or the true length of her legs. A bare foot peeped out from beneath the hem. The toes wiggled.

Grey smiled slightly. He was familiar with that foot. Everything else was a revelation.

"A comb?" she asked again.

"I heard you the first time."

Which meant, Berkeley supposed, that he simply wasn't going to give her one until he was ready.

Grey stood, opened the trunk, and found a comb and a brush.

As an afterthought he also handed her his mirror. She took all three items eagerly and fled immediately into the empty bedroom. Grey followed at a more leisurely pace. He stood just inside the doorway and leaned against the wall. Berkeley had already pushed the sleeping cat out of the shaft of sunlight and taken the same position for herself on the window seat. Damp and tangled, her hair was a gossamer halo about her head. The pale threads reflected sunlight.

Berkeley put down the brush and mirror but kept the comb. She began working it through her hair, starting at the ends. She was very much aware that Grey's eyes hadn't left her. "You must have something else to do," she said, sparing him a glance.

"I can't think of anything."

"I wish you wouldn't stare."

"You have to be used to it. You must know you're a beautiful woman."

Berkeley didn't flush. She thought the compliment too outrageous to take seriously. "I know nothing of the kind, Mr. Janeway." Still, she was used to being watched. Anderson did it all the time, though not in precisely the same way as Grey. It was very much as if she had acquired a keeper after all. What she didn't know any longer was how she felt about it.

Grey watched Berkeley's fingers move deftly through her hair. There was a graceful sweep to her hands that wasn't practiced or planned. The movement was as hypnotically soothing as the rise and fall of the tides. He had no intention of looking away.

"May I ask you a question?" Berkeley said.

"Of course."

"This morning . . . at the wharf . . . how did you know I wasn't a boy?"

Grey's flinty stare easily stopped Berkeley's hand and pinned her just where she sat.

"Are you certain you want to know?" he asked flatly.

She thought she did when she asked the question. Now she wasn't as sure. "Yes."

"I didn't know immediately, if it's any consolation. I didn't know when you were darting back and forth along the dock. When you were flinging fish at the Ducks I still had no idea. But after you came running at me and attached yourself to my back like a—"

"Limpet?" she suggested. It sounded so much nicer than barnacle.

"Leech," he corrected. "Just like a leech. It was then that two particularly interesting things about your anatomy became known to me."

"You mean my—" She broke off and merely looked down at herself. The slippery material of the dressing gown had parted, and the gap gave her an unrestricted view.

Grey watched her yank the lapels closed, denying him even a hint of her rosy skin. "I mean your breasts," he said.

Berkeley's mouth twisted to one side. Her expression was disapproving. "I know the circumstances of our meeting were unusual, Mr. Janeway, and I haven't given you reason to think highly of me, but I'm unaccustomed to vulgarities. I do wish you'd refrain from—"

"They're *your* breasts, Miss Shaw, and you pressed them flat against my back. You may want to refrain from doing that in the future or bringing them into conversation at all."

"But I didn't," she defended. "You're the one who—"

He interrupted her. "You're the one who wanted to know how I knew you weren't a boy. I remember giving you the opportunity to take back your question. You didn't, and I politely answered it. In any event, breasts are not vulgar at all."

"I liked it better when I was a boy," she muttered.

Grey cleared his throat to cover his short laugh. "If it will be a small comfort, Miss Shaw, I shall try to choose my words more carefully and not give offense."

Berkeley wondered if he was serious. His eyes were solemn, and there was no amused slant to his mouth. She decided to believe him. He was not entirely without manners, and his treatment of her, though brusque at times, had been far short of abominable.

Grey pushed away from the wall as Berkeley resumed combing her hair. "So how do we go on from here?" he asked.

"I expect I shall have to find employment," she said.

"Can you cook?"

"No," she said regretfully. "Not so that I could earn my way."

"That's unfortunate. The last woman who got off one of the packet boats and could cook is now earning a thousand dollars a month at the El Dorado. I know because I bid for her services. I drove the price up so they didn't get her cheaply, but I would have liked to have hired her here."

"A thousand dollars." Berkeley's tone was awed. "Perhaps I could learn."

Grey shook his head. "Not in the Phoenix's kitchen. This city has enough problems with fires." He noticed she didn't appear hurt by his refusal. He remembered she had mentioned a talent earlier. "Do you sing? Dance? Play an instrument?"

"Not so that I could earn my way," she repeated.

"Do you know anything about gaming? Faro? Dice? Poker?"

"No."

"Needlework?"

"No."

"And you don't want to whore."

"No!"

It was the answer Grey had expected, but her vehemence made it difficult to keep his smile in check. "Well then, what is it you *can* do, Miss Shaw?"

Berkeley set down the comb. "Give me your hand, Mr. Janeway, and I'll show you."

Chapter Four

Berkeley's request brought the full force of Grey's skeptical gaze. "You know some parlor trick with palms and fortunes?" he asked incredulously. *"That's* your talent?"

"Please," she said, nudging the cat aside. "Sit down. I don't believe you'll be disappointed."

His short laugh scoffed her. "I can't be. I have absolutely no expectations."

She noticed that in spite of his words he still hadn't moved. One of her eyebrows arched, and she patted the space beside her. "Come," she said. "You're not afraid, are you?"

It hadn't occurred to Grey that he might be hesitating because of fear. "Now you're being absurd," he told her. But he was staring at her deeply green eyes and wondering suddenly if she sensed something he was denying. Grey walked to the window bench and sat. He held out his left hand.

Berkeley only glanced at it. "Your right one, please. You're right-handed."

"How did you know?" Then he remembered she had seen him writing at his desk. This *was* just a parlor trick, he reminded himself.

"There are signs in your palm," she said.

"Yes, of course." His tone was clearly disbelieving, but he dutifully raised his right hand.

Berkeley took his hand in both of hers and turned it palm up. She supported the back of it with her left hand and laid her right one over the top. Her fingers trailed lightly across his skin, and her head lowered in the same motion. She inched closer.

She no longer smelled of fish. It was the wayward thought that occurred to Grey as he stared at her bent head. The faint scent of his soap clung to her skin and pale hair. Then there was something else, another fragrance, more subtle and vaguely tantalizing, one he couldn't define but that might have been just her.

Her fingertips were cool, her touch like threads of silk crossing his palm. The hand that supported his was strong. She seemed unaware of how close she held him to her breast.

"How peculiar," she said softly.

Grey waited, but she didn't enlighten him. She probably had no idea what to say, he realized. She was making this up as she went along. It didn't really matter. Berkeley Shaw could say most anything. The men who came to gamble in his house would put down gold just to have her hold their hand—especially if she took it directly to her breast.

Unaware of Grey's straying thoughts, Berkeley began to tell him what his palm revealed. "You're quite intelligent," she said quietly. "And clever. They're not the same thing at all, you know, and you're both. You're a kind man, though perhaps it is not something you wish others to know. I do not even think you permit yourself to believe it." She glanced up at him, but his expression was guarded in a way his palm could not be. The implacable blue-gray eyes were mirrorlike, drawing in her gaze, then reflecting it back. She did not see kindness there.

Berkeley's eyes dropped away. Her finger traced his heart line. "It is in your nature to help others even though you resist the notion. You have given a great deal of thought to your beliefs, and you act on them, in spite of what those close to you may think.''

Grey permitted himself a small, archly satisfied smile. There *was* no one close to him.

''You are rather an insular man,'' Berkeley went on. ''There is a certain amount of pride in your self-sufficiency. The secrets that you keep in your heart keep others away, and that's important to you. It has become a way of life.'' She paused, retracing the line lightly. ''It has been this way for a very long time.''

''Do you know my secrets, Miss Shaw?'' Grey asked.

She shook her head. ''Only that you have them.''

''What man doesn't?''

Berkeley's smile was gentle. ''Just so, Mr. Janeway. Do you want to know more?''

''Please, by all means.''

Ignoring the challenge in his invitation, Berkeley studied the marks of his life again. His hand was large, capable. The fingers were lean and strong, and the tips were rough from hard, physical labor. There was evidence of a callus on the heel of his hand. ''You have no difficulty giving orders. Other men look to you for leadership, and you take on that responsibility somewhat reluctantly. You prefer to provide it by example, working alongside those you lead.''

Berkeley's fingers drew over his palm again. A small shiver passed through her. The response was so unexpected that she almost dropped his hand. ''I'm sorry,'' she said. ''I'm not certain what—''

''It's a good effect,'' Grey said. ''You should keep it in. Adds an authentic touch.''

Berkeley didn't defend herself or try to explain what had just occurred. The truth was, she didn't know. ''You've had one love in your life,'' she said, keeping her voice steady. ''But not a true love.''

''What makes you say that?''

She pointed to the small lines on the side of his hand just below his little finger. ''This first one is weak and only faintly traced,'' she said. "It's shallow and without purpose. Perhaps you imagined yourself in love.''

"Don't all men do that?''

"I don't know,'' she said. Her glance was curious. "Did you?''

Grey didn't know either. He often wondered if there was a woman his damaged memory had left behind, but he had never felt compelled to find out. He had imagined that if there had been someone—a true love, as Berkeley named her—then he would have known somehow, and been moved by forces beyond reason and past explanation to find her. "Yes,'' Grey said at last. He found himself not wanting to disappoint Berkeley. She obviously believed what she was telling him. "There was a love, just as you said.''

Berkeley nodded. "But nothing came of it.''

"No,'' he said, smiling. "Not a thing.''

"I wasn't entirely certain,'' she admitted now. "You see, your lines are quite odd. It's almost as if you have two lives. Or have had two. I can't get any sense of the time of it all. It can be interpreted in different ways, I suppose. This lifeline is broken right here.'' She pointed to the distinct unmarked space in his palm.

Grey found himself bending his own head. "What does it mean?''

"What it means doesn't make sense,'' she said. Berkeley looked up and found herself directly in the line of his gaze, his face very close to hers.

"How do you mean?'' Grey asked.

"By all rights, Mr. Janeway, you should be dead.''

Grey simply stared at her. It took considerable effort not to show that she had struck him this time. "As you said, it doesn't make sense. I'm quite alive.''

"Yes, I know.'' Berkeley pulled back a little, uncomfortable with the narrowing space between them. His posture hadn't changed at all. He gave the appearance of being relaxed, even slightly amused, but there was a tension in his hand that he couldn't hide from her now. She was aware of the potential strength in his fingers and the grip he could make around her own wrist. She had a sense suddenly that she held him only because he permitted it, and that it could easily have been the other way around, that perhaps he even wished now that it was.

Feeling trapped, Berkeley tore her eyes away from his and willed herself to breathe evenly. "It's only one possible interpretation," she said. "It easily could be explained by a separation of your public and private self. Two faces. Two lives. Or just that you've put some important part of your past behind you. You've obviously experienced a great deal of turmoil. There have been enormous hardships and losses. A betrayal. You're very much alone, Mr. Janeway, but it's by your own choice."

Grey frowned slightly. Intrigued in spite of himself, he said, "Explain yourself."

"Here," she said, pointing to the beginning of his lifeline. "This cluster of lines. Your family roots."

"I don't have any family."

"You don't recognize them," she corrected, watching him closely. "There's a difference."

Grey's remote eyes didn't flicker. "If you say so, Miss Shaw."

Berkeley lowered his hand. "You're a rather lucky man," she said. "Though it may be more accurate to say that you have the ability to recognize a change in your fortunes and use it to your advantage."

"Yes," he said dryly. "That would be more accurate."

She ignored his tone. "You can depend on a long life, though not one that will be without its difficulties. I suspect you will marry."

"You only suspect?"

"It's clear that you will have children, Mr. Janeway." She held up four fingers, paused, and then extended her thumb. "Five." Berkeley looked at him. "Do you already have a child?"

He didn't know. "No."

She frowned. "I don't know what to make of that. It's clearly there."

"I would know if I had a child, Miss Shaw." But he wouldn't, he thought, and he didn't.

"I think the child isn't yours."

That made no sense to Grey. "Do I have a child or not?" he demanded.

Berkeley started at his tone. "I can't really say. You've said you don't, and that's probably true, but your palm says one of your children won't be yours." Agitation made her voice rise a notch. "I can't do any better than that, Mr. Janeway. It's up to you to make some sense of it. I can only tell you what I see."

"You can't say whether I'll marry or not. That shouldn't be so difficult to make out."

"It has everything to do with you," she said tartly. "You could always choose not to marry the mother of your children."

"And perhaps I'll choose to marry the mother of the child who isn't mine. That should nicely twist my life."

"She's one and the same," Berkeley told him. "And don't ask me to explain. I can't." It wasn't even what the lines of his life told her. It was what she *felt.* "In any event, your life will be rather complicated by her. Interesting, I think, but complicated."

"It became that this morning," he said under his breath. He surprised himself by thrusting out his hand again. "What can you tell me about wealth, Miss Shaw? If you're going to read palms to miners, then you have to be very clear about money."

Berkeley hesitated. She really had no desire to hold his hand again. There was a certain amount of discomfort in touching him that owed nothing to reading his palm. He made her aware of herself, of her breathing, of her rapid pulse, of the tremor in her own fingers.

Attempting to hide her reluctance, Berkeley accepted his palm. She could feel him start to withdraw even as she took it. She raised her eyes curiously.

"I don't expect you to do something you find distasteful," Grey said. "It's clear you're having second thoughts."

"No," she said. "You don't understand. It has nothing to do with you, not the way you obviously think."

"Suppose you explain."

"No, I don't think I will." She would not make herself the object of his amusement by admitting he made her heart beat a little unsteadily. Berkeley drew Grey's attention back to his palm. "Wealth is the one constant in your life, Mr. Janeway. You've always been a rich man."

Grey almost laughed aloud. It hadn't been very many years ago that he had been fighting for food scraps. If the hardtack had only one wormhole, it was fit for eating. He could have been moved to kill for a mouthful of biscuit that wasn't mealy, if there had been such a thing. "You may want to look at that again," he said.

She did. "No, I'm not mistaken. You have quite a lot of money. You always have." She put down his hand again. "I find it odd that you came to San Francisco at all."

"Oh? Why odd?"

"I imagine that most men come here for the same reasons as my . . . my father. Because they entertain some hope of a rich strike and wealth beyond what they can spend in their own lifetime. You have that already. I would say you were born into it."

"You're wrong there," Grey said. "But I've made my fortune, so I won't quibble with your interpretation. Can I expect not to lose it?"

"I believe it's safe to say that."

Now Grey did laugh. "You don't want to give away the game, do you? Too many particulars might spoil it for some people, is that the way it works?"

Berkeley didn't deny it. What would have been the point? she thought. "Something like that," she offered.

"Another enigmatic reply," he said approvingly. "I rather think you *do* have a talent, though what can be made of it remains to be seen." Grey stood. Without explaining himself, he left the bedroom, then the suite.

Berkeley heard the door of the sitting room open, and his footsteps receded in the hall. She looked at the cat in bewilderment but the tabby accepted her notice as an invitation and launched herself onto Berkeley's lap. Her claws dug painfully into the satin dressing gown, causing Berkeley to give a little yelp. She pulled the cat away, held her at eye level, and spoke to her sternly. She was developing the finer points of her lecture when Grey returned.

"Oh," she said softly, lowering the much chastised cat onto her lap. "I didn't hear you come in."

"So I gathered." He remained just inside the doorway. "I've asked Shawn to come up here. And we're also going to get some food. I assume you're hungry."

She was almost sick with hunger, but it was of little consequence to her. Berkeley looked down at herself, then at Grey. "I'm not dressed to receive a visitor."

Grey watched her yank the robe's sash more tightly around her. It caused the lapels to part again and presented a glimpse of the high curves of her breasts. No, she was not dressed to receive a visitor. "See what you can find in my trunk," he said. Grey checked his pocket watch. "I would have thought Sam would have been back by now."

Berkeley barely heard him. Cat in tow, she hurried into the dressing room and shut the door. Knowing that Grey would probably consult his watch as she performed her change, Berkeley flung open the trunk and rooted through it quickly. She appeared in the bedroom a few minutes later wearing a blue-chambray shirt, denim trousers, and a pair of thick socks. The long tails of the shirt were bunched inside the trousers, while the trouser legs were bunched inside the socks. Her hair was once again tucked inside a hat, this time one of his.

Grey stared at her. "You look . . ." He paused, searching for an adequate description. "Thick."

Berkeley flashed him an uncertain smile. "Yes, I do rather. I can't help it though. You really have nothing suitable."

"Yes, well, Sam can't get here soon enough to my way of thinking." He turned as he heard Shawn's approach behind him. "This way, Shawn."

Berkeley had hoped to see a tray of food in the worker's hands, but they were empty. Her stomach rolled again, this time with dread.

Grey directed them both to sit down on the window seat, then motioned Berkeley to take the bewildered worker's callused hand. "Miss Shaw has a bit of a trick, Shawn. I'd like to hear your opinion of it."

Berkeley lifted Shawn's palm, supporting the back of his hand in the same manner she had Grey's. "You've had a hard life," she said quietly, "but no harder than you expected. There was an important loss early on. One of your parents." She shook her head. "No, that's not quite right. It was your grandmother who was raising you; she's the one you miss." Berkeley didn't look up to see Shawn's astounded expression. "You can expect to live a long life and marry again but you won't have any children. Any *more* children, I should say. You'll prosper here in San Francisco though not in the goldfields." She raised her face and smiled at him. "Watch Mr. Janeway," she said. "And learn from him. He can make you a rich man."

Shawn Kelly snatched his hand back and cradled it against his chest as if he had suffered an injury. "She's bewitched, Mr. Janeway, and that's a fact."

"Yes." Grey sighed. "I suspect she is."

The thickly muscled laborer stood up, clearly stunned by what he'd heard. "Not a soul here knows about my grandmother," he said. "I never said a word."

"Are you married?" asked Grey.

Shawn shook his head. "I was though. My Meg died. And we have two children, just like she said. A boy and a girl. Meg's mother's bringin' them up, and I'm to send for them when I'm settled myself." He looked down at Berkeley. "And you think if I take my cue from Mr. Janeway, I'll make my fortune?"

"I know you'll prosper," she said.

"Oh my," he said, awed.

Grey's tone was dry. "Indeed." He blocked Shawn's path as the worker would have made a quick exit. "What I'm interested in, Mr. Kelly, is if you would have paid Miss Shaw for the information she just gave you."

Shawn's black brows came together in a single line above his eyes. "Hope's a precious thing," he said. "I'd pay for a piece of it, Mr. Janeway. Sure, and I would."

Grey nodded. "You can go."

Shawn backed out of the room, thanking Berkeley as he went. He excused himself when he bumped into Grey, then he hurried out.

Grey was grimacing as his attention turned to Berkeley. "Thank you very much."

His tone made no sense to her. He didn't sound pleased at all, and she had only done as he asked. "I don't understand. You asked me to—"

"I didn't think you were going to tell him to watch me. I won't be able to turn around without seeing him. The idea that I can make him a fortune is absurd."

"He didn't think so."

Grey had to agree with her. Shawn took the information in stride. "Let us establish right now that whatever else you choose to tell these men about their futures and fortunes, my name will not come up in it."

"But—"

"Miss Shaw, I can't very well have a band of miners in step behind me."

"But you can't dictate that sort of thing. I shall have to find some other way to say it if it comes up again."

Grey decided he could be satisfied with that for now. "What about his family?" he said. "How did you know he was married?"

"There were two marriages indicated in his palm. It was safe to assume that at his age one had already taken place."

"No, Miss Shaw, I mean *truly,* how did you know?"

Berkeley remained silent.

"So I'm not the only one with secrets," Grey said.

"Believe as you like, but don't ask me again how it's done when you don't want to hear the answer."

Grey was considering how to reply to that when his thoughts were interrupted by a shout from the hallway. He heard Berkeley following him as he went to the sitting room to get the door. "Luncheon," he said, taking the tray. "Where'd you get this, Mike?"

"The El Dorado."

Grey knew it would be better than edible. It would be delicious. He thanked Mike but saw that the worker was hesitating, shuffling slightly and trying to glimpse past him into the interior of the sitting room. "Is there something else?" asked Grey. He had a fairly good idea of what it might be.

"Well, sir," Mike began somewhat uneasily. "Shawn stopped me as I was coming in the front and told me the oddest thing. I was . . . well, I was wondering, Mr. Janeway, if the lady would have a go at my hand. Sort of set me on the right path, so to speak."

Grey turned to Berkeley. She was staring hard at the tray of food in his hands. "Perhaps later, Mike. The lady's hungry—"

"No," Berkeley said. "I'll do it."

Shrugging, Grey let Mike pass and set the tray on the desk. He sat on the pine crate behind it and began uncovering dishes. The El Dorado's cook had prepared the seafood gumbo that was her particular specialty. The stew was so spicy the aroma alone burned the back of Grey's throat. Somewhere in the French Quarter of New Orleans there was a brothel sadly missing Annie Jack's fine cooking. It was San Francisco's gain.

Grey scooped rice into a large bowl and added a substantial helping of the gumbo. He tore the crust off the slab of warm bread, then began eating while he watched Berkeley draw Mike in with a few words and a shy, sideways look.

"Right here," she said, tracing his lifeline. "See how it branches? This is a picture of the confusion you sometimes experience. You've had choices in your life, not too few, but too many, and you wonder about some of them. You wonder

how different your life might be if you had stayed on the farm."
She paused. "Ohio? Is your family's farm in Ohio?"

"Yes, miss," he said eagerly. "It is."

Grey almost choked on his second mouthful of gumbo.
"Mike, I thought you were from Kentucky."

"I am. Directly south of Cincinnati. Part of the farm borders
the Ohio River. Easy enough for her to get confused about a
little thing like that."

"Yes, isn't it," Grey said.

Berkeley ignored him. "Do you have a question for me?"
she asked Mike.

"What?" Grey said, feigning surprise. "You don't know
what he wants to know?"

This time Berkeley's mouth pursed to one side, and she had
to draw on a well of patience to keep silent.

It was Mike who defended her. "Please, Mr. Janeway, she
can't think if you keep interrupting."

"I apologize." He noticed that the cat was circling his legs,
and he dropped her a bit of shrimp. "You'd think she would
know," he whispered to the tabby.

"Your question?" Berkeley asked again.

Mike thought he was going to ask if he would strike gold.
Instead, he heard himself say, "Will I see my family again?"

Berkeley Shaw felt the full measure of yearning that
prompted that question. She looked down at his palm and
answered the only way that she could. "Yes, you'll see them
again. Sooner, rather than later. You should write to them. Let
them know that you miss them." Her voice was hushed. "That
you love them."

Mike drew back his hand and offered thanks that was heart-
felt. "You don't know . . . this means . . . thank you . . ." He
couldn't manage to quell his youthful grin and walked out of
the suite looking even younger than his twenty-four years.

Berkeley closed the door after him, but she didn't move
away from it. It took a moment to collect herself. In spite of
the heat of the day and the warmth of clothes she was wearing,
she was cold. It was a deep, abiding cold, the kind that made

her bones ache and drew her muscles taut. She also knew she was its source and there was no escaping it.

Carefully, feeling brittle and unsteady, Berkeley crossed the room. She put a hand on the back of the chair, held her place, then sat down slowly. Taking off the hat, she placed it on one corner of the desk.

"Are you all right?" Grey asked. His eyes had narrowed as he watched her at the door. He continued to scrutinize her.

"I'm fine." She had been showing off, she thought. She had no one to blame but herself. In order to prove her talent, she had to allow herself to be vulnerable, and this was the price of pride. "It takes a while sometimes to recover."

"Very affecting."

Berkeley didn't respond. She gathered her damp hair in a fist and drew it around her shoulder. Silently, she began plaiting it.

"How did you know he was a farmer?"

He had already proven he didn't want to hear the answer. Grey Janeway was not so different from anyone else of her experience. She knew what to say. Living with Anderson had taught her that. "He had calluses consistent with holding a plow. If you do enough of this sort of thing, Mr. Janeway, certain marks of a person's life become apparent. It merely takes some careful study to recognize the characteristics for what they are."

"I thought it might be something like that."

"Yes," she said, smiling weakly. "I was sure you did."

Grey put down his spoon and served her up a bowl of rice and gumbo. "Careful, this is hot even when it's stone cold. Taste it, you'll see what I mean." He watched, satisfied when she took a tentative bite. "Hot as hell, isn't it?"

That was the exact description that came to Berkeley's mind. Her eyes widened a little as the gumbo settled in the pit of her empty stomach. There was a trail of fire all the way down her throat, but she gamely took another bite.

"Bread?" Grey asked. She nodded, and he gave her a chunk. "Now tell me how you settled on Ohio as Mike's home."

"His accent. I've met people from that area before. Two, in fact, on the ship coming here. Mike was willing to make some allowance for my mistake."

"Yes, I found that interesting. Does it happen often that you're wrong?"

"It happens, but usually it's an error like the one I made with Mike. If the person wants to believe, he will find some way to make the information fit. If he's a skeptic, he will always find something wrong."

"And Shawn Kelly? You didn't see a thing in his palm, did you?"

She smiled slightly, shaking her head. "There's no doubting that you're a skeptic. Mr. Kelly had evidence on his left hand of a ring that he had only recently removed. That's what made me offer the information that he would marry again."

"You said he would have no more children."

"It's a simple enough subterfuge, Mr. Janeway. It makes me sound as though I know more than I do. People give themselves away in subtle ways. When I said he would marry again there was a slight tension in Mr. Kelly's hand that seemed to confirm he had been married before. Knowing that, it was logical to assume he had children. So I told him he wouldn't have any more. Later he offered that he had two. When he tells the story to others, he'll forget that he gave me that information. He'll repeat to others that I *knew* he had a boy and a girl."

"And his grandmother? How did you arrive at that conclusion?"

Berkeley waved her spoon with an air of nonchalance. "Most people his age have experienced some loss in their life. It merely requires a bit of refined guesswork to get to the root of it. I pay attention to the signals that people give me when I hold their hand. I watch their faces when they're looking at their own palm. I listen to the tone of their voice and the rhythm of their speech. I hear what they say and, more importantly, hear how they say it. There's nothing more to it than that, Mr. Janeway, but it takes practice. Years of it if one's going to be good."

"And it helps if you look as if you've been touched by the fairies themselves."

Berkeley's fathomless green eyes grew a shade wider and deeper. "What an odd thing to say. I wouldn't know about that."

Grey wasn't sure he believed her. "Have you ever tried to make money from this talent of yours?"

"No. It's a parlor trick, just as you suggested. I entertained Ander—" Berkeley caught herself again. She quickly took a mouthful of gumbo and considered how to correct herself. "I entertained and, er, amused my father's friends. Why? Do you think I *could* earn a living with it?"

"Don't you?"

Her short laugh was a bit uneasy. "I don't know. I mean, I hadn't given it serious thought. When I told you I had a talent, well, I said it just so you wouldn't think I was completely useless. I was rather feeling that way, you know, and you were goading me, not intentionally perhaps, but I'm sensitive about not being able to cook or sew or sing or—"

Grey held up his hand. "I believe I understand," he said dryly.

Her expression became wary as she returned his considering gaze. She could not interpret his long silence or guess at his thoughts.

"Do you want to work for me?" Grey said finally.

Berkeley blinked. She exhaled slowly, softly, trying not to appear eager or desperate. "I should like that," she said quietly.

Grey studied her a moment longer, then he nodded once, satisfied with her answer. "Finish your gumbo," he said.

It was dusk before Sam Hartford returned to the Phoenix. He arrived with gowns, petticoats, drawers, nightgowns, stockings, shoes, and one corset. Berkeley was overwhelmed by the generosity of Ivory DuPree. Grey was skeptical. While Berkeley carried off her secondhand wardrobe to a small suite down the hall, Grey questioned Sam about the unexpected bounty.

Sam pulled on one eyebrow and shifted a bit uncomfortably. "Miss Edwards ... I mean, Miss DuPree ... gave me a bill for the things," he said. He reached into his wrinkled vest pocket and extracted a ragged piece of brown paper. The writing was Ivory's own, painstakingly neat but perfectly legible. All of the clothing was itemized and a value was placed on each. He handed it to Grey. "I haggled a bit with her, Mr. Janeway, I don't mind sayin', but Miss DuPree wouldn't hear any of it. She insisted on taking me around to the shops herself, just to prove she wasn't asking more than the worth. Then she added a little bit to each piece, for the inconvenience to her."

"The inconvenience?" asked Grey.

"Yes, sir. Miss DuPree had to try on all the clothing first, everything but that blue-spangled gown—she tossed that at me and said whoever needed it was welcome to it. You were particular that the clothes should be too small for her, and she made a point to show me that was just the way of it."

It must have been quite a show, Grey thought. He said nothing and let Sam go on.

"So after she figured out what fit and what didn't, that's when she set a price."

"And that's when you haggled with her."

"Yes, sir. So she decides to take me around to the shops, like I said, and prove her point. I didn't mind too much, since you asked me to find out where you could buy a lady fashions and notions and such." Sam stopped pulling on his wiry brow and rocked forward on the balls of his feet. "So that's why I'm so late gettin' back. But you got your list right there on one side and the shops on the other, and if you don't mind, Mr. Janeway, I'd be plumb grateful if you'd find someone else to go lookin' at ladies' furbelows and geegaws next time out."

Grey cleared his throat to suppress the laugh caught there. His expression remained grave. "You've done admirably, Sam. I won't call on you in the future for similar duties."

"Thank you, sir." Sam stopped rocking in place. "It's a relief, I must say. I really don't have a liking for—" He stopped, his attention straying to the doorway where Berkeley Shaw suddenly appeared. Without hesitation Sam removed his hat. It was more difficult not to gape.

Grey turned. One of his dark brows arched slightly as he regarded Berkeley. She had lost no time changing into one of Ivory DuPree's castoffs. The navy blue day dress, with its tightly fitted sleeves and lack of ornamentation, made a slim silhouette of her figure. In dramatic contrast, her fine, pale hair was its own radiant light. Her smile was tentative, a shade wistful. "Yes, Miss Shaw?" Grey said.

She stepped into the room. "I wanted to thank you. The gowns are surpassingly lovely, all of them, though I really think this is the only one suited for everyday. The others are quite fine, and I shouldn't—"

Grey interrupted her. "Wear them or don't wear them. They're yours now."

His abruptness startled Berkeley. Had she offended him? Her fingers moved a bit nervously over her midriff. She smoothed the fabric where it gathered at her waist and looked at Sam. "And thank you, Mr. Hartford. You were very kind to—"

Grey stopped her again. "He's my employee, Miss Shaw. Kindness has no place here."

Bewildered, Berkeley's smile faltered, then faded. "Yes," she said. "I can see that. Am I permitted to express my thanks to Miss DuPree?"

"Here." Grey held out the ragged and wrinkled bill presented to him by Sam. "Thank Ivory by paying this."

Berkeley took the paper and examined it. Her brow creased as she totaled the items. One gown was valued at two hundred dollars. Another at three hundred fifty. The simple, serviceable dress she was wearing now had been assigned a worth of one hundred twenty-five dollars. Oddly, Ivory DuPree's most beautiful offering, a sapphire satin evening gown embellished with blue glass beads, had no dollar amount attached to it. To be certain no one thought this was an oversight on Ivory's part, she had placed a thick slash next to the gown's description.

Berkeley's eyes moved along the list. Shoes: eighty dollars.

Stockings: fifteen dollars per pair. The undergarments came to one hundred eighty-five dollars.

"So much," she said softly. Berkeley looked up at Grey. "This is a fortune. I can't accept them when I can never hope to pay. I'll have to return everything to Miss DuPree." She turned hopefully to Sam. "You'll assist me, won't you, Mr. Hartford? I shouldn't know where to go if you don't accompany me."

Sam started to sputter and rock on his feet again. Whether he was trying to form the words to agree to Berkeley's request or refuse her was never clear. Grey cut him off, thanking him again, then dismissing him. Sam tipped his hat in Berkeley's direction as he hurried from the room.

"Was that necessary?" asked Berkeley. "Mr. Hartford had not answered me yet."

Grey waved aside her objection. "Sam would have hemmed and hawed for ten minutes without any direction from me. He's not in a position to offer his assistance to you without clearing it with me."

"You're very arrogant, aren't you?" she said baldly.

Grey's smile, the one that did not quite reach his eyes, appeared. "I'm the owner of the Phoenix, and I care very much that the people in my employ do as I request."

"Order, you mean."

He shrugged. "Order, if you wish. I believe it's my right." His gunmetal glance was steady on her upturned face. "And if you wish to work for me, Miss Shaw, it will be your responsibility."

Berkeley knew she had choices. One of them was to go back to living on the streets, hiding in a masculine disguise until she could steal aboard a Remington ship. She could also present herself to another gaming house and hope they saw the same potential in her talent as the owner of the Phoenix. Whoring was another solution. There were probably other alternatives available to her, but Berkeley couldn't think of them now. She knew, as Grey Janeway did, that employment with his gaming house presented itself as her best opportunity.

Berkeley's chin lifted, and, at her side, her hands stilled. "Yes," she said. "I can accept that."

"Good." He held out his hand, not to close this agreement with a shake, but to take back the bill. "Give that to me."

She immediately shook her head. "I fully intend to return these clothes to Miss DuPree."

Grey's hand remained extended, and his mouth thinned a little with impatience. "What? And wear my shirts and trousers while your own wardrobe is being assembled? Endeavor to use your head, Miss Shaw. Clothes made specifically for you will cost every bit as much as what Ivory scrawled on her bill, and perhaps even more."

"Then I can't afford any of it."

Rather than argue, Grey took the scrap of bill from between Berkeley's twisting fingers. She had rolled it as tightly as a candlewick. "You can't afford *not* to have it. Anyway, you won't owe this to Ivory. I'll pay what she's asked and you'll owe me."

"If that is supposed to ease my mind, Mr. Janeway, it's wide of the mark."

"I have no idea what would ease your mind," he said without inflection. "I've merely explained the way I intend things to be. Do you have some difficulty with it?"

Of course she did, though there was probably little point in voicing it now. "As you wish," she said.

Grey wondered that Berkeley could make those three words of acquiescence sound so quietly defiant. "I *do* wish, Miss Shaw."

"You realize that it will take me years to repay you, though. You may grow tired of having me forever underfoot."

"I regularly clean my boots. It won't present a problem."

Berkeley blinked at his perfectly expressed indifference. He gave her no indication that he was amused in the least. "I believe I'd like to return to my room," she said. "If you'll excuse me."

"But I don't."

She had already started to turn when the import of his words reached her. "I beg your pardon?"

"Sit down, Miss Shaw." He indicated the room's only chair again in the event she pretended to misunderstand. Grey moved to the desk directly in front of her and leaned back against the edge. He put down Ivory's bill. "Are your rooms satisfactory?" he asked.

"Yes. Yes, of course." There was virtually no furniture, but Donnel Kincaid had assured her that would be remedied quickly. A cot had been moved into the bedroom, and Donnel had ordered the hasty construction of an armoire in expectation of her receiving clothes from Ivory. Uncertain of her precise arrangement with Grey Janeway, the workers considered Berkeley the hotel's first real guest. There were many small attempts throughout the afternoon to make her rooms more livable. While Grey was gone from the Phoenix on other business, workers arrived at odd intervals offering blankets, oil lamps, towels, and freshly plucked wildflowers. One of the carpenters gave her an exquisitely carved figurine he had whittled to place on her mantel. Except in size, it was virtually identical to the figurehead of Rhea that adorned the front of the Phoenix. Mike and Shawn presented her with one of the mirrors they weren't prepared to install until later in the week, and they also carried in a large pine crate for her to use as a table in her sitting room. Someone else cut a square of muslin to fit it exactly and serve as a tablecloth.

These spontaneous gestures touched her deeply. "Everyone has been very kind," she told Grey.

"That isn't what I asked. I was inquiring about your rooms."

"You must know they're satisfactory," she said.

He didn't deny it. "I wanted your opinion," he said. "I understand that my men have been generous with some personal items."

"Yes." She did not elaborate on their kindness again.

"You realize that Shawn and Mike have already spread the word of your special talent."

She nodded. "I thought the men's interest might have something to do with that."

Grey knew it was only part of their expressed interest. She seemed to have no idea of her own appeal. "Did you read their palms? Tell their fortunes?"

"No, no one asked me to."

"Which is to say that you would have had any of them gotten the nerve to ask."

Knowing that he was prepared to object, Berkeley answered truthfully. "Yes, I would have."

"In the future, if asked, you will refuse. If you're going to earn your living this way, then you can't read a palm without gold crossing yours. Are you clear on that point, Miss Shaw?"

"Yes."

"Good. Now, to the matter of your room and board." He saw Berkeley's eyes widen slightly. "Did you think I would allow you to live at the Phoenix at no charge?"

"I hadn't given it any thought at all."

It was precisely what Grey suspected, though he was surprised that she admitted it so easily. "You should attempt to do it more often, Miss Shaw. Think, that is."

His honeyed drawl was absent, she noticed, when he took her to task. On those occasions, which seemed to be more frequent as his acquaintance with her grew longer, his tone and manner had the brusque accents of a Yankee clipper captain. There seemed to be nothing to say to his reprimand, so Berkeley remained silent.

"Since the gold strike," Grey went on, "sleeping space in San Francisco has always been difficult to come by. Therefore it's expensive. Men have paid as much as twenty-five dollars a night to sleep two on a tabletop. An individual room can cost a thousand dollars a month."

Berkeley actually gasped. "But I couldn't possibly—"

"No, you couldn't," he said flatly. "Which is why I'm prepared to offer you room and board at the Phoenix for six hundred dollars each month. That's roughly two hundred dollars less than I'd be getting if the rooms were rented to anyone else."

His offer didn't help color return to Berkeley's complexion. She nodded dumbly.

Approving of her silence, Grey smiled faintly. "It's imperative that you remain at the Phoenix to sustain mystery and interest in your gift. It would be wise for you not to refer to it again as a parlor trick. That will remain between us. Word will spread as easily as the last Frisco fire that the Phoenix has a very special hostess. The less you're seen, the fewer details known about your talent, the more we can expect in the way of a steady turnout."

"Hostess?" she said weakly.

"Yes. How did you imagine I'd employ you? No, don't tell me. You didn't think about it."

"Of course I did," she said stoutly. "But you know very well I thought I would tell a few fortunes each evening. Nothing more."

"That's not so far off the mark," he told her. "You'll greet the gamblers, talk to them, observe them. That's necessary, isn't it, to make your readings more persuasive?"

Berkeley knew it would do no good to tell him otherwise, and the truth was, it *would* be helpful. The more she knew about each person, the less she had to make herself vulnerable and rely on her peculiar talent. "Do you mean for me to choose whose palms I'll read?"

"Exactly. The less left to chance, the better you'll be received."

Anderson Shaw and Grey Janeway were cut from the same cloth, Berkeley thought. Perhaps God had only one bolt of fabric at His disposal. Recalling the deception Connor and Decker Thorne had tried with the earrings, it seemed likely. Deception came more easily to men, it seemed. "Tell me more," she said, pretending an interest she no longer felt.

"Your duties will require an extensive wardrobe."

"Which you'll choose."

"That's correct."

Berkeley sighed. Her life wouldn't be so different from the one she had known with Anderson. It made her more determined to leave San Francisco. The largest obstacle confronting her, as she understood it, would be the enormous debt to Grey Janeway. With what she would owe him for her room and board and wardrobe, she would never have enough to purchase her passage east.

"The fittings will be done here," Grey explained. "You won't have to venture out."

It was just as she had expected. She nodded dully and looked down at her lap. Her hands rested there, folded together in an attitude of quiet contemplation.

"I've had to revise the Phoenix's opening to September 26. That's a little better than a month from now. Things are going to be very busy around here. You will have to be ready by then as well."

"You won't be disappointed, Mr. Janeway."

He stared at her bent head. Threads of her radiant hair had escaped the loose plait. Short tendrils brushed her forehead. "No," he said. "I don't think I will be." He was quiet a moment, wondering at the direction of her thoughts. "You haven't asked about your wage."

She raised her head and met his level gaze. "I've never had any sort of position before. I thought it was proper for you to broach the subject."

"So it is. I'm prepared to offer you a thousand dollars a month." He saw her mouth open and spoke quickly to cut her off. "Before you try to negotiate, remember that's what Annie Jack is getting at the El Dorado—and she can cook."

Berkeley was well aware how paltry her talent was compared to Annie Jack's gumbo. Grey's offer left her without words.

"Say something, Miss Shaw."

"Yes. I say yes."

"Good. Now do you see that it's not impossible for you to be rid of your debt?"

She nodded.

"I believe you'll be an asset to the Phoenix. I wouldn't offer that salary if I didn't think you'd earn it. You're going to draw a crowd, and that crowd is going to spend money right here.''

''Are your games quite honest?'' she asked before considering her words.

Both of Grey's brows rose. ''They are. Do you doubt it?''

''Frankly, I don't know what to make of you or the Phoenix.''

One corner of Grey's mouth lifted in a narrow smile. ''And here I was thinking you knew all about me, Miss Shaw. Isn't that what you tried to prove this morning? After all, you read my palm.''

''I learned what was important.''

''Oh? What's that?''

''You're not the man I first thought you were.''

Chapter Five

You're not the man I first thought you were. Grey found himself mulling over Berkeley's words late into that first evening and at odd times during the next four weeks. She had refused to explain herself, and Grey had not insisted because her meaning was clear enough to him. He had only, briefly, wanted to hear it from her. In retrospect it was just as well she had remained silent. Berkeley's explanation was more likely to confuse his mind than clear it. She had that effect on him.

Grey was sitting alone in the Phoenix's great hall. The chairs and gaming tables were all uncovered now. The mirrors behind the mahogany bar reflected light from the oil lamps all around the room. Just outside the Phoenix men swaggered or staggered on the rough sidewalks of Portsmouth Square, all of them looking for a lively place to set down their gold. Tomorrow night their choices would include the Phoenix.

Grey rubbed the back of his neck, massaging away the stiffness that had crept up on him while he worked. Financial sheets and ledgers were spread across the table so that none of the polished surface was visible. He could have worked in his suite at his desk, where his new burgundy-leather chair would have provided some measure of comfort for his aching muscles. Instead, he had chosen the solitude of the great hall on one of the last nights he could be alone in it. He appreciated the open, empty space around him. He liked the fact that outside the Phoenix it was an evening with no moon, while inside the mirrors magnified lamplight.

Raking back his thick hair, Grey bent over the papers in front of him and began adding a column of figures for the second time. He paused only once, and only for a moment, when someone jerked on the locked entrance to the gaming hall. The large doors rattled, a stranger shouted, then the drunken miner was dragged off by his friends in search of a door that wasn't barred.

The column totaled the same amount in both directions. Satisfied, Grey moved on. He had no idea when the cat joined him, just that at some point he looked up and found her curled on top of the ledger he needed. He gingerly slid the book out from under her, smiling to himself for accomplishing the feat without disturbing her slumber.

Something Berkeley said came back to him now. *You're a kind man, though perhaps it's not something you wish others to know.* Grey didn't know where the precise truth lay in her words, but some part of it resonated as fact. If he was a kind man, and he didn't know that he was, then it was true that he didn't want others to know. He'd had cause a number of times later to tell her kindness had no place here, and he'd meant it. So there also was a truth.

As if to punctuate his thought, Grey opened the ledger so hard the frontboard landed heavily on the table. The cat bounded to her feet as a shock wave vibrated under her. Frightened, she meowed plaintively and prepared to leap to another table. Half-standing himself, Grey made a grab for her and knocked his chair sideways. Papers scattered when he flung his arm out, and the ledger spun off the edge. It thumped to the floor, but not before the corner of it squarely struck Grey's toes. The table wobbled when his knee jerked reflexively and caught the underframe. He grunted. The cat hissed.

From another part of the great hall the sound of light laughter washed over them both.

The cat recovered before Grey. Using the tables like lily pads on a pond, she jumped from one to the other until she reached the grand, curving staircase. Only then did her feet finally touch the floor. It took two more jumps before she was wrapped safely in Berkeley's arms. Grey managed to right the table by the time the cat reached her refuge. He was picking up the chair when Berkeley joined him.

She didn't ask if she could help. Her offer would have been refused. Instead, she secured the cat under one arm and knelt on the floor to gather the fallen papers. Grey didn't thank her when she handed them over, and he didn't extend a hand to help her to her feet. Berkeley expected neither from him.

At no time in the last month was Grey Janeway as attentive as he had been that very first day. Far from being under his feet, Berkeley came to realize entire days passed where she didn't see him at all. His presence, though, was keenly felt.

Nothing happened in the Phoenix that wasn't directed, suggested, or approved by Grey Janeway. When seamstresses began to arrive with yards of fabric and fashion books, Berkeley knew it was at Grey's insistence. She was measured and poked and fitted in front of the large mirror in her bedroom, while Grey was consulted wherever he happened to be working at the time.

In spite of Sam Hartford's earlier wish to be relieved of all millinery duties, he was the one who volunteered to relay messages between the seamstresses and his employer. He grew red-faced and breathless in the process, taking the stairs two and three at a time when the remote discussions between the two parties became somewhat heated. His head was muddled with flounces and fluting and frills, but he learned the difference between passementerie and twisted floss silk. On one occasion he grew bold enough with his newfound knowledge to recommend a carriage dress of gray silk rather than the blue the head seamstress had suggested.

''She's being swallowed by the furbelows,'' he warned Grey

at the third fitting. His voice had carried through an open window back to Berkeley and the seamstresses.

"Is that dangerous?" Grey asked dryly.

"It surely is, sir. She needs smartly cut lines to give her boldness."

"Well, for God's sake, save her."

By the time Sam returned to Berkeley's suite the seamstresses had removed all but the last set of ribbon flounces. When he saw the result he beamed proudly, immensely satisfied with his timely rescue.

Berkeley straightened, stroking the cat lightly. The tabby's face was pressed into the crook of her elbow. Her face nuzzled the soft cotton wrapper that Berkeley wore over her nightshift. The wrapper was without any ornamentation, and the nightshift had only an edge of lace along its scooped neckline. Thanks to Sam Hartford and Grey's distant oversight, Berkeley's slender lines were not obliterated by a gauzy cloud of ruffles. It was in the very absence of softly rounded fashions that Berkeley's feminine nature could be found.

Still petting the cat, she looked at Grey sideways. His mouth was set rather grimly, and he appeared to be staring at her bare feet. She curled her toes as if she could hide the offending parts.

"Do you want something to drink?" he asked abruptly.

Berkeley had been on the point of excusing herself, certain her presence was unwelcome. His question startled her. "Yes," she said after a small hesitation. "I should like that."

"Whiskey?"

She had been thinking tea. Or warm milk. Both those things would require fussing in the kitchen. "Whiskey will be fine."

Grey dropped the haphazardly stacked papers he was holding on the table and went to the bar. "What brings you down here?" he asked, searching out an open bottle and two glasses.

"I came looking for the cat. If I don't let her in, she'll scratch at my door to get in later."

She also would cry mournfully, Grey recalled. He'd awakened one night to exactly that pitiful cacophony and left his room with every intention of throwing the cat out. He'd been stopped in his tracks by the light from Berkeley's room as she opened her own door. She had knelt in the hallway and taken the cat in her arms. She had stroked her cheek against the tabby's face and murmured something nonsensical into its ear. She and the cat disappeared a moment later, and the door clicked closed behind them. Grey was cast in darkness again, but he stood there for a long moment and wondered at the wash of tears he had glimpsed on Berkeley's face.

Grey studied her reflection in the mirror as he poured their drinks. She didn't look as if she'd been crying tonight. Her eyelids were vaguely swollen and heavy with the effects of a deep sleep. There was a rosy flush to her complexion that all the light in the gaming hall couldn't wash out. She had taken up the chair beside his and drawn her knees up to her chest. The cat was balanced across the top and displayed no signs of discomfort on her knobby perch.

Grey carried the drinks over, sat down, and pushed one tumbler in Berkeley's direction. She was forced to dislodge the cat in order to drink from it. He watched the cat stalk off, making quite a show of her independent nature. "When are you going to name her?" he asked somewhat brusquely.

Berkeley's eyes widened a little. "You mean I may?"

"Of course. Why shouldn't you?"

"Well, she's *your* cat."

"She's not mine," he corrected. He sipped his drink. "I suffer her presence. That would be the accurate description of our association."

Berkeley thought it was an apt description of Grey's arrangement with her as well. "I've had a name in mind," she offered somewhat shyly. "What do you think of Pandora?"

Grey looked at the mess his pile of papers had become, thanks in no small part to the cat's curious nature. "I think it's perfect."

Berkeley's smile radiated her pleasure. "Then she'll be Pandora from now on, though I doubt it will make any difference to her. She's never seemed in particular need of a name." Her smile became a shade wistful as Pandora sprinted lightly up the staircase. "She comes and goes as she pleases."

"Unlike you," Grey said, a certain edge in his tone. "Is that what you're trying to tell me?"

Berkeley's head swiveled in his direction. "I wasn't making comparisons," she said quietly. "But yes, since you've mentioned it, she is rather unlike me in that regard. I don't mind terribly. I've felt safe here. I simply didn't expect the confinement to be as wearing as it is."

He wondered at her use of the word safe. It was almost as if she imagined herself hiding out from some danger. "Where would you like to go?"

"Oh, I don't know. The bay perhaps, or out to one of the hills." She realized he was starting to get up. He stood and regarded her with a mixture of patience and amusement. "What?" Berkeley asked, surprised. "You mean right now? You were asking where I would like to go this minute?"

"This very minute," he confirmed. "Do you have a coat?"

She shook her head. "It's not finished. Mrs. Irvin still—" Berkeley stopped as her hand was taken and she was drawn to her feet. Grey took off his own jacket and wrapped it around her shoulders.

"You'll be fine," he said.

Berkeley's protest was halfhearted at best. She made it because the circumstances demanded one. "It's after midnight, Mr. Janeway."

"I'm aware of the time."

She was being pulled toward the rear of the gaming hall. "But I'm in my nightgown."

"No one will know that."

"*I'll* know."

Grey opened the back door and stepped out into the cool night air. A breeze ruffled his dark hair. "Wait here while I get the carriage." He took a lamp from its hook just inside the door and crossed the yard to the stables at the rear of his property. Berkeley could hear him talking to someone but couldn't make out the words. She imagined that one of his employees had just been roused from a deep slumber.

A few minutes later Grey returned for her. She was about to call his attention to her shoeless state when he made the point of no account by picking her up. She fell silent, which she suspected suited him just fine, and let herself be carried across the yard. When they reached the carriage Berkeley noticed only one of them was breathless, and it wasn't Grey.

He lifted her into the open carriage and deposited her on the cool leather seat. Berkeley's teeth were already beginning to chatter, and the seat under her only added to her discomfort. Grey began tucking thick woolen blankets all around her until Berkeley's muffled voice called a halt.

"I promise you I'm quite warm now," she said.

Grey held up the lantern and looked her over. Her eyes regarded him from under a cloud of pale hair. The curve of her upper lip hinted at her smile. When she looked at him like that he forgot he was the one with good sense.

Tearing himself away from her gaze, Grey sat down beside Berkeley and passed the lantern back to the stable attendant. He took up the reins. "We won't be gone long, Emmet, but don't try to stay awake."

Emmet's sleepy nod indicated he would have no trouble sleeping in the interim. "Just as you wish, Mr. Janeway." He lifted the lantern to light their way out and waved them off.

Berkeley lowered the blankets so that her chin rested outside them. Her first deep breath of the night air was immensely satisfying. She selectively filtered out the odors of horse dung and stale liquor and concentrated on the scent of salt water. "Where are we going?" she asked, as they turned away from entering Portsmouth Square.

"Out to the Point."

"I don't think I've ever been there."

Grey didn't doubt it. "It's not far."

Berkeley fell silent again. In time she relaxed. The city's noise gradually faded, and she became aware of the wind's soft sigh through the trees. An owl followed their trail, his gentle call repeating itself as they rounded a bend in the road. She looked behind her once and saw the center of San Francisco was awash in light. It leaked through cracks in ramshackle buildings and poured openly from windows of the gaming halls and brothels. In Sydney Town open fires marked the places where the Ducks gathered to discuss their business. Torches led the way for small gangs already on the move.

Berkeley's glance strayed back to Grey. He was concentrating on keeping the carriage on the path that passed for a road. With no moonlight to guide him, their pace had slowed. "You didn't bring the lantern," she said, missing it for the first time. "Did you mean to leave it behind?"

He had. "There's no point calling attention to ourselves."

"But you're not afraid of the Ducks," she said.

"Only fools aren't afraid of the Ducks. I hope you're not saying I'm a fool."

A small crease appeared between Berkeley's brows. "But you didn't show the least fear when you met them on the wharf."

He smiled a little at her misplaced confidence. "That's because I had you to watch my back."

"I'm serious," she protested.

"So am I. I saw how you flung those fish. I figured I was safe enough."

Berkeley sighed. She remembered the weapon he had carried that day in his boot. "Do you have your knife?"

"Yes, I always carry it." He glanced down at her. He could only make out her eyes. Starshine made them luminous. "Does that make you feel better?"

When she nodded, her cheek rubbed against his shoulder. It made her realize how close she was to him. Berkeley lifted her head and began to move away.

"Stay where you are," he said.

Convinced he was cold, Berkeley threw two of her blankets across his lap, brushing his hard thighs as she arranged and rearranged them. His sudden shiver seemed to confirm her fears, and she burrowed beside him, lending her body heat.

"Can you not be still?" he asked, his voice rough.

Berkeley became still as stone. She was almost twisted backward in her seat. One hand rested on his knee, the other held his shoulder. Her breast pressed against his upper arm. "I don't think I can manage this for long," she whispered.

It was a small mercy, Grey was thinking. He lowered the reins and the horse came to a halt. The carriage rocked on the uneven ground a moment before it was as still as Berkeley. "What do you think you're doing?" he asked quietly.

"Weren't you cold?"

"Did I say I was?"

"No." Berkeley's voice was barely audible. His silence was almost unbearable, and the tension that ran through Grey's body became a vibration in her own. The sense that it was not entirely born of anger came to her without warning. Not trusting what she felt, Berkeley's eyes darted across the darkened planes of his face.

"Perhaps there is something to this touching gift of yours."

Berkeley hardly knew what he said. His breath was warm against her cheek. His head bent closer, and she only had to lean into him to close the gap and feel his mouth on hers. The moment stretched, held. Without warning it snapped and became another that was only slightly less fraught with anticipation. Then it passed also. Slowly she withdrew, and the space between them widened.

Grey took Berkeley gently by her arms and turned her on the carriage bench. Her hands slid away from his shoulder and his knee and fell on her lap. He tucked the blankets across them both and took up the reins. "We're almost there," he said.

She nodded again. This time her cheek did not brush his shoulder.

The Point overlooked the cliffs that stretched vertically from the bay. It was deserted at this time of night, and, except for the occasional bark of a sea lion below, it was quiet.

He had brought her to the bay and the hills in a single journey, Berkeley realized. A canopy of stars hung above them.

Below was an endlessly unrolling carpet of waves. For a month she had been certain she had existed only as an afterthought in his life, if she had been given any thought at all. Then, for no reason that she could discern other than it was in his power to do so, he had given her exactly what she asked for.

"Thank you," she said.

Grey nodded. The curve of the carriage sheltered them a little from the breeze, but he doubted it was enough warmth for her. He put one arm around Berkeley's shoulders and leaned back against the padded cushions. For a long time they sat like that, heads almost touching, staring at the sky and listening to the breaking waves.

"Have you been lonely, Berkeley?" Grey asked.

His familiar use of her name struck her almost as forcefully as his question. She was caught off guard by both, and the truth tumbled out before she thought better of it. "A little, yes."

"Mrs. Irvin was no company?"

The dressmaker had been company, of course, but she wasn't a companion. "Mrs. Irvin was busy with her fashion books and her seamstresses had pins in their mouths. They could talk to each other that way, but I couldn't understand them." Berkeley felt Grey's low chuckle rumble pleasantly in his chest.

"What about Sam?" asked Grey.

"He was always there and always willing to talk. It's the sad truth that he learned more about the cut of velvet fabrics than I'll ever know. He tried to teach me, but I'm afraid I wasn't very interested."

Under cover of darkness, Grey's rare smile deepened. "What about the other workers? They were in and out of your rooms, weren't they?"

"Well, yes, that's true, and they did everything quite beautifully." Berkeley thought he must have known that. Donnel told her Grey Janeway had approved every piece himself. "But no one stayed long in completing their tasks. Shawn and Mike put up the bed rather quickly. Jordan hung drapes. Harry and

Sam brought in the new armoire and transferred my wardrobe. Things came and went, and my presence was rather incidental.''

"You were a regular visitor to the kitchen, weren't you? What about Annie Jack?"

"You only managed to secure Annie's services three days ago," Berkeley reminded him. "And she's been very busy organizing the kitchen the way *she* wants it. Another instance where I've been more in the way, than in the way of help. In any event, Annie Jack isn't certain what to make of me."

Neither was Grey, but he doubted he and his new cook were thinking along the same lines. "What does that mean?"

"She says I'm a spirit woman."

"A what?"

Berkeley shook her head. "You'll have to ask her. She won't explain it to me, but she doesn't allow me near her."

Annie Jack was a Negress of considerable size and substantial spirit herself. He could not imagine that Annie was seriously concerned by Berkeley Shaw. "I'll speak to her," Grey said.

"You can't make her like me," Berkeley told him. Any more than he couldn't make her be less lonely by filling her time with fittings and renovations and cookery. She hadn't recognized these events as anything but Grey Janeway getting on with his business of managing the Phoenix; now she wondered if that were strictly true. He had found no time for her, but he had made certain that others were supposed to.

"I'll speak to her anyway," Grey repeated. He felt her reluctant nod. Apparently she accepted his right to do so, but she didn't have to like it. He doubted she would like what he had to say next. "I've made some inquiries about your father, Berkeley."

She sat straight up, her spine rigid. The blankets covering her shoulders fell to her waist, and she didn't feel the cold at all. His statement robbed her of breath, then of coherent thought. She raised her hand, and for a moment she believed she meant to strike him. She covered her mouth instead.

Grey sat up as well. He took her wrist in his hand and drew

it away from her mouth. "You deserved to know. One way or the other."

She drew in a sharp breath, and it became a dry sob. It was not grief that made her cry out, but a deep abiding sense of guilt. She had thought of Anderson Shaw a hundred times since finding herself at the Phoenix and not one of those thoughts was about missing him. Grey hadn't said it yet, but Berkeley knew Anderson was dead. She turned her head and stared back at the city, dry-eyed and almost without expression.

When Grey touched her shoulder she tried to shrug him off. She had no use for his pity. She certainly didn't deserve it. "You can tell me," she said. "I won't cry."

He wished she would. There was some sense to tears. "He's buried in a graveyard usually reserved for Sydney Town felons," he said. "The story isn't clear. Some say he was a victim from the beginning. Some say he started the fight. He didn't have a chance once he wandered into that part of town. Your father must have given a good account of himself. It's the reason people remembered his name."

"I want to see his grave," she said.

Grey was shaking his head before she finished. "You can't go there."

"You can take me. The Ducks don't bother you. If I'm under your protection, they won't bother me."

"The Ducks bother me. They haven't figured how to get rid of me. There's a difference." He watched Berkeley shift toward him. She was hugging herself under his jacket now, and he drew it more closely around her shoulders. She was not arguing with him, but Grey didn't mistake her silence for surrender. He understood the problem he had just created for himself by telling her the truth about her father.

"Did you bring me up here to tell me?" she asked.

"No. I didn't think I was going to tell you at all tonight. I didn't expect to see you."

"How long have you known about him?"

"Since this afternoon. You had already eaten dinner and

were in your room when I got back. I was prepared to tell you in the morning.''

It didn't matter that she wished he had told her earlier. Her reasons were entirely selfish ones. Anderson had found a way, even in death, to deny her a single evening's peace.

''Berkeley?'' Grey's voice prompted her to look at him again. ''Is there no one at all you can go to?''

She shook her head and pushed back strands of hair that brushed her cheek. Being alone was usually different than being lonely. Tonight they felt very much the same. ''No one,'' she said.

''But your letter—''

Berkeley didn't allow him to finish. ''It was to a business acquaintance of my father's. I can't expect help there.'' She leaned back. Beneath the blankets her shoulders were slumped. She crossed her arms, hugging herself for warmth and comfort. ''It no longer matters where I am; I have nowhere to go.''

''Then there's no urgency for you to leave San Francisco.''

''None at all,'' she said a little dully.

Grey wondered at her answer. ''Berkeley?''

''Hmmm?''

''Were you trying to get away from your father?''

She didn't look at him, but stared straight ahead. ''Yes.''

''But you suspected he was dead.''

''I did, but it's not the same as knowing.''

And as long as she wasn't certain, Grey realized, she had her sights set on leaving. The importance she placed on seeing her father's grave was clearer to him now. He also understood why she had not been overly disturbed by her virtual confinement in the Phoenix these past four weeks. He realized why she had felt safe in the hotel. ''You've been hiding from him,'' Grey said.

''You're supposing that he wanted to find me. He left me, not the other way around.'' Berkeley let her head fall back against the cushion and closed her eyes. ''But there's truth in what you say. I was panicked at first, not knowing where he was or what I would do without him; then I managed it. More importantly, I realized I was managing it.''

"By dressing in a man's clothing?'' he asked. "Bathing in the bay? Sleeping in the streets? That's your idea of managing?''

"It's my idea of surviving. I did it on my own. You can't know what that meant to me.''

Grey thought he did know. He said nothing for a long time. While silence filled the passing minutes he stared at her, trying to make out the features of her upturned face. It wasn't composure that he observed in her expression, but exhaustion. Then there was the tear he saw slip from between her closed lashes. She made no effort to brush it away, almost as if she was denying its existence. Grey leaned toward her and raised his hand. His fingers hovered just above her cheek, then he brushed her face with the lightest of touches.

He wondered if she knew how often his thoughts were occupied with her, or how often his eyes strayed from any task at hand to observe her. Since her arrival he had had his men stepping lively to see to her personal needs and comfort, and what he noticed was that none of them complained. Even Sam Hartford, who had made noises about not wanting to be involved in furbelows and geegaws, took up Berkeley's standard after he saw her in one of Ivory's gowns. Donnel, Mike, Shawn, and half a dozen others were no different. The special attention that was given to Berkeley's suite was initiated by him, but fulfilled by everyone else. When Grey saw the manner in which they cheerfully carried out his instructions he realized they were all looking for excuses to spend time with her.

He was no different. He only held himself back.

Until now. His fingertips touched her cheek, and he felt the damp evidence of her tears. She didn't stir. "Berkeley?''

Her eyes opened. They glistened. Another tear fell. It didn't matter if she had his permission or not, she did not want to cry in front of him. "Can we go now, Mr. Janeway?''

His hand dropped to her throat. His fingers slipped behind the nape of her neck and his thumb brushed the underside of her chin. "Grey," he said. "I think you'd better start calling me Grey."

She didn't question him. At this moment she wasn't even curious why he should say that. "I'd like to go home."

He didn't press her. Instead he tucked her in beside him and sheltered her with one arm. He took up the reins in his free hand, and, with a flick of his wrist, the carriage began to roll forward slowly. Berkeley Shaw was asleep by the time they reached the Phoenix.

The morning was shrouded with fog. It suited Berkeley's mood and her movements. When she unbarred the gaming house's door and stepped onto the sidewalk, the whole of Portsmouth Square was swallowed by the thick, damp mist. Diffuse light from an invisible sun made it possible for her to see a few feet beyond each step she took. Behind her the fog closed like a curtain, removing every trace of her path.

Berkeley's shoes tapped out a light staccato beat as she hurried along the rough wooden sidewalk. Confident that she could pass unobserved because of the fog, she did not try to keep her head down or shade her face with the hat she wore. Wearing the clothes she had never returned to Grey, Berkeley knew that a passing glance would only mark her as one of the last of the city's late-night revelers.

Venturing into Sydney Town was not something Berkeley would have done in broad daylight. Night was certainly no safer. But a San Francisco morning, with its lowering clouds from the bay as thick as cotton batting, presented itself as the perfect time. The shanties and tents, the clapboard hovels and crudely built gaming hells, were clustered near the waterfront and rose up the slope of Telegraph Hill.

It was toward the hill that Berkeley made her way. Her progress was slowed by the deeply rutted street and the occasional drunkard or brawler staggering out from one of the saloons. The area was quiet, almost eerily so. She was aware of her own breathing and the soft rustle of her clothes as her arms brushed her sides. Water splashed loudly as she stepped into a puddle, and she picked up her pace to get away from the sound.

Berkeley didn't know the precise location of Sydney Town's cemetery and doubted that it was connected to anything remotely resembling a church. She had, however, once observed an unruly group of mourners following a hearse on the outskirts of Sydney Town, and she took that same direction now.

She came upon the cemetery literally by accident as she tripped over stones that marked the entrance. Hastily she replaced the stones in something resembling a pyramid and righted the wooden cross that had landed on its side the same time she did.

The fog that had served to cloak Berkeley's journey from the Phoenix now worked against her. There were no granite slabs to indicate where a body was buried, and the crosses were difficult to see except when she was standing beside them. Some of the graves were marked only with stones arranged in a pile similar to the one at the entrance. Crouching low, Berkeley worked her way through the rows of graves more by feel than by sight.

Sydney Town's cemetery was populated by men who bore an odd assortment of names when they had been among the living. There was Luckless Bill, English Joe, One-Chance Charlie, and Eddie Smiles. Berkeley found wooden crosses with names as plain as Mr. Smith and Mr. Jones burned into them. Seldom were dates revealed. More often she found the manner of death. Gunshot in the back. Hanged. Drowned. Demon Rum. Sometimes the crime was noted. Card cheat. Liar. Traitor.

Berkeley shivered and pulled her jacket more closely around her shoulders. The Sydney Ducks apparently had their own code. Murdering others could be forgiven. Betraying a fellow Duck was a death sentence. Immoral or amoral, it didn't matter. It was what they lived and died by.

Anderson Shaw. Berkeley's fingers trembled when she reached out to touch the cross. It leaned a little to the side, and she straightened it. It inclined again as soon as she let it go.

She mounded some dirt at its base and pushed it deeper in place. The cross was no better made, but no worse than any of the others. No information about the manner of his death was burned into the wood; nothing to indicate if he was sinner or saint in the eyes of the Ducks.

Around the edge of the grave the grass was wet. Berkeley sat down anyway, crossing her legs tailor-fashion. She plucked a piece of long grass and chewed on the end while her eyes remained riveted on the marker. It must be true, she thought, and still she could not believe what she was seeing. Berkeley would not have been surprised at all if Anderson had simply materialized out of the mist. She could imagine him standing just behind her, his hand pressing into the small of her back, his knuckle digging sharply into her spine. He would incline his head toward her and make a comment that only she could hear. Other people would remark on his solicitousness. Only she would know the truth.

When she had set out this morning Berkeley's head had been filled with things she wanted to say to Anderson; now it was curiously blank. Nothing came to mind. She wasn't angry or bitter or triumphant. Guilt and shame no longer bore down on her. There had never been any real sadness, only fear, and that, too, was receding. She was no longer prompted to speak by any thoughts of hurting or insulting him. Words that she couldn't have imagined saying to him when he was alive had occurred to her earlier. Now she remained silent.

Peace was unfamiliar to her, and the irony for Berkeley was that at the moment she felt it, recognized it, and tried to embrace it, she was also disquieted by it. She drew her knees up to her chest, hugged them, and rocked gently back and forth. She hummed softly, a song her mother had sung to her, and when the tears finally came they were because her own arms were small comfort when the ones she wanted were her mother's.

It was the warmth of the sun on her back that made Berkeley aware of the passage of time. Around her the fog was thinning. She could see an entire row of crosses now, and when she squinted through the mist she could even see the listing cross

at the entrance. Berkeley jumped to her feet. She tugged on
the brim of her hat and walked quickly around Anderson's
grave. On her way out of the cemetery she straightened the
cross again before she hurried down the hill.

The citizens of Sydney Town were starting to stir. Barkeeps
were shoving sleepy-eyed patrons out the doors so they could
clean liquor, blood, and vomit off their floors. Half-dressed
men stepped out of brothels and completed fastening their
trousers or buttoning their shirts on narrow stoops or in the
streets. Berkeley only just managed to avoid one who relieved
himself as she walked by.

Colorful names that spoke to the origins of Sydney Town
were attached to the saloons. She passed the Rum Punch and
Judy, the Noggin of Ale, and the Bay of Biscay. She crossed
to the other side of the street before she reached the Fierce
Grizzly, a groggery she'd heard about from Shawn, so named
because the owner actually kept a female bear chained beside
the door. Men slept in various contorted states outside lodging
houses, where signs in the curtainless windows indicated there
were no rooms or beds to let. Berkeley picked her way past
all of them and knew herself to be more wary now than she
had been earlier.

The slowly lifting fog was revealing Sydney Town in all its
tawdry and dangerous glory.

"Pssst. You. Boy. Come here."

Berkeley was halfway between two buildings. The Tam
O'Shanter tavern was behind her. The red glass globe of a
brothel lay ahead. The low-pitched voice came from the narrow
alley on her left. She did not wait to find out what the gravel-
throated stranger wanted with her. The pause in her step was
only because she was surprised. It did not signal her intention
to stop.

The hand that clamped over her mouth was a hard one. It
fit itself so securely over her lips that Berkeley could not get
any leverage to bite or scream. She sucked in air through her
nose as she was dragged into the alley.

"Empty your pockets."

Berkeley was hanging on to her assailant's forearm with both hands. The grip he had on her face made her aware of how easily he could break her neck, even if it was not his intention to do so. Only the tips of her toes touched the ground. She had neither balance nor purchase, and the last thing she was able to do was show him her empty pockets.

He gave the order again, hissing this time. His breath was sour from a combination of stale spirits and rotting teeth. When she was still unable to respond he began an impatient search of her person himself.

Berkeley's hat was the first thing to go. A tidal wave of pale hair spilled over his forearm. She heard his grunt of surprise but he recovered quickly. His free hand went directly to the front of her jacket. He pawed her breasts through the material. Behind the hand that covered her mouth, Berkeley began to gag.

"Let her go."

Relief washed through Berkeley when she heard Mike Winston's voice. The hesitating, respectful tone that she usually associated with him was absent now. He spoke flatly, with an edge of real menace, and Berkeley realized that she was not the only one who understood it. The hand on her mouth eased enough for her to draw a gasping breath, and she was lowered so that her heels touched the ground.

Mike produced a knife and waved it close enough for Berkeley's captor to see. "Let her go," he repeated softly.

Berkeley twisted free and leaped away from her attacker. The man's hand still grazed her hip and thigh before she was free. She was breathing hard and trying not to retch.

"Get out of here," Mike told her. "Run as if your life depends on it. Because it does."

She started forward, hesitated, then began to run. When she turned the corner she saw two men approaching the alley from across the street. She shouted a warning to Mike and kept on running. Looking over her shoulder, she saw the men halt and turn in her direction. For a moment she thought she had diverted their attention from the alley, but then they went on. The last thing she saw before she turned another corner was Mike emerging from the alley only to be dragged back into its shadowy interior.

Berkeley sprinted down the street, hurdling over refuse and dodging hungover stragglers. She was winded by the time she reached Portsmouth Square, but she didn't slow perceptibly until she was standing in the Phoenix's grand gaming hall.

Sam was polishing the bar. Shawn was leaning against the banister, whittling. Donnel Kincaid and three other workers were eating their breakfast at one of the gaming tables. Everyone looked up when Berkeley came crashing through the entrance, but no one moved. Astonishment held them still until Grey Janeway appeared at the top of the stairs and began barking orders.

"Sam. Donnel. Get your guns. The rest of you take a weapon from my case." He was down the steps in the time it took him to finish rapping out the commands. He threw Shawn a key and pointed to the storeroom at the back of the hall. "You know where I keep them." Grey was carrying a pistol in his right hand. The cast of the barrel was the same shade as his eyes.

Berkeley flinched when both were turned in her direction, but she didn't back away. "It's Mike," she said.

Grey already knew that. He had been standing on his balcony when Berkeley made her wild dash across Portsmouth Square, her hair trailing like an unfurled flag behind her. Until he saw her he hadn't known she was gone. That was Mike's assignment. Expecting to see that it was Mike chasing her, Grey had permitted himself a small smile. It vanished when Mike didn't appear, and Berkeley's face betrayed the depth of her fear as she approached the Phoenix.

He knew then that it was Berkeley's protector who was in trouble. "Did you leave him in Sydney Town?"

She felt the question as an accusation but she didn't attempt to defend herself or explain. "Yes. The Ducks. They—"

"Where?" he asked abruptly. Behind him Shawn, Sam, Donnel, and the others had gathered.

"I'll show you." Berkeley turned swiftly only to be hauled back hard before she had taken a single step. She winced as Grey's fingers tangled in her hair and pulled on her scalp. "The Tam O'Shanter. On the waterfront. There's an alley that—"

Shawn brushed past Grey. "I know the place," he said. "Let's go."

Grey let the others leave before he released Berkeley. She staggered away from him but didn't cry out. "You shouldn't have gone there," he said tersely.

She didn't respond to the reprimand. "Please," she said instead. "You have to find him quickly. I'm afraid for him."

"You should be."

Berkeley shook her head. "You don't understand at all. His palm . . . when I touched his palm . . ." She couldn't say any more. She turned and fled in the direction of the storeroom. When she came back carrying a shotgun, Grey was already gone.

Except for a few broken bottles, a pile of rags, and Berkeley's battered hat, the alley beside the Tam O'Shanter was empty when Grey and his men arrived. Sam found a fresh blood trail near the wall of the tavern, and there was evidence of a stampede of men in the swirl of footprints marking the ground.

"You don't suppose they pitched him in the drink already?" Sam asked. He scratched his head while he looked warily at the small gathering of Ducks across the street. He thrust his chin in that direction. "Looks like we got a few of the flock cackling over yonder."

Donnel's dark red brows drew together. "I don't think we'd do well to be trapped in this alley. Seems to be a dead end from what I can tell."

Grey scooped up the hat and motioned them all onto the street. "Keep your weapons in plain sight but don't draw on any of them."

A husky, though unmistakably feminine voice called to them. "You boys looking for something special this morning?" Amelia Flowers stood in the doorway of her brothel and gave the men on both sides of the street a full view of her ample bosom. "Or are you just looking for a fight?"

"You got something special, Amelia?" one of the Ducks called. "Or is it the same thing you've been giving everyone on the waterfront? Namely the clap." His friends laughed at his humor, slapped him on the back, and started walking away.

Grey watched them go. He stepped on the brothel's small porch. "Thank you, Miss—"

"Mrs.," she corrected. "Mrs. Flowers. Your friend's in here. Leastways I assume he belongs to you." She stepped aside to allow Grey in. She motioned to the others, and most of them followed. Donnel and Sam took up sentinel positions on either side of the door.

They found Mike in the dining room, lying on the table. Two of Amelia's girls were hovering over him. They didn't move aside even when it was clear that Grey wanted a closer look at his man.

Mike was bruised and cut, but he was alive and he was conscious. He turned his head when he heard Grey's voice. Only one of his eyes opened. He looked at Grey through the narrow slit. "Is she all right?" he rasped. "It happened so fast . . . the fog . . . I couldn't—"

"You have nothing to apologize for," Grey said. He placed his hand lightly on Mike's shoulder. "Do you think we can move you?"

Mike nodded. "I can walk." He started to sit up, but Grey pushed him back. The pressure was enough to cause him to groan.

"We can make a litter," one of the girls suggested. "You can carry him that way."

In the end they used two sheets to make a sling. Mike passed out when they lifted him, and that was just fine with Grey and the others. It took four of them to hoist Mike, but it was manageable, even with weapons in their free hands. Grey drew a handful of gold coins from his jacket pocket and gave one to each of the girls and the rest to Amelia Flowers.

"Anytime," the madam said softly in response to Grey's thanks.

Grey caught up with his men just as Berkeley reached them from the other direction. She was limping slightly but trudging along gamely, the shotgun raised over her shoulder. Her relief in finding them with Mike in tow was short-lived. Grey tore the shotgun out of her hands and gave it to Sam. "You must have the sense of a slug," he said. He swore under his breath when the look she gave him showed neither fear nor regret. She only appeared hurt. "Sam?" Grey said. "What has less sense than a slug?"

"Not rightly sure." He grinned a little as his boss thrust the hat he'd been carrying into Berkeley's hands and told her to put it on. She jammed it on her head so forcefully that it almost swallowed her eyes. "Reckon it might be one of those jackaroos you tell about from time to time."

Donnel spoke up. "A bag of hair."

Grey had a firm grip on Berkeley's upper arm and was pulling her along. "How's that again?" he asked.

Donnel shrugged. "A bag of hair's got less sense than a slug or a jackaroo."

Shawn nodded. "A bag of hair's got as much sense as a brick. I'd say Miss Shaw's got about that much sense."

Berkeley tried to pull away, but Grey held her fast and drew her close. He made her keep pace with him in spite of her limp. "A brick it is," he told Berkeley. His voice lowered so that only she could hear him. "When Mike comes around he might come up with something even less flattering about your intelligence."

Berkeley let the comment pass. She twisted around far enough to glimpse Mike. "Is he going to be all right?"

Grey didn't know the answer to that. "Shawn will get a doctor as soon as we're back at the Phoenix."

"I want to take care of him," Berkeley said. "You can put him in my suite."

He didn't answer her. Grey was aware of the attention they were drawing as their armed group crossed Portsmouth Square.

He saw Berkeley glancing around and lowering her head as she realized the same thing. Giving her a little shake, he brought her head up again. "We could have a parade of Ducks following us," he said. "Remember that. Mike took a beating for you. By all rights it should be you in that sheet."

Berkeley lost her footing as she shuddered. "Don't you think I know how fortunate I am that Mike came along?"

"Fortunate? Luck had nothing to do with it. Mike was there because I asked him to watch after you."

"You what?"

Grey didn't understand her astonishment. "I hoped you'd prove me wrong and not venture into Sydney Town," he said. "Mike took up the watch last night in the event I was right."

Berkeley's raised face was pale as salt. Her eyes held enormous pain. "Then I've killed him," she said on a thread of sound. "It will be my fault when he dies."

Chapter Six

Grey held Berkeley beside him while he directed the men to take Mike upstairs. He dispatched Sam to find a doctor and when Annie Jack pounded out of the kitchen demanding to know what was going on, he sent her back to make poultices and cut bandages. Berkeley tried twice more to wrest free of Grey, but he held her fast. The imprint of his fingers bruised her fair skin and made her arm tingle and finally go numb. In spite of her desire to remain stoic, she heard herself whimper pitifully.

Grey didn't ease his grip on her arm. He steered her up the steps after the others had gone. At the top he turned them toward his suite and away from Mike's room.

Berkeley dug in her heels when she realized where she was going. Her resistance meant only that Grey had to pull her harder. Her heels bumped along the floor until she stumbled forward and her feet caught up with the rest of her. She accompanied him quietly after that.

At the entrance to his suite Grey trapped her between outstretched arms while he opened the door. He placed one hand squarely on the center of her back and pushed, easily sending her far enough in the room for him to close the door and lock it before she understood his intention. He was moving down the hall before he heard her twist the handle and make her first demand to be let out. He was out of earshot when she asked again.

Berkeley did not repeat herself a third time. She slumped against the door and remained there the better part of half an hour. She scrambled to her feet and moved quickly to the green-velvet settee when she recognized Annie Jack's heavy tread in the hallway. The door was unlocked and thrust open. Annie carried a tray in front of her, and for a moment her wide shoulders filled the frame as she hesitated on the threshold.

"Don't be tryin' to sneak out while Annie's hands are busy," she said. It was Annie's peculiarity to always refer to herself in the third person. "Mista Janeway will take a pound of flesh from you and more than twice that from Annie Jack. He says Annie's supposed to bring you breakfast, and that's what she's doin'."

Berkeley stood, but her movement immediately made the cook wary. She sat down slowly. "I meant to help you, Miss Jack."

Annie bristled. Her coffee-colored complexion darkened a shade as her brow furrowed. "Now don't give me your airs. No one calls Annie Miss Jack, and no one's startin' now." She placed the tray on the pie table just inside the door. "There's eggs and tomatoes and Annie's spicy hash. Don't expect you'll be gettin' this personal service again. Never had to serve no man's mistress at the El Dorado, and this is the last time here. Mista Janeway's got another think comin' if he expects Annie's goin' to be his house nigra."

Annie's plain speaking simply took Berkeley's breath away. She nodded numbly.

"Now what's wrong with you?" Annie demanded. "It's a fact you're lookin' sadder than a wet puppy. You just realizin' now how upsettin' your voodoo is to some people?"

"Voodoo?" Berkeley's head came up. She frowned. "I don't know anything about that."

Annie shrugged. "You cast a spell on Mike, sure enough. Got him followin' you around like he was a pup himself. Near to got himself killed, that's what the doctor says. Annie says it's your spirit that almost done him in. Mista Janeway's done the right thing, keepin' you here. Safer for everyone if you can't get to your charms and powders."

Agitated, but not wanting to frighten Annie off, Berkeley slid forward to the edge of the settee. "What are you talking about, Miss . . . Annie? What charms and powders?"

"Annie knows what a spirit woman needs to make her magic." Her tone clearly indicated she would hear nothing to the contrary. "She's seen your amulet."

"My amulet? I have none."

Annie stared her down, her eyes very nearly black in her dark face. "Annie's seen it, she's tellin' you. With these eyes. A pearl, it is. In a crown setting. A teardrop of pure gold hangs from it."

Berkeley's face cleared. "You mean the earring," she said.

"Earrings come in twos, same as your ears. You only have one of these. It's a charm, plain and simple."

There was no point in arguing with Annie's reasoning, but the fact that the cook had seen the earring was worth discussing. "It would seem you've been searching through my room," Berkeley said. "I know where I keep that earring, and it's not in plain view. You couldn't have seen it unless—"

Annie's substantial girth shook a moment as she set her shoulders rigidly. That she had just been offended was made abundantly clear. "Unless Annie had been chasin' down that cat of yours with her broom and the evil thing hightailed it straight to your rooms lookin' for a safe place to hide her sorry self. And Annie, thinkin' she'll save herself another chase later in the day, lets the cat into your sittin' space all quiet like so you ain't disturbed a lick in your bedchamber. The cat takes herself right up that high-backed wing chair you got by the fireplace and jumps on the mantel, where she knocks over a little treasure box that's sitting right there on the edge, so precious and unassumin' it makes a body forget what kind of magic might be inside. So Annie picks up the box and sees the charm, and the cat pounces straight away on Annie's arm, scratchin' fierce.'' The cook thrust her arm forward and rolled up the sleeve to her elbow. Two raised welts almost four inches long were plainly visible. ''Annie pushes the charm back in the box with the point of her broom and puts the box back on the mantel. That's when the cat lets go, but before Annie can swat her good she's run off.'' Annie pointed her thick index finger in Berkeley's direction and waggled it hard. ''Now you can believe Annie's searchin' your rooms or you can believe the truth. It's no account unless you're fixin' to put a spell on Annie.''

Berkeley sighed. ''I'm not going to put a spell on you,'' she said tiredly. ''I believe you.'' Yesterday morning the cat had bounded into her room and taken refuge under the covers. Berkeley had a dim memory of something crashing to the floor in her sitting room, but when she got up later there was nothing out of order. She had dismissed it as part of a dream and never given it another thought—until now. ''I'm sorry, Annie. I didn't know about Pandora's trip to your kitchen. I try to keep her in at night.''

Annie gave no indication that she was appeased. ''Pandora,'' she said under her breath. ''That's a spirit woman's cat if ever there was one.'' She was still muttering as she let herself out. The door was locked again and given a shake for good measure. Annie's footsteps quieted gradually, like thunder rolling in the distance.

Berkeley picked up the tray and moved it to Grey's dining table. She was not hungry but she went through the motions of fixing a plate with small portions. She ate a little and pushed more around. The tea was hot and soothing. She drank it without milk or sugar and was pouring herself a second cup when Grey's return drew her attention to the door.

She put down the teapot. Her cup clattered in the saucer as she laid them on the table. Berkeley's eyes searched his features for some sign that would answer the question uppermost in her mind. His gunmetal glance was shuttered. There were small lines etched at the corners of his eyes and mouth. Everywhere else his skin was pulled taut over the bones of his face. A muscle worked in his jaw. He leaned against the door, not looking at Berkeley, but looking right through her. It was tension that kept him upright, nothing else.

Berkeley could not assign meaning to anything she observed. She did not know if she was looking at anger or the last tenuous hold Grey had on his emotions. She remained silent, her eyes following him warily as he finally pushed away from the door and crossed the room.

Grey pulled out a chair, but he didn't sit down on it. Instead, he sat on the table and used the chair as a stool for his feet. His position was no accident, but a compromise of sorts, better than towering over her, but still with the advantage of the high ground.

"The doctor thinks Mike will survive," he said, watching Berkeley carefully. He saw no relief in her pale features. The words didn't comfort her because there was no assurance in them. "His shoulder's been set, and the cuts are all stitched. There's bruising on his belly and back that might mean he's bleeding on the inside." Her head bowed but she accepted the news calmly. Her hands folded in her lap and remained still. "If he makes it through the night, he'll probably recover fully."

Berkeley nodded once. It would be a long night. "May I sit with him?"

"Look at me, Berkeley." Her head came up, but she stared at a point past his shoulder. Tears hovered on the rim of her lashes. "You expect him to die, don't you?"

She nodded. The movement was enough to make the tears fall. She knuckled them away impatiently. "I . . . I know . . ." She stopped and tried to gather her thoughts. Finally she said, "Yes, I expect Mike to die."

Grey waited for her to say something else. When she didn't he made his appeal in a tone that was meant to be answered. "Talk to me, Berkeley. Tell me the whole of it."

She bit her lower lip and said nothing. Grey's own silence didn't prompt her to speak any more than his command had.

"This has something to do with what you saw in his palm," Grey said. "Are you telling me you really believe your own parlor tricks?"

"I know what I felt," she said quietly. "I believe I know what it meant."

The heel of Grey's hand struck the edge of the table sharply. Berkeley jumped, darting him an uncertain glance. His hand was steady, not raised, and he was watching narrowly. "Look at me," he said when she would have turned away again. "You're acting as though you knew all along this would happen."

"I didn't know *this* would happen. Only that *something* would. I never felt anything like it before. I didn't understand that Mike's life was somehow caught up in mine. I didn't realize I would have some part in his death."

"You don't," Grey said tightly. "He's not dead."

Berkeley said nothing to that.

"I was there, remember? When you read his palm. You never warned him about any accident. You never told him he had only a short time to live."

"What would you have had me say? He asked about his family, and I told him he'd see them sooner rather than later. I told him to write to them and tell them he loved them. I gave him the answers he wanted to hear because the truth would have served no purpose. If he listened to me, if he did as I suggested, then at least his family will derive some comfort from his words." Her voice had risen slightly, then it fell off. Her tone was quiet, deliberate. It felt as if her heart were in her throat. "Not all of us get that same chance."

Berkeley's eyes implored him. "Please, let me go to Mike."

"And do what?" Grey asked. "Do you really think you can give him a measure of peace when you expect him to die?"

She flinched as though he'd struck her. Berkeley thought she finally understood why she had been locked in his suite. "You're afraid I'll hurt him, aren't you? You think I'd actually do Mike some harm to make you believe my prediction." Wounded, she squeezed herself into one corner of the chair.

The distance between her and Grey still wasn't enough. The chair scraped harshly against the floor as she pushed it back.

"I never said that," Grey told her. "I put you in here to keep you from saying something rash in front of the others. No one needs to hear that you hold yourself responsible for Mike's injuries—least of all Mike. And certainly I don't want you telling anyone that you *saw* this in his palm a month ago."

"Don't you believe me?"

"I believe there is no such thing as a foregone conclusion," he said. "I don't want anyone giving up on Mike because you're acting as if he's already dead. That's why you're going to do exactly what I say. You're going to sit with Mike while I'm there to monitor every word, and you're going to thank him for saving you. Then you're going to pick up his hand, and you'll study it, and you're going to tell him that what you see in his future is a long life, a happy marriage, and three towheaded boys all farming in Kentucky. You can elaborate any way you like, but you're going to convince him that his life is all in front of him, not behind him." His eyes were the exact steely color of a razor's edge. Their intensity held Berkeley still. "Now, can you do that?"

She nodded.

"Good," he said. But he wasn't finished. "Afterward you're going to go to your own rooms and begin preparation for this evening. The Phoenix is going to open as scheduled at six o'clock, and you're going to make your first appearance on my arm at seven. You will greet our guests graciously and you'll read the palms of a few I've chosen for you. I've made some notes on these guests, and this afternoon I'll have them delivered to your room. You can study them at your leisure. It's not complicated information, just some basic facts that will embellish your performance and make it more convincing. Are you clear on what I expect?"

She nodded again, more slowly this time, her leaf green eyes a little dazed.

"Tonight I want you to call me Grey, never Mr. Janeway."

A small crease appeared between Berkeley's brows. She

worried her lower lip before she spoke. "People will think you and I . . . that is, they'll probably believe that . . ." She didn't finish, couldn't really, not when Grey's eyes mocked her.

"That you're my mistress?" he asked. "Is that what you can't quite bring yourself to say?"

"You know it is. I thought that was settled between us."

"It's never been fully *discussed* between us. No, don't start going on about not being my whore. I have no desire to hear all that again. I'm talking about appearance here, not fact. In fact, you have your own rooms. The appearance, however, should be otherwise. It's for your own safety, and when you allow yourself the time to think about it you'll realize I'm right. You'll find that people will believe you're my mistress whether you encourage them to or not. You may as well encourage them. It will afford you considerable protection and leave you free from constant propositions."

One of Grey's brows arched. "Unless you wish to be propositioned? Do you, Berkeley?"

"No." Her voice was barely audible. "No, I don't."

"Not all of them will be unseemly," he said. "I imagine you can expect to get more than a few for marriage."

Her throat was dry. She eyed her cup of tea and would have picked it up if her hands had been steadier. She swallowed with difficulty. "I don't want to be married."

There was no mistaking her sincerity. Grey wondered at it, wondered at the experiences that had led her to it. "Very well," he said quietly. "Then you'd do well to follow my lead this evening. Actually, I'll expect that from you." Grey pushed aside the chair where his feet rested and stood. "Do you have any questions?"

There was one. Her tongue seemed to grow thick in her mouth with the prospect of asking it. She forced herself to do it because anticipation was worse than knowing. "You haven't mentioned how I'm to be punished," she said.

Grey stared at her. "How you're to be punished," he repeated slowly. "No, you're right, I haven't mentioned it. I'll have to give it some thought." If anything, she grew paler. Grey raked his hair and swore softly under his breath. "God, Berkeley, I have no intention of laying a hand on you. Is that what you're expecting?"

Her eyes betrayed her. She answered him without saying a word.

"Mike could die," he said quietly.

Berkeley sucked in her breath. She wished he had hit her instead.

Grey took her by the wrist and drew Berkeley to her feet. "Let's go," he said. "Remember what I want you to tell Mike. Convince him that you mean every bit of it." He dropped her hand and, without a backward glance, preceded her out of the room.

Berkeley closed her eyes. Steam rose like twisted threads of silk above the water. She rested her head against the back of the tub, exposing the length of her slender throat. The fragrance of lavender was released as her fingers made a sweep across the water. She palmed the soap and raised it to her damp shoulder, then let it fall again.

She lay there, breathing slowly, evenly, unwilling to move until the water cooled to the point she was forced out. Berkeley did not think it was possible to be so exhausted and still be alive.

Sitting with Mike had taken its toll on her spirit; taking his hand had robbed her of strength.

With her eyes closed, Berkeley had no difficulty bringing Mike's face to mind. Even bruised and swollen his mouth had managed an endearingly lopsided smile. Two pillows had been tucked under his head so he didn't have to raise it to see her. Behind the slit that passed for his left eye, he watched her walk up to his bedside and take a seat on the very edge.

She thanked him for his rescue and told him no one had ever risked so much for her. He blushed. Leaning forward, she kissed him lightly on the mouth. His flush deepened, and he looked past Berkeley's shoulder to where Grey stood.

''She makes me wish I was where you are,'' Grey said easily. Mike would have to believe him because he meant it. ''The next time she needs rescuing I won't leave the heroics to you.''

Low laughter rumbled in Mike's broad chest. He began to cough hard. A spittle of blood appeared on his lips, but he managed to get out the words, ''Like hell.''

Berkeley took the handkerchief Grey handed her and wiped Mike's mouth. She wet one corner of it in the basin at Mike's bedside and dabbed at his split lip again. The blood hadn't come from there. ''Do you have a loose tooth?'' she asked.

Mike's brows lifted slightly. He ran his tongue around the interior of his mouth. He held up three fingers.

Berkeley allowed herself to believe the blood had come from any one of them. She tucked the handkerchief under her cuff in the event she needed it again. ''Would you like to hear what your future holds, Mike? It will give you something pleasant to think while your bones knit.'' In spite of his battered face, Berkeley could tell he was wary of what she might see in his palm. She saw him look to Grey again.

Grey shrugged. ''It's up to you, Mike, but I'd be curious. Four weeks ago she told you you'd be seeing your family soon, and right now Donnel Kincaid is making arrangements so you can be on the next clipper out of San Francisco if that's what you want. Return is guaranteed if you decide to make the trip west again. I can't say that I like how it's all come to pass, but I don't suppose Miss Shaw has any control over that.''

Berkeley glanced over her shoulder at Grey, her expression a mixture of surprise and gratitude. ''Did you write to your family, Mike?''

He nodded, then grimaced.

''I won't ask any more questions,'' she promised. Berkeley took the hand he extended but held it in only one of hers. She girded herself for the shock of the first touch and threw up all her defenses. Still, she sucked in her breath at the depth of the pain. ''Your hand's very cold,'' she said, smiling weakly to cover her lapse. ''I wasn't expecting that.'' Behind her she heard Grey take a step forward. His shadow hovered like a bird of prey.

Berkeley examined Mike's palm and cautiously allowed herself to feel something beyond his pain. "Why, Mike, you've never mentioned this before. There's a girl sweet on you back home in Kentucky. Did you think Shawn would never give you peace about her?" She felt his hand stiffen slightly, and she managed a teasing smile. "You know it's more likely that he'd be jealous. It's a certain thing you're going to marry her, probably before he marries again. I don't think you realize how deeply she cares for you, Mike. She's a bit shy, like you, and never wanted to seem forward. You broke her heart when you left your farm. I suspect she'll be waiting for you when you go back, sitting on your mama's porch, helping her snap beans for canning. She won't know which way to look when she sees you. She'll be thinking she looks a fright, and you'll be thinking there's never been anyone prettier."

Berkeley was aware her breath was coming shallowly. The pain in her arm was intense. The skin from her fingertips to her shoulder felt like a single exposed nerve. "There will be children," she whispered. She bent over his palm. "I can't make out if you'll have five or six. Oh, I see it now. There are six. You're going to have twins." She dropped his hand and stood up quickly. She rubbed her arm but tried to make it look like an absent gesture. Tilting her head to one side, the smile she offered him was a playful one. "At least I think it's twins. You have a lot of scratches on your palm, Mike. It could be you'll only have three beautiful babies."

Mike stared at her. Berkeley thought he was seeing more clearly through that single slit of his than he ever had with two good eyes. It had never been so important to him to know the truth before. Her own gaze didn't waver in the least. She held his stare, her features untroubled and serene, and willed him to believe every bit of what she had just told him.

When he finally spoke, Mike's voice was the clearest it had been since the beating. "Do you suppose it's Bonnie Sue McMasters?" he asked.

Berkeley's laughter was part relief and part unfettered, youthful joy. "Oh yes," she said, dropping to her knees beside the bed. "Yes, Mike. I think it's Bonnie Sue McMasters you're meant to marry."

Mike laid his hand over the crown of Berkeley's head. Her pale hair was like silk under his palm. His fingertips passed through it lightly, then fell down her cheeks and rested on her shoulder. He could feel her trembling, but she didn't move away from him or seem to want to. Her eyes appeared too large for her small face, but they were shining, awash with tears that she wouldn't shed. Most important was the complete absence of pity in their depths.

Berkeley felt Mike's hand fall away as Grey helped her to her feet. "He needs to rest," Grey said. "Find someone to come and stay with him. I'll be here until I'm relieved." He followed her into the hallway, leaving the door opened a crack in case Mike called for him. He spoke in a whisper that didn't carry beyond Berkeley's ears. "You couldn't have done it any better," he said. "Thank you."

"It wasn't a performance," she said. Berkeley left him alone to think about what that meant.

The water was cooler now, and Berkeley realized she had slept a little while her thoughts drifted back. She found the soap and rubbed it across her shoulders and arms. Her skin tingled. Washing didn't erase the sensation; it aroused it. Berkeley soaped her breasts. They were faintly swollen, and the nipples were taut. She caught sight of her flushed face in the cheval glass near the fireplace. Her eyelids were heavy, and her damp skin glowed. Then she saw Grey Janeway's reflection as he stepped up to the tub behind her. He knelt and took the soap from her hands.

Berkeley's breath caught. There was an unfamiliar pressure in her chest, a deep, abiding ache that made her want to draw her knees up close to her breasts. She didn't. Couldn't. Grey's hand lay on her naked shoulder. The soap was gone and it was just his palm against her skin. His thumb moved back and forth over the ridge of her collarbone, and in the mirror his eyes held hers.

She watched his hand as his fingers trailed slowly down her arm and disappeared under the water. She bit her lower lip, her eyes darkening, when she felt him graze her thigh. The water rippled. Berkeley shivered.

His hand was on her hip, then the curve of her bottom. Without a word passing between them he conveyed his need for her to lean forward. When she did, his thumb traced her spine with enough pressure to make her arch. She saw herself unfold under his touch, her breasts lifting, her shoulders rising. When he held the nape of her neck her chin came up, and the length of her slender throat was exposed.

His mouth settled first on the curve of her shoulder. He held her still and touched the hollow of her throat. She felt the damp edge of his tongue. The breath that she seemed to have been holding for an eternity was finally released in a ragged little sigh. She gripped the sides of the tub. His mouth lifted, then it came down on hers. Her heart hammered . . .

Berkeley shot up suddenly. Water splashed the floor as a small tidal wave was raised around her. Her heart *was* thudding loudly, but then so was the door to her suite. Heat rushed her as she stared at the cheval glass and saw only her own reflection. Grey wasn't there. She had always been alone.

"Just a moment," she called. Her voice was hardly more than a whisper, and the insistent knocking at the door continued unabated. Berkeley stepped out of the tub and slipped into her wrapper. She hurried to the door, water dripping in her wake. Her fingers were on the handle, prepared to twist it when something made her pause. "Who is it?"

Just as if she didn't know, Grey thought. Her voice came to him cool and sweet and clear. "Berkeley," he said, a thread of impatience running through the single word, "open this door."

Berkeley turned the key and pulled on the handle. She cracked the door and peered out through the opening. It was impossible not to stare at him. Less than a minute had passed since she had held the vision of him in her mind's eye. She could still feel the heat where he had touched her, or where she thought he had.

Grey was regarding her with more distant interest, his flint-colored eyes slightly remote as he took in her flushed complexion and the beads of water that glistened on her naked throat. Her mouth was damp, and the centers of her darkening eyes were wide enough to hold his reflection. She was holding her wrapper closed at the waist as if she didn't trust her efforts to belt it. The lapels gaped above her fist, and Grey watched a diamond water drop run its course from the tendril of hair curling around her neck to the shadowed curve of her breasts.

Berkeley did not think her dream had played her false in any detail about Grey Janeway. Only what he had done to her had been imagined. Looking at him now, she was struck by how clearly she had brought him to mind. She had captured the perpetually wind-ruffled look of his dark sable hair and the way it just touched his collar at the back. She had recalled the clarity of his blue-gray eyes and the way his smile, reserved and faintly cynical, did not touch their steely depths. His lean frame filled the space she allowed him, and the casual grace with which he rested against the wall spoke to the aristocratic manner he could not entirely shed.

Berkeley blinked as he leaned forward and rested one hand on the doorjamb. He did not try to force his way in. He simply stood there, somehow negligently braced against her door, looking vaguely amused and annoyed at the same time. And while Berkeley took in the contradictions of his expression, she could only think of his hand and the lean fingers that had trailed with such perfect gentleness across her skin.

Her mouth parted. She felt her breath catching again.

"Are you quite all right?" Grey asked.

Berkeley nodded.

Grey was unconvinced. He inclined his head forward and tried to see into her suite. "Do you have someone in there?"

"No." She expelled the word more than spoke it. "No," she said again, this time with more certainty. With some effort

Berkeley gathered the errant threads of her thoughts. "Has something happened to Mike?" she asked.

"He's resting comfortably. I just came from there. Shawn's sitting with him now." Grey reached inside his vest and pulled out a neatly folded paper. "I have the information I promised. May I come in?"

"I'm not dressed," she said. "I haven't finished bathing." Berkeley noticed that neither of these excuses were particularly discouraging to Grey. He didn't move away from the door. She opened it wide enough to extend her hand. "Let me have the paper, and I'll study it."

"I'd like to go over it with you."

Berkeley considered closing the door and locking it. "You have a key to all the rooms, don't you?"

One corner of Grey's mouth kicked up. "Hm-mmm." He was genuinely amused now and didn't mind that Berkeley knew it. He waited her out, watching her animated features change as she considered her options. "Thank you," he said dryly as the door opened wide to admit him. His eyes followed the trail of wet footprints from the doorway to where they disappeared into her bedroom. "If you'd like to finish your bath, I'll wait here." Grey watched, fascinated, as a wave of heat flushed Berkeley's porcelain-smooth skin. "You don't want the water to get cold."

The way he was looking at her made it difficult for Berkeley not to stammer. She stared at the paper in his hand rather than subject herself to his scrutiny. Knowing that she was being teased did not make her feel better; it only made her feel hopelessly young. "May I?" she said, holding out her hand.

Grey gave her the paper. He chose the ice-blue-brocade wing chair to lounge in while she unfolded the paper and studied its contents. Stretching out, his long legs extending toward the barren fireplace, Grey let his eyes wander around the room. The suite was not so different from the ones that would soon be occupied by the Phoenix's regular guests. The drapes were cut from the same brocade that upholstered the wing chair. The settee was a contrast in navy blue velvet. There was a small oval dining table near the window with a chair at each end. One of the chairs was pushed slightly to the side, and the table's walnut surface was littered with stationery, an inkwell, and several pens. Grey imagined the arrival of her bathwater had been the interruption that stopped her work. He wondered at the contents of the crumpled, discarded vellum sheets. It hadn't occurred to him that Berkeley would have need of a writing desk.

Grey's eyes didn't linger long on the table, but they strayed back there from time to time, his curiosity engaged. He continued to look about the room, noting the workmanship of the end tables, the vase of fresh flowers, and the handsomely carved box on the mantel. He was satisfied that Berkeley could be comfortable in this sitting room and in the whole of her suite, but he also was aware she hadn't done anything to make it her own. Not that he had any idea of how she could have accomplished that when she had been confined to the Phoenix.

Berkeley looked up from the paper and found herself being regarded rather distantly by Grey Janeway. His aquiline nose gave him a certain arrogant appeal. She tried to imagine what he was thinking and found that she couldn't. No one had ever looked at her in quite that way, as if she were more than a curiosity, but interesting in her own right. She folded the paper and returned it to him.

Grey didn't put it away. "You'll need to memorize it," he said.

"I already have. Excuse me." She disappeared into the bedroom, shut the door, and returned a few minutes later wearing a plain gray gown. The sleeves were rolled up to her elbows, and the neck was open. A towel was draped around her shoulders, and she was combing through her damp hair. Her feet were bare. "Mr. Sam Brannan used to operate a general store. He's a Mormon elder but no longer one of Brigham Young's trusted confidants. There's a matter of money owed to the Lord in the form of tithes and Mr. Young would like to collect it. It would be a considerable sum now that Mr. Brannan is rich from the gold strike and the businesses he owns. Mr. Brannan is also head of the Vigilance Committee here in San Francisco, which he organized to run out the Sydney Ducks.''

Grey smiled. Berkeley Shaw was a quick study. ''Lorne Fitch?'' he asked.

''Mr. Fitch is the president of the First Bank of California. He's building a granite-stone mansion northeast of the city. He owns shares in the railroad and in some piece of most everything else. He's married to Marilyn Adams, and they have four children.''

Grey held up his hand. He had given her more information but he was satisfied she knew it all. ''Enough. I'm convinced.''

''There's still Anthony Bottoms,'' Berkeley said. ''He's a favorite of Miss Ivory DuPree.''

''Enough,'' he repeated.

Berkeley made one final pass through her hair with the comb, then placed it on the mantel. She picked up the treasure box that Shawn had fashioned for her and carried it over to Grey. ''I wonder if you would look at this,'' she said, opening the lid. ''Do you think I could have it fashioned into a pendant?''

Grey said nothing for a moment. His attention was not on the box at all but on her. ''You're still limping,'' he said.

''I'm sorry.'' She looked at her feet. Her weight rested mainly on her right foot. Uncomfortable with his scrutiny, Berkeley's toes curled. ''I shall be careful this evening not to embarrass—''

Those wriggling bare toes undid him. ''Do I need to have the doctor see you as well?'' he asked irritably.

''No, I'm—''

''What did you do to yourself anyway?''

''I twisted it when I was running after—''

Grey interrupted her again, this time speaking with a clenched jaw. ''Miss Shaw, will you *please* stop wiggling your toes?''

Berkeley came sharply to attention.

''That's better,'' he said. It was difficult not to smile. Grey pointed to the box. ''Show me what you have there.''

Berkeley tilted the open box toward him. The earring lay alone inside. The engraved letters were not immediately visible.

Berkeley nudged the golden raindrop so the delicately inscribed ER could be seen. She fixed her eyes on Grey while he studied the earring.

Grey drew it out of the box and laid it across his palm. "Is this yours?" he asked.

"In a manner of speaking."

"You stole it."

Berkeley didn't flinch at his conclusion. There was no accusation in Grey's tone and no judgment. There was also no recognition in his features as he studied the piece. Berkeley knew he could keep his thoughts guarded and his expression distanced, but she knew he was not without emotion. She didn't believe he could look at the earring and not reveal his connection to it—if there was one.

Her glance slipped to the table, where the evidence of her frustrating attempt to write to Decker and Colin Thorne was strewn across the polished surface. She had found no easy way to tell them that she knew Graham Denison was dead and Greydon Thorne had never really existed. She didn't have the proof they expected, but Berkeley had known both these truths when she had taken Grey Janeway's hand in hers. *He was not the man she had first thought he was.*

Still, there were doubts. She found them unsettling because they were so unfamiliar to her. They made it impossible for her to reveal anything to the Thornes. There was a link between Grey Janeway and Graham Denison, but it was not one she was certain she wanted to share. It was that link that she wanted to be wrong about.

Her hope that it would come to pass ended when he merely returned the earring to the box.

"You should have taken the pair," Grey said. "Then you wouldn't have to worry what to do with the only one you have."

Berkeley closed the lid and replaced it on the mantel. "I didn't steal it. It was given to me, and whether you believe that is of no concern. I only wanted your advice."

"I know someone who can put it on a necklace. If you want,

I'll take it with me." His dark brows drew together slightly. "Who's ER?"

"Elizabeth Regina," she said. "I was told the earring is one of a pair made for the queen's coronation."

Grey laughed. "I hope you didn't believe that."

"No, but I like the story."

"It would make the earring worth a great deal if it were true."

She nodded. "Priceless if I had the pair."

"Who gave it to you?" He was surprised by how much he wanted to know the answer.

Decker Thorne's wry smile came to Berkeley's mind. *I trust you to make the right decision, Mrs. Shaw. This is the final test.* "Someone who trusted me."

The enigmatic reply did not satisfy Grey, but he refused to let her know he was bothered by it. He stood. "Show me your gowns," he said.

Berkeley was taken back by his abrupt change in subject, but she led the way into her bedroom and opened the armoire. She watched Grey examine the evening dresses critically, holding several of them up to her. He finally chose a rich green gown with short puffed sleeves and a deep neckline.

"I can't wear that," she told him. "Not this evening. Not for several evenings, I imagine."

"Why the devil can't you? It fits, doesn't it?"

"It fits. Of course, it fits. It was made for me."

"My point exactly."

"But not mine. I can't wear it because of the sleeves."

Grey pulled the gown out and hung it from a hook on the back of the armoire's open door. "What's wrong with them?"

"They're short."

"Sam says it's the fashion." A small crooked smile touched Grey's mouth. It sounded ridiculous to his own ears. Sam Hartford. Arbiter of fashion. "All right, Berkeley, what's wrong with short sleeves?"

Berkeley found herself staring at him, staring at the smile that flickered behind his eyes. Suddenly she didn't want to tell him. "Nothing," she said. "I didn't think they would be right. The evenings are cool here, aren't they? And I don't have a proper shawl."

"You'll be inside," Grey said.

"I know. There'll be a crush of people. I probably won't feel chilled at all. I shouldn't have said anything about it. The gown's quite perfect, Mr. Jane—"

"Grey."

"Grey," Berkeley repeated quietly. "Really, it's quite perfect."

The doors to the Phoenix opened at six o'clock. The first guests were there by invitation. The Alcalde arrived with his wife. Sam Brannan came with his entourage of bodyguards. Bankers and businessmen and speculators and claim holders filed in. Outside, in Portsmouth Square, the uninvited carried themselves off gloomily to the El Dorado or the Palace or stood three deep at the windows to get a glimpse of the longest bar in San Francisco. By six-thirty two hundred of the city's most prominent citizens were enjoying roulette and faro and poker at the tables, toasting their reflections in the mirror-lined wall, and whispering about Grey's hostess, who had yet to make her appearance.

Chandeliers brightened the grand hall. There were fewer than twenty women in attendance, each of them with an escort. Among the black top hats and stiff collars, they flashed like starshine on a dark sea. Combs sparkled in their hair, and chokers glittered around their necks. The mistresses avoided the wives, and they all avoided congregating, thereby not inviting comparisons. Not one of them was looking forward to meeting Grey Janeway's new hostess.

Abovestairs Berkeley Shaw slipped out of Mike's room and hurried back to her own. He had been sleeping quietly when she entered his room but in time he woke and she modeled the gown Grey had chosen for her. Her awkward pirouette had coaxed a smile from Mike. She felt his forehead with the back of her hand and found it cool, not fevered. It was another encouraging sign.

Berkeley did not want to think about what waited below. The sounds had been filtering up the stairs and down the hallway for almost an hour. She had gone to Mike's room as much to deny the music and constant hum of voices as to assure herself that Mike was improving. Now it was more difficult to pretend that she couldn't hear, harder still to pretend she wasn't afraid.

Grey's steps announced his presence in the corridor. Berkeley was opening her door as he was reaching out to knock on it. "Please," she said, her fixed smile wavering ever so slightly. "Come in."

Berkeley thought that he shouldn't be so handsome or quite so much at ease. He was elegantly turned out in a formal black tailcoat and trousers. His waistcoat was black satin. In contrast his shirt and flat tie gleamed whitely. Gold studs flashed on his cuffs. He looked for all the world as if he wore these clothes daily, as if they more perfectly suited to his leanly muscled frame than his own skin.

Grey's smile slowly appeared. "I believe I'm flattered," he drawled softly.

Berkeley flushed. "I'll only be a moment," she said quickly. "I need my gloves." She would have backed away and fled the room for no other reason than to compose herself, but Grey was standing there, shaking his head slowly and holding her in place with the strength of a look.

"If I may return the compliment," he said. The words were almost spoken in the manner of one asking permission. Almost. Grey did not want to take the chance that he would be refused, and he did most definitely want to return the compliment.

It was not the gown he noticed, but how she looked in it. Her skin was radiant against the rich iridescent shades of green in the satin. Her heavy cascade of pale hair had been lifted off her neck. It was smoothly curved at the back of her head and secured with ebony combs. Her beautifully sculpted throat was bare. The deeply cut bodice laid open most of her white shoulders and revealed the delicate line of her collarbones.

Grey watched her take a steadying breath, her reed-slender body swaying slightly. The cut of the gown accented her small waist and long leg line. It dipped fashionably low to expose the high curves of her breasts. Berkeley Shaw was not swallowed by flounces and trimming. The gown served her, not the other way around.

"Lovely," Grey said. "Sam's hard work has done you justice."

Berkeley said nothing. She had not been warmed by his appreciative study. She had only suffered it.

Grey frowned. Berkeley's radiance did not extend to her eyes. She looked pained, not pleased. "What is it?" he asked.

"I don't think I can do this," she whispered raggedly. "I thought I could, but I can't. I'm sorry." At her sides her fingers clenched. She wanted to look anywhere but at him. She forced herself not to look away. "I'm sorry I gave you the impression that I could. I'm not so worldly that I can find it a compliment when a man looks at me the way you just did. The thought of the others . . . downstairs . . . I simply can't . . ." Berkeley's voice trailed off as she ran out of steam.

"If another man looks at you the way I just did," Grey said slowly, "I'll kill him."

Nervous laughter bubbled in Berkeley's throat. She hiccuped. Her hand flew to her mouth, her eyes wide above it.

"Get your gloves, Berkeley." Grey's tone did not encourage refusal.

She found herself turning and picking up the long white gloves from where they lay on the dining table. The papers and inkwell and pens had long since been removed; the letters remained unwritten. She slipped the first glove on her right arm, adjusted it above her elbow, then raised her left arm to do the same.

"What the devil?" Grey started forward even as Berkeley was retracting her arm and attempting to hide it behind her back. He held out his hand. "Give me your wrist." Berkeley offered her arm reluctantly. Grey took her wrist and raised it, lifting it out to the side so he could see the soft inside of her elbow and upper arm. There had been an attempt to hide the bruises with powder, but it was not as effective as Berkeley might have wished. "This is what's wrong with short sleeves," Grey said.

Berkeley nodded. There was no recrimination in her eyes. "The gloves will cover some of it."

"Not enough." He dropped her wrist. "I did that to you this morning, didn't I?" He recalled grabbing her tightly and keeping her close the entire way from Sydney Town to Portsmouth Square. He had forced her to keep up with him. Had he even realized she had been limping then? Would it have mattered if he had? Now his fingerprints marred her delicate skin like a brutish brand. "Why didn't you tell me?" he asked. "You started to."

She looked away, unaccountably shy. Berkeley ducked her head and shrugged her beautiful shoulders. "You didn't do it intentionally."

That wasn't entirely true, Grey remembered. He had been furious with her. He'd meant to hurt her, or at least show her the hard edge of his anger. What he hadn't meant to do was leave marks. "Did you think I would feel bad about this?" he asked. "Were you trying to protect me? Look at me, Berkeley. Were you trying to protect me?"

She stared at him. "Something like that."

For a moment a muscle worked in Grey's cheek. "Don't assume you know what I feel and don't try to shield me from my own blunders."

"All right," she said softly. "Shall I find something else to wear?"

"God, yes."

Trying not to show her smile, Berkeley hurried into the bedroom. "Do you think the red velvet will do?" she called back to him.

"No. What about the blue-beaded gown? The one Ivory gave you."

Berkeley pulled it from the armoire. She had never even tried it on. There was something about it that unsettled her each time she picked it up. It had been thrust to the back of her wardrobe. Trust Grey to remember it. "I don't think it will fit."

"It will fit," he said with assurance. "Put it on." He consulted his pocket watch. "You have three minutes."

Berkeley wiggled out of her gown and tossed it on the bed. She stripped out of two petticoats that had added fullness to the last gown but which were unnecessary for this one. Stepping into the gown, she pulled it up to her shoulders. The sleeves were long and tapered. They flared at the shoulders and were cut narrowly around her wrists. The bodice was heart-shaped and decorated with hundreds of tiny glass beads that shimmered like sapphires when she moved. Berkeley carefully smoothed the silk across her midriff and made a quarter turn to each side in front of the cheval glass. The gown was not as revealing as the green satin, yet she was infinitely more uncomfortable in it.

"Do you need help with the back?" Grey asked from the doorway.

Berkeley was grateful for the interruption. She knew she required a diversion. She had to steel herself. Ivory DuPree's gown was tugging on her senses.

Chapter Seven

Berkeley faltered at the top of the stairs. Her fingers dug into Grey's arm as she was seized by a wave of light-headedness and stomach-churning anxiety.

Beneath his sleeve, Grey could make out the crescent shape of Berkeley's nails. He winced as she pressed harder. "You'll leave bruises," he whispered. "What will my guests think?"

She gave him a quick sidelong glance. "I'm sorry." It was an effort to uncurl her nearly bloodless fingers from his forearm.

Grey laid a hand over hers before she removed herself from his support entirely. "I was teasing, Berkeley. Are you all right?"

She only nodded. Her throat felt as if it were stuffed with cotton. It was difficult to draw a breath deep enough to fill her lungs.

"Courage," Grey said. "You're going to be the belle of the ball."

Berkeley expected him to begin the descent down the curving stairs. When he didn't move she cast him another glance and glimpsed an expression of pure puzzlement on his face. "Are you all right?" she asked.

He was, Grey thought. And he wasn't. He had never experienced a moment from the past with such overwhelming clarity. He knew without any doubt that he had done this before. The staircase. The woman. The people waiting for them. *You're going to be the belle of the ball.* Those had been his words. Everything was the same, yet not the same at all.

Too quickly the moment passed. The freshness of the experience vanished with it. He repeated the words to himself but there was no recapturing it. His certainty of having gone through these motions before faded as well, yet there was the beginning of a headache as muscles corded at his nape, reminding him this was not his imagination.

Grey resisted the urge to rub the back of his neck. He patted Berkeley's hand lightly. To all appearances he was comforting her. The reality was a little different than that. "Shall we?"

The noisy throng of guests quieted as Grey Janeway and his hostess appeared at the curve of the grand staircase. Grey had greeted guests when the doors opened, but this was the first opportunity for them to acknowledge his accomplishment en masse. The initial light applause swelled to thunder. Empty glasses on the bar actually inched forward with the strength of the vibration. Grey inclined his head, accepting the accolades in an aristocratic manner that was bred in the bone. Some of the rowdier guests hooted gleefully at the airs they thought he affected. Grey chuckled deeply and smiled at their reminder that he had no special claim on good breeding and inherited wealth. He had scrapped and scrabbled like everyone else in the hall. He'd been less fortunate than some, luckier than most. No one among the two hundred present tonight thought he deserved anything less than what he had earned.

But to a man they were wondering what Grey Janeway had done to deserve the woman on his arm.

Grey held up one hand to silence the crowd. "Ladies." Grey made a point to single them out and give each one a moment's attention. "Gentlemen." In some corners of the hall this distinction was greeted by a low rumble of laughter. "It is my very great pleasure to introduce you to the Phoenix's hostess, Miss Berkeley Shaw. Miss Shaw, my friends.''

Berkeley's beaded gown flashed as she was turned toward Grey. He lifted the hand that was lying over his forearm and brought it to his lips. Surprise held Berkeley still. She was unaware of the collective groan that was offered up by most of Grey's male guests as her unavailability was confirmed.

"Can you smile at least?" Grey asked over her hand. His lips brushed her skin as he spoke. His eyes were focused on hers. "They shouldn't be left with the impression that you're terrified.''

Her smile was reflexive. "But I *am* terrified."

"Good." Grey was encouraging her smile, not her state of mind. He lowered her hand, placed it on his arm again, and turned to the crowd. Applause swelled again as they began their descent. Grey scanned the faces lifted in their direction while he tilted his head toward Berkeley. His faint grin was still in place. "You will have them quite literally in the palm of your hand," he whispered. "Let's see what you can do with it.''

The first hour passed in a blur of faces that Berkeley could barely distinguish and names she would not remember. She knew she fixed her smile and extended her hand and made socially appropriate comments, but it was done by rote. The real effort she made went unnoticed by everyone, including the man who rarely left her side. Grey could not know, nor could Berkeley adequately explain, the sensations that were making her skin crawl and her heart beat like a trip-hammer.

She was mounting all her defenses to sustain the pretense of normality while terror defined the only emotion she felt.

Berkeley smiled warmly at Samuel Brannan. He was a large, blustering sort of man, the kind who brought attention to himself even when he traveled without six bodyguards. He pumped Berkeley's hand before he seated himself across the table from her. His protectors formed a phalanx on either side and curious onlookers squeezed in where they could.

Grey stood just behind the table, in clear view of Sam but

not close enough to Berkeley to be accused of giving her any signals.

"I don't know what you have in mind, Grey," Brannan said. "I don't exactly need an excuse to take a beautiful woman's hand."

"Perhaps she needs an excuse to take yours," someone in the pressing crowd called.

Brannan laughed good-naturedly. "There's the truth of it." He placed his hand in the middle of the narrow table. "Well, Miss Shaw? Even if you don't tell me anything out of the ordinary, I'll still leave this table a satisfied man."

Berkeley turned Sam Brannan's large palm over in hers. She held his eyes steadily with hers. "I hope I can do more than merely satisfy you," she said huskily.

Behind her, Grey's dark brows drew together. He had never heard Berkeley's voice fall to quite that suggestive pitch before. If he'd had to make a wager on it, he would have said it wasn't possible. He glanced around at the men and women watching her. Her comment hadn't gone unnoticed and wasn't going to pass unremarked. Sam Brannan's complexion, he saw, had turned a ruddy hue beneath his large side whiskers. He was still game, though, looking infinitely more honored than offended.

Berkeley had no idea that she had displeased Grey or elicited any comment from the crowd of onlookers. She stroked Sam Brannan's palm several times, tracing the curve of his mounts with her fingertips. Berkeley spoke as if she and Sam were alone in the great hall. "You have always been a powerful man," she said quietly. "Your strength comes from your conviction and your faith. You are a leader among men even when you do not position yourself that way. You take a stand for yourself, and others simply follow whether you ask it of them or not."

Sam Brannan was smiling broadly. "If that don't beat all," he said. "You tell her to say that, Grey?"

"I don't put words in her mouth," Grey said. "And if I did, those wouldn't be the ones I'd want her to tell you."

Sam chuckled. "Just so," he said. "Go on, Miss Shaw. I can stand to hear more."

Berkeley continued for a few minutes in the same vein, relating the traits she sensed in his character. Finally she said, "Do you have a question for me, Mr. Brannan?"

He didn't respond immediately, but gave her query full consideration. "I believe I do," he said, stroking his beard. "I'm engaged in a new struggle, and though I feel the rightness of it, I have my doubts that it can succeed. What do you give for my chances?"

Berkeley leaned closer. "The answer to that doesn't rest in your palm," she told him. "But in your heart and head. Your Vigilance Committee may have a good intent, but it exists outside the law. It can't hope to operate within the structures of justice when there are no trials for the accused. Good intentions do not necessarily lead to good decisions. You and your committee will drive the Ducks out but not without claiming some innocents. You will be successful, Mr. Brannan. The cost will be your peace of mind."

Samuel Brannan slowly withdrew his hand from Berkeley's. She had spoken only to him, her voice low and intent. Now the gathering was waiting for him to pass judgment on what he had heard. His thoughtful gaze told her she had given him something to think about, but it was his cocksure, brash personality that spoke to the crowd. "Miss Shaw is confident of our success," he boomed as he came to his feet. He raised his glass of seltzer, saluting Berkeley and the future of the Vigilance Committee.

Grey's light touch on her shoulders kept Berkeley in her seat as drinks were lifted and a raucous cheer went up. He bent toward her ear and whispered, "Can you do another?"

She nodded. Lorne Fitch sat down next, his wife beside him. Berkeley took most of the cues from her. She went carefully through the information Grey had provided for her earlier and gathered new insights along the way. She told him that he came from a large family in New England and eventually identified the city as Providence. She discovered he met his wife at a church social and was so taken by her that he stammered through most of their first conversation. Berkeley's recitation not only won over Lorne Fitch, but his wife as well, as they both were skillfully guided through fond memories of courtship and marriage, giving up secrets they believed they hadn't given up at all. The banker's question had nothing to do with the success of his business ventures. He wanted to know something far more personal.

"Tell me if you can, Miss Shaw, will my wife and I be blessed with another child?"

It was then that Berkeley dropped Mr. Fitch's palm and took up his wife's. She only had to lower her guard a bit to know the truth, and if she hadn't felt the life force in Marilyn Fitch's touch, she would have known by the look in the other woman's eyes. Berkeley hesitated, silently asking Mrs. Fitch's permission to give up this secret. The banker's wife offered her a blissful smile and nodded.

Berkeley's glance slid to Mr. Fitch. "When you ask about another blessing," she said, "I assume you mean one beyond the child your wife's carrying now."

Fitch leaped up from the table, toppling the chair behind him. He lifted his wife by the elbows and searched her face. The truth of Berkeley's words were plain on Marilyn's glowing skin and beatific smile. He'd been blind not to have seen it before. "I'll be damned," he said, grinning widely. "Will it be a boy this time, Miss Shaw?"

It was Grey who responded. "You only get one question," he said. "If you want to know the answer to that, then you can pay for the privilege or wait nine months."

The gathering laughed heartily as the banker was put to a blush. It was Marilyn Fitch who laid down two pieces of gold from her reticule and slid them toward Berkeley.

"A boy," Berkeley said confidently. She palmed the gold pieces and they disappeared down the front of her beaded bodice with credible sleight of hand.

It was the second time that evening she drew Grey Janeway's displeasure.

Anthony Bottoms was the final guest to be invited to Berkeley's table. It was nearing midnight when Grey pretended to relent his previous decree that Berkeley had finished performing for the evening. It had been Shawn's idea to let some time elapse between the first two readings and the last one. In the future there would always be the question of whether or not Berkeley was truly done for the night. Men who wanted her attention would be encouraged to stay at the tables longer. As long as the possibility existed that she might have time to take their hand, they would wait for her.

Berkeley wished now that Shawn had not gone to Grey with his idea or that Grey had not received it so well. She wished she had done more than smile wanly when Grey asked if she was still prepared to meet Mr. Bottoms. And when she touched the gambler's cool hand she wished she was wearing gloves.

Anthony Bottoms was a dandy, smooth and polished and without substance. Touching him was like licking icing from a cake, sweet at first, sickening when repeated. Berkeley's exhaustion left her defenseless.

The first contact raised the flesh on Berkeley's arm. The shiver that rippled through her was quite real, though not caused by an attraction to Anthony Bottoms as the onlookers thought. Berkeley's exotically colored eyes darkened at the centers. She drew her chair closer to the gambler's, and when she bent forward her breasts swelled slightly against the beaded neckline of her gown. Her voice was quiet, just as it had been with the others, but it was intimate as well. She reached the husky pitch she had hit once with Sam Brannan and stayed there throughout the interview with Anthony Bottoms.

"You're a bit of a confidence man," Berkeley told him. "It's in your blood. Generations of gamblers. Is that right, Tony?"

The man who had always despised the shortening of his Christian name, swallowed hard and nodded.

"I thought so," she said. Her smile was a shade wicked. "You're good at it though. You watch others, make a note of their weaknesses, their habits under stress. Your father taught you how to do that. Would you say you exploit others, Tony? Take advantage of their weaknesses? No, that isn't how you describe what it is you do. It's all fair in your mind because others enter into the game with you willingly. They like your style. Some of them even envy it.''

Berkeley raised her eyes to him and gave his palm an imperceptible squeeze. "I like your style," she said deeply. "Very much indeed.''

Grey Janeway was certain he didn't like what he was hearing. He stepped closer to where Berkeley was sitting, not touching her yet but close enough that he knew she could feel his presence. He wasn't worried that Anthony Bottoms would take Berkeley's revelations too seriously, especially not when Grey's flinty stare was leveled on him, but Grey could not say the same for the men who were pressing in, intrigued by the intimate nature of her conversation with the gambler.

Anthony Bottoms fingered his mustache. It was an unconscious gesture he made when he was nervous, an emotional state that was largely unfamiliar to him. He felt the force of Grey's coldly remote eyes and the searing heat of Berkeley's. He was not a man accustomed to these extremes. At a gambling table he was used to making others uncomfortable. Charm and polish did not serve him well in these circumstances.

"Do you have a question for me, Tony?" Berkeley asked. One brow was lifted archly. "Would you like to know if you've sparked the interest of a certain woman?"

Anthony Bottoms felt beads of sweat forming just under his mustache.

"Perhaps you want to learn if the luck you've had this evening will continue the rest of the week." There was the suggestion in her voice that she was not speaking of his good fortune at the gaming tables. Berkeley crooked her finger at him and beckoned him closer. "Do you want everyone to know the suit and royal line of the card you have up your sleeve?" she whispered. Berkeley sat back, her smile secretive as Anthony Bottoms leaped to his feet.

"What did she tell you, Bottoms?" someone in the crowd asked.

"Out with it," another voice prompted. "Don't leave us in suspense."

"We're not bloody mind readers, you know," said a third. This roused a round of laughter and more insistence that Anthony share what Berkeley had whispered to him.

Anthony pulled at his mustache and forced a smile behind his hand. "She's says I'm going on a trip back East," he told them. He reached inside his jacket and pulled out a receipt. "I only bought this today, gentlemen, and I haven't told a soul."

Berkeley shrugged off Grey's light touch and stood. She looped her arm through Anthony's and sidled close to him. Her saucy wink was meant for him alone, but the men crowding in saw it. "Why I do believe you're a knave, Tony Bottoms. And you've quite captured my black heart."

Anthony Bottoms thought of the jack of spades secreted in the cuff of his shirt. It was just as well he was planning to leave Frisco. This woman could ruin him, and she had let him know it in no uncertain terms. He had thanked her in the only way he could, by cementing her reputation as someone who knew more about the future than the rest of them. He envied Grey Janeway. The man was going to make a fortune with her.

"Step aside," Anthony told his friends smoothly. "I want a farewell dance with Miss Shaw." The sea of men parted, and he spun Berkeley away as the music swelled.

Grey let them go, but his eyes followed. He accepted the congratulations of his guests with little comment. Berkeley Shaw was a success, and it was because he had insisted she not back away from her opening night commitment. He wondered that he did not feel better about it.

"I'd like to retire," Berkeley told her dancing partner. After taking the floor with Anthony Bottoms, she found herself in the arms of a succession of men. She smiled gaily and laughed from time to time and tried not to think about the strangers who put their hands in hers or laid their open palms against her waist. She tried not to think about the fact that none of the men were Grey Janeway. "Would you mind escorting me to the stairs?"

Martin Reade bowed with correct formality. He was a tall man, slenderly built, and rather endearingly awkward. "I'd be happy to escort you safely to your room."

Berkeley didn't tell him that her safety was not at issue. None of the upstairs rooms and suites would be given out until tomorrow. Except for Mike and Grey she was quite alone on the floor. "Yes, thank you. I'd like that." The waves of dizziness were coming at her now with little respite between each crest. The curving staircase presented a more intimidating climb than any three of San Francisco's hills.

"You're very pale, Miss Shaw," Martin noted. "Should I find Grey?"

"No. No, he doesn't need to be disturbed. Please, just get me through this crush."

Martin took Berkeley's arm and began to wend both of them toward the stairs. Berkeley had to turn away three prospective dancing partners before Martin took over the duty by saying she was unavailable. It wasn't until they reached the foot of the wide staircase that Berkeley knew she couldn't make the ascent. She placed her hand flat in the middle of Martin Reade's chest to stop him.

"There are stairs at the back through the kitchen," she said, her voice hardly above a whisper. "Take me there."

He regarded the distance to be traveled skeptically. "I'll carry you up this way."

"No! Not in front of everyone. Please, help me get to the back stairs."

By keeping to the perimeter of the large hall, Martin and Berkeley were able to reach the kitchen with relative ease. Annie Jack's domain was still a hive of activity, even at this late hour. The cook and her helpers were putting the finishing touches on a four-tier cake.

"Out!" Annie yelled at them. She went immediately back to the work, proof that she expected to be obeyed.

Berkeley could feel Martin begin to retreat. "The stairs are that way." She pointed past the table of hovering helpers toward the pantry. "She doesn't bite."

"Annie *do* bite," the cook said. "She's fixin' to tear a leg off someone if they trespass in her kitchen."

Martin hesitated. It was Berkeley who pulled him along. Annie Jack actually raised her frosting knife at them and waggled it threateningly as they passed her table. A dollop of buttercream icing landed on the sleeve of Martin's jacket. Berkeley didn't wait for more to follow. She jerked him by the elbow and hustled him to the base of the stairs.

"Ignore her," Berkeley said, referring to Annie's bellowing. "She's not going to follow us, and I require your help."

Martin Reade rose to the occasion. He helped Berkeley steady herself by offering his arm so they could climb the narrow stairs together. It was a satisfactory arrangement for half the trip. Martin carried her the remainder.

"I think I should get Grey," he said as he lowered her feet to the floor in front of her door.

"No. There's really no need." She turned the handle. "If you'd just come inside a moment in the event I need you. Perhaps you would help me out of this gown?" Berkeley pulled on his hand, not giving him time to refuse her. "It won't take long. Here, this way. My bedroom's through here."

Martin stumbled after her, bewildered by her insistence and more than a little uneasy by the possible consequences. He looked over his shoulder several times, expecting to see Grey Janeway standing in the doorway with loaded pistols.

It wasn't Grey who eventually appeared but one of Sam Brannan's bodyguards. The man's broad shoulders filled the doorframe. He had a thick neck and legs as solid as pier pilings. His arms were crossed in front of his chest, but there was nothing in his posture to indicate patience. His squarely cut chin lifted aggressively as he indicated Martin should leave.

"Mr. Brannan sent me to look after the lady," he said. "You can go, Reade."

"I don't know, Hank. Grey should know Miss Shaw doesn't feel well."

"He knows." Hank Brock stepped aside. "Mr. Brannan told him. Go on, with you, Reade."

Martin made a stiff bow in Berkeley's direction and missed the frightened appeal in her eyes. He slipped past Brock and hurried out of the suite.

Hank Brock was handsome in a rough-hewn fashion. His face looked as if it had been carved with a thick chisel and a heavy hand. The strokes were broad and blunt. His hair was a shade darker than his eyes, and both were very nearly black.

Berkeley sat down slowly on the edge of her bed. "I'm going to be sick, Mr.—" She stopped. She couldn't remember his name.

"Brock," he told her. He started to come toward her but halted when Berkeley pushed herself back. Hank reached for the basin on her washstand and held it out to her. "Be sick in this."

Berkeley accepted the basin but did not move any closer. "You can go now." Her voice reverberated eerily as she bent over the porcelain bowl. She closed her eyes.

"If you don't mind, Miss Shaw, I'll wait right here. Mr. Brannan was insistent that I tend to your needs."

Berkeley's knuckles were almost as white as the basin she held on to. She suspected her face was approaching that color. She wanted nothing more than to be sick right now, to clear her stomach and perhaps her head.

"Maybe you're not so ill after all," Hank said. He tugged on the basin and removed it from her hands, noticing the faint trembling in her fingers as he did so. "Do you want a damp cloth for your head? No? What if you lie down?"

Berkeley avoided the hand he extended toward her shoulder by pushing even farther back on the bed. Her back was pressed solidly against the headboard when she finally stopped. "Leave, please," she told him. "I want you to leave."

"You didn't seem to mind Reade's presence," he said musingly. "Now, why is that?"

"Mr. Reade wasn't carrying a gun."

Hank Brock mentally gave her full marks for being aware

of what others often missed. He opened his jacket slowly and took out the pistol that was tucked into the waistband of his trousers. He laid it on the nightstand beside the unused basin. "Now neither am I."

"I'm feeling better," Berkeley said. In fact, she was feeling worse. Crowded by his nearness and panicked by his size, she thought she might actually faint.

"I'm glad to hear it," he said pleasantly. One of his knees depressed the edge of the bed as he moved closer. "Then you won't mind answering a question I've had since I first saw you this evening. I'm real curious to hear where you came by that gown."

Berkeley looked down at herself. The glass beads sewn into the bodice were struck by a combination of moonlight and lamplight, one cool, one warm. "It was a gift."

"Is that right?" he said as if the answer was only of mild interest now. One of his hands brushed the hem. He felt Berkeley try to retract her leg, but she wasn't fast enough for him. Brock caught her ankle and yanked her toward him. Her head bumped the headboard, not hard enough to hurt her seriously but more than enough to stun her. Her instinctive struggle stopped, and he had her trapped, his arms braced on either side of her shoulders and one of his heavy legs securing both of hers. "Tell me about the gown, Miss Shaw. I'll warn you, though. I've seen it before."

Berkeley put her hands on his chest and shoved. It was like pushing on a boulder. Her hands dropped to her sides and she drew a ragged breath.

"You were eager to get out of this gown before," Brock said. "I heard you ask Reade to help you. Shall I?" His knee nudged the hem higher. He glanced down at the exposed length of her legs. "Very nice. What else do you have to show me?"

Berkeley opened her mouth to scream and abruptly shut it again. There was only one person on the floor who might hear her, and Mike was in no condition to mount a rescue. Berkeley quieted because she knew he would try, and then most assuredly, she would be responsible for his death. One of

Brock's hands slipped under the small of her back. When he started to turn her over Berkeley jammed her fist into her mouth to keep from crying out.

It was Brock's gun settled firmly against his temple that gave him pause. He knew it was his own weapon because the moment he felt the cold steel on his skin his eyes strayed to the washstand.

"Back away, Brock," Grey said. "Easy. Keep your hands very still." Grey pulled the pistol back so Hank Brock could move. There was already a red crescent where Grey had jammed the barrel against his skin. Brock was lucky, Grey thought. There should have been a hole. He noticed that Brock had raised his hands to shoulder height. The man knew how to position himself for surrender. "Turn around slowly. Face the door and start walking." Grey followed the bodyguard in the hallway and as far as the top of the back stairs. "Get out," he said. "And don't return here with Brannan again. You'd do well to find a replacement when Sam decides to come around."

Hank Brock's broad features were stoic. He did not offer any explanation for what Grey had seen in Berkeley's bedroom. The fact that he was still alive was proof enough that Grey had singled out his mistress for most of the blame. Hank was not going to say anything that might alter that opinion. "I need my gun, Mr. Janeway."

"Get out," Grey repeated. He kept the pistol level. Brock's barrel chest made a large target, and the distance between them meant Grey couldn't miss placing his shot. He watched Brock consider his options, then decide on the one that would mean his life could continue. The bodyguard turned slowly and headed down the stairs. Grey lowered the weapon when Hank Brock left by the back door.

Berkeley was kneeling on the floor hovering over the basin when Grey returned. She had finally managed to empty the contents of her stomach. There wasn't much. Most of what she did was heave dryly, wrenching her diaphragm and throat. Her shoulders and head sagged weakly. She didn't look up as he walked past her.

Grey put the gun on the washstand and poured Berkeley a glass of water. He hunkered beside her and handed her the glass. "Rinse and spit. Do you have any liquor?"

She shook her head but didn't raise it. "The water's fine." She gave him back the glass when she was finished. "Thank you."

Grey replaced it then hauled Berkeley to her feet as he stood. "Come on."

Berkeley stumbled after him, almost knocking the basin over. "Where are we going?"

"You don't just leave your guests," he said coldly. "You certainly don't sneak out on them towing your lover."

"My what?" she said weakly. "You mean Mr. Reade?"

"What has he to do with anything?" Grey jerked her along.

"Oh, please," Berkeley said as she was pulled into the hallway. "Don't make me go back there. I can't. I really can't. Mr. Janeway . . . Grey . . . please . . . I need to get out of this gown. Oh, God." She was shaking now and tears hovered at the edge of her lower lashes. "You don't understand. I need . . . you're hurting me. My arm . . ." She tried to wrest herself away from him. His grip was exactly the same as the one he had used earlier in the day. She could feel his fingertips pressing on her bruised flesh.

Grey stopped long enough to turn her in his arms. His hold on her eased marginally, but he didn't let her go. "You can explain what you think I don't understand in a moment. Right now you're going to come with me and bid your guests good night. Don't you dare cry in front of them, and don't you dare affect that, fey, wounded look of yours. I haven't done a thing to you. Yet. And I don't want you looking contrite. The point of this exercise is to show them that nothing happened, that nothing is wrong. You can't convince them if you look repentant."

Grey took out a handkerchief and wiped her eyes. He pinched color in her pale cheeks, smoothed back several loose tendrils of hair, and studied her critically. "Pretend you're hurling fish at them. That should see you through."

Somehow it did. Berkeley stood on the curved landing at Grey's side while he thanked his guests for graciously helping him open the Phoenix. He thanked them also for the warm welcome they extended his gaming hall's hostess and spoke for both of them when he said he hoped they would return soon. The gambling, he told them, could continue until dawn, but he and his lady were retiring. He raised Berekely's hand then, almost as if he were offering her to the crowd, but after holding it up just long enough to make them wonder at his intention, Grey smiled wickedly and drew it back to his lips.

Only Berkeley Shaw knew how cold those lips were.

Grey did not return Berkeley to her own suite. At the top of the stairs he steered her in the direction of his own rooms. Once inside he locked the door, dropped the key on a table, and gave her a small push toward the long sofa. Grey went immediately to his newest acquisition, an ornately carved walnut sideboard. He opened the cabinet on the left and took out a decanter of bourbon and two tumblers. He splashed both with liquor and gave one to Berkeley.

"*Now* you can look apologetic," he said. "A certain amount of contrition would serve you well."

Berkeley was too miserable to be angry. "I don't know what you think I've done. I felt ill. I asked Mr. Reade to escort me to the stairs."

"Reade? Martin Reade?"

"Yes."

"What about Hank Brock?"

Berkeley used both hands to lift her drink to her mouth. She sipped it carefully. "I was light-headed," she continued, staring at her drink rather than at Grey. "I didn't want to create a scene if I fainted, so I showed Mr. Reade to the back. We went through Annie's kitchen. You can ask her if you'd like."

"I will."

Berkeley knew he would. "Mr. Reade brought me to my room. I asked him inside." Her voice dropped to a barely audible whisper. "I required some assistance to remove my gown."

"What's that?" Grey asked. He knocked back his drink and poured another. "It sounded as if you said you invited him to undress you."

Berkeley knew he didn't really require confirmation. She went on. "I don't know where Mr. Brannan's man came from. I didn't hear the outer door open."

"But it wasn't locked," said Grey.

"No, I didn't think it was necessary. There's only—"

"I mean you didn't lock it when you invited Reade inside."

"No!" Berkeley's head came up. "It wasn't like that. Please let me return to my room. I want to get out of this gown. You don't—"

Grey held up his hand, stopping her. "Finish your story. What about Hank Brock?"

"I don't know. He was just there. Perhaps he was waiting for me. I tell you, I don't know anything else."

"You're lying. You've been teasing the men all night. You put Sam Brannan to a blush. Bottoms, too. Didn't you listen to yourself?"

"It wasn't me." Berkeley pressed one side of the tumbler to her temple. Her head was pounding, and a dark curtain was being drawn across the corners of her vision.

"Not you? Did I hear you right? Brock was in your bed. You weren't struggling. You weren't pushing him away."

"I tried. You just didn't see me." She closed her eyes. "I'm not lying," she whispered. "I'm not."

"You never called for help."

"I was afraid Mike would be the only one to hear me. I couldn't risk that."

"He was starting to undress you."

Berkeley's agitation became impossible for her to contain. She stood. The glass fell through her nerveless fingers and thudded on the carpet. "He wanted this gown," she told him, pulling at the tight sleeves and bodice. Dozens of blue glass beads were torn free. They scattered at her feet like icy raindrops. Almost frantic now with her need to be out of the evening dress, Berkeley yanked one shoulder seam and rent it. Jerking harder, she managed to free one arm as Grey crossed the room to stop her. She warded him off, her breath coming on the back of a sob. "He knew it was Ivory's!" She was suddenly pulled into Grey's arms and held there. She couldn't move, couldn't fight, and the very strength of him was her undoing. Berkeley pressed her face against his shoulder. Her body trembled with the intensity of the emotion coursing through her. She closed her eyes and held on, her fingers curling around his jacket. "This is the gown she was wearing when he raped her!"

Berkeley would only ever have a hazy recollection of what happened after that. She knew the floor slid away from her feet, and there was a sense of floating. Something cool and damp touched her face. Hands, gentle hands this time, saw to her comfort. She lay very still in a warm cocoon and dreamed of emerging as a gossamer winged fairy.

"You're awake."

It was Grey's voice. Berkeley searched the shadowed corners of the room for the source. She saw him when he shifted in the wing chair, swinging his leg from the curved arm to the floor. Something slid from his lap and landed heavily on the floor. He ignored it and lit the lamp on the table beside him. He turned back the wick so only a thin flame flickered. Berkeley saw it was a book that had fallen.

She wondered how he had known she was awake. Surely his eyes were no keener in the dark than hers, yet he had seemed to be aware of the precise moment she opened hers. "Have I been sleeping long?"

Grey shrugged. He didn't know himself. He had drifted off while reading and let the lamp burn itself out. "As long as you needed to," he said. "How are you feeling?"

Berkeley pushed herself upright. The sheet and blanket that covered her shoulders fell to her waist. She was no longer wearing the hateful beaded blue gown. It had been replaced, along with her corset and camisole and half a dozen petticoats, by a fine, sheer linen nightshift. The lawn fabric could have been gossamer wings. She leaned against the headboard and drew her knees toward her chest.

"Berkeley?"

"I'm better, I think."

"Perhaps you should take inventory."

She didn't smile. Her features remained grave. "I'm fine."

Grey nodded. He could see for himself that she had a measure of natural color in her cheeks. Her eyes were clear, and if she was still suffering from a headache, then it had at least become tolerable. He looked at the clock on his mantel. It was after five. The musicians had stopped playing downstairs more than two hours ago. The last of the revelers had left shortly afterward.

"Did I faint?" Berkeley asked.

"Not quite that. Until you went to sleep you never lost consciousness."

"You undressed me?"

"Yes."

Berkeley pressed her forehead against her knees. "I don't suppose you considered asking for Annie's help?"

"Considered and dismissed," he said. "It seemed getting you out of that dress was the most important thing."

"Yes," she said quietly, lifting her head and looking at him. "Yes, it was. Thank you."

"Is it true what you told me about Ivory?"

Berkeley nodded.

"I know you believe it's true," he said. "But do you *know* it?"

"Have I heard it from Ivory, you mean?" she asked. "No. How could I? I've never met her. Hank Brock certainly didn't tell me. I *know* it because I felt it. All evening. From the moment I put that gown on I knew something horrible had happened in it. When I was on the gaming floor . . . with the men . . . sometimes it was as if . . ." But she didn't go on. What she had felt wearing that gown, the things she'd said, the way she'd said them, it was not like her. It was not *her*. Not entirely. Berkeley moved to the edge of the bed and slid her legs over the side. "What have you done with it?"

"It's safe."

"I don't want it to be safe. I want it burned." She started

to get out of bed, but Grey got to his feet first. He crossed to where she sat in three easy, nearly soundless strides. Berkeley looked up at him. "Do you intend to keep me here?" she asked.

Grey's fingers raked his dark hair. When his hand reached the back of his neck it stayed there, massaging away kinks and tension. "Don't make it sound as though it's against your will," he said wearily. He pointed to the window. "It's not even light yet. Go back to sleep."

She was struck by how tired he looked. There were tiny lines at the corners of his mouth; the usually intense eyes were dull. His skin was stretched tautly over the bones of his face. Quite unexpectedly Berkeley reached up and touched his gaunt cheek with her fingertips. "What about you? Have you slept?"

He didn't answer her question. He captured her hand instead. "Why did you do that?"

Her eyes were large, luminous. "I . . . I don't know." It had seemed the most natural thing in the world to touch him in just such a manner. "Was it wrong?"

"Wrong?" he asked softly. "No, it wasn't wrong."

Berkeley felt his hold on her hand relax. She twisted her wrist, not to release herself, but so that she was the one holding him. She tugged once, just enough to encourage him. He lowered himself to the bed beside her slowly, as if he was still unsure it was what she wanted. Berkeley laced her fingers between his and drew his hand onto her lap. She stared at the contrasts in the clasp. The inherent strength in his long, lean fingers made her own hand seem more delicate than it actually was. His rough fingertips were a counterpoint to her soft ones, and her skin looked as smooth and white as polished ivory next to his darker complexion.

Berkeley spared him a glance before her eyes returned to the safety of her lap. "I wanted to say I'm grateful," she said. She hooked her heels on the bed frame. "For noticing I was missing from the crowd. For taking the time to look for me. I know what you thought I was doing, but you were mistaken.

I didn't encourage him, or at least I didn't mean to." She took a short breath. "I wish—"

"Berkeley," Grey said quietly. "There's no need to—"

"You shouldn't be afraid to hear me out." She realized suddenly that she was squeezing his hand harder than was ever her intention. She relaxed her grip. Her brief sidelong glance caught Grey's brief smile.

"Go on," he said. "You were wishing . . ."

She nodded slowly. "I was wishing I had given you some reason to think better of me. I've allowed you to set me up in my own rooms and purchase clothes for me and make certain I have enough to eat. That I came to the Phoenix at all doesn't speak well of me. Then I disobeyed one of the few demands you made by going to Sydney Town. I disobeyed you again by following you back when you went to get Mike. It seems when I try to be independent I only make myself foolish."

The corners of Berkeley's mouth turned in a self-deprecating smile. "In any event it's clear you do not regard me in a favorable light. I only mention this because it makes it all the more astonishing that you would put yourself out this evening on my account. I realize that in part your were acting to protect your investment—"

"Investment? You, you mean?"

"Yes, of course. In coming to find me, Hank Brock might very well have hurt you." Having said her piece, Berkeley slipped her fingers from in between Grey's. She wondered if it had been clear that she was thanking him.

Grey let the silence that followed stretch. He withdrew his hand from her lap. "Are you quite finished?" he said at last.

Berkeley nodded once.

"Will you look at me, Miss Shaw?" His fingertips touched her chin. With no real urging on his part, she turned to face him.

"You may call me Berkeley," she said, raising her eyes to his. "I don't mind."

"I thought some formality was in order now. I'm trying very hard not to take advantage of you."

"I don't mind."

Grey blinked, not certain he'd heard her correctly. "Perhaps you don't know what I mean when I say 'take advantage of.' "

"I think I do," she said.

He merely stared at her, and this time she did not look away. "Yes," she whispered, as his head lowered toward her. "Yes."

Grey's mouth came down on hers. Her lips were soft, pliant. They moved under his tentatively at first, then more eagerly. Her hands lay flat on his chest. Her fingers slowly curved in the fabric of his shirt, and she raised herself up a little, pulling herself closer to him. Their mouths parted briefly, and it was Berkeley who strained forward to press her lips to his. They shared a single breath as her spontaneous sigh of satisfaction was swallowed by him.

Grey's hands slid around her waist. He held her against him, his fingers threaded at the small of her back. Their slow descent to the bed started with an almost infinitesimal shift in weight and balance. Berkeley's fingers eased around Grey's shoulders as she was lowered under him. The delicious pressure of his chest on her breasts made her breath catch. Her lips parted.

It was the opening Grey had been waiting for. He learned the shape of her mouth with his tongue. He teased the soft and sensitive line of her upper lip and nibbled gently on her generous lower one. The damp edge of his tongue pressed for entry and found it. The kiss deepened. Grey swept her mouth, teasing again, tasting. Her response was no mere imitation of what was done to her, but somehow richer. She seduced where he teased, savored where he tasted. She drew him in more deeply and made what was an entirely new experience for her exactly the same for him.

Berkeley Shaw was outside all that was familiar to Grey Janeway.

He broke the kiss, his breathing ragged. He cupped her face and searched her features. Light from the room's single lamp flickered across her skin as he raised himself higher. Her eyes were wide, her lips faintly bruised and damp. "You *know* where this is going, don't you?"

Berkeley was held too tightly simply to nod her answer. She had to say it aloud. "Yes," she whispered. "I know." *I've always known.*

Grey did nothing for a moment, merely continued to watch her, then he felt her body lift under him, arching delicately in a movement she couldn't quite contain, pressing her breasts against his chest, her thighs against his hip, and he knew he needed to believe her. His groan was as involuntary as the sweet, helpless curve of her body rising to meet his.

"Berkeley." Then his mouth covered hers again.

She closed her eyes. It was a surrender of sorts, this loss of one of her senses, but every other sense was enriched by it. Berkeley heard the sounds made by the damp heat of their mouths joining and parting, slanting first one way, then another. There was rustling of the sheets and straining in the bed supports as they shifted positions. The fabric of her lawn nightshift sliding over her shoulder was like a whisper.

His kisses tasted faintly of bourbon, and Berkeley knew that if given a choice she would always drink from his mouth. At the curve of his neck and the underside of his jaw, she had no comparison for the salty-sweet taste of him or the musky fragrance that she breathed in deeply. Grey himself became the point of reference.

Berkeley's hands slid under his shirt, and she felt the bunched muscles of his back and shoulders. Her fingertips glided across his chest and dipped just inside his trousers. His skin retracted under her touch. The sound he made was born of both pleasure and pain.

She couldn't help her small, satisfied smile.

Grey's teeth caught her ear and tugged gently. "You like that, don't you?"

Did he mean what she had done to him or what he was doing to her? She supposed it didn't matter. She liked both. Berkeley twisted her head. "Yes," she whispered against his cheek. "I like all of it."

Grey managed to trap laughter at the back of his throat. "You haven't experienced half of it."

Berkeley knew that far better than he did.

Grey rolled away and sat up. He removed his shirt and tossed it toward the foot of the bed. He intercepted her startled glance. "Would you like me to turn back the lamp?"

She shook her head slowly. "No, I like looking at you," she said, surprising them both with her frankness. She cleared her throat and tried to explain. "It's just that you're rather more than I thought you would be." Berkeley pushed herself up. One strap of her filmy shift fell farther down her arm. She didn't notice at all. Grey was kneeling beside her, his fingers on the front fly of his trousers. His erection was clearly outlined. Her mouth went dry. Indeed, rather more summed it up nicely.

Berkeley cleared her throat. "Perhaps the lamp . . ." She cast suddenly nervous eyes in the direction of the table.

Grey's fingers stilled. His mouth tightened marginally, not with displeasure, but with the demand this change in plans placed on him. "Very well." He gracefully vaulted over Berkeley and landed lightly on his feet. The lamp was extinguished quickly, and he returned to the bedside. He saw the worry still etched in her features and went immediately to close the drapes. He approached the bed again, this time more slowly while his eyes accustomed themselves to the dark, wondering all the while if Berkeley had changed her mind.

Something sailed past his face in the dark. Something almost insubstantial, like the brush of a butterfly's wing. It took him a moment to recognize it for what it was: the fine sheer linen of Berkeley's nightgown.

Grey Janeway's rare smile was shuttered by darkness.

Chapter Eight

Berkeley moved to one side to make room for him. Her hand brushed his naked hip. She retracted it quickly. She hadn't heard him remove his trousers or drawers.

Grey found her hand with unerring ease. He drew her back to his hip first, then to his heavy, hard erection. The muscles across his back tightened as her fingers curled around it. He showed her how to move her hand along the length of him and when her nails lightly scored the underside he hauled her up hard against him and buried his mouth in her hair.

They fell on their sides on the bed. Berkeley found herself almost immediately under him. Where she had cradled him in her hand, now she cradled him in the cleft of her thighs. She arched, rubbing herself against him. His mouth was hot on hers, and his tongue speared her. It glided past her teeth and circled hers. He suckled her, drawing out her breath and laying her open to him.

She was fearless. She let him see she was vulnerable, that he could do anything to her. His hands slipped into her hair, stroking it, letting the corn silk strands fall between his splayed fingers like rainwater. He turned her head and kissed the back of her neck. His mouth sought the shell of her ear, and he whispered her name. He kissed her eyes, her cheeks. He sipped her skin at her shoulder and at the hollow of her throat. His tongue made a pass across her collarbone and dropped vertically, between her breasts at first, then flicking each nipple in turn.

He caressed her breasts, and they swelled under his palms. She moved restlessly, stretching, reaching. Her abdomen lifted as her back arched. She felt her thighs parting naturally around his hips. He stroked her from the underside of her breasts to her waist, then cupped her bottom. The sweet, musky fragrance of her moist sex was as heady as incense. Grey drew back and positioned himself between her thighs. He felt her hands brush his arms. She was reaching for him.

"In a moment," he said hoarsely. Then he bent his head and took her with his mouth.

Air spilled from Berkeley's lungs at this first touch of his lips. His tongue darted along her damp skin. He plunged, jabbed. The intimate caress deepened. His teeth scraped the fleshy hood. His tongue flicked again, snakelike in the beginning, tormenting her, then finally came more evenly, with soft insistent strokes that were like velvet over sandpaper. Berkeley's fingers fell away from Grey's shoulders and curled in the sheets. Her head tilted back. She pressed her lips together. A soundless cry vibrated in her throat.

Threads of tension pulled her legs taut. Pleasure spiraled outward to the tips of her fingers. She radiated heat as a flush swept just below the surface of her skin.

Grey raised his head. He leaned over her. "I want to hear you," he whispered against her mouth. His hips twisted; he ground himself against her open thighs. "Let me hear you."

Berkeley's jaw unclenched as she drew in a ragged breath. She sipped the air, her inarticulate moan the beginning of her first wild cry. She clutched him, his name coming from her lips as if torn from her.

"Oh, sweet . . . sweet." Grey covered her mouth with his and absorbed her cries after that. "I need to be inside you," he told her. Urgency and hunger made his voice hoarse and almost unrecognizable. The words were muffled against her lips. "Take me in."

Berkeley felt Grey's hips rise, then her bottom was lifted and he surged forward. He took her deeply with the first stroke, plunging past every point of resistance before he recognized them for what they were.

He held himself still. She surrounded him so tightly he could feel when she drew her first uneven sob. He didn't have to see her eyes to know they were wounded, and he didn't have to feel her flinch to know he had hurt her. Grey swore softly when her muscles contracted around him. "For God's sake, don't do that," he whispered harshly. "Don't move."

Berkeley didn't think she had moved at all. Now she tried not to breathe.

"You can breathe," he told her. "Just don't do the other."

Not certain what "the other" was, Berkeley just inhaled very slowly.

"Bloody, bloody hell." He began to withdraw.

Berkeley winced. She reached for his shoulders and grasped them. "Please, not yet . . . not yet."

"You don't know what you're asking." In spite of that, Grey remained exactly where he was.

Berkeley's breathing calmed. The pain of his entry had disappeared. What she felt now was a heavy pressure as her body strove to accommodate him. By slow degrees she began to relax. It didn't matter that he was still hard inside her; what mattered was that she could be soft around him and still hold him there. "I don't want it to be over," she said softly. "Is it over? I think there should be more. I can stand it now. I promise you that I can."

Grey wished he could see her face clearly. It would be worth seeing for that look of earnestness and innocence. And she was still innocent. Berkeley Shaw was probably the single woman in the whole of the world that he could bury himself in to the hilt and she would remain unquestionably innocent.

"It's not over," he said. Then he began to move slowly.

Berkeley sighed and closed her eyes. The pressure had become an aching fullness that was actually quite nice. There was a rhythm here, a natural cadence like the ebb and flow of the tides. She let the power of it wash over her at first, then rose up to meet it. Her hips lifted and fell as he surged forward and withdrew. She held him loosely with her arms and more tightly and most intimately where they were joined.

Berkeley touched his face. Her fingertips brushed his cheek. His skin was warm, taut. She wished she had not asked him to turn back the lamp.

It was unexpected that she would feel heat uncurl at the center of her again. She had only been meeting the waves, then suddenly she was riding one of the crests. Pleasure skimmed her. Her entire body arched as Grey's rhythm changed and his thrusts shallowed and quickened. It was his breathing that matched hers now, a slightly strained rasp as his breath caught in his throat. He pushed into her again, and this time her body contracted around him. He was not proof against that. Every taut nerve vibrated with pleasure as he sank himself into her with one deeply satisfying final thrust.

The air was cool on her flushed and heated body. Berkeley tugged a sheet as high as her breasts when Grey moved away from her and onto his side. She supposed she should say something to him, though she hadn't any idea what it might be. She fell asleep mulling over the possibilities.

Grey slipped out of bed and padded quietly to the dressing room. He closed the door before he lit one of the lamps but did nothing about the thin stream of yellow light that slid under it. He poured water into the basin and washed himself. The cloth came away tinged pink with Berkeley's blood. Grey wrung it out. He opened a window and tossed out the water. Someone below shouted, but Grey didn't hear. He pulled on a pair of drawers and tied the drawstring loosely around his waist. He sat down in a wing chair next to the open window and propped his feet on a padded stool. A breeze eddied into the room and ruffled his hair. Grey let his head fall back and closed his eyes.

Falling asleep was the farthest thing from his mind when he did it.

The bed was stripped and Berkeley was gone when Grey woke a few hours later. Pandora slipped into his suite as soon as he opened the door. Except for the cat, the hallway was empty. Grey visited Mike before performing any of his usual morning rituals. He discovered that not only was Mike able to sit up in bed, but that it had been Berkeley who had helped him there. She had also been responsible for carrying his breakfast tray from the kitchen to his room. "Busy, busy lady," he muttered to himself on the journey back to his room.

Pandora was still there, and she puttered around Grey's legs while he washed, shaved, and cleaned his teeth. "Water's not the only thing I can toss out that window," he told the cat. As if daring him, she leaped up to the open sill and rested herself upon it with an air of supreme confidence. Grey stared at her a moment, then walked over and closed the window. "Stupid cat, you could have fallen."

Grey ate breakfast in Annie Jack's kitchen. He wasn't entirely certain the cook had ever been to sleep, but lack of shut-eye didn't affect her mood or her energy. She still ordered her helpers around in a tone that was just short of thunderous and completed tasks herself when everyone else was too slow for her tastes. Grey sat on a stool beside the butcher's block while he ate flapjacks and watched the goings-on with interest and no comment. "I think I'm terrified of you, Annie," he told the cook when he finished his plate.

She stopped in her tracks and blushed deeply beneath her coffee-colored skin. The assistant she had been haranguing slunk away while Annie's head was turned. "Go on with you, Mr. Janeway," she said as though accepting a pretty compliment. "Ain't no cause for you to be 'fraid of Annie. Leastways, not if you've done nothin' wrong." She gave him a mock-serious look. "You haven't done nothin' wrong, have you?"

Grey decided to leave quickly before he admitted to all his

sins, real and imagined. He complimented Annie and her helpers on last evening's success and thanked her for breakfast. "Has anyone here seen Miss Shaw this morning?" he asked casually as he was on the point of going.

All three of Annie's assistants raised their hands with some reluctance and looked to the cook for guidance. Annie stood there with both her hands firmly on her hips, her generous mouth pursing in disapproval. "She was here just about an hour ago and lookin' like the stuffin' was knocked out of her. Didn't bat an eye when Annie shooed her out."

"You gave her something to eat, didn't you?" Grey asked.

" 'Course Annie did. Miss Berkeley had herself two soft-cooked eggs and finished them just yonder on the other side of that door. Mark my words, Mr. Janeway, that girl's got somethin' inside her that's purely unnatural. You shouldn't make her call up the spirits to your friends like she did last night. Can't be a good thing come of it."

"I'll take it under advisement," Grey said dryly. He started to leave again and stopped. "One more thing, Annie. Did Miss Shaw come through here with someone yesterday evening?"

"More like the wee hours of the morning," Annie told him. She looked to her assistants for confirmation. There was unanimous agreement through a show of head nodding. "Don't rightly know the gentleman's name. Tall drink of water though. Looked a might uncomfortable. Not the same man who tore out of here later. Annie didn't get a good look at that one."

"It's all right," Grey said. "I know who the second man was." He left the kitchen for the gaming hall. Sam Hartford was at the bar supervising the delivery and stocking of liquor. Shawn and Donnel Kincaid were sharing a table while they looked over plans spread across the top. They all greeted Grey with congratulations on the successful opening.

Grey met with them briefly and reviewed plans for taking in the Phoenix's first overnight guests that afternoon. Donnel had a list of employees for Grey to look over. Most of the rooms were already spoken for. Some men had reserved space for themselves almost as soon as Grey announced he was rebuilding the Phoenix after the last quake. When word got around that he intended to have permanent rooms to let, the clamor for them began. With Mike occupying one until he was fit to leave California and Berkeley in a suite of her own, there were only three rooms that hadn't been reserved. It was Grey's belief that they remained because no one knew they were still available. "They'll fill up today," he told the others. "As soon as someone realizes there's a bed to be had."

"A clean one to boot," Shawn chuckled. "God, when I first came here I slept on a table and paid the owner dearly for it."

"I had the ground," Donnel told them. "It was free. Blankets were five dollars each and that was to rent one, not own it."

Sam spoke from behind the bar he was rubbing down. "Slept my first two nights in a trough. First one didn't cost me a penny. Second night, though, when the owner found me, damn if it didn't cost me plenty to keep him from filling it with water."

Grey watched them all turn in his direction. It was clear they expected him to share a similar story about his early days in the city. The bed he was thinking about, however, was the one upstairs. "Have any of you seen Miss Shaw this morning?" he asked.

"She went out as the liquor was coming in," Sam said. "Said something about a walk. I offered to go with her, but she didn't want the company. I don't imagine she'll be gone long, and there's no need to worry that she'll end up in Sydney Town. Not after yesterday."

Grey's mouth flattened, not liking what he heard. What he liked even less was that he couldn't do anything about it. "Sam, do you remember what Miss Shaw was wearing last night?"

Sam Hartford grinned. His eyes creased deeply at the corners. "It was the royal blue gown with the beaded bodice, fitted sleeves, and the plain skirt. Her train had a contrasting border of blue floss silk, and she wore little satin boots that laced on the inside." He ignored Grey's scowl and accepted the light, humorous applause from Shawn and Donnel. "It was one of the gowns Ivory gave me, remember? The one she offered to you at no cost.''

Grey *did* remember now that Sam jogged his memory. His chair scraped the floor hard as he pushed away from the table. ''I'll be back in an hour or so. If Miss Shaw returns, don't let her leave again without seeing me first.''

Ivory DuPree was not alone in her room when Grey came calling. Grey waited patiently by the fireplace, his smile in check, while Anthony Bottoms gathered up his trousers, shirt, and stockings and was shooed into the hall. Ivory tossed his boots out a moment later. Their odd thumping sound as they landed made Grey think at least one of them caught Anthony squarely in the back.

Ivory flounced back to bed. It was something of an accomplishment given the fact she was quite naked. She picked up her silk wrapper and slipped it on. ''I hope you have a very good reason for being here,'' she said, casting him a stern glance over her shoulder. ''Anthony was one of my better customers, and I just sent him packing.''

Grey distinctly remembered the gambler holding up proof that he was taking a clipper out of San Francisco. ''Isn't he leaving the city today?''

''Of course he is, but that doesn't mean he won't be back. Now I doubt he'll recall much about our evening except that it ended rather badly.'' She turned around and belted her robe. ''So, what's this about, Mr. Janeway? I haven't seen you since you latched on to that . . . umm, *hostess* of yours. Miss Shaw, is it?''

God, Grey thought wearily, Ivory was angry at him. The very last thing he felt like doing this morning was smoothing her ruffled flounces. ''I'm sorry, Ivory, about not thanking you personally for the gowns you gave up. It was generous of you.''

This didn't mollify her in the least. ''I was hoping you'd have a job for me,'' she said. ''You let me believe something like that could be in the offing last month. Or has your . . . umm, *association* with Miss Shaw changed that?''

Grey ignored Ivory's second flagrant attempt to needle him. ''There's a position for you anytime you want to work the tables at my place,'' he said. ''But no whoring with the overnight guests. The Phoenix isn't a brothel.''

''Go to hell.''

''I'll take that as a 'no.' ''

''Take that as 'I'll-think-about-it.' I haven't heard what you'll pay.''

He named an amount that was less than Annie Jack was getting in his kitchen but more than Ivory received at the Palace. ''I don't care what you do at your own place,'' he said.

''You mean I can't live at the Phoenix?''

''No, you can't live there. If I put up everyone who worked for me, there'd be no room for guests.'' He held up his hand as Ivory's dark eyes sparkled with her intent to argue. ''I'm here about one of the gowns you gave Sam,'' he said. ''Maybe you'd better sit down, Ivory. You're not going to like this much.''

Without quite knowing why, Ivory sat. She felt her skin grow cold as Grey put forth his question and explained some of the circumstances surrounding his asking it. She'd heard of Berkeley Shaw's special talent before it was put on display last night. There had been rumors that Grey's new hostess had some second sight or sixth sense. Ivory hadn't given it much credence. More than rumors surfaced yesterday evening when a few of the witnesses at the Phoenix's gala opening wound their home through the Palace. They couldn't stop talking about what they'd heard and seen Grey's hostess do with the likes of Sam Brannan and Lorne Fitch. She'd heard Anthony's story from the gambler himself. Anthony was something of a cipher, but he wasn't easily impressed. Miss Shaw had made a thorough job of that.

''So is it true?'' Grey asked when he came to the end of his recitation. ''Does Miss Shaw know what she's talking about?''

Ivory's gaze had swung to the window. Now she stood and

drew back the drapes. Her view was the alleyway behind the Palace. She saw a milk wagon negotiate a tight corner and head for the square. A drunk appeared from behind one of the outbuildings and hitched a ride on the back. He passed out among the clattering milk containers. Her eyes followed a customer of one of the other girls as he stumbled toward the privy. Apparently he decided he couldn't make it and proceeded to relieve himself where he stood. The strikingly blue, cloudless sky didn't make anything she witnessed less tawdry.

"I wasn't always a whore, Mr. Janeway. I grew up in a God-fearing family, and I expected to marry and have babies and raise them the same way." Ivory pulled her glossy black hair over her shoulder and clipped it with a comb she picked up from her vanity. "We came out here with Brannan's group in '46. That's right. I'm a Mormon. Or I was. My father was one of the leaders Brannan dismissed for breaking with church law. My father never broke with anything. He was dismissed for accusing Brannan of misusing the communal funds. My parents and I lived separate from the rest of Brannan's flock after that. When it became clear that Brigham Young wasn't going to change his plans for settling in the Salt Lake Valley, things only became worse for my parents. They decided to head overland to meet with Young."

Ivory sat down on the stool in front of her vanity. "There were twenty of us in the party that set out to cross the Sierra Nevadas. Three of us survived. The two men didn't want to go on, and I couldn't go alone. I was lucky to make it back to San Francisco but not so fortunate that I knew how to protect myself."

"Hank Brock was one of the other survivors?" Grey asked.

Ivory nodded. Her slight smile was mocking. "I thought he loved me," she said. Her short laugh rang hollow. "Do you know any woman who makes love the first time without being in love? Or thinking it's returned?"

Grey thought he might know exactly one. "I suppose not," he said as expected. "But making love isn't rape. Miss Shaw was certain it was rape."

Ivory didn't respond to this overture. She told her story at her own pace, in her own way. "The first I realized that Hank had no intention of marrying me was when I became pregnant. He was actually grateful when I lost the baby. He thought we could continue just as we had been. I was the one who said no. I turned down half a dozen other offers of marriage because I was spoiled goods. None of those men cared about that; some of them didn't know. *I* knew. *I* cared. And when men all around me began to make money with the gold strike I realized I could make it, too."

She looked at Grey, her head lifted defiantly, her eyes unashamed. "I'm good at what I do," she said. "You know I am."

"Ivory." Grey said her name gently. The truth was he couldn't recall much about their encounters together. Beyond a moment's pleasure and release, they had meant little to him. He felt sick to his stomach. "Ivory, you don't have to unburden yourself to me."

"Is that what you think I'm doing?" She came to her feet. *"You* came here asking the questions, Mr. Janeway. If you're feeling some burden, then look to yourself for the cause of it."

Grey thought having a shoe hurled at him would have hurt less. He actually winced. "I'm sorry," he said. "You're right."

Ivory DuPree relaxed her militant stance. "It was last winter," she said. "Hank had made some money in the goldfields, and he was working for Mr. Brannan as one of his exterminators. He was feeling pretty full of himself when he came here one night and got liquored up. He asked for me. I told him no. He asked Howard for me, and Howard told him I wasn't interested. I thought that was the end of it. People don't generally cross Howard, after all. That would be like crossing you in your own place."

Grey nodded. "What happened?"

"Hank got me alone upstairs. He pushed me down on the floor and threw up my royal blue skirts and had me right there. I didn't scream. I didn't cry. I was too bitterly ashamed to do either of those things. I thought I had some control over who

used me, you see. Hank showed me that night that I didn't.''
She sat down again, carefully this time, as if she were a child's
balloon being slowly deflated. ''Your Miss Shaw was correct
in the details she supplied you,'' Ivory said finally. ''Did Hank
Brock accompany Brannan to the Phoenix last night?''

''He was there.''

''I can't imagine why he'd tell Miss Shaw what happened
between us unless it was in the way of a warning.''

''She didn't say she learned anything from Brock.''

''Then how?'' asked Ivory. ''I've never told another soul
until now.''

''Didn't I mention that part?'' Grey said, thinking back.
''No, I suppose I didn't. I didn't want to lead you.''

Ivory's dark eyes merely grew puzzled.

Grey sighed. ''Miss Shaw was wearing your gown last
night.''

''You mean she *felt* what happened to me in it?''

''More than that. There were moments in the gaming hall
when it seemed she *was* you.''

Ivory's jaw sagged a little. ''That's quite incredible . . . if
it's true.''

''That's what I thought . . . if it's true.''

''Wait right here,'' Berkeley told the boy she had deposited
at the end of the long bar. She turned to go, stopped, and went
back to straighten his collar and the shoulders of his ragged
jacket. ''Stand up straight and don't look around as if you mean
to steal something. And definitely don't steal something. Mr.
Janeway will never let you in again if you do that. He'd never
let *me* in again.''

Berkeley hurried to the kitchen, where she doggedly ignored
Annie's efforts to evict her while Berkeley helped herself to
fruit, warm bread, and a bowl of stew. She carried her load
back to the gaming hall and placed it on the bar. ''You can
eat this here,'' she said. ''I'm going to find Sam.''

''Thank you, ma'am.'' The boy whipped off his hat and

revealed a thick shock of hair every bit as pale as Berkeley's. He crumpled the hat and stuffed it under his jacket behind his back. He dipped a chunk of the bread into the stew and began eating hungrily.

Berkeley watched him a moment, remembering all too well what that gnawing hunger felt like. "I won't be long."

The boy didn't lift his thin face to acknowledge her departure. He scooped up another portion of stew and jammed it in his mouth.

Grey Janeway took two steps into the Phoenix before what he saw brought him to an abrupt halt. "For God's sake, tell me you didn't go out dressed like that."

Nathaniel Corbett lifted his head. He didn't turn because he could see the man speaking to him quite clearly in the mirror. "No," he said somewhat defiantly, "but I came in this way."

Grey recognized his mistake as soon as the towhead had come up. The eyes that watched him with a mixture of rancor and wariness were closer to his own shade of tempered steel than Berkeley's leaf green ones. "Who the hell are you?" he demanded.

Nat did not answer immediately. His eyes shifted to the staircase.

Grey almost groaned aloud when he saw the boy look for rescue from above. He knew instantly who the angel was. "Did *she* bring you here?"

Nat's mouth closed tightly.

"I'm not going to torture you, boy," Grey said, shaking his head in disgust. "Give me a name to call you by."

"Nathaniel Corbett. Mostly I'm called Nat." He pushed his plate away though he wasn't close to eating his fill. "You can't make me say anything about the lady. I'm not giving her up."

Berkeley appeared at the top of the steps, Sam in tow. She made her descent quickly, seeing that everything was not quite as it should be. "Mr. Janeway," she said pleasantly. "Have you been properly introduced? This is Nathaniel Corbett. Nat, this is Mr. Janeway, the owner of the Phoenix. The one I was telling you about. He might have a job for you here."

Nat brushed off remnants of stew on his trousers and extended his hand to Grey. "Pleasure, sir."

Grey stared at the thin hand. There was dirt beaten into the whorls of his fingerprints. Grey took the hand and shook it. "Job?" He was looking at Berkeley.

"Yes," she said with complete confidence. "I thought there might be something. Sam seems to think so, don't you, Sam?"

Sam was pulling on his eyebrow and rocking back and forth on his heels. "I said we might have use for a lad that could run the stairs, fetching for guests and whatnot. That's all I said."

"It doesn't matter, Sam. She would have come up with something if you hadn't. Where did you find him, Berkeley?"

"I'd seen him around before. This morning he was rummaging in the refuse behind the Nip and Tucker. It's not right for anyone to live that way."

Grey didn't disagree. "How old are you, Nat?"

"Twelve." He felt the full force of Grey's flinty stare. "That is, I will be in a year."

God help him, Grey thought. Another orphan in the storm. "Where the hell are your parents?"

"Dead, sir. I have an uncle in Virginia that I lived with."

Berkeley sidled up beside Grey and said under her breath. "He ran away."

"I figured that out all on my own, Miss Shaw." He regarded the boy again. "You had some notion of making your fortune in the goldfields. Is that it?"

"No, not exactly, sir. Thought I'd just get away from my uncle."

"And how long have you been here?"

"About eight weeks."

"He fell in with the Ducks at first," Berkeley said. "They used him for getting into places they couldn't, then he'd have to let them in."

"Are you done with the Ducks?" Grey asked. He watched the boy's narrow face carefully as the youth nodded vigorously. "If I find out differently, Miss Shaw here won't be able to save you. Is that clear? You'll be on your own, and I'll make you wish you had stayed in Virginia with your uncle.''

"Grey!" Berkeley pulled on his sleeve, trying to get him to reconsider his words. "He's just a—''

"Is that clear?'' Grey asked Nat again.

"Yes, sir.''

Grey nodded, satisfied for now. "Sam, find him some decent clothes, then take him around and show him what you want him to do. You can fix him a room above the stable.''

Berkeley yanked hard on Grey's jacket. "Not the stable. You can do better than that.''

"I could,'' he agreed, "but I'm running a hotel here, not an asylum for foundlings.'' Whether he was just running an asylum was open for debate. He saw that Berkeley was prepared to argue with him. "All right, Miss Shaw, what would you offer as an alternative?''

"There are a few empty rooms. Sam told me.'' Out of the corner of her eye she saw Sam quickly duck his head as if he could disavow all knowledge of their earlier conversation. "Nat can have one of those.''

"He can't afford it.''

"Then I'll pay for his room.''

"*You* can't afford it.''

"Then he can stay with me. There's room enough for both of us. Shawn can bring a cot in and—''

Grey caught Berkeley's wrist. "Give us a moment,'' he told Sam and Nat. His smile did not reach his eyes. "This way, Miss Shaw.''

Berkeley allowed herself to be escorted to the farthest corner of the gaming hall. "I don't think they can hear us here,'' she said. "I'm not certain they can even *see* us.''

Grey was not amused. "That boy is *not* going to share your suite,'' he whispered roughly.

"I don't see why not. It's mine. I'm paying for it.''

"But you're there at my sufferance.''

Her eyes widened. "I beg your pardon? Do you mean you'd pitch me in the street if I went against your wishes?''

"That's precisely my meaning."

"But—" She broke off when she realized that not a single argument occurred to her. "That's really very small of you, Mr. Janeway."

"I never said I was a kind man," he told her. "You did."

"Well, I'm reconsidering."

"Good. Now let me put this to you: The boy can have your rooms under one condition."

"But you just said—"

"I said he couldn't *share* the suite with you. There's a difference if you're not living there."

Berkeley frowned. For all her prescience in other moments she was blind to the outcome of this one. "I don't understand," she said. "Where would I live?"

"With me."

Berkeley sat on the window seat in Grey's bedroom. As long as she stroked Pandora's back the cat remained comfortably curled in her lap. Behind her the window was open a few inches. It was enough that she could hear that Portsmouth Square was finally quieting. There were occasional shouts and some off-key singing, but most of the adventurers and risk-takers had found their homes for the night. Berkeley could make out the strains of music coming from downstairs in the Phoenix's gaming hall. It would be hours yet before the band was allowed to leave. The musicians had agreed to play until daybreak.

Berkeley yawned hugely. She had greeted hotel guests and would-be gamers from eight until ten. Afterward she moved among the crowd in exactly the way Grey had asked her to, staying longer at tables where there was a run of good luck for the customer and moving quickly away when it ran for the house. It wasn't long before the illusion of cause and effect was firmly established in the minds of most of the players. In addition to the rumors about Berkeley's special sighted gifts, she also appeared to be blessed by an aura of good fortune.

It was after midnight before she chose a palm to read. She was so tired by that time Berkeley thought she might very well fall asleep over it. The miner hailed from Texas, was unmarried, and had enjoyed a fair amount of luck in the goldfields and at the gaming tables. She predicted he would hit another vein inside of three months and draw to an inside straight this evening. She had no idea if either of those things would happen but when she left him, he was sitting at the poker table waiting for the lucky draw. If he had enough money, Berkeley supposed the odds would eventually favor him.

She had excused herself after that, but not without first asking Grey's permission. He had bent his head toward her solicitously and posed a single question that was overheard by no one: "Where's the boy sleeping?"

"In my room," she said.

"Then I can expect to find you in mine."

Berkeley hadn't confirmed it then. There was still the matter of her pride. It wasn't important to her that Grey was certain of her final response; she needed to wait as long as possible to give it.

"Perhaps he means to turn in with Nat," she whispered to the cat as she glanced at the mantel clock again. It was almost two. "He might, you know. He would let me worry all day long, then do the unexpected." Pandora raised her head and offered Berkeley a frankly skeptical look. "What do you know? It's not beyond all possible reason."

Berkeley had spent the day considering her choices. Sitting with Mike, helping Sam at the bar, or offering her opinion of the menu to Annie, were merely things she did to cover the direction of her thoughts. She joined the search for suitable clothes for Nat and assisted Shawn with the new employees, but all the while she was contemplating her dilemma.

She could go to the El Dorado or the Palace or any of the other gambling houses now. Grey Janeway had crafted a reputation for her that any of the gaming establishments would have been happy to employ. What was less certain to her was how willing the other owners would be to cross Grey. The fact that he'd managed to get Annie Jack from the El Dorado made Berkeley suspect there was at least one owner who would eagerly take her on. It didn't follow that she would be any safer there.

She had choices. They just weren't particularly good ones.

Berkeley gently moved the cat from her lap and stood. She picked up the throw at the foot of Grey's bed and wrapped it around her shoulders. The bed looked inviting. She had made it that way, in the precise fashion that Anderson had taught her, squaring off the clean sheets, turning down the coverlet, plumping the pillows. The wayward thought of her late husband made Berkeley shiver. She returned to the window seat and curled in the corner. Pandora approached again, stretched, and laid her forepaws on Berkeley's bare feet. Berkeley smiled sleepily as the cat began to lick her toes.

An hour later she was not entirely uncooperative when Grey helped her out of her gown and dressed her for bed. She held on to his shoulders while he unfastened the tiny ivory buttons at her back and laid her forehead wearily against his chest while he lifted her out of the yards of silk. A little later she stumbled out of all six of her petticoats and made a halting pirouette to present her back for the removal of her corset. She missed Grey's indulgent smile.

Berkeley raised her arms obediently so he could remove her chemise, and they remained that way while he slipped her sheer nightshift over her head. Her head lolled forward. He lowered her arms and kissed the silky back of her neck. A gentle push was all she required to move toward the bed.

A few minutes later Grey turned back the lamps and crawled in beside her. Berkeley rolled toward him. She rubbed her chilled, slightly damp toes against his legs. Grey pushed Pandora out of bed before she burrowed under the covers and began licking his feet. He slipped one arm under Berkeley's pillow. Their foreheads almost touched. Her palm lay flat against his chest, and he covered it with his hand.

Grey thought about what she'd said when she held his palm in her hands. His voice barely reached the level of a whisper.

"Did you know you were the woman who would complicate my life?"

Dawn came to San Francisco in all its monochromatic splendor. Milky and murky, fog blanketed the city. Cool gray fingers of it crept into the room from the square. Berkeley remembered that she hadn't closed the window. She opened one eye and promptly closed it again.

"You're awake," Grey said quietly.

"No," she said. "I'm not."

One of his dark brows arched lazily. "Oh."

Berkeley became aware of how close she was to him. She did not need to open her eyes to understand the band of heat around her waist was Grey's arm or that the warmth she felt between her legs was because he had insinuated one of his own there. Her nightdress had risen almost to the level of her hips. She reached under the blankets to push the hem lower and her hand brushed Grey's erection. His flannel drawers covered his arousal. They also outlined it.

"I know I'm awake," Grey said.

Berkeley did not move away. She moved closer. Grey's hand pressed the base of her spine, and her hips tilted forward. She held him in the cleft of her thighs. She raised her face and kissed the underside of his chin. His mouth came down on hers. The touch was soft, sweet. There was no hurry here. The exploration was languorous, vaguely sleepy in spite of Grey's words to the contrary.

"Berkeley?"

"Hmmm?"

"You do know what you're doing, don't you?"

What she was doing was tugging at the string securing his drawers. When the knot gave way her fingers slipped under the material. She cupped him in her hands. Her lips tickled his as she whispered against his mouth. "You showed me yesterday."

A chuckle vibrated at the back of Grey's throat. Her fingers tightened, and the short laugh melted into a groan. He had no choice, Grey thought, he had to believe she was awake.

He kissed the corner of her mouth, her jaw, then the sensitive spot just below her ear. He breathed in the lavender fragrance of her unbound hair. His fingers made a trail from her temple to her throat and then to her breast. He lowered his lips over her nipple and raised it to hard arousal through the thin fabric of her shift. She moaned softly. His teeth caught a little of the material and a little of her. Berkeley arched, crying out.

Grey's head came up. "Did I hurt you? I didn't mean—" He stopped because she was already shaking her head no, and her eyes were darkening with the proof of her arousal. She shouldn't look at him like that, he thought. Everything he meant to say to her went out of his head. The things he wanted to hear from her were going to be left unspoken.

Grey raised himself just enough to be rid of his drawers. They were pushed under the covers to the foot of the bed. Berkeley's slender thighs came around him as he laid her on her back. He kissed her again, deeply and slowly, and erased the moment's look of unease that he saw shadow her features. He was determined to go very carefully this morning. There would be no pain for her this time.

Her hands rested lightly on his shoulders at first. Her mouth softened as he looked at her. He was being very patient, she thought. Considerate. She stroked his upper arms, then his back. She felt the matched pair of divots at the base of his spine. Berkeley's smile had a secretive cast.

Grey felt as if she'd reached inside his chest and pulled out his heart. He groaned softly in protest, then once more in surrender.

"Have I hurt you?" she asked. Her faint smile disappeared altogether.

"No."

"Good." Berkeley let him kiss her. "You have two dimples here." She knuckled them lightly to indicate her discovery. It had the effect of pressing Grey's arousal more firmly against her. Her eyes widened.

"You weren't expecting that," he whispered.

Berkeley shook her head.

One of his hands stroked her from breast to hip. He lifted himself off her and let his fingers dip between her thighs. She was small and tight and completely ready for him. Still, he stroked her. Her body accommodated one finger, then two. She sucked in her lower lip and pressed her mons against his palm. The pale triangle of hair was as soft as fleece beneath the heel of his hand.

Berkeley was turned toward him. Her thigh hooked over his hip. She was lifted slightly, held there while he probed, then settled by slow degrees until she had all of him inside her.

Berkeley spoke her thoughts aloud. Her voice was husky, almost inaudible. "It doesn't hurt this time."

Grey was gratified to hear it, but he didn't miss the underlying surprise in her voice. His lips brushed her mouth. He held himself still inside her. It had been his fault that she'd had pain before. Mostly his fault, he amended. Her omission that she was without experience had contributed to some of her discomfort and lingering fears. "I will never hurt you again," he said against her lips.

He was struck suddenly by what he heard himself say. He'd meant *it* not I. *It will never hurt you again.* The act. Not him personally. How was he supposed to manage that?

Berkeley drew his head back to hers. "You're a very good man," she said softly.

Grey almost believed her.

They stayed in bed until long after sunshine burned through the fog. Grey made love to her a second time as she came out of a light doze. He hadn't slept at all. She couldn't seem to help herself.

Grey leaned back against the headboard. His fingers sifted lightly through Berkeley's silky hair. Her eyes were closed, but this time he knew she wasn't sleeping. Beneath the sheet her hand stroked his thigh. It was almost too much. Almost.

He remembered how easily she had taken him into her that second time, how snugly she held him. She had explored him with her hands and fingers and finally her mouth. She had a generous mouth, soft and succulent lips. Her kisses were heady. She had moved over him slowly, tasting him, but more than that. Savoring. She did not seem to find anything about him uninteresting.

She hadn't shied away from the puckered scar on his side or the three stripes on his back. She'd kissed them without comment, her fingertips gentle in their search. Her touch raised heat under his skin that didn't dissipate once her hand moved on. She didn't talk at all. Except for a slight murmur, the hum of her pleasure, she was silent.

He moved over her and in her. Their bodies rose and fell in splendid unison. The tension and hunger had been there from the beginning. They had nurtured and sustained it with their searching mouths and hands and when they sought the final expression of it, pleasure surged over them.

It was Grey who came first, burying himself deeply inside her. He spilled into her while her fingers pressed whitely into his back. The tremor that rippled through him rippled into her, and she came under him, her body stretched taut, her head thrown back, her beautiful mouth parting on a sharply drawn breath.

Grey touched Berkeley's cheeks with the backs of his fingers. "Why did you run off this morning?" he asked.

Her smile was a trifle bittersweet. "To avoid this, I expect."

"This?"

Berkeley's hand stopped moving along his thigh. She opened her eyes and sat up. The strap of her shift fell over her shoulder, and she raised it back into place. "This," she repeated. "The questions. You have them, I suppose."

"A few," he said mildly. His eyes narrowed slightly as the strap slipped over her shoulder again. This time he put it up. He touched her chin and lifted it. "Don't you? Or did you really learn everything about me when I put my palm in your hand?"

She merely regarded him steadily. He had asked the question with too much lightness for her to answer. No matter how it appeared to Grey Janeway, there had been nothing impulsive about her decision to share his bed. Not last night and not tonight. "What do you want to know?" Berkeley brushed a strand of hair away from her cheek.

"You'd never been with any man until yesterday," he said. "Why didn't you tell me?"

"Was it so very important?"

Grey thought about it. "I suppose not. It's done. I would have rather not hurt you."

She shrugged. A light flush filled her cheeks with color in spite of her seeming indifference. "It wasn't so bad."

One corner of Grey's mouth lifted wryly. "Damned with faint praise," he said under his breath.

"What?"

He shook his head. "Nothing. It doesn't matter." Grey picked up her hand and laced his fingers with hers. He was struck again by the contrasts. His hand nearly swallowed hers. "Anyway," he said, "I think I did know the truth in the beginning. I let myself believe what I wanted to later on."

Berkeley raised his hand and brushed her lips against his knuckle. It wasn't simply that he understood what she had known all along, but that he had said it aloud. At his core Grey Janeway was an honorable man. A sweetly decent, honorable man.

Berkeley found she could take solace from that, even while it made the other things she sensed about him all the more confusing.

"Would you have come back this evening?" Grey asked.

"You mean if you had asked?" she said. "Instead of threatening Nat with eviction?" Berkeley felt the intensity of his blue-gray stare. His honesty deserved hers. "Yes. I would have come back to your bed."

Grey knew himself to be a coward then because he didn't ask the obvious question. He didn't ask why. "You didn't move any of your things here."

"That's not true. I brought the box Shawn made for me and my earring. I don't own anything else."

He gave her a stern look. "Berkeley. I don't think of you as an investment like the carpets and mirrors and gaming tables. The gowns are yours."

"When I pay for them." She relented when she saw his mouth thin. "Very well. They're mine. I'll move them in later today." Berkeley slipped her hand free of his. "Sam told me you went to see Ivory DuPree."

"Sam talks too much."

"Well?" Berkeley asked.

Grey thought he heard about a half dozen questions in that single one. "She confirmed your story. She told me no one knew about it."

Berkeley nodded. She looked down at her hands. "She was bitterly ashamed."

Grey sat up a little straighter. "Those are the same words she used. How did you—"

"You don't understand yet, do you?" Berkeley's large, expressive eyes betrayed her disappointment. "It's what I *felt.*"

"I can't accept that," Grey said. "Brock told you something."

"He didn't, but I can't prove it." She touched his wrist. "Does it frighten you, Grey? This gift I have, does it bother you so much?"

"It scares the hell out of me."

"Why?"

He was stubbornly silent.

Berkeley leaned forward. Her voice was gentle. "Do you think I'll tell someone about the man you killed?"

Chapter Nine

Grey stared at Berkeley. Nothing about his features changed but incredulous was inadequate to describe what he was feeling. After a moment he shook his head as if recovering from a blow. "The man I killed?" he repeated under his breath. Before she could answer, Grey held up one hand. "Never mind." His hand stayed in midair long enough to halt Berkeley, then went to the back of his neck. He bent his head and rubbed the corded muscles. When he looked up again he noticed her expression was one of concern. *She* was concerned for *him.* Clearly she had no idea that he was at all worried about her. "Why in the world would you think I've killed someone?" he asked gently.

Berkeley's mouth flattened a little. "I'm not a child," she said. "And I'm not addled. There's no need for you to condescend to me."

Grey thought it best not to say anything.

"Are you denying it?" asked Berkeley.

That he had been condescending? he wondered. Or that he had committed murder? Grey thought one of them should strive for clarity. "Berkeley, I haven't killed anyone." To the best of his knowledge, it was true. "Now, tell me why you don't believe me."

"I know what I felt when I held your hand," she said.

"That was your reasoning when you expected Mike to die."

Berkeley looked away. "I'm not sorry Mike's recovering. I never wanted him to die to prove myself. But I wasn't entirely wrong either. I *did* sense he was going away. I merely mistook the cause. And I told him he would see his family."

"Those things are going to happen because I'm making them happen," he reminded her. "I'm the one making the arrangements and paying for his passage."

Berkeley's head came up. Her expression was earnest. "Don't you understand, Grey? It doesn't matter how the end comes to pass, just that it does. Your interference was critical to make things come about. You were part of the outcome all along."

"With that sort of thinking you can make most anything seem as if you predicted it."

"Isn't that the point downstairs?" she asked. "Isn't that what I've been hired to do with the Phoenix's patrons?"

"Yes," he said slowly. He could tell Berkeley was warming up to something.

"But you don't like that I *believe* I can do it. Is that it?" She waved a hand dismissively, not waiting for his reply. "Don't bother to answer. You're quite content thinking it's all a parlor trick. I don't know why I'm surprised. Anderson . . . my father was the same way. He was never really certain about my gift, but he never took any chances with it either. He kept me close. He was always watchful. He insisted I do exactly as I was told." Berkeley gave Grey a frank look. "You're not so very different."

"I don't think you're a performing bear," he said.

Her short laugh held no humor. "I've been to Sydney Town, Grey. I've seen that poor animal chained in front of the Fierce Grizzly. My leash is only a little longer than hers."

Grey reached for Berkeley, but she was like quicksilver. She slipped free of the fingers that just touched her wrist and slid out of bed. Without a backward glance she walked into the dressing room and closed the door.

Berkeley did not move her clothes into Grey's suite that afternoon, and she did not return to his bed that night. She removed the box that held the earring from his mantel and replaced it on her own.

Grey did not insist that she join him that evening or any of the ones that followed. Except for the fact that he gave Nat Corbett his own room on the third floor, Berkeley could have believed Grey didn't notice her absence from his bed or her presence anywhere else.

They were coolly polite in public and never spoke in private. For her own protection, Berkeley continued to address him as Grey when they were together in the gaming hall. The illusion that they were lovers did indeed keep the majority of men from propositioning her. In front of those who worked for him there was no illusion, he was Mr. Janeway and she was Miss Shaw.

"Sam says he's getting himself an ice pick," Nat told Berkeley.

She tapped the page he was supposed to be reading. They were sitting at one of the gaming tables near the Phoenix's entrance. Except for Sam stocking behind the bar, the hall was empty. The Phoenix was closed all morning and several hours each afternoon to everyone except its boarders and employees. It was then that the business of operating the establishment took place. Sam Hartford completed his inventory, wrote out his order, and restocked the bar. Donnel Kincaid inspected for damages made each night by a few rowdy miners and oversaw the repairs to the main hall or the rooms above it. From the kitchen at the rear, Annie Jack's stentorian voice was always audible as she ordered her assistants around but did most of the work herself. The Phoenix required a staff of thirty to keep her boarders happy and the gaming tables filled. There were dealers and musicians and housekeepers and waiters. Now that all the living quarters were spoken for, the second-floor dining room was always occupied by a few of the boarders. No matter the time of day, the back stairs from the kitchen to the dining room was the busiest thoroughfare in the hotel.

Grey avoided most of the daily rumblings. If he was not at the bank or the wharf or haggling with one of his suppliers, then he was in his office with Shawn going over the books and supervising his other investments.

The hours when the Phoenix was closed were not so demanding on Berkeley. Now that Mike was recovered and on his way east, she kept a closer eye on Nat, making certain he didn't run afoul of Grey. The simplest way to keep that from happening was to keep him busy. While the boy made himself useful to everyone at the Phoenix, he was most attentive to her. When she suggested tutoring him each morning following breakfast, he fell in with her plan without complaint. If she wanted to go shopping or simply for a walk, he was invariably at her side. He accompanied her on errands and sat beside her at meals when she didn't take them by herself. She kept him out of mischief, and he kept her from being alone.

It was an arrangement that seemed to be working remarkably well. Which was why Berkeley was surprised when Nat closed Emerson's first series of essays over her tapping finger.

"Must I?" he asked plaintively.

Berkeley withdrew her finger from the book. "What are you asking me, Nat? A moment ago you were talking about ice picks. Really, I can't follow your conversation sometimes."

Nat's face had filled out since he'd come to the Phoenix, but it still retained its narrow shape. His grin was almost too big to be contained in its width. "Do you know that Mr. Janeway often remarks the same about you?"

She sighed. For once Nat's toothsome smile did not melt her heart. "Mr. Janeway and I understand each other perfectly. And you shouldn't repeat things you don't necessarily understand, Nathaniel."

The use of his full Christian name brought Nat to attention in his seat. "Then I shouldn't have told you what Sam said about the ice pick."

"I don't even know what that means," she said. Berkeley held up her abused finger to keep him from explaining. "Let's inquire of Sam, shall we?" She had raised her voice just enough to carry to the bar. "Sam, I know very well you heard both of us. Stop hiding back there. Why is Nat thinking I should know you want an ice pick?"

Sam's head rose slowly above the mahogany horizon of the bar. "To chip ice?" he said.

Nat completely ignored Sam's sour look in his direction. "No, Sam. Remember you said it this morning, just after breakfast? We were all still sitting around the table except for Mr. Janeway and Miss Shaw. Donnel said it was getting colder and colder between the two of them and Shawn said he was wearing a coat at breakfast from now on. You kinda laughed and said you were getting yourself a damn ice pick." Nat's mouth screwed up to one side. "Sorry for cussin'," he apologized to Berkeley. "It sorta slipped." He glanced back at Sam. "You remember that, Sam?"

"I sure as hell don't remember cussin'," he said, his flushed expression both stern and cautionary. "Miss Shaw's been particular that no one does that in front of you."

Berkeley raised a brow at Sam. "Does Nat remember most of it correctly?" she asked.

"I reckon so," he said. He began polishing an imaginary smear off the top of the bar.

"You and the others talk about me and Mr. Janeway?"

"No, ma'am. We don't. Leastways not regular-like." He polished harder. "But this morning it was pretty chilly at breakfast. Thought Annie's pancakes would get a touch of frost on them the way you two were pleasin' and thankin' each other just like you meant it when you didn't mean it at all. It don't take someone with your gift to see you ain't happy and that he's worse off than you. Donnel and me, we figure it's been goin' on since about the time Nat here came. Six weeks, give or take a day. 'Bout time someone says somethin'."

Berkeley didn't respond immediately. She took Emerson's essays from Nat and came slowly to her feet. "I'm sorry it's

been so uncomfortable for you and the others," she said carefully.

Sam stopped polishing and pulled at his eyebrow again.
"Awww," he said, shifting his weight. "Now see here, Miss
Shaw, there's no need to take it like that. I collect I put it all
wrong."

"No, I think you said it exactly right." She pressed her lips
together in a flat, cheerless smile. "If you'll excuse me?"

Nat pushed his chair back and stood. Sam tipped his hat.
They waited until she had disappeared up the stairs before they
exchanged worried and slightly accusatory glances.

Berkeley reappeared in the main hall at six. Grey had arrived
minutes before and was at his customary place at the end of
the bar, greeting guests as they passed. He watched Berkeley's
reflection in the mirror as she came down the stairs. The skirt
of her cream-silk gown shifted gently. She did nothing so
human as merely walk down the steps. She floated. From where
Grey stood it looked as if her hand glided along the banister.
It was there not to steady her, but to ground her.

Grey saw heads turn in her direction as one after another of
the men glimpsed her arrival. Her fixed smile was for all of
them collectively and none of them individually. Their reflec-
tive glances touched briefly. When he turned she wouldn't meet
his eyes at all.

He had no complaints about her work. She moved easily
among the crowd, chatting with the regulars, acquainting herself
with the first-timers. She stood at the tables, watching the play.
Sometimes someone would let her take a hand or give her
money so she could play her own. She never won. The miners
laughed about it; even teased her good-naturedly about her
poor luck. They found it ironic that she couldn't make her
extraordinary talent work for her at the tables. Not one of them
seemed to understand it was impossible for someone to lose
as consistently as she did.

Berkeley Shaw, Grey thought, was slow-witted like a fox.

Every loss for her was a win for the house and every win for the house put money in her coffers. She was simply more patient about getting it than the men who frequented the Phoenix.

Grey's attention strayed from Berkeley as he saw Donnel approaching. The man's fiery brows were a single furrowed ridge above his eyes. "What is it?"

"Have you seen Nat?" asked Donnel.

"I better not see him down here. Why? What do you need?"

"I need Nat," he said. "He's supposed to be delivering coals to the rooms. We're in for a cold night."

"You can look in my apartments," Grey said. "The last time I saw him he was returning *The Three Musketeers* to my library. Miss Shaw has him reading Emerson." Grey shook his head, plainly sorry for the boy. "Has to be painful for him."

Donnel grunted. "Oh, I think he'll find *all* reading painful if he has to sit down for it." He began to stalk off, but Grey brought him up short. Donnel's surprised expression froze when he saw his employer's face.

"Don't lay a hand on him," Grey said. His voice was steady. His eyes were like ice chips. "Find him, have him do his work, then send him to me. You might want to check with Miss Shaw. She may know where he is." He took his hand from Donnel Kincaid's muscular forearm. "We'll talk later."

Donnel nodded once, then wended his way through the crowd.

Several hours later Grey noticed Donnel again. This time the redhead was moving more gingerly among the guests, almost as if he didn't want to touch them. When Grey saw Donnel bend close to Berkeley, getting her ear while she was engaged in a palm reading, Grey saw the reason for his foreman's circumspect tour of the tables. Donnel's hands were as black as the coal he had been carrying to the rooms.

Grey saw Berkeley's features pale as Donnel spoke to her. To her credit she didn't jump away from her customer and follow Donnel immediately. She completed her recitation before excusing herself. There was the usual clamoring for her to do another, but she declined as she always did. When she retired to her rooms the guests didn't know, as Grey did, that she had no intention of returning to the hall this evening.

By the time Grey reached her room Berkeley was on the point of stepping out. She wore a black woolen mantle with a hood that was pulled up over her hair. Her head was bent as her fingers twisted around the silk frogs. She almost barreled into him.

Grey caught Berkeley by the elbows to steady her. It was the first time in six weeks that he had touched her unexpectedly. She looked up at him, not merely startled, but shocked. His hands fell away slowly. He didn't know if he should apologize or shake her. In the end he did neither. While he was contemplating his options she was brushing past him.

Grey fell in step beside her. "Talk to me, Berkeley. What's happened? Where are you going?"

"Nat's missing. Donnel's searched everywhere. He took on Nat's chores himself to make certain Nat wasn't in one of the boarders' rooms. He wasn't. Donnel had looked all around before that. Donnel says you saw him in your library this morning. That was after Sam and I saw him. As near as Donnel can tell he hasn't been seen by anyone since."

"But that was twelve hours ago."

"Exactly." She paused on the landing at the back stairs. "Sam's going to drive me. There's no need for you to bother yourself."

"Like hell." He followed her closely. "Why do you think it's a bother? Do you think you're the only one who cares what happens to the boy?"

"I'd say we're all suspect where caring is concerned. As you pointed out, it's been twelve hours." Berkeley drew on her gloves when she reached the kitchen. Her back was rigid with anger. "Excuse me."

Grey waved Annie and her helpers back to work and stepped outside behind Berkeley. "I'm going with you."

She shrugged. "Suit yourself."

Grey stepped around her and blocked her path to the stable.

Her face was lifted defiantly. "Dammit, Berkeley, this isn't my fault!"

"You're wrong," she said. "It's yours and it's mine. Ask Sam."

Sam was looking miserable himself when Grey took the reins from him and told him to step down. "Don't mind helpin' out," Sam said. He assisted Berkeley into the carriage, then jumped down. "No tellin' where Nat's like to end up."

"I'll drive her," Grey said. "Berkeley says I should ask you why this is my fault."

"I said it was mine, too." She sat down, her eyes straight ahead.

Sam tugged on his hat. "Miss Shaw thinks that something I said this mornin' mighta got Nat thinking he wasn't welcome. I was explainin'—and you know I don't get the words right sometimes, Mr. Janeway—anyway, I was sayin' how everyone knows you and Miss Shaw ain't been exactly gettin' along. I recollected that it had been like that since about the same time Miss Shaw brought Nat here. I didn't mean one had anything to do with the other."

"I know, Sam." Grey placed one hand on the older man's shoulder and squeezed it briefly. "Get the doors, will you?"

The night air was every bit as cold as Donnel had predicted. Berkeley took a blanket from beneath the seat and laid it across their laps.

"I take it you have some idea where he'll go," Grey said. "You'll have to direct me."

"There's a warehouse on Jackson Street. It's filled with building supplies and paint. Nat's stayed there before."

Grey wondered if Berkeley had. "I know the place. John Hardy owns it." He snapped the reins and the double team of horses took the corner smartly.

The building occupied the full length of the block from front to back. Under Berkeley's instructions Grey guided the carriage to the narrow side alley. Before he could secure the horses she had alighted from the carriage and was hurrying to a window directly at ground level. When Grey caught up to her Berkeley was on her hands and knees trying to force it open. He hunkered down beside her. "Get up," he said. "I'll do it. You'll ruin your gown."

"I'm paying for it," she snapped.

Grey sighed. The window creaked. "If it's that hard to open, Nat probably hasn't used it recently."

"It's always this hard to open."

Which answered, he supposed, his question about whether she had ever used the entrance. "Are you going to slither in there?"

"There's no other way."

"There is," he said. "I can go to John's house and ask him to take us in the front entrance."

"Nat would be long gone."

"I'm going in with you."

"You'll never fit." Berkeley let the window close gingerly so she wouldn't have to force it a second time, then she stood, hiked her gown, and began removing petticoats. She took off her mantle as well and thrust all of it at Grey. "Put this in the carriage."

"Berkeley, so help me God—"

"I'll open a door for you," she promised. "Give me a moment." She dropped to her knees again and opened the casement with her forearm. She poked her head inside, inched forward until she had wriggled her shoulders in, then extended her arms and dropped hands and head first onto the dirt floor of the basement. Berkeley's tumble was not acrobatic, but neither did she hurt herself. She brushed herself off and stood on tiptoe to close the window firmly behind her.

Outside Grey paced. The horses stamped restlessly as he passed back and forth in front of them. He considered what he would tell Brannan's patrolling Vigilantes if he was caught in this alley. He wasn't a Sydney Duck, just a sitting one. "Damn her," he muttered. "She's not going to—"

"Grey! Down here!"

Berkeley's voice reached him from the back of the warehouse. Grey turned. He could just distinguish the dark outline of a door she had swung out. Grey squeezed past the horses and the carriage and sprinted to the entrance she held open for him.

Berkeley spared him an assessing glance. "You didn't think I'd let you in."

"Not true," he lied baldly.

She didn't believe him but didn't argue. "Shut the door. You'll have to be careful in here. There're stockpiles everywhere, and we can't risk lighting a lantern. Do you want to search separately or stay together?"

Grey could only imagine one reason why Berkeley would pose the question: She was afraid to be on her own. "We'll stay together."

Their progress was slow and not without mishap. Grey jammed his knee into a board that was sticking out in their path and Berkeley fell backward onto some sandbags. "He's bound to have heard that," Grey whispered after he knocked over a paint can.

"Shhh."

"What makes you think he'll run from us?"

"What makes you think he won't?" she said. Berkeley shook his arm as he recovered from stumbling over some bricks. "Can you *not* be quiet?"

They continued to pick their way through rows of squarely stacked lumber and pallets of bricks. "Do you have some destination in mind?" Grey finally asked. "Or could he be anywhere among this rubble?"

Berkeley stopped and pointed up and in front of her. "There."

Grey squinted in the darkness. He saw the shadow that ran almost the width of the warehouse had rectangular form and substance. It was a storage loft. Berkeley led him the last few yards to the ladder without incident.

"I've never been up there," she said. "I never slept anywhere but the cellar. Nat told me about this loft."

"You can't go up there in your gown," Grey said. The ladder was in a fixed position. It was a straight vertical climb from the floor of the warehouse. He took hold of the rung at shoulder height, then paused, waiting for Berkeley's inevitable argument.

Berkeley sensed his waiting attitude. "I can't go up there in any circumstances," she admitted finally.

"What's up there?"

"Height."

Grey smiled. "All right," he said. "I'll flush him out if he's up there, and you hold on to him when he gets down."

"I can do that," she said.

"I never doubted it." Without knowing he was going to do it until it was done, Grey placed a kiss on Berkeley's forehead. He thought she might have even leaned a little toward him for it. "Promise me we'll talk later," he said.

Berkeley nodded. It was an easy promise to make and keep. Later was anytime short of forever. She gave him a nudge to start his climb, then stood back and watched his shadowed ascent.

Grey came across Nat more by accident than design. The boy was curled comfortably in a pile of gunnysacks that Grey tried to step over. Yelping, Nat bolted upright. He scrambled to his feet and on instinct alone tried to elude his would-be captor. Nat dived sideways as a pair of arms tried to restrain him. He somersaulted smoothly to his feet and vaulted over a sawhorse.

"Nat!" Grey called. "It's Mr. Janeway. I'm not going to hurt you." Grey didn't think his announcement gave the boy any pause at all. Afraid Nat would kill himself hurtling down the ladder, Grey tried to capture him before he got that far.

Nat felt fingers brush the back of his neck a moment before they securely caught his collar. He wiggled out of his jacket and flung himself toward the ladder. He grabbed the side rail in one hand and let his small body swing free of the loft. His feet caught one of the rungs and his free hand found the other side rail. With the fearlessness and agility only a young boy can muster, Nat was down the ladder in seconds.

And into Berkeley's waiting arms.

Nat struggled at first. He fell still when he caught the fragrances that identified his captor, the sweet lavender scent of her hair, the hint of roses that clung to her gown.

"Stay right where you are, Nathaniel," she said. Her arms were hard around him, part hug, part restraint. "Are you all right?" She loosened her grip just enough to pat him down. Berkeley touched his face, his shoulders, his wrists, then she gave him a little shake. "You scared us, you know. Donnel. Sam. Shawn. Annie Jack's beside herself."

Grey jumped the last few feet to the ground. He brushed himself off. "Is he all right?"

"I don't know. He hasn't said."

"Have you given him a chance?"

Nat wriggled out of Berkeley's arms. "I ain't hurt myself," he said somewhat defiantly. "I know how to get on."

"Of course you do," Grey said. "You got the entire way to San Francisco without mishap. You can certainly manage a few city blocks without coming to grief."

"Can I have my jacket?" Nat asked.

Grey handed it over. "What are your plans?"

Nat jammed his arms into the sleeves and pulled the jacket on. "What do you mean?"

"I mean do you intend to bolt again or are you coming back to the Phoenix with us?"

"Grey," Berkeley began. "He's coming—"

"He needs to make up his own mind," Grey said firmly.

Nat's eyes darted from Grey to Berkeley and back again. It was difficult to make out their features, and he was wary of good intentions. "You'd take me back?"

Grey expelled a breath slowly and kneaded the nape of his neck. "I didn't come here to tuck you in, Nat. Of course I want you back at the Phoenix." Grey thought that would be enough for the boy. Instead Nat turned to Berkeley.

"What about you, Miss Shaw?"

Grey started to protest. "Nat, Miss Shaw's the one who insisted—"

Berkeley caught the edge of Grey's sleeve and tugged. "No,

Grey, you don't understand all of it. Nat wants to know if I only came looking for him because of the earring.'' She reached out. The tips of her fingers brushed Nat's cheek. ''It's part of the reason I came,'' she told him. ''But I think you were afraid I wouldn't otherwise. That's why you took it from the box on my mantel. You still have it, don't you? You haven't pawned it.''

In answer, Nat reached in his jacket pocket and withdrew the earring. Even in the poor light it shone splendidly at the center of his palm. He dropped it into hers and watched it disappear as her fingers closed over it.

Berkeley gave the earring to Grey for safekeeping. She dropped to her knees in front of Nat and took his hands in hers. She had to look up at him, and she held him fast when he would have pulled away. ''Listen to me, Nat,'' she said, her voice imploring him. ''That earring isn't properly mine. I had to find it. But I would have come after you regardless, and I would have asked you to come back even if you'd sold it. I hope you believe me because I don't know any other way to say it. You've practically lived in my pockets these past six weeks. I'd miss you dreadfully if you stayed away now. I care very much what happens to you.''

Nat felt his eyes well up with tears. He couldn't brush them away because Berkeley held his hands. He blinked them back and sniffed hard. ''But you've been so unhappy,'' he said, his voice quavering. ''Sam said you've been like that since I came.'' He didn't give Berkeley an opportunity to answer. His head swiveled to Grey. ''And you, Mr. Janeway. I've been a sore disappointment to you. The only job you asked me to do for you, I managed to make a mess of.''

Grey tried to silence the boy with a warning look, but the darkness of the warehouse shrouded his expression.

''I'm supposed to be looking after her, not the other way around.''

Berkeley's attention swung fast in Grey's direction. ''Did I

hear him correctly?'' she demanded softly. ''Did you set Nat
the task of keeping an eye on me?''

''Both eyes,'' Nat interjected.

Grey sighed. ''It was a good job for him. He needed something important to occupy him.''

''But *I* was looking out for him.''

''I know. You needed something worthwhile to occupy you.''
Berkeley glanced back at Nat. ''What was he paying you?''

''Two bits a day and my room and board.''

She didn't blink at Grey's generosity. Instead she felt her
heart swell. ''You're a shrewd bargainer, Nat,'' she said, trying
to keep her voice steady. Berkeley managed a wry chuckle. ''I
worked for nothing.''

''I would've, too,'' the boy offered earnestly. ''I didn't mind
at all livin' in your pockets.''

Berkeley allowed Grey to help her to her feet. ''It seems to
me you're not entirely to be trusted,'' she said to him softly.

Grinning, Grey put his hand behind Nat's shoulders and gave
him a nudge. ''Let's go. Can we use the door and lock it behind
us?''

''Sure,'' Nat said. ''I never leave by the window.''

A few minutes later they were settled in the carriage. Berkeley put on her mantle but sat on the petticoats. She made Nat
squeeze between her and Grey and covered him with the blanket. She slipped one arm around his thin shoulders while Grey
took the reins. ''You know, Nat,'' she said, ''whether or not
Mr. Janeway and I get along, it has nothing to do with you.
Sam didn't mean for you to think that. And looking after me
doesn't make you responsible for my actions or my moods. I
don't want you to come back to the Phoenix because Mr.
Janeway and I want you there. I hope you're coming back
because it's where you want to be.''

The carriage passed under a street lantern. Grey looked over
the top of Nat's bright hair at Berkeley. His eyes caught hers,
and for once he let her see the unshuttered depths.

"I know it's why I'm going back," she said quietly, answering the question Grey hadn't had to ask.

Sam Hartford inspected the brass rail of the bar for scratches and spots. He tapped a fitting with the toe of his boot. "Missed something here," he said.

Nat stooped obediently, rag in hand, and began furiously wiping away the offending dullness.

Sam eyed the boy suspiciously. Nat's eagerness to make himself helpful raised a few questions in Sam's mind. "You sure Miss Shaw said I was supposed to put you to work this morning?" he asked. "This is the time she usually makes for your lesson."

"You saw yourself how she was at breakfast," Nat said.

"Near pale as that rag you're usin'," Sam said. "Not a kind comparison, but then I was never good with words."

Nat glanced at the rag. It was a light gray color. "She was about this shade, all right. She's having a lie-down now. I don't expect she'll be up again for another hour." Nat plopped himself on the floor and crossed his legs tailor-fashion. "You notice there's been a thaw, Sam? Between Miss Shaw and Mr. Janeway, I mean."

Sam stretched his neck and scratched the underside of his chin. "I been noticin' it for 'bout a month now. Reckon it started around the time you took off." He gave Nat a stern look. "Now don't be making too much of that. It's probably just a coincidence that they've been chippin' away at the ice since then."

"What do you make of it?"

"I think Mr. Janeway's courtin' her."

Nat's head bobbed once. "Damn if I don't think the same thing."

"Watch your mouth, Nat. There'll be hell to pay if Miss Shaw hears you."

Nat accepted the rebuke with a grin and bent to his task.

One of Sam's wiry brows kicked up. "What are you really supposed to be doing right now?"

"It's what *you're* supposed to be doing," Nat said. "Teaching me from *A Moral System of Philosophy*."

Sam made a face. "You still got that magazine Mr. Janeway slipped you yesterday?"

"It's in my room."

"Well, go get it. Seems I recollect seein' 'Murders in the Rue Morgue' by that Poe fella. I suppose we can do some moral philosophizin' about that. Killin' ain't right, you know."

Upstairs in her suite Berkeley was blissfully unaware that her teaching methods were being subverted. She lay on her side in bed, a cool compress across her forehead. She fingered the delicate gold chain around her neck until she touched the pendant that dangled from it. The pearl was smooth under her fingertips. The golden teardrop beneath it was warm from resting against her skin.

Grey hadn't returned the earring to her for more than a week after they had retrieved Nat from the warehouse. She had asked for it several times, but he either changed the subject or simply promised he would get it from his safe later. When he did return the earring it was in a cherry wood box with its own secret drawer. The fittings were so tight it had the appearance of a solid block of beautifully burnished wood. He had to show her how to slide one of the pieces to reveal the contents.

Berkeley had no difficulty recognizing the earring for what it had become: a peace offering.

She knew he had heard her tell Nat that the earring wasn't properly hers, but he didn't question her about it. He never once reminded her that she had said outright that it had been a gift. He let the fact that she lied to him become unimportant. Instead he made the earring hers by having it fashioned into the necklace she wanted. She had allowed him to place it around her throat. His fingers had been very gentle as they brushed her skin. She thought he might kiss her then, but he hadn't.

They spoke several times a day after that, always briefly but without strain. In the beginning it was mostly of inconsequential things. He remarked on the gown she had chosen; she complimented his jacket. They compared notes about the evening meal. Later Grey began to ask about Nat's promise as a student and Berkeley would inquire about the business. They stopped passing comments about the weather and spent more time in the gaming hall in each other's company.

Berkeley found reasons to search him out in the crowd of gamblers. He found excuses to touch her.

She noticed things about him that she had not seen clearly before. He was reserved among the men who came to the Phoenix and called him friend. Grey was polite but distant. He was warmer to the men who worked for him than he was to any of the ones he entertained or did business with. He did not extend trust easily and was wary when others did.

Berkeley had seen him being approached by Sam Brannan on two different occasions. Grey declined to serve on the Vigilance Committee both times, but he managed not to make an enemy of the powerful Brannan in the process.

He was a careful man, thoughtful and considerate. She had been wrong to think there was ever a time he hadn't paid attention to her. It was his nature to pay attention to everything. He knew when Sam's rheumatism was paining the older man. He knew exactly what to say to end one of Annie Jack's tirades. He performed sleight of hand for Nat's amusement and knew exactly where the boy was in his lessons. There wasn't an employee whose name he didn't use with ease. That everyone had a sense of their own importance in the running of the hall was Grey's doing. George Pettigrew, the effusive greeter from the El Dorado, came to work at the Phoenix. So did a number of others who were valuable in their positions at equally profitable gaming houses. Without ingratiating himself to anyone, Grey Janeway attracted people who wanted to work for him.

He took care of the people he cared about and did it in ways that weren't obvious. A colorful apron, with strings long enough to get around Annie's ample waist, would suddenly appear in her kitchen. Sam would find a new bottle of liniment for his aching bones while he was sorting out the bar stock. There were books for Nat, tools for Donnel, and for Ivory DuPree there had been the settling of an old score.

Berkeley felt strongly that she was never meant to know about the beating that Hank Brock endured, or at least never know the origin of the fists that pummeled him. The item in the *Gazette* that caught her eye was an account of the attempt on Sam Brannan's life. Offering no proof, the reporter and Brannan surmised that it was the work of the Sydney Ducks, a response to their displeasure with the Vigilance Committee. Brannan himself was unhurt, and in fact hadn't been present when the Ducks made their strike. The attack had been more in the nature of a warning, the reporter wrote, and one of Brannan's bodyguards, a Mr. Henry "Hank" Brock, took the severe beating for being associated with Brannan and responsible for his protection.

Berkeley never asked Grey what part he had played in serving up Ivory DuPree's retribution. His slightly swollen hands and grazed knuckles were proof enough that he had seen to the problem of Hank Brock personally.

Pandora made a graceful leap to the bed and drew Berkeley out of her musings. "Where did you come from?" she asked the cat. "I thought you were downstairs with Nat." The ever-inscrutable Pandora simply stared back at her. Berkeley scratched her neck. "Did I leave the door ajar? Is that what I did?"

"Berkeley? May I come in?"

It was Grey's voice that filtered in from the adjoining room. Berkeley was trying to sit up to make a better presence when he poked his head around the bedroom door. "Stay where you are," he ordered quietly. "My objective wasn't to disturb you. I was on my way downstairs when I saw Pandora slip in here. I thought I could get her before she made a run at your bed." He gave the cat an arch look. "It appears I'm too late."

"I don't mind Pandora's company," Berkeley said. She lowered her head back to the pillow and didn't replace the compress. "Or yours."

This last was spoken so softly that Grey took his cue from

the movement of her lips. "I'll only stay a moment." He pushed the door wider and came through. There was a rocker by the window, and Grey moved it closer to the bed. "Annie tells me you left breakfast just after I did this morning. She's wondering if something she prepared disagreed with you."

Berkeley slipped one arm under her pillow, raising her head a few inches. "She's afraid I'll put a spell on her if I suspect she's trying to poison me."

"Something like that," Grey admitted. "I'm supposed to look around here for charms and potions, and if you have a doll that looks like Annie, I'm supposed to take it with me— or at least get the pins out."

Berkeley laughed. "Poor Annie. She doesn't know what to make of me."

Grey's smile faded. He let silence draw out a beat longer before he said, "Neither do I."

The expression in her leaf green eyes was gentle. "I know."

His intention not to linger fell by the wayside. "Do you mind?" he asked. "I'd like to talk about that. There are some questions . . ." His voice trailed off because he felt the full force of her extraordinary smile. It was at once wistful and shy, yet somehow encouraging. Her skin glowed, and the gentleness of her expression was replaced by an unusual serenity. It was almost as if she knew what he was going to ask. "I think I'm prepared to hear your answers," he said finally.

Berkeley nodded. "I think you are, too."

"You've been enormously patient, waiting me out like this."

"Enormously stubborn," she said. "Intractable."

"A little," he allowed. He leaned forward in the rocker, stopping its motion cold while he rested his forearms on his knees. "There's something to this talent of yours, isn't there? It's not merely clever parlor tricks."

"Do you want an answer?" she asked. "Or confirmation of what you've been observing. I can't tell."

Grey hesitated. "Confirmation," he said at last.

"Then you're right. There is something to my talent. It's not merely clever parlor tricks."

"But sometimes it *is* fakery."

"Actually quite a lot of the time that's exactly what it is." She saw Grey's fingers press together at the tips as he frowned. "Do you think I'm being contradictory? My special gift is incredibly wearing. I can't sustain what's required of me to use it day after day. I can't let myself be that vulnerable. So, yes, often I rely on other means to enhance it."

"Like watching how people carry themselves and listening for their accents. You wait for the small expressions and movements that give them away."

"Exactly like that. I told you that's what I did from the first. You weren't prepared then to hear that it might be anything else."

"But when you looked at my palm it was—"

"It was never about looking at your palm." Berkeley carefully pushed herself upright. She smoothed the fringed coverlet across her legs. "I have almost no idea what the lines and mounts on anyone's palm mean. It was because I touched you and allowed myself to *feel* something that I know what I know."

"Ivory's gown," Grey said. "You allowed yourself to feel that?"

"No," she said quickly, shaking her head. "Oh God, no. I couldn't help myself that night. Sometimes there's an intensity about an object I'm touching that I'm helpless to ignore. It was like that with Ivory's gown. Perhaps if I hadn't been wearing it . . ." She shrugged. "I don't know. It was very powerful. It may not have made any difference."

"And with my hand? The intensity was there?"

Berkeley understood what Grey was really asking. "That's more difficult to explain, and I don't know that I can or that it would make any sense to you. You're still wondering how I know about the man you killed."

"Yes."

"There was no trickery involved," she said. "You're very guarded, Grey. There's little you give away casually."

His features were perfectly schooled now. There was only a slight narrowing of his eyes as he searched her face.

Berkeley fingered the earring pendant. "Shall I tell you something about Graham Denison?"

Grey's glance strayed to her throat. "Is that who gave you the earring?"

"In a way," she said, watching him closely. "It's also the name of the man you killed."

Grey came up out of the rocker as if shot from a cannon. Pandora's back arched, then she crouched and prepared to pounce. "You can't know that," he said, glaring at the cat. His long-legged stride took him to the window. He stared out, his arms rigid at his side. "It's not possible." This last was said softly, more to himself than to Berkeley. "You couldn't know."

Berkeley drew Pandora onto her lap and stroked her absently. Was she wrong? Her eyes traveled over the taut line of Grey's lean frame. His jaw was fixed, his shoulders braced. He had the look of a man who had taken one blow and was preparing himself to receive another.

"You're correct," Berkeley said and readied herself to deliver it. "Under any usual circumstances, I couldn't know, but there's nothing usual about my situation here. I wouldn't find myself in San Francisco if not, in part, for Mr. Denison. And I wouldn't be here with you if not for your rather surprising likeness to him."

Grey turned slowly to face her. A small vertical crease appeared between his dark brows. "I look like him?"

"Yes." Berkeley frowned. "Don't you know?"

"No," he said. "I don't. You're going to have to accept that."

"Perhaps you didn't get a clear look at his face before you—"

"Have a care," he interrupted. "You're close to accusing me of stabbing him in the back."

"No, I wasn't thinking that at all. I thought . . . well, I thought it might have been dark."

Grey advanced on the bed. Pandora didn't snarl at him this time. She simply leaped out of the way when he sat on the edge of the bed. "Do I frighten you?" he asked Berkeley. She shook her head and reached for his hand. Grey withdrew it slightly, keeping it just beyond her easy grasp. "Are you certain you want to touch me?"

"Are you certain you want me to?" She showed him again her uncommon patience by turning her palm over and waiting for him to place his hand in hers. It was a long minute later when her fingers closed over his. "I'm only holding your hand, Grey, not probing your guarded feelings or your past. I don't want to know anything from now on that you don't tell me freely."

"Do you mean that?"

"I mean it. But you have to remember that sometimes not wanting to know isn't sufficient protection. I only can exercise a certain amount of control. I didn't want the knowledge that was revealed in Ivory's gown, and it came to me anyway."

"And what about Graham Denison? Did you come across what I revealed then by accident or design?"

"Design," she admitted.

"You were looking for his murderer?"

"I was looking for *him.*"

Grey looked at her oddly. "You thought I would know?"

"I thought you *were* him."

"That doesn't make any sense."

"No," she sighed. "It doesn't. Not when you have to look at things from your point of view. That would make things rather confusing."

"Incredibly," he said dryly. "Berkeley, you have to strive for some clarity here. You said I bore a surprising likeness to this Mr. Denison."

"You do."

"Can't I assume from that that you've met him?"

"I suppose you can assume anything you like, but it doesn't follow that you'll be right. This time you took a meaning I didn't intend."

"I see that now. And the earring? What was I supposed to understand when you said he'd given it to you 'in a way'?"

"I didn't mean for you to understand at all," she said candidly. "I was being purposely evasive."

"Yes," he said. "You were. Does that mean you're not truly prepared to tell me about Graham Denison?"

Berkeley hesitated. She squeezed his fingers because she could not quite meet his eyes. She knew herself to be a coward. "It means I'm not prepared to tell you anything about myself," she said quietly. She risked a glance at him. "I'm sorry, Grey. I am."

"I'm sorry, too. I'd hoped ..." He touched her chin and brought her eyes back to him. "Perhaps after we're married it will be easier."

Chapter Ten

Nat won the wager. He won because he was the only employee or guest of the Phoenix who thought it would take Grey Janeway an entire week to wear Berkeley down. When asked how he arrived at the winning number for his submission, Nat's answer was simple: He thought God Himself would have needed the seventh day if Miss Shaw had been around to try His patience. Amid the raucous laughter, Nat was very happy to collect three hundred dollars.

Courting in earnest was an exhausting business, Grey decided as he leaned against the bar. First there had been the matter of flowers. He had filled Berkeley's suite with them. He surprised her with carriage rides in the afternoon, theater and opera tickets in the evening, and a Sunday steamer trip up the Sacramento River. Grey had no plan except to keep her so busy she'd marry him simply to get a rest. At the very least she would have to move in with him to make room for the flowers.

Grey followed Berkeley's progress as she wended her way through the crowd toward him. She was stopped several times by guests and gamblers and always spent a moment with each one, but her beautiful eyes invariably darted toward him, seeking him out as if he were her calm in the storm. He thought how odd that was, that she should see him in that light when he rarely experienced the kind of peace she gave him credit for. He found himself straightening at the bar, wanting to go to her. He held back, not certain she really needed or desired to be rescued, and selfishly, because he wanted her to come to him.

Then she was there, standing in front of him, her fingers lightly brushing his hand. "Is everything all right?" she asked, searching his face. His jaw was set, and a muscle worked faintly in his cheek. His eyes radiated intensity.

Grey caught her fingers and drew her inches closer. "Everything's fine," he said deeply. And it was. She was here, with him, and she had come of her own accord. "No regrets."

Berkeley's smile was uncertain. "Are you asking if I have any?" she said. "Or telling me that you did?"

"I was asking."

She glanced behind her. The Phoenix was crowded this evening, but a small protective semicircle had been invisibly drawn around where she and Grey stood. Berkeley felt quite alone with him, quite safe. "No regrets. I held out for seven days because I wanted to be sure." And she had given in because there could be no assurances where Grey was concerned.

"I thought you held out because you wanted Nat to win the pool."

Berkeley's smile was secretive. "You're not going to get me to admit I knew anything about that."

Grey let go of her hand and slipped his own about her waist. "Do you want to go up early this evening?" he asked. "Everyone will understand if you want a few more hours' rest on the eve of your wedding day."

His thoughtfulness touched her. His arm was a warm band at her back, and she was comforted being held by him. "Yes, please. I'd like that."

Grey nodded. "Of course." He released her. It was what she had come to ask him, he realized, and he was glad he had thought of it first. He couldn't help but be aware that she had been tired recently, that she often slept past breakfast and began yawning early in the evening. Most days, until he drew her out, Berkeley kept to her room. It seemed as if she would have been content with that. The flowers, the theater, the carriage rides had all been his idea. She didn't expect it, and Grey saw that she didn't know quite what to make of the attention. Sometimes Grey thought he had overwhelmed her. *Did I wear you down, Berkeley? Or did I wear you out?*

"Grey?" Berkeley asked. "What is it?"

For a moment he wondered if he had given voice to his thoughts. No, he'd said nothing. She'd only seen something in his face, glimpsed his uncertainty. Grey carefully shuttered his expression. A faint smile eclipsed the edgy, uneasy set of his mouth. "Go on," he said. "Use the stairs from the kitchen. It will take the men a little longer to realize you're gone."

Berkeley hesitated, searching his face again. As much as she wanted to leave the hall, she did not really want to leave Grey. Had she been possessed of even a thimble's worth of courage, she would have asked him to come with her, to sit with her until she fell asleep, perhaps even to lie with her, to hold her, touch her, place his lips upon hers, allow her to open her arms, her mouth, all of her body to him. She wanted him like that again. In spite of her gift, Berkeley was much less certain what it was he wanted. Tomorrow afternoon they would be married, and he had never once said that he loved her. Sharing those words had not been part of Grey's strategy to court her. "Good night," she said.

Grey nodded once, then watched her go. For a moment he had half expected that she would ask him to accompany her. Foolish, he told himself now. She hadn't let her guard slip all this long week, if indeed she had been guarded at all. It may have been that she simply didn't love him.

"I'll take that drink now, Sam," Grey said, turning back to the bar. "In fact, just slide the bottle this way."

* * *

Nat stepped outside with a bucket of scraps from the kitchen. Annie Jack's voice carried to him even after the door closed. "Take them all the way to the alley," she yelled. "Annie don't want the dogs nosin' around her kitchen." Dutifully, Nat hopped off the porch and marched across the yard. He was on the point of letting the scraps fly when the bucket was yanked out of his hand and he was hauled upward by the scruff of his neck.

"This way," a voice said close to his ear. "I believe you have some explaining to do."

Berkeley was passing through the kitchen on her way upstairs when Annie flung open the back door and called to Nat to take a second bucket. "That boy," she said to no one in particular. "He can't make it from A to B without losin' his way. Now where'd he go?"

"Can I help you?" Berkeley asked.

Annie eyed Berkeley's ivory gown and her matching kid boots skeptically. "That'd be somethin' to see, you traipsin' across the yard in *that* dress with *these* scraps."

Berkeley took the bucket right out of Annie's hand. "That would be something to see," she said politely. Squeezing past the cook's ample form, Berkeley went as far as the lip of the porch. "Nat! You forgot this other—" She fell silent when she heard some scuffling and a muffled cry from the direction of the stable. She cocked her head. "Nat! Is something wrong? Is there someone with you?"

"I'm coming!" he called.

Behind her, Annie began to say something, but Berkeley waved at her to be quiet. She squinted in the darkness, trying to make out the deeper shadows against the side of the stable. She was preparing to step off the porch when one part of the shadow separated itself from the rest. Her eyes shifted to Nat's small form as he came running toward her. When she looked back toward the stable there was nothing left for her to see.

Nat held out his hand for the bucket. "I'll take it, Miss Shaw."

Berkeley shook her head. "Annie can find someone else. You're coming with me." To be certain he obeyed, she took his outstretched hand. "Now," she said.

Grey saw light seeping from under the door as he approached his room. He couldn't remember leaving a lamp burning, but he supposed he must have. It didn't occur to him that he would find his suite occupied. Berkeley was curled in the large chair next to the fireplace. She had a shawl around her shoulders, and her boots were tucked neatly under the chair. Nat was lying on the sofa, one stockinged foot dangling awkwardly over the side, the other over the arm. Both of them were asleep.

He wondered which one of them had picked the lock, then decided it had been a joint effort, or at least that's the story they would tell. Neither one of them was likely to let the other take full responsibility. Shaking his head, wryly amused, Grey hunkered beside Berkeley's chair and placed one hand over her knee. He whispered her name several times before she finally responded.

"Oh," she said softly. "You're back."

She had a perfectly lovely, drowsy smile to welcome him, and for a moment he was transfixed. He didn't want to ask the obvious question. It came out anyway. "What are you doing here?"

Her sleepy eyes strayed to Nat's prostrate form. "Will you take him to his room? He wanted to wait up for you, to tell you himself, but he's too tired." She pressed back her own yawn by knuckling her mouth. "You won't make much sense of it now. I'll explain everything." She intercepted his skeptical glance. "I promise you'll understand."

"All right. Come with me. You can open his door."

Grey fished Nat's key out of his pocket and gave it to Berkeley. He scooped the boy up in his arms. Nat would have cringed if he had known he was being carried like a young child, but he slept through the walk down the hall and didn't wake even when he was stripped down to his drawers and tucked into bed. Grey watched Berkeley stroke Nat's fair head. She bent and kissed him, then turned back the lamp.

"You're like a mother to him," Grey said when they had stepped out of the room. "He calls you Miss Shaw, but he thinks of you as his mother."

"I know." She glanced at him sideways. "You don't find that objectionable?"

"No. Why?"

"It rather makes him your responsibility as well."

"I accepted that the day you brought him here." Grey opened the door to his room for her and ushered her inside. "He could be our son, you know. His hair. The shape of his face. They're both like yours. He has my eyes, though."

"And your cleverness." She turned on him suddenly, her expression earnest. Her eyes shone, and there was a knot in her throat that gave her voice a vaguely desperate quality. "Can you love him, Grey? As if he were your own? Would you be able to forgive him if he'd done something that could—"

"Berkeley." Grey took her wrists. "What is this? What's wrong? Here, sit down." He drew her over to the sofa. "Do you want something to drink?"

She shook her head as she sat. Her hands slipped out of his, and she stared at them after they came to rest in her lap. "Could you forgive me?"

He touched her chin and raised her face. "I think you'd better explain yourself."

"Nat and I," she began slowly, "we've placed you in danger. Someone's found out about you and Graham Denison." She saw that Grey's features were not cleared in the least by this information. "The man you killed, Grey. Others know now."

Grey's hand dropped away from her face. He slowly let out the breath he'd been holding. Berkeley was quite sincere about what she was saying, but Grey did not accept her alarm. "Who?" he asked calmly. "Who knows?"

"Decker and Colin Thorne."

"I see." Though of course he didn't. "And they would be exactly who?"

Berkeley touched the earring pendant at her throat. She fingered the dangling raindrop of pure gold. "They would be the ones who gave me this earring. They paid for my father and me to come to San Francisco. We were supposed to find Graham Denison for them, but their faith and money was misplaced with us. It was all a hoax on my father's part." Her eyes fell away from his. "No," she said quietly. "That's not entirely true. I was there, helping him carry it out. It was as much my fault that we ended up here as Anderson's."

Grey felt a tightening in his chest. Here were the things she had been unwilling to tell him a week ago and now, on the eve of their wedding, she was revealing them, not because she wanted to, Grey realized, but because she believed she had no choice. "Go on," he heard himself say. It was odd that he should say that, he thought. What he had wanted to do was stop her. "Tell me about the hoax."

"I don't know how my . . . my father first learned about the Thornes. He was very good at finding people who thought they needed him. He never left much to chance. He knew more about Colin and Decker Thorne than they could possibly have imagined, and he knew all of it before we were ever invited to their home in Boston. That's what we did, you see. Made ourselves useful to people, convinced them we could help with some particular task. My father's special talent was making it seem as if it were entirely their idea. My very special talent was . . ." Her voice trailed off. She looked away, her smile mocking and sad. "Well, you know what it was even if you don't quite accept it."

"No," Grey said. "I'm not sure that I do." He stood and went to his sideboard. He had a need for a drink even if Berkeley didn't. He poured himself half a tumbler of whiskey. "What exactly is it that you did for people?"

Berkeley's hands turned over helplessly, almost as if she were at a loss to explain it herself. "Find things, I suppose. That's what most of the work was. Lost family treasures. Missing documents. I authenticated antiques and approved the worth of certain pieces of jewelry. Occasionally I was asked to find a person.''

''And how often did you rely on your talent?'' Grey asked. ''And how often was the outcome determined by Anderson's research?''

Berkeley shrugged. ''I can't really say. He never completely trusted me, but he was more than a bit afraid not to. It was just as well he left so little to chance. I didn't like helping him, and he knew it. Mother was the one who told him I had the gift, but he didn't know if he could believe her. It was a dying confession. It made him doubt her. Still, she was able to extract a promise from him not to abandon me.''

''So he didn't.''

''No,'' she said on a thread of sound. ''He kept me very close.''

Grey studied her profile. Anxiety had made her complexion pale. When she brushed back a corn silk strand of hair he saw a faint throbbing in her temple. His eyes moved to her jaw. The line of it was rigid as she clenched her teeth. ''What else do I need to know, Berkeley?''

She started a little as his voice drew her back to the present. ''Colin and Decker Thorne are brothers,'' she said. ''There's also a third brother, the youngest one. Greydon. They were all separated in London as children, after their parents were murdered, when Greydon was a mere infant. The only clue to his identity is an earring almost identical to the one around my neck. This is a replica that Colin commissioned. The real pair date back to Queen Elizabeth's coronation.'' She saw his skepticism. ''It's true. The earrings now are in Boston with Decker's wife. You may have even heard of her. Jonna Remington.''

Grey lowered his tumbler. ''Remington Shipping? That Remington?''

Berkeley nodded. ''She's the one who first contacted my father. She wanted to help her husband and Colin find Greydon. Anderson Shaw had become known to her, but you musn't think it was serendipitous. My father had been looking for a way to California. He really did have it in his mind that he could become a wealthy man out here. What he required was a sponsor.''

"The Thornes.''

"Exactly. We made a good living from our work. People could be very generous when we were successful in recovering an object or pointing out a fraud. My father, however, had a difficult time holding on to our money. He gambled much of it away.'' *What he didn't drink. What he didn't give to whores.* "There was never enough to suit him. Certainly not enough to buy two passages to California.''

Grey sat in the wing chair. He leaned forward, forearms resting on his knees, and rolled the tumbler between his palms. "So he convinced them to hire you to find Greydon.''

"Almost,'' she said. "The last person known to be in possession of the earring—the real one—was Graham Denison. Decker didn't know about the earring until Graham disappeared. It turned up in the Remington mansion shortly after Graham visited there.''

"So Decker and Graham knew each other.''

"Yes.''

"But Graham's not the brother.''

"No one knows. That's what finding Graham would have helped to determine. He could have explained his connection to the earring.''

Grey was quiet. He stared at the tumbler of whiskey. The slight trembling in his hands caused a ripple across the surface of the amber liquid. "If you had found him,'' he said slowly. "If I hadn't killed him.''

"Yes.'' Berkeley stood long enough to cross to Grey's side. She knelt in front of him and carefully lifted the tumbler and set it aside. She folded her hands around his. "I didn't want to come here,'' she said. "From the beginning I tried to tell Anderson we shouldn't use the Thornes. I knew it before we met them and . . . and afterward I was certain. They're not the sort of men you can cross and expect nothing to come of it.''

"Yet you fell in with your father's plan.''

"It wasn't so simple as saying no to him. You don't know how he was. And you don't understand about my gift. I've explained before that I'm not entirely in control of it. When I met the Thornes and realized how dangerous it would be to make enemies of them, I thought I could manage to get us out of it. But the earrings . . . they were very powerful. Holding them was like wearing Ivory's gown. I couldn't seem to help what I said. I couldn't pretend I didn't feel anything, and I couldn't lie. I told them what I knew: Graham Denison was dead. It was my . . . it was my father who told them what else I tried to say before I fainted. He's the one who said we would find the proof in San Francisco."

"Then you didn't really expect to find Mr. Denison here."

Berkeley shook her head. "I didn't expect to find him *anywhere*. I certainly didn't expect to find his killer here."

Grey slipped his hands out of hers and leaned back in his chair. He sighed heavily. "I *do* wish you'd stop saying that."

"I wish I had never told you. That's how Nat found out. Not because I said anything to him," she added quickly, "but because he overheard me telling you."

"God," Grey said under his breath. "What a mess." He rubbed the back of his stiffening neck. "You may as well tell me the rest of it."

"I wrote to Decker Thorne quite some time ago and informed him of Mr. Denison's death. Of course I could offer no proof and I didn't want to bring your name into it—"

"Thank you," he said dryly.

"So I simply restated what I knew to be true: the search for Greydon Thorne had reached an impasse. Something about my correspondence, perhaps the brevity of it, must have aroused their suspicions. Apparently they're here looking for the earring. I know it's worth a great deal, but it's not one of the heirloom pieces. Colin Thorne had it made with the intent of exposing me as a fraud. I knew it was a fake as soon as I held it. I thought I'd earned this one."

"They may have a different idea."

"I'm realizing that now." Berkeley pulled up a footstool

and sat on that. She hugged her knees and regarded Grey over the top of them. "You can't imagine how wealthy they are, Grey. It seems odd they would want this earring so badly."

Grey was reserving judgment. "How does Nat fit into this?"

"They approached him after they located me at the Phoenix. I can't divine their reasoning, but they wouldn't do it this way without some purpose in mind."

"You're certain it's them?"

"I've never seen them here, but Nat gave me their names."

Grey's brows pulled together slightly. "Go on."

"Remember when Nat disappeared a few weeks ago?"

"Yes."

"At the time I thought he took the earring because he *wanted* me to come after him. He says now that he had it because the Thornes asked for it. They were going to give him a good deal of money for it."

Grey considered this, his flinty stare fixed on a point past Berkeley's shoulder. "Nat had second thoughts?"

"Yes. He decided not to meet with them, and he's stayed close to the Phoenix ever since. That seems to have forced their hand. They came here this evening looking for him."

"They were in the hall tonight?"

"No. Lurking about outside."

One corner of Grey's mouth twitched. Lurking. Berkeley presented an interesting picture. "I take it they managed to get Nat alone."

"Just briefly," she said. "While he was doing a chore for Annie out back. They frightened him. He told them he couldn't get the earring for them any longer. He thought that would be the end of it."

"It's never the end. What did they manage to get out of him? Something about Graham Denison?" Grey knew the truth a moment before he saw it in Berkeley's eyes. "Nat told them I killed Denison."

Berkeley bit her lower lip and nodded. "I told you he'd overheard me talking to you. He didn't mean to tell them, Grey. They frightened him terribly."

Grey thought he knew a little bit about Nathaniel Corbett's developing character. It would take quite a threat to get him to say something so damaging, and Nat himself wouldn't have been the target. "They threatened to hurt you," Grey said. "Nat told them what he did because he was afraid for you."

Tears welled again in Berkeley's eyes. Her voice was raw, pained. "He was asked to make a horrible choice. Please don't blame him."

Grey reached for Berkeley and drew her onto his lap. She didn't resist him. She buried her face against the side of his neck and wept. His fingers sifted through her hair. "I don't blame him," he whispered against her ear. "How could I? He wasn't given a choice, no matter what you think. He loves you. Nat did exactly what I would have wanted him to do."

"He loves you, too."

"He respects me. He might even admire—"

Berkeley raised her head. Her eyes glistened. "It's more than that. You said so yourself. Nat could be our son. He has a son's feelings for you. I know he does. It's why he feels so terrible about what happened this evening."

"All right," he said gently. "But it doesn't change what's been done."

Berkeley impatiently dashed away several tears. "I know that. Nat does, too. We talked about it tonight. Perhaps it would be better if we went away."

"Desert me, you mean."

"No!" She shook her head vehemently. "No, it wouldn't be like that."

"It would be *exactly* like that because that's how I'd feel about it. And I'm not going anywhere. This is my home." He withdrew a handkerchief from his pocket and gave it to her. "Tell me something, Berkeley. When you told me a woman would complicate my life, did you know that you were that woman?"

"I haven't deliberately set about complicating things, if that's what you're thinking."

"I wasn't thinking that at all," he said. "I was wondering if you knew earlier than me that I would come to this."

Berkeley had the handkerchief up to her nose. "Come to what?" She blew inelegantly.

Watching her, Grey's mouth twitched. It was not an auspicious moment to make his declaration, but it did speak eloquently to the perfect madness of what he felt. "That I would come to be this hopelessly in love with you."

Berkeley's mouth sagged a little behind the square of linen. She gathered some measure of poise as she finished using the handkerchief, folded it neatly, and tucked it under the sleeve of her gown. "You might have waited," she said, striving for a dignified tone. "I was not at my best just then."

"No, you weren't, were you?"

"You needn't agree."

Grey's fingers closed around a thick rope of Berkeley's hair. He tugged lightly so that her face was angled toward him. Her beautiful mouth was lifted like an offering. "I find that arguing with you generally serves no purpose."

"Oh."

With that faint expulsion of air Berkeley found her breath was taken away. Grey's mouth covered hers and drew out an immediate response. Her hands went to his shoulders, and she arched into him. Her tongue touched his lips, the ridge of his teeth, and finally was thrust into his mouth. She tasted whiskey and peppermint. She settled herself against him as he murmured her name.

Grey's fingers trailed along the neckline of her gown. He pushed the material farther down her shoulders until her breasts swelled above the satin bodice. He caressed her and felt Berkeley's heart beat fiercely under his palm. She laid her hands over his and held him there a moment, gathering her breath and perhaps a little of her courage. Slowly she lifted herself so the bodice was caught under his thumbs. The fabric inched lower and her breasts swelled in his hands.

She kissed him deeply, moaning at the back of her throat when his fingers circled her nipples. His touch was exquisitely maddening. She couldn't think clearly, but she could react without thinking. Her body seemed to know what to do without any conscious command. Touching him in return came to her as simply as breathing.

A trail of clothes marked the path they took to Grey's bedroom. Her gown in the sitting room. His shirt in the library. A puddle of petticoats indicated a considerable pause by the bedroom fireplace. Trousers. Stockings. A corset. Drawers. They tumbled into bed naked.

Berkeley was stretched out beneath him. He held her wrists lightly. His nose nudged hers as his mouth settled over her lips. He kissed her thoroughly and thought the taste of her was very much as she was, both sweet and tart. The notion made him smile.

Berkeley caught that smile as he drew back. It was more than a little wicked, perhaps just a bit self-congratulatory. She found she didn't mind at all. It was beautiful to her, as he was: proud, perhaps even arrogant, but wonderfully rakish. Gentleman pirate, she thought. And the notion raised her own compelling smile.

Grey watched her with darkening eyes. His voice rasped. "Open for me."

"Yes," she said simply.

Her wrists were released and she circled his neck. Berkeley's thighs parted around him. She raised her knees and lifted her hips. He would find her body was prepared for him, that she was warm and moist and aching to take him in her. She almost cried out when she felt his first slow thrust. Instead she pressed her lips together and closed her eyes.

"Sweet, sweet Berkeley," he whispered. "Still so shy. Let me see you."

Her lashes fluttered as he settled deeply inside her. She searched his face.

"And let me hear you." He began to withdraw. Her tiny moan made him sink himself inside her again. "Just that way," he told her. His mouth hovered above hers. "Just that way."

Berkeley's fingers ran down the muscled ridges of his back.

She felt a tremor go through him that was taken up by her own body. They matched rhythms and heartbeats. The same rush of blood dulled their hearing and made their pulses pound. It was more than the movement inside her. He seemed to move through her.

It would have been the hardest thing she had ever done, not to fall in love with him.

Grey felt Berkeley's inner thighs tighten against his hips. Her feet skittered across his calves. She was sipping the air now, drawing in breath a little at a time as she rose up to meet him. He held himself back waiting for her release, and when it came he gathered her up in his arms and held her tightly, rocking powerfully against her, harder and faster, until his hoarse cry rent the silence.

Berkeley stroked the back of his neck. Her fingertips flicked his dark hair, smoothing the perpetually ruffled strands. She kissed him softly, her lips damp, her mouth warm, as he withdrew. She felt herself contract around him a final time, a movement she couldn't help and wouldn't have wanted to. A shiver caught them both unaware. He closed his eyes as the vibration rippled through him.

Grey lifted himself away from Berkeley and rolled onto his back. His heartbeat slowed. His forearm lay across his eyes. He felt her nudge him with her knee but didn't stir. She wasn't insistent about getting his attention. She didn't seem to require anything but to remain close to him. Grey obligingly let her drape one arm across his chest. The crook of his shoulder cradled her head.

Several minutes passed. He thought she had fallen asleep. He was surprised when she asked softly if he had.

"No," he said. "I'm awake."

"Hmmm."

Grey waited. Berkeley didn't say a thing. "Was there something you wanted?"

"No."

"I see," he said slowly.

She smiled. "No, you don't. You say that when you're confused."

"I see," he said again. "You know me so well."

Berkeley levered herself up on one elbow. "That's *exactly* what I was thinking. But the opposite."

"Exactly the opposite." Grey lifted the arm that covered his eyes and gave her an arch look. "I see."

She poked him in his chest with her index finger and was quite unrepentant when he winced. "It's true," she said. "I know a lot of important things about you, but very little of the details."

"Give me an example."

"I know you're a careful man, for instance. But I don't know where you were born."

"You can't tell by my accent?" he drawled softly.

"It's a practiced accent. You know it is. Soft as honey one moment, clipped and cool in another. Very deliberate. You could be a plantation aristocrat or a Yankee trader."

"Perhaps I'm both."

"Are you?"

Grey frowned a little. "You know what I am, Berkeley. I operate a gaming house and hotel. I own some prime San Francisco real estate I plan to develop someday, and I have shares in the railroad ventures. That makes me a businessman, as dull and steady as all the other bankers and merchants in the city. You're right. I'm a careful man."

"And you were born . . ."

"On a ship," he said.

Berkeley's leaf green eyes widened a little. "On a ship," she repeated softly.

He nodded. "In the Middle Atlantic a few hundred miles from Charleston. I've been to harbors in London and Paris. Boston. Shanghai. Buenos Aires. Rome. I grew up on that ship. Perhaps that explains my accent."

"I suppose," Berkeley said, not entirely convinced. "Your parents weren't simply passengers then."

"No. They weren't passengers."

Berkeley waited for him to elaborate. When he didn't, she didn't press. "How did you come to San Francisco?"

"Chance. Our hull was damaged by a whale. We had to put ashore, and this is where we limped in. News of the gold strike had just reached the cove. The tents and shanties were almost all deserted. Our ship was the first one abandoned in the bay."

"So you didn't really have any choice about staying."

"Not much. It didn't matter. This is where I wanted to be. I struck a small vein of gold early on. I took what I could get at easily, then sold the claim to some men willing to break their backs for the rest of it. I came back here and saw the possibilities of making a real fortune. My first gaming house was on that ship."

"Is she still out there?"

Grey shook his head. "No, she burned. I saved her figure-head."

"Rhea."

"That's right. I've managed to save that lady in spite of two fires destroying just about everything else."

"I've heard about the fires," she said. "I arrived just after the last one. I never could have imagined anything like that. Donnel said it took most of the city."

"He's right. The rebuilding begins as soon as the debris cools."

"That's why you call this place the Phoenix. You've built her from the ashes."

Grey wound a lock of Berkeley's hair around his fingers. "Come here," he said quietly. He hardly had to tug at all. Berkeley leaned over him and placed her lips warmly over his. He kissed her a very long time. She seemed to melt into his side. Her head came to rest on his shoulder again. Grey was comfortable with that.

"You'll spend the night here," he said.

"What's left of it."

"And you'll be here in the morning."

"Yes, Grey," she said dutifully. "I'll be here."

He glanced down at the crown of her gold-and-platinum hair.

He wasn't entirely certain of her, especially since she'd made noises about leaving him. "What about Nat?"

"He'll be there, but you'll have to talk to him before then. He needs to understand you don't blame him for what he's done."

Grey was very clear on his need to talk to Nat. "I'm not convinced that he's done anything. At least not with the Thornes."

Berkeley's eyes lost their sleepy appeal. "What do you mean by that?"

"I don't have it all worked out yet," he told her. "There are some things that don't make sense to me." His fingers trailed lightly across her naked shoulder. "Why would these men not confront you themselves? Why use Nat?"

"I don't know."

"And if I bear some resemblance to this Graham Denison, as you say I do, then wouldn't Decker Thorne be curious about me? You said I was his friend."

"Perhaps the resemblance is only in my eye. Captain Thorne might see none at all. I've only seen a newspaper sketch."

"Possibly. It's not so important as the earring itself. If it's really a replica, why would they want it back so badly?"

At first Berkeley thought he was doubting her. She closed her fist around the earring. "It *is* the replica."

"I believe you," Grey said gently.

It took Berkeley a moment to hear what he was saying, to hear the absolute conviction in his quietly spoken words. "I'm sorry. I wasn't sure you . . ." She raised her head and looked at him. It was there in his eyes, his frank acceptance and his willingness to wait her out until she was satisfied. "Captain Thorne almost dared me to choose one of the others," she said at last. "I knew what Anderson wanted me to do, and I chose this one anyway."

"Did you ever tell him?"

"No. I wasn't that foolish. He thought it was the one that should have been Greydon's."

Grey considered that. "Do you think he might have told anyone about it?"

Berkeley understood immediately where Grey's thoughts were headed. "Like one of the Sydney Ducks, you mean? Perhaps even the man who killed him?"

Grey nodded. "We don't know much about the fight that ended in his death. It's not beyond all possibility that your father talked about the earring. He may have promised it as collateral against a gambling debt."

"And when he couldn't produce it . . ." It wasn't necessary to finish. It was all too much like Anderson Shaw to have engaged in a game where he couldn't match the stakes. He had paid with his life. "There may be other reasons he told someone."

"Dozens probably. It doesn't matter why, only that he might have."

"You think the men who threatened Nat are Ducks?"

He nodded. "I told you once they could come after me . . . they just never figured how. Now there's Nat and there's you. They must know they can hurt me through both of you."

Berkeley didn't say anything. She had come to a similar conclusion.

Grey felt her stillness. She might as well have telegraphed her thoughts to him. "Stop it," he said. "You're not responsible for what they do. Neither is Nat. The last thing I want either of you to do is think you're protecting me by disappearing. Do I have to ask you again if you'll be at my wedding tomorrow?"

She turned her head to look at him. "Perhaps we should consider putting the wedding off a few weeks. Nat and I could go somewhere, and you could settle this with the Ducks. You wouldn't be vulnerable because of us."

"Not vulnerable at all," he said dryly. "I would be out of my head wondering if the two of you were safe."

"Nat and I could manage."

"Listen to me, Berkeley: *I couldn't.*"

Berkeley sat up. She touched the side of Grey's beautifully

angled face with her fingertips. Her voice was slightly awed. "You mean that, don't you? We've become necessary."

"How can you not have known?"

"Because I was afraid," she said softly. "It's not so easy to look into someone else's heart when you're afraid of what's in your own."

"I know." He took her hand and kissed her fingertips. "And now? Are you still afraid?"

"A little."

"So am I."

Berkeley blinked. She hadn't expected that.

Grey's hands closed over hers. "Loving you is outside my experience, Berkeley. It's like diving into a breaking wave. I don't know if I'm going to be crushed or carried. I don't know if I've waited too long or jumped too soon. I don't know until I'm in it." The planes and angles of his face softened as he watched Berkeley's shy glance evade him. "You might want to say something here," he prompted gently.

Berkeley stared at Grey's large hand enclosing hers. "Everything about you is beyond my experience," she said at last. "Not just loving you. Your kindness. Your decency. Your strength. I'm afraid I'll be a poor sort of partner for someone like you. I can be petty, you know. Perfectly jealous. And I'm not decent. You know I'm not. The games here at the Phoenix are more honest than anything Anderson and I have ever done. I've lied to you and I've been unfair, but mostly I've been an irritant. I came with a cat and found a boy and nearly got one of your men killed. I've brought the Ducks to your door and I don't—"

He kissed her. Thoroughly.

Berkeley found her hands resting on his shoulders when he drew back. She stared at him through eyes that were slightly dazed. "And I don't know that I could ever leave you," she whispered.

"Good." He paused a beat. "I did hear you say you loved me, didn't I?"

"With all my heart." Berkeley smiled when she saw both

relief and satisfaction expressed in his features. She leaned into him and laid her mouth across his. He offered no resistance to her overture. His arms slipped around her back, and he drew her closer.

They both dived headlong into the breaking wave.

Nat spit on his fingers, then used them to flatten the stubborn cowlick at the crown of his hair. He grimaced when the effect was less than he hoped for.

"Try this," Grey said. He handed the boy a small jar of pomade from his bureau. "A bit goes a long way. Use it sparingly." Standing behind his little best man, Grey watched Nat in the mirror. He nodded approvingly as Nat took less than a fingernail's amount of the fragrant cream and dabbed it over the offending stem of hair. "Just so. Here, take this comb and run it through."

Nat's eyes lifted gratefully as he accepted the comb. "You're a good one, Mr. Janeway, helping me out like you have. I know it's because you don't want me to embarrass you and all, but I sure do appreciate it. Truth is, I wouldn't want to make a bad show of it today. Sam says spit and polish is what's called for."

Grey touched Nat's shoulder lightly. "And you have plenty of both." He took back the pomade and set it aside, then he lifted the comb from Nat's hand and straightened the boy's part. The cowlick disappeared. "As for embarrassing me, that's not possible. You've already shown considerable courage by not running off this morning."

"I wanted to. I thought you'd be angry."

"Not at you, Nat. Only at the men who are using you to get to me. You can be proud that you told Miss Shaw the truth last night and that you stayed to tell me the same."

Nat ducked his head but not before Grey glimpsed his small, pleased smile. "Thank you, sir."

Grey ruffled Nat's hair.

"Sir!" Nat clamped his hands over his head, protecting it from another surge of Grey's affection.

It took a mighty effort on Grey's part not to laugh. Young Nat's hair was a veritable garden of shoots, strands of hair sprouting in every direction. Dutifully he smoothed it all back in place with the comb. "There. You're quite turned out." He straightened the shoulders of Nat's black jacket and patted the collar. "And handsome. I don't suppose you'll have any trouble finding a dance partner at the reception."

A flush touched Nat's cheeks. "You think Miss Shaw will dance with me?"

Grey turned Nat away from the mirror, then hunkered down to be at eye level. "I think I couldn't stop her," he said. "Do you know Miss Shaw told me once that I would have four children?"

Nat's narrow face puckered in a vague frown. "I didn't know that, sir."

"Well, she did. And she also insisted that there was another child. One that was mine and yet not mine. She said I would have a child who wasn't mine."

Nat's frown deepened. "She says some odd things, Miss Shaw does. You shouldn't take it—"

"She was talking about you, Nat. She didn't know it at the time, but she was talking about you. Miss Shaw said I would marry the mother of the son who wasn't mine. She's that woman, and you're that son."

"I don't know what she's been tellin' you, Mr. Janeway, but Miss Shaw's not my mother."

"I know that," he said. "She makes it a bit complicated, but I find that she's usually right. She was telling me I would think of you as my son. That's what's come to pass, Nat. I think of you in exactly that way."

Nathaniel Corbett sucked in one side of his cheek and worried it between his teeth. He bit down a little harder so he had an excuse for the tears welling up in his eyes. "I didn't want to come to the Phoenix," he said.

Grey smiled. "Miss Shaw made you?"

"She grabbed me by the arm and marched me across six blocks to bring me here. Do you know what she told me, Mr. Janeway?"

Grey shook his head.

"She said you had a tender heart for throwaways."

Grey's head tilted to one side. "Stowaways, you mean?"

"No." Nat gave his head a vigorous shake. "Throwaways. Like me. Like her. People that don't matter to anybody else. She said they mattered to you, that *we* would matter to you."

"And so you do," Grey said quietly. "I told you, Miss Shaw's usually right." He stood, his very tender heart recovering its normal rhythm slowly. He cleared his throat, his voice a bit hoarse. "Do you have the ring?"

Nat patted himself down until he felt the familiar shape of the ring in his vest pocket. "Yes, sir. Right here. Would you like to see it?"

"No. Keep it there and keep it safe."

"I will." Nat glanced over his shoulder at the clock. "Don't you think we should be going downstairs? Seems like we should get there before Miss Shaw."

Grey laughed. "An excellent notion."

The gathering in the gaming hall was a small one. Sam Hartford was there. So were Donnel and Shawn. Annie had just hurried in from the kitchen and was still out of breath. Berkeley had balked at the idea of exchanging vows with Grey in front of all and sundry. The reception was open to anyone who wanted to wish them well, but the ceremony was meant for those close enough to be family.

The Reverend Amos Watkins had no objection to performing the service in the gaming house. He'd had three churches destroyed by quakes and fires and his current meeting place was a large canvas tent that yawed uneasily with the winds. For the amount Grey was going to donate to the building fund, the good Reverend was willing to yaw a little himself. The Phoenix would do just fine.

Grey was speaking to the minister, Nat close by his side, when he felt the attention of those around him shift. He followed the path of their collective interest until his eyes came to rest on Berkeley.

He smiled. She didn't seem to notice that she was holding them captive. She had lifted the hem of her gown a few inches and was carefully making her way down the steps. Sam rushed to the staircase and in three mighty strides heaved himself up beside her to offer his elbow. She seized it gratefully and faltered only when she realized she was the object of all of their attention.

Berkeley sought out Grey, and it was like stepping into sunshine. She basked in the warmth she saw in his eyes. The last of her doubts melted, and she wondered that she had had them at all. It would be fine. *This* would be fine. What other course could her life have taken but this one? Hadn't she always known this end was inevitable?

Grey's eyes moved over Berkeley's spare figure as she approached him. Seed pearls that gave luster to the combs in her hair also illuminated the bodice of her gown. Satin and lace shimmered, and the contrasting textures rustled lightly as she stepped forward. Her complexion glowed. Save for the pendant earring she wore at her throat, her neck and shoulders were splendidly bare. The gown's tightly fitting sleeves gave her porcelain elegance; the length of her from wrist to shoulder was smooth and gracefully curved. Her unusual, otherworldly aura had not had full expression until now. She didn't seem quite real to him. Berkeley did not merely radiate light; she was its source.

Grey welcomed the first touch of her fingers as her hand brushed his. She was not insubstantial at all but flesh and bone and beauty. She could be held in his hand, in his arms, against his side.

He wondered then at the odd tremor that suddenly tripped his heart.

Chapter Eleven

Berkeley darted Grey an uncertain glance. He was staring straight ahead, unmoved in any outward way by what he had experienced. He was pretending as though he didn't know he had just shared her premonition, yet he was fairly vibrating with the force of what she felt. The heartbeat she heard in her ears wasn't only her own. Grey's blood seemed to thrum through her veins.

The minister was speaking to her. She saw his mouth opening and closing with crisp precision, but Berkeley could not make out a single word or any sense of the whole. Every sound reached her vaguely distorted. Panic and dread were tangible forces that roiled through her. The knot in her stomach went as high as her throat and lodged there.

She felt Grey's eyes on her, and when she looked at him she saw that his expression was merely expectant. He didn't seem afraid. He wasn't accusing or concerned. There was a hint of a smile about his mouth that was both indulgent and encouraging. Berkeley wondered that he could project such a calm presence when she was on the verge of collapse.

The Reverend Amos Watkins shifted his spindly frame and

his attention to Grey. Berkeley swayed a little on her feet as her hand was being lifted. Nat was there suddenly, extending his own hand, dangling a ring between his thumb and forefinger. He was looking up at her, his mouth set in a solemn smile befitting the occasion. Berkeley's glimpse of him was brief as he ducked behind Grey again. The gold ring in Grey's hand was left to mark the completion of his duty.

Grey spoke to her as he slipped the band over her finger. Out of the corner of her eye Berkeley saw the minister nod approvingly. In the other direction Donnel, Sam, and Shawn were grinning while Annie Jack clutched her handkerchief.

It was over with a kiss. Or perhaps it had begun with one. Berkeley couldn't be sure. She found herself in the circle of Grey's arms, and his head was being lowered while her face was raised. His mouth was gentle on hers, reverent and somehow very sweet. When he drew back she was aware her vision of him was not quite as clear as before, that his features shimmered in and out of focus, and that he seemed to waver on his feet. It was the first she understood that her eyes were wet with tears.

Grey found a scrap of linen and lace folded neatly beneath the fitted wrist of Berkeley's gown. "Something old?" he asked, pressing it into her hand.

She gave him a watery smile. "Something new. A gift from Annie." Berkeley dabbed at her eyes and tucked the handkerchief away before turning to face the witnesses. Sam's eyes looked suspiciously wet, and Shawn was blinking rapidly. Donnel Kincaid's fiery brows were drawn together, and he was staring at the floor.

Annie Jack stepped out of the semicircle and wrapped her arms around Berkeley. "This only proves Annie was right all along about your powers," she said. "You put a spell on Mr. Janeway pure and simple. You'll never convince Annie it was anythin' else."

"I wouldn't try."

Grey was still chuckling when Annie took his hand and pumped it fiercely. "Mark my words, Mr. Janeway. You do right by your wife or there will be hell to pay. Pardon Annie's cussin', Reverend, but some things got to be said so there's no mistakin' their meaning."

"I understand, Annie." Grey drew back his hand and laid it lightly on her shoulder. He kissed her on the cheek and brought a flush to her coffee-colored skin.

"Mind yourself," she said, wagging a finger at him. "Annie don't want trouble with Miz Berkeley herself."

When Annie stepped aside the others moved forward, offering kisses and congratulations, and in the case of Sam Hartford, an approving aside about Berkeley's wedding finery. Only Nat hung back. He had seen Pandora slinking along the foot rail during the ceremony and at his earliest opportunity he had cornered her. Now he stood by the mahogany bar clutching the cat and wondering if he could put any stock in what Grey Janeway had told him that morning.

Berkeley made a subtle gesture with her chin and eyes in Nat's direction. Grey followed it and saw the boy leaning against the bar pretending to enjoy holding the squirming, clawing cat in his arms. Separating himself from the gathering around Berkeley, Grey walked over to Nat.

"I think you saved the day," Grey said. "Remembering the ring *and* keeping Pandora from destroying Berkeley's gown."

Nat's head lifted. "You think so?"

"Oh, I'm certain of it. The cat's been eyeing Miss Shaw like she's a saucer of cream."

Nat's eyes darted toward Berkeley. The seed pearls in her bodice glowed. "She's a bucket of it, sir."

"Exactly." Grey gingerly separated cat from boy. "Perhaps you could go over there and wish her happy. I'll keep Pandora away from all that satin and lace froth." He gave Nat an encouraging nod and watched the boy trot off obediently before he released Pandora up the stairs. By the time he rejoined the group Nat was looking quite cheerfully at ease at Berkeley's side. Grey found himself satisfied with that.

Annie Jack and her assistants had prepared a wedding supper for the bride and groom and selected guests and a feast for all the well-wishers who would come when the Phoenix opened its doors that evening. Roast beef, salmon, trout, golden potato medallions, carrots, peas, and mushrooms, sourdough rolls, salads and sauces and raspberry ices were carried out and laid along the length of the bar and replenished by a parade of servers. The gaming house was transformed into a banquet hall with a fountain of punch which no one touched and a dozen kegs of beer that were tapped out before midnight.

There was no one who wasn't welcome at the Phoenix. Berkeley and Grey, with Nat beside them, greeted everyone who came through the wide double doors. Some came with the express intention of extending their best wishes, others because word that drinks were on the house and all bets were off was a message difficult to resist. The music was lively and the dancing was energetic. The women in attendance never lacked for partners. Neither did Nat. Twice Berkeley made Grey rescue him from the crush of generous breasts. It was when she sent him into the fray a third time that Grey escorted the tired, but very happy boy up to his room and tucked him in for the night.

"Buckets of cream," Nat whispered sleepily as he turned on his side. "Every one of them."

Grey chuckled softly and drew the covers over Nat's shoulders. "Exactly," he agreed. Grey looked down at his feet when he felt the familiar press of fur against his legs. He scooped Pandora up, scratched her under the neck, then placed her on the bed beside Nat. She nestled in the crook of the boy's thin arm and gave Grey a look that said she was in charge now.

Berkeley was no longer among the hundreds of guests in the gaming hall when Grey returned. He felt her absence almost immediately. He stood on the stairs, scanning the swirling figures on the dance floor, the throngs at the bar, the press of bodies near the entrance, and she was at the center of none of them. He looked for her in the kitchen and on the back porch. He offered to bring up a case of liquor from the basement simply to have an excuse to look for her there.

No one seemed to realize she was missing, or at least no one offered to tell him where she had gone. Grey stepped outside the Phoenix and into the open courtyard of Portsmouth Square. The night was unusually warm for so late in the year but Grey saw men walking with their shoulders hunched and collars lifted as if they were experiencing something far different.

Grey stood on the lip of the sidewalk while his eyes moved around the square. In the moonlight Berkeley's gown would have shone like a beacon. She hadn't come this way to remove herself from the heat and stale air of the gaming hall. Still, he stepped off the sidewalk and began walking away from the Phoenix, drawn toward the center of the square by something he could neither identify nor define. It was only when he reached the middle and realized that indeed, there was nothing there, that he turned and finally saw what he was seeking.

Berkeley stood on the balcony outside his sitting room. Her arms were braced on the balustrade, and she leaned forward, her posture a mix of anticipation and defiance. Her hair had been released from the pearl-encrusted combs and was lifted on the back of a warm breeze.

She could have been Rhea, the exquisitely lovely and proud figurehead of the *Lady Jane Grey*.

His heart tripped again when he saw her move away from the balustrade. It was everything he had felt when he took her hand at the beginning of the wedding ceremony, and ten times more. Blood roared in his ears, and his heartbeat slammed against his chest. He began running toward the Phoenix, his breathing labored even before he hit his stride. It took him minutes longer to make his way back through the crowd once he was in the hall. Now it seemed that everyone knew he was trying to get to Berkeley, and they all thought they knew why. Grey had no choice but to accept their good-natured teasing and suggestions about how he should proceed with his wedding night. His progress to the staircase was marked by improvised percussion. Hands solidly clapped his back, and glasses of beer were thumped loudly on tabletops. Miners applied their large boots rhythmically against the floor in a foot-stomping serenade that vibrated the hall.

The Phoenix erupted into enthusiastic applause when Grey finally reached the top of the stairs. He did not stop to acknowledge it.

The warm breeze that had met him in Portsmouth Square now circulated through his apartment. The balcony doors were wide-open. Drapes fluttered at the windows on either side. Lamplight flickered. A small, mostly ornamental fire had been laid in the grate. Slim fingers of orange-and-yellow flames wound around the kindling. They almost disappeared until the night air breathed life into them again.

Grey closed the door behind him. The drapes, the lamplight, the fingers of flame all stilled. Then Berkeley was there, in the center of the balcony, framed by the open doors as if she had been captured on canvas.

He went to her.

His worst fears were realized when she took a step back.

"Berkeley." His voice was hoarse and almost without sound. She did not regard him with the wariness she would have reserved for a stranger, but with the contempt that was due a liar. "I can explain."

"Who are you?"

"Please. Come inside. We can talk there."

She ignored him and stayed her ground. "I've seen Rhea. I've seen the inscription below her. You should have had it sanded away when you brought her here. It's too obvious to be a mere coincidence." She gathered the slender threads of her composure and asked him again, "So tell me, who *are* you?"

"Grey Janeway."

Berkeley took another step backward, unsatisfied with his answer. Her thighs struck the heavy stone balustrade, and she was brought up short. Her eyes darted to her left, and she pointed to the ship's figurehead mounted not far from the edge of the balcony. "It's from the ship where you were born," she said.

"Yes. I told you that."

"But not all of it. You were being evasive and clever when you said that. You didn't tell me *when* you were born."

He told her now. "Five and a half years ago." Grey reached for her, but she twisted sideways and eluded his outstretched arm. He made no attempt to follow when she went toward the figurehead.

Moonlight lent Rhea's perfect features a blue cast. She could have been sculpted in granite, not wood. Berkeley gave her back to Grey and turned toward the goddess. She was careful not to look down as she stretched out over the balustrade and touched one of Rhea's curving locks. Her fingers slipped across the warm, smoothly polished shoulder. Berkeley's eyes fell to the ornate script carved below the figurehead's breasts. It was not the goddess's name, but the name of the ship that had carried her.

Lady Jane Grey.

Berkeley let her arm fall back and she stepped away from the rail. She didn't turn to look at Grey, but she knew he was just behind her now. "Grey Janeway is a name," she said quietly. "Not who you are."

"Then you have no cause to be angry with me. You know who I am."

She shook her head. "You deceived me."

"No, I didn't. Or at least no more than I've deceived myself."

"You're Graham Denison."

"It's only a name."

Berkeley hugged herself. Cornered, her back still to him, she had nowhere to go when Grey's fingers lightly traced the curve of her bare shoulder. "Why couldn't you tell me?" she whispered. "You let me think you murdered him. Why did it have to be a secret?"

Grey's hand slipped under the silky fall of her hair. His thumb rubbed gently up and down her sensitive nape. He felt tension cord the slender muscles in her neck. "Because I don't know the truth of it myself," he said. "If I was Graham Denison, he has nothing to do with my life now." He eased her around and now his thumb pressed upward on the thrust of her small chin. "Do you understand, Berkeley? I didn't tell you because I don't know if it's true, and if it's true, it doesn't matter."

"How can that be?"

Grey could tell she wanted to believe him. Her eyes were wide and clear as she stared up at him. It was her mouth that hinted at her misgivings. It trembled. He bent his head and touched his lips to hers. There was more promise than substance in the kiss, but it was enough. He felt her still. Her hands dropped to her sides, and she breathed softly and evenly. When he drew back her face was raised and her eyes were closed.

"Come inside," he said. "Please."

Berkeley opened her eyes slowly. "You know I'm afraid."

"Yes."

"Since this afternoon, at the moment you touched my hand, I felt a threat I couldn't name. I thought you would be torn from me, from my heart. I thought it started with you, and I imagined you felt it as strongly as I did. Was I wrong, Grey?"

He didn't admit it immediately. He would have liked to have told her the explanation lay in their own apprehension as they faced the minister, but he couldn't belittle what she had sensed with a lie. He hadn't been afraid of what they would face together, only that he might face it apart from her. "I felt *something.*"

"Do you think this is what it was?"

"I hope so." He cupped the side of her face when she frowned. "Because it's nothing. When you hear me out, you'll know it doesn't have to threaten us at all."

She leaned her cheek into his hand and held it in place with her own. After a moment she signaled her readiness by kissing the heart of his palm. Berkeley lowered his hand and threaded her fingers through his. She led him into the sitting room.

Grey closed the balcony doors while Berkeley laid a small log on the fire. He sat on the sofa, but she took the wing chair, perching on the edge with her hands lying open in her lap. She looked as if a drink wouldn't come amiss, but he didn't offer, knowing that she would refuse. He realized his eyes must have strayed toward the sideboard because she was on her feet suddenly. Without a word of her intention she poured two fingers of bourbon in a crystal tumbler and carried it over to him.

He didn't think she could possibly know how much he loved her. "Thank you," he said, accepting the glass.

Berkeley returned to the chair. This time she sat back far enough to curl her legs under her. Her gown spilled over the edge like a cascade of white water. She touched the pendant at her throat. "You told me you didn't recognize this."

His eyes fell to the earring. "I don't. As far as I know I've never seen it before. I haven't lied to you, Berkeley, not in the manner you think. I took my name from the *Lady Jane Grey*. She was a clipper registered to the Asbury Line out of London. I was a member of her crew from '45 until she was abandoned in San Francisco Bay."

"Graham Denison disappeared in 1845. In the spring, I think."

"It was April when I began my service."

"He was sailing with a Remington clipper. *Siren*. He disembarked in Philadelphia, then . . ." She shrugged helplessly.

"*Lady Jane Grey*'s port of call before I joined her was Charleston. I don't know anything about a Remington clipper."

"I don't understand," said Berkeley. "How can you *not* know?"

"Because I simply have no memory of any part of my life before I awoke on *Jane Grey*." One corner of his mouth lifted in a wry smile. Berkeley was sitting at attention now, her features a mixture of curiosity and disbelief. "It happens, I'm told. I'm not the first person to suffer this affliction. I've talked to one London physician about it, someone who's made a study of amnesia. That was a few years ago and more than eighteen months after I came aboard *Jane Grey*. He gave me no assurances that I would recover what I'd lost. There was nothing much he could tell me at all."

"But how does it happen?"

"Some injury to the head provokes it."

Berkeley's eyes lifted to the crown of Grey's head. She made a thorough examination, as if the damage done to him might still be visible. "You appear perfectly fine to me."

Grey's smile was wry. "Thank you for that, but it's nothing you can see. There's no wound to speak of."

"How were you hurt?"

He hesitated, uncertain he wanted her to know.

"Please don't lie to me, Grey," Berkeley said. "What can be the harm if I know the truth?"

"I was beaten," he said finally.

Berkeley's mouth parted fractionally. It wasn't at all what she expected to hear. "Beaten? By whom?"

Grey shrugged. "I have no memory of it, Berkeley. The bruises I wore for nearly a month afterward suggest that more than one man took part and fists weren't the only weapons used. The beating took place in Charleston harbor, not on the clipper. I learned later that I was taken aboard *Jane Grey* by two of her crew. They happened upon the fight and frightened off my assailants." He raised the tumbler of bourbon in a mocking salute to his rescuers, then he knocked back a mouthful. "At least that's what they always told me."

"You don't believe them?"

"No," he said quietly. "I never believed them. Sheffield and Hanks were not inclined to put themselves out for anyone. Knowing them as I came to, the notion that they acted in my defense is hardly likely. I never saw any evidence that they were the thugs who beat me, but I think they were paid to take me aboard *Jane Grey*. I also think that if it hadn't been for my memory loss, I would have been met with an accident at sea. As it was, they saw no purpose in killing me. I presented no threat to them or the men who insisted on my disappearance. By the time we reached London, they were quite sure of that. Rather than bring any suspicion down on their heads, they elected to let me keep mine."

"You told me once the clipper had been abandoned here. Does that mean those two men are in San Francisco?"

"No. They left the ship in London five years ago. I've never seen them again. I imagine they were paid rather handsomely for getting me away from Charleston. There was no reason for them to stay with *Lady Jane Grey.*"

"And you were satisfied with that?" asked Berkeley.

"I was." One corner of his mouth lifted in a wry smile. "Oh, I see. You think I should have forced some answers from them. Perhaps do the same turn to them that was done to me." Grey shook his head. "The truth is, I was glad to see them gone. Trying to force answers from them would have most likely resulted in my untimely death, not theirs. I wasn't all that well healed by the time we reached London. I managed enough work to keep the ship's master from tossing me overboard, but I was in no position to act on my suspicions about Sheffield and Hanks."

Berkeley believed that was only part of the truth. "You didn't want to know," she said quietly.

Grey didn't answer immediately. He finished his bourbon and set the crystal tumbler aside. "No," he said. "I didn't. Can you appreciate that?" He didn't wait for her response. "Do you think I haven't wondered why someone would want me dead or, at the very least, out of the way? Hardly a day passes that I haven't considered it. Did I hurt someone? Did I pose a threat? Perhaps I had gambling debts. Perhaps I was a thief. I don't presume I was innocent in what happened, Berkeley, and neither should you. I may well have deserved what was done to me. I could have wronged someone. A woman. A partner. A friend. That's what I didn't want to know. If it was revenge that led to my beating, then I was willing to let it be."

"And if it wasn't? Your past was taken from you, Grey. What about your family? Didn't you ever think that someone deserved to know what had happened to you?"

"Of course I thought about it. Over the years I learned enough to know there were never any inquiries made out of Charleston. No one there was trying to find me, not in any obvious way. There were no rewards offered. More attention was given to runaway slaves. No one was looking for anyone matching my description.''

"That's not true," she said. "The Thornes were looking for you. But you're correct in that their search was not conducted in any obvious way. They were paying for the discretion of their investigators. Decker and Jonna Thorne recognized there were some reasons for you to desire anonymity. They were trying to honor that while attempting to find you for their own purposes.''

"We don't know that I'm Graham Denison. And if I am, what does it matter? There's nothing I can do to help the Thornes now. I certainly can't identify that earring. If they expect I can lead them to the youngest brother, then they're sadly out of it there.'' Grey rubbed the back of his neck. Tension had corded the muscles. He felt the beginnings of a blinding headache.

Berkeley watched the grooves deepen at the corners of his mouth. He looked weary suddenly, and she recognized it was pain giving his eyes their cool, distancing look. She stood and extended her hand. He didn't seem to know what to make of her offer at first, then he stood himself and placed his hand in hers. She led him into the bedroom.

After lighting the lamps, Berkeley helped him out of his jacket and loosened the collar of his shirt. "Sit there," she said, pointing to the bed. "I'll only be a minute." She disappeared into the adjoining dressing room.

Grey was pulling off his shoes and stockings when she returned. He frowned a little when he saw she was wearing her nightshift. "I would have helped you out of your wedding gown," he said. "In fact, I was rather looking forward to it.''

Berkeley took the shoe he was dangling from the end of his index finger and placed it beside the other. "I'm sure you were," she said. She knelt in front of him, removed his sock, and dropped it inside his shoe. "Lie back.''

Grey scooted backward and stretched out. His eyes closed immediately. He felt Berkeley crawl onto the bed beside him. His head was gingerly raised and laid on her lap. He heard himself actually sigh when her fingertips began massaging his temples. "It was so obvious, was it?" he asked, referring to his headache.

"You were white around the mouth," she said. "Do you get the headaches often?"

"No, not often."

"Another good reason, I suppose, not to call up the past."

Grey looked up at her, surprised that she had divined the connection.

"That's what brought this on, isn't it? Or have I mistaken the matter?"

He closed his eyes again as her fingers pressed against his scalp. "You're not wrong," he said tiredly. "It's always been this way. Sometimes I think I'm on the point of remembering something, then there will be a flash of hot, white light behind my eyes. The recollection, if there was one to be had, is gone in the explosion."

"So there's nothing," she said. "Nothing at all that you remember."

"Not exactly. It's when I try to dredge up my past that I'm rewarded with this pain. You're right that I don't like to try very often. But there are occasions when it seems as though a memory slips through. I can't predict it or even account for it fully. I believe that it has something to do with what I'm engaged in at the time. As if I'm going through the motions of some activity I've done before." There was a heaviness in Grey's shoulders as tension seeped out of him. Berkeley's fingers ruffled the fringe of hair across his forehead. She touched his cheek. "The first night I stood with you on the stairs, introducing you to the crowd in the gaming hall, I had a sense that I had done something like it before. It was a glimpse into my past. Nothing more. It only lasted a few seconds. There have been other moments like that over the years."

"Tell me about them."

"There's not much to tell. I was sitting in a Paris brothel once, playing whist with the madam, when I was struck by that sense of repetition."

Berkeley tugged on his hair. "You might have spared me that one."

Grey drew her hand to his mouth and kissed her. "It was only once."

"And you were only there to play cards."

"That's right." He risked a peek at her and caught her trying to tamp down her smile. Grey let her withdraw her hand. Her fingers returned to his scalp. "When I was drawing up the plans for the Phoenix there was something about it that was familiar to me."

"You mean the act of designing?" she asked. "Or the plans themselves?"

"The plans."

"Perhaps this hotel is very much like the house you lived in."

"I thought of that. I don't know. I suppose it could be. Or perhaps I always lived in hotels."

"Graham Denison comes from Southern aristocracy. His family has money, land, and privilege that predates the Revolution by a hundred years."

"Have you ever seen his home?"

"No. I was never a visitor to Beau Rivage. My family moved away from Charleston when I was six. In any event, we weren't likely to have been invited to one of the parties the Denisons, or any other of the plantation owners gave. My mother wouldn't have been welcome."

"Why not?"

"She was a reminder of how far one of their own could fall from grace."

Grey opened his eyes and stared up at her. "What do you mean?" But he knew the answer. Suddenly it was very clear to him.

Berkeley saw it in his face. "My mother and father weren't married," she said. "Anderson Shaw was my stepfather."

Grey wondered that he hadn't realized it before. There had always been a hesitation on Berkeley's part when she spoke of Anderson Shaw. Had she thought he would care she was a bastard? "And your mother? Who was she?"

"Virginia Lerner. She was born at Summerfield, west of the city. The plantation was old and relatively profitable. She was the youngest of four. All girls. My mother was a disappointment, she told me once, from the moment of her birth. She was supposed to have been a boy, you see, and spent most of her growing-up years pretending she could be one. Then at sixteen she committed her one unforgivable act of rebellion."

"She became pregnant."

"That was only part of it. She refused to name the father of her child. *My* father. For that, more than mere fact of her pregnancy, she was forced to leave Summerfield."

"Marriages are arranged all the time in those circumstances," Grey said.

"My mother wouldn't accept that. Her father caned her across the back to force her to change her mind. I saw the scars once. I wouldn't have been so stubborn. I couldn't have taken the beating she did."

Grey didn't believe it. "So she left?" he asked.

"Yes. She was afraid she'd lose the baby if she stayed. She never told me that. Anderson did. With few exceptions, Mother never spoke much about the past, but I don't think leaving Summerfield was nearly as difficult for her as leaving Charleston was years later. She cried most of the day. I remember being frightened for her. Her complexion was colorless, and her eyes were vacant of any expression. The tears simply drained from her. I thought she was dying. When I think on it now, I'm sure part of her was."

"Do you know why?"

Berkeley didn't answer for a moment. Her fingers stilled. "I think she was leaving her lover . . . my father."

Grey rolled away, then drew Berkeley down beside him. He propped himself on one elbow. "Do you know who he was?"

She shook her head. "There was someone," she said slowly. "Someone who visited our home from time to time. I saw him on only a few occasions, but I think he may have come to see my mother more often. I remember being sent out of the house without warning. There was a woman who lived with us, a Negress. She cooked and cleaned and took care of me. I think she took care of Mother as well. There would be times when she would hustle me out of the house in the middle of the afternoon, mumbling all the while that it wasn't right. I didn't understand it then. I thought I must have done something wrong, though I never really believed she was angry with me. Lizzie didn't come with us when we moved. Anderson wouldn't let her."

"Did you ever ask your mother about your father?"

"No. Does that seem odd to you? It was something I knew I shouldn't talk about. She never said I couldn't. I just knew it would have made her sad."

"So you were protecting her."

"I never thought of it that way. I suppose I was."

"And after she died? Did you ask Anderson about him?"

"Once. He told me he didn't know who my father was." Berkeley brushed a pale strand of hair from her cheek. Her eyes lowered a fraction, and she stared at Grey's strong throat. Her voice was barely audible. "I didn't believe him."

"Why wouldn't he want you to know?"

She shrugged. "My mother may have asked him not to tell me. I'd like to think it was her wishes he was following and not some purpose of his own." Berkeley's mouth parted on a soft sigh. "But knowing him as I did, I suspect he had his own reasons. I can't fathom them though." She darted him a glance, her smile apologetic. "I hadn't meant to go on about me. You're very good at doing that, making me say things I didn't think I would."

"Really? I don't think we talk about you nearly often enough." He took her hand and unfolded her fingers so he could trace the lines of her palm. "I need someone to interpret these for me."

"Why don't you try?"

"All right." He looked at the array of lines. "It shows right here that you'll be married."

"You should have looked at that a week ago," she said. "It would have saved you seven days, dozens of bouquets, and two nights at the opera."

"You would have insisted I was making it up."

She laughed. "Go on. Tell me something else."

"Well, it's very clear that you'll be married only once."

Berkeley's smile faltered. "Is that so?"

"Yes. And you'll have four . . . no, five children."

"Interesting. That's the same number I said you would have."

"Fancy that." Grey feigned innocence. "I'd forgotten."

"What else?"

"You'll be mother to a child who isn't yours."

"Nat."

"My thought exactly." Grey's finger went to another line. "This shows clearly that you'll have one great love."

"Oh." She pretended interest in her hand. "Can you tell when I may expect to meet him?" Berkeley found herself pinned to the bed, her wrists at the level of her shoulders. Her girlish giggle disappeared the moment Grey's mouth covered hers. His kiss was hard and thorough, and it made her ache for him almost instantly. She gave herself up to the kiss, the moment, the weight of his body pressing against the length of hers.

Grey drew back slowly, just far enough to see her face. Her breath was warm on his skin; her mouth was damp. "I want to be your one great love," he said.

"You are."

His eyes held hers, and he saw the truth in their depths. His own mirrored the same. "Aaah, sweet Berkeley." His mouth touched hers briefly. "I like the way you complicate my life."

She smiled at that. "You know you were right," she whispered. Berkeley saw one of his dark brows kick up. "About your name . . . about who you might be and who you might have been . . . it doesn't matter. I love *you.*"

Grey released her wrists. She immediately looped her arms around his neck and drew him closer. She kissed the corner of his mouth, his jaw, the curve of his neck. He turned them both so he lay on his back and her slight weight was stretched along the length of him. His fingers gathered the light linen fabric of her nightshift until it reached the back of her thighs. He made several deliberate passes across her silky skin. Grey felt the long, smooth muscles in her legs relax. Her thighs parted, then she was straddling him. He cupped her buttocks. The pressure he applied with his hands secured her over his erection.

Berkeley raised herself and looked down on Grey. He was watching her intently, his eyes darkening at their centers. The breath he was holding was released in a controlled sigh as she began to unfasten his shirt studs. They littered the bed like bits of gold ore until her arm swept the sheet and brushed them aside. She opened his shirt, sliding her palms across his skin from navel to shoulders. He sucked in another breath, his skin retracting in anticipation of her touch.

With Berkeley's help Grey shrugged out of the shirt. Her palms lay flat against his shoulders as she bent and lowered her mouth on his. The kiss was a teasing one, light at first, then with pressure behind it, deliberate and leisurely. She touched him with unhurried familiarity, nudging his lips open with her own, playing her tongue against his. Her body became an instrument of exquisite torture as she moved over him with sinuous grace. Each shift in her position, in the balance of her weight, brought pleasure to bear and the agony of anticipation to endure.

Seated over Grey, Berkeley's open thighs rubbed against him. The barrier of his trousers was both maddening and arousing. To both of them.

Grey's fingers curled in her hair, drawing it over her shoulders so that it fell like a curtain on either side of her face. He relaxed his grip as she moved lower, kissing his throat, then his collarbone. Her mouth settled over his heartbeat, and he felt the warm flick of her tongue. She turned her head and kissed his nipple. The edge of her teeth caught his flesh and tugged gently. His hips thrust upward, but she was no longer intimately cradling him there. He groaned softly and felt the outline of her small, satisfied smile against his skin.

Berkeley's mouth made a trail down the center of his chest. Her fingers slipped below Grey's trousers. He started to help her with the buttons, but she brushed his hands aside. She worked his trousers and drawers over his hips and let him finally push them off moments before she took him in her mouth.

Grey's eyes closed. There were her hands, and there was the hot suck of her mouth. It was all he knew. He thought he might have said her name but wasn't sure. Pressure built in his chest as his heart hammered and his breath caught. His hearing was dulled by the steady roar in his ears. Sensation was confined to the rigid length of him where Berkeley's mouth held him so intimately. The caress of her tongue, the sweet damp tug of her lips, pulled a low, inarticulate sound of pleasure from the back of his throat. He reached for her. Her silky fall of hair slipped through his fingers like a shower of water, and he came away with nothing.

The arching thrust of his body brought her closer. He caught her arm. She raised her head slowly, kissing him, tasting the first pearly drops of his seed on the tip of her tongue. Her eyes were dark, slightly glazed, but her focus was clear. The look he gave her made heat rush through her body. She was lifted over him. His mouth devoured hers and they shared the taste of him on their tongues. He palmed her bottom, his fingers pressing whitely into her taut flesh. She was lifted and guided and fitted against him, sheathing him with the warm, wet walls of her body.

Berkeley contracted around him. They both were speared by the sensation. Heat uncurled between them, and they shared in it equally. Pleasure stirred. Tension drew the muscles in their legs taut. The straps of Berkeley's shift slipped over her shoulders. The soft linen hovered for a moment at the level of her breasts, then fell past them. The tips of her rose-colored nipples were achingly hard buds now. He cupped her swollen breasts, liking the heaviness of them against his palms. His thumbnails lightly scored her nipples, and he heard her soft cry. He drew her down, wanting the taste of her in his mouth.

She drank the air, none of her breaths deep, none of them completely satisfying. Grey's mouth tugged on her breast; his tongue laved her nipple. It was a powerful feeling, this knowledge that he controlled even the breath she took. Then he heard his own harsh, husky cry and knew that he wasn't alone in wielding that power.

Berkeley's hips lifted and fell. She rode him smoothly, wet and tight around him, controlling the thrust and rhythm of their bodies. Her slender frame arched sleekly above him. His hands slid over her rib cage, her waist. She looked down at herself and the sight of his fingers sliding over her thighs, disappearing between her legs, was unbearably erotic.

Grey only had to touch her. The pressure of his fingertips brought her release from the first, but he kept his hand there, the caress maddeningly insistent, allowing her to experience how long the skimming force of pleasure could stay on the surface.

It was inevitable that she would draw him in. Her pleasure eddied around him, and the energy she expended she also generated. He took it in as she had taken him, absorbing her shudder and finding that it triggered one of his own. She was turned under him as his thrusts quickened. Her thighs gripped him. Her fingers slipped under the hair at the nape of his neck. She tugged. His mouth slanted across hers, his lips hard. The pressure was almost pain.

Almost.

Berkeley swallowed his hoarse cry. Tears blurred her vision for a moment. She had blinked them back by the time he rolled away from her. They lay side by side, their breathing a heartbeat out of synchrony. Perspiration gave their limbs sheen; lamplight rendered them glowing. Bunched under their bodies were the coverlet and sheets. In time they drew them up and laid their heads on plump pillows.

Grey turned to face Berkeley. Her lashes fluttered once, twice, then closed completely. He made no move to touch her.

He stared at the elegant purity of her face, the perfect arc of her brows, the slender shape of her nose. With her eyes closed, their leaf green color and fey, otherworldly appeal was lost to him, but it took no effort on his part to bring them to mind. Her mouth was damp and slightly parted; her breath came even and sweet. Her cheeks were washed with pale rose color. Grey remembered that her nipples were only several shades darker and exactly the same hue as her lips.

He leaned toward her. His mouth brushed her forehead. A smile hovered briefly on Berkeley's lips, but she didn't stir. Grey reached past her for the bedside lamp and turned it back. He let the one on his side of the bed keep a mere fingernail of flame. Slipping an arm across Berkeley's waist, Grey closed his eyes.

It was still dark outside when Berkeley woke. She couldn't say whether she had slept only minutes or a few hours. She felt rested, yet vaguely restless. Easing herself out from Grey's arm, Berkeley padded quietly into the dressing room. In the morning she would have all of her things moved in here, she thought. She would share this space with Grey, her gowns crowding his silver-threaded vests and perfectly cut jackets. Her gloves and linens would fill one drawer, his cravats and stockings would take another. She found it odd that she was looking forward to it. There had been no sense of sharing with Anderson. Everything had belonged to him. She was no less his possession than his walking stick and shoes.

Berkeley shook off the unpleasant sensation. She fixed the strap of her shift over her shoulders and poured cool water from the pitcher on the washstand into the basin. She washed her face and arms with a damp cloth. Water trickled down her throat and disappeared between her breasts. She squeezed more droplets out. The linen shift clung wetly to her skin. Opening the first buttons, she separated the material enough to slide the cloth over her breasts. Their swollen curves still ached a little.

A rivulet of water ran over her abdomen and nestled in the triangle of hair between her legs. Berkeley raised one leg on a stool and lifted the hem of her shift. She ran the wet cloth along the length of her inner thigh and finally between her legs.

Some sound she couldn't identify turned her toward the doorway. Grey stood on the threshold, his figure backlit by the bedroom lamp. His frame and features existed entirely in shadow. The sound she had heard was his single strangled breath.

Berkeley wondered if she should be embarrassed that he had been watching her. She straightened, easing the cloth out from under her shift, and let her foot fall from the stool. She stood there uncertainly while droplets of water beat a tattoo against the floor.

Grey stepped into the room and took the cloth from her hand. He wrung it out, wet it again, and squeezed a little more water from it. Without a word he raised her shift and completed her ablutions. His hand lingered between her thighs just once before he withdrew. Her silky skin was cool and damp. His thumb skimmed her inner thigh as he dragged the cloth along her leg. Grey dropped the cloth into the basin and cupped her face. Her shift fell back in place, the hem brushing against her ankles.

He kissed her, his lips rubbing hers. She leaned into him. Her breasts were pressed to his naked chest. "I want you," he said against her mouth. "I woke up wanting you." He backed her against the wall and heard her gasp as his hips ground hers. "Is it too much?" he asked. "Too soon?" He would stop, he told himself. If it was what she wanted, he would stop. But it wasn't the answer she gave him. "It's not enough," she said. "Not yet."

There was a rending of material as the linen shift was torn at her shoulder. Berkeley felt the fabric whisper against her skin all the way to the floor. She stood on tiptoe, her lean muscles stretching to fit herself to the length of him, then she was lifted and held to the wall by Grey's hands and the hard, violent thrust of his body.

Her fingernails pressed into his shoulders. Her throat was arched. She felt his mouth on her skin and knew he would leave a mark there, a brand of sorts. The entire time he possessed her she never once felt like his possession. What was done to her was also done with her.

Grey's breathing came harshly. He thrust into her again and again, rocking her back. Her mouth opened, but her cry was nearly soundless. She was nearly weightless in his arms. He pushed into her harder, grinding his hips against hers. Her bottom rose in his hands, her fingers curled whitely against his shoulders, then her slender frame shattered under him and she was still. He spent himself inside her and held her until she had taken all of him.

Berkeley felt herself sliding down the wall. She clutched Grey as he eased himself out of her and lowered her to the floor. They sat there a full minute, slightly dazed and fully sated, neither of them inclined to speak. Finally Grey picked up Berkeley's shift and handed it to her. "I think I tore this."

"I'm quite certain you did." She found the rent shoulder seam with her fingers. "I can repair it."

He didn't give a damn about the shift, he thought. It was a bloody stupid conversation to be having with her. God, he could still feel her all around him. He could feel himself pounding into her, forcing her roughly back against the wall. Other than the whimper he trapped at the back of her throat, she hadn't made a sound. "Did I hurt you?" he asked. "When I came in here . . . I didn't expect . . . I didn't think—"

"You didn't hurt me. You've never hurt me."

"That's not true," he said. "The first time there was pain . . . and blood. You left me. You took the sheets and disappeared. I know I hurt you then."

She found his face and cupped his cheek. Leaning toward him, Berkeley kissed him lightly. "You gave me pleasure. Every other thing is of no account." She raised herself to her knees and lifted the nightshift modestly in front of her. Faint lamplight from the adjoining bedroom limned her shoulder. "Will you excuse me? I'll join you in a moment." Berkeley watched him rise in an athletic, fluid motion. Indeed, it would have been difficult for her to look anywhere else. His body unfolded with grace and power, his muscles sleek and taut. Her eyes followed his progress to the door. "Leave it open just a bit."

His inclination had been to leave it open all the way, but he knew why she wanted it otherwise. Grey was flattered Berkeley thought he could still act on a sexual impulse when it required most of his strength to walk to the bed. Grinning to himself, he tumbled on it and drew the covers over him. A few minutes later she joined him, smelling faintly of soap and lavender. She was not wearing or carrying her shift. She slipped in beside him wearing nothing but her fragrance.

"Was our wedding quite all right?" she asked. "I mean, did I say everything properly? I didn't embarrass myself, did I?"

He turned his head. His flinty eyes grazed her face. "It was perfect," he said. "*You* were perfect. Don't you remember any of it?"

"You're not in any position to take me to task for faults in my memory. And no, I don't remember a thing after you took my hand. Not of what was going on. I remember what I was feeling quite clearly, but nothing of what I was doing."

"You said all the proper words. I can find a number of witnesses who will swear to it, and you signed your name to our license."

Berkeley saw he was grinning at her, but his eyes looked vaguely disturbed by the direction of her conversation. "What name did you sign?" she asked.

His grin faded. "Mine. Grey Janeway. That's who I am here. It doesn't matter who I was anywhere else or in any other time."

"Doesn't it?" She raised herself on one elbow and looked down on him. "Haven't you ever wondered about the name you chose? I know you took it from the clipper, but you could have taken it from anywhere, chosen anything."

"What of it?"

"Didn't it strike you as even remotely familiar?" she asked.

Grey's hand went immediately to the back of his neck. He remembered the violent headache that had visited him the first time he announced his name on board the *Lady Jane Grey*. He had no difficulty bringing it to mind now. It was returning with the same vengeance.

Chapter Twelve

Berkeley saw that Grey's headache was returning. It was difficult to watch pain dulling the color of his eyes and not do something to help him. She forced herself to hold back when all she wanted to do was go to his rescue. "Please, Grey," she whispered. "You must listen to me. You deserve to know that Graham Denison was a good and decent man."

Grey massaged the back of his neck. "I suppose the Thornes were your source on that count."

"Decker and Jonna," she said. "Colin Thorne and his wife never met Mr. Denison, but Decker seems to have thought of Graham as someone more than a business acquaintance. I believe there was a friendship there. Certainly mutual respect."

Grey closed his eyes. Lamplight pressed against his lids and slipped under his lashes. He couldn't contain the soft groan that had rested for a while at the back of his throat.

Berkeley reached across him to turn back the lamp on his side of the bed, then she did the same on her own. "Is that better?"

He couldn't nod. His mouth formed around the word "yes,"

but there was no sound. Grey found Berkeley's hand and squeezed it.

It was more than she could stand. Pushing herself upright, Berkeley once again drew Grey's head onto her lap. She pressed her fingers to his temples and scalp and began a gentle massage. More than a minute passed before she felt any softening in the rigid set of his shoulders and the corded muscles of his neck.

"Go on." Grey's voice was deep, guttural. Even to his own ears, the words were almost indistinguishable from a low cry of pain. He forced himself to say more. "Tell me what you know."

Berkeley's fingers stilled. She couldn't absorb any more of his hurt, and she couldn't make herself say anything that would give rise to it.

Grey gripped her wrist. The tension in his arm and fingers made his hold painfully strong. He heard her wince, but she didn't ask to be released. "You started this," he said. "Finish it now."

"Graham Denison was also known as Falconer," she whispered. "He was a conductor on the Underground Railroad that brings fugitive slaves north, sometimes as far north as Canada."

"I've heard of the Railroad," he said. He let his silence speak to the fact that he knew nothing about Falconer.

"I believe Decker and Jonna Thorne were involved with the Underground and that it was through their work that they met Mr. Denison. I have no proof. They denied any involvement before it was raised as a question. Their wanting to find him had nothing to do with the Underground, but it hobbled their ability to search for him. They respected what appeared to be his desire to disappear from public view. He became rather notorious after his identity was revealed. You can imagine that as a member of the plantation aristocracy he was something of a peculiarity to everyone. Southern papers reviled him, while the abolitionists made him their hero. He was sought after for lectures and asked to write a book. The Thornes indicated they understood Mr. Denison wanted to put it behind him. They helped him by arranging his passage on one of their clippers."

"Then they found the earring he left behind."

"Yes. And he disappeared. They considered that he could have taken up the cause of the abolitionists again. That mandated the Thornes be discreet in their inquiries. They didn't want to be the cause of his capture if he was operating in the South. Their search came to nothing."

"So they sought you out."

"In a manner of speaking. I've told you before that Anderson had a way of finding people who needed us. Jonna Thorne was desperate to help her husband, desperate enough to believe that she initiated the contact, not that it was the other way around. By the time she met us she was no longer thinking about how she had first come to learn about us. She'd made a careful study of our references, but Anderson always anticipated that. Jonna and Mercedes Thorne were prepared to be convinced that I could help them."

"Decker and Colin?"

"Skeptical," she said. "More than that. Fearful. Afraid they would be disappointed again. Graham Denison is their only link to the earring and, therefore, to their brother. It's you they need to talk to, Grey. You're Graham Denison."

Grey's fingers eased open around Berkeley's wrist. "It's no good, Berkeley. I don't remember. I *can't* remember."

"Tell me about those scars on your back," she said. "The three stripes." Berkeley doubted she was the first woman who had asked about them. Anyone who had run their fingers along the length of his back would have felt the distinguishing marks. "What did you tell the others?"

It was too much effort to make a denial. The truth served him better. "I told them it happened at sea. They were satisfied with that."

"But it didn't, did it?"

"No. I went to sea with them."

"Were they part of the beating you took?"

"No. They're old wounds. I don't know how I came by them."

"They're cane marks. I've seen those same stripes on my

mother's back. You didn't get them from a whip. Did you know that?''

''Yes.''

''It's a harsh discipline. You angered someone terribly.''

Tension knotted Grey's neck again. ''I've thought of that.''

Berkeley felt the rigidity in his muscles. She repositioned herself to cradle him better. Her palms stroked his shoulders. ''What about that pistol wound?'' she asked.

Grey touched the puckered scar at his side. ''I don't know how I came by it. I seem to be disposed to making people want to kill me.''

Berkeley didn't smile at his black humor. ''I think we need to discover who the men were that approached Nat,'' she said. ''We need to know if Decker Thorne is really here with his brother, or if Anderson spoke to someone about the earring before he was killed.''

''It's the Ducks,'' Grey said. ''You know it.''

''I want to be certain. If that's true, then I need to write Captain Thorne and tell him that I've found you. It doesn't matter that you may never be able to help him. I think he was your friend. He has a right to know that you're alive.''

Grey opened his eyes and looked up at her. ''What if he wasn't my friend? And you still don't know that I'm Gray Denison.''

''What did you say?'' She didn't give him time to repeat himself. ''You called him Gray, not Graham.''

''Wasn't that your point earlier?'' he asked. ''The names are similar. Gray is an acceptable way to shorten Graham.''

''It was the way you said it. It came out so naturally, as if it were familiar to you. I've never thought of him as anyone but Graham. Captain Thorne didn't call him Gray.''

''Then he probably wasn't the friend you suspect he was. He has very selfish reasons for wanting to find me.''

Berkeley smoothed the small vertical crease between Grey's brows. She wished she had not been so quick to turn back the lamps. She wanted to see his face more clearly. ''Have you remembered something?'' she asked.

"No," he said firmly. "And I'm not likely to. Ever. You shouldn't expect differently. But I've been thinking for some time that it's likely I'm Gray Denison. You were so certain I'd killed him, and I realized that I probably had, but not in the way you thought. He's dead to me, Berkeley. He can't help the Thornes or anyone else. He can't help himself."

Berkeley ruffled his hair gently, then smoothed it again. "He has a family," she said. "The Denisons are well-known and highly regarded. Anderson learned all about them before we ever met the Thornes. Joel Denison is the family's patriarch. By all accounts a hard taskmaster and set in his ways. Anne-Marie was his wife. She died three years ago. I was led to believe that Graham was her particular favorite."

Grey closed his eyes. There was no relief for the dull, incessant roar in his ears. "Then I have brothers and sisters," he said with no inflection.

"A brother. Garret, I think. Your father is James and your mother is Evaline."

The names meant nothing to him, but he was aware of a deepening ache behind his eyes. "Falconer's activities must have been an embarrassment to them."

"Yes. That seems likely. They're slave owners. Beau Rivage has always had slaves. It couldn't have been easy for them to learn that Graham was working with the Underground."

"You said Graham disappeared in Philadelphia."

"That's right. From the *Siren*."

"But *Jane Grey*'s last port of call was Charleston. What would I have been doing there?"

"Perhaps you didn't go there willingly," she said. "Or perhaps you did and encountered problems when you arrived. We can't know that without knowing who attacked you."

Grey's short laugh held no humor. "It seems that anyone who found fault with Falconer's work would have had reason. Was there a reward for him?"

Berkeley found it odd how Grey distanced himself from Falconer. He could accept that he was probably Graham Denison, but not that it made him Falconer. "There was money offered by different slaveholders, but it wasn't generally made public. What you did was against the law. You didn't have Northern sympathizers to protect you after you left Boston. Going South at all was a risk. Returning to Charleston was dangerous.'' Her fingers threaded through his dark hair. ''But then you know that firsthand.''

''Apparently so.'' Grey eased himself off Berkeley's lap. He turned on his side and accepted the pillow she slipped under his head. ''It's easier to understand why no one in my family mounted a search. They didn't want me found.''

''Grey,'' Berkeley said quietly, ''you don't know that.''

''No, you listen to me now. Perhaps not looking for me was for my own protection, but there's no escaping the fact that dead or alive I could only bring more shame to them. It was better for my family that I was simply forgotten. The real question for me is one of motive. If I really did act to help slaves move along the Underground, was I acting on my convictions or out of revenge?''

Berkeley frowned. ''Why would you think it was revenge? Why must you judge your character in the poorest light?''

''Because evil is often done by men with good intentions and apparently selfless acts can be rooted in profoundly selfish motives. I believe something provoked me to disregard my family's interests and take up an abolitionist's cause.''

''Graham Denison had a great respect for freedom.''

''So does Grey Janeway. Especially his own. I'm not eager to lose it. I want to give this matter of Decker and Colin Thorne some thought.'' He waited until Berkeley stretched out beside him before he continued. ''I'll speak to Nat myself, and I'll decide what's to be done from there. Can you accept that?''

Berkeley fingered the earring pendant around her throat. ''Your headache's better, isn't it?''

He realized suddenly that it had almost completely vanished. ''Yes.'' He waited, thinking she intended to move him from his purpose. He was mildly surprised when she answered his earlier question.

''I can accept that you want time to think about these things,'' she said. "But I know something about Grey Janeway myself. I suspect he acts with a bit more nobility of purpose than he would like anyone to believe."

"Then you continue to deceive yourself."

"You saved me at the wharf," she pointed out.

"I thought you were a child."

"You took me in."

"I realized you were a woman."

"Pandora?"

He shrugged. "You seemed to have some affection for her. I was still trying to get in your good graces."

"You put Mike on my trail to watch over me."

"By that time I was trying to get into your bed."

"You arranged for his care and passage home."

"I sent him away because I thought he entertained a certain affection for you. I was jealous."

Berkeley's eyes widened a little. She wondered if she could believe him when he was bent on making her see him in a different light. "What about Nat?"

"Would you be with me now if I had turned Nathaniel Corbett away?" He found her hand and drew it toward him. "I only want you to understand that I don't act out of selflessness."

Berkeley fell silent, considering that. "What about Ivory DuPree?" she asked, suddenly inspired.

"What about her?"

"Hank Brock was injured not long after you found out he'd raped her."

"Do you believe taking the matter into my own hands was somehow high-minded or moral? It was neither. There are courts to pass judgment, Berkeley. I acted with the same disregard for their justice as Sam Brannan's vigilantes. And I despise their methods. It was chivalrous perhaps, dangerous certainly, and it was wrong. Given the same circumstances, I would do it again."

Berkeley raised his hand toward her mouth. She kissed his knuckles. "I can accept that," she said quietly.

* * *

Grey picked up a deck of cards lying on the gaming table in front of him and began to cut them. The ace of spades appeared on the first cut. He closed the deck and cut again. This time he revealed the ace of hearts. The third cut showed the ace of diamonds. It was only on the fourth cut that he missed finding an ace. He had to go behind Nat's ear to bring out the club.

Nat's jaw slackened a bit in amazement. "I want to learn that, Mr. Janeway."

Grey glanced sideways at Berkeley. She had Nat's lessons spread out in front of him. There was a slate of sums, a map of Europe, and Irving's "Rip van Winkle." "Some other time," he said, pocketing the cards. "You have these lessons first." It was difficult not to be sympathetic to Nat's disappointment. The best he could do was postpone them a little longer. "Is there nothing else you can tell us about the men?" he asked. "Are you certain you've remembered everything?"

Nat's pale brows came together in a parody of concentration. He was willing to think on it all day if it kept him from doing sums. "I think I should be excused from lessons to consider it," he said seriously. "It's hard to recall things when you're expected to name all the capitals of places you've never been and ain't likely to get to."

"And are not likely to visit," Berkeley said, correcting him. She looked at Grey, who was not being entirely successful at keeping his grin in check. "You can't possibly have any more questions for him. I'm satisfied that neither of the men asking after the earring is Decker or Colin Thorne."

"I'm satisfied on that count," Grey admitted. "But Nat hasn't provided enough detail to identify who they might be."

"And he can't. He's too young to establish their ages with any certainty. You heard him. He thinks you're forty-one." She smiled sweetly when Grey winced at that reminder. She couldn't resist adding, "And Sam, who's twenty-five years older than you, he thinks is forty-two."

Grey picked up the slate and passed it to Nat. "Write down thirty and add twenty-five. That will give you Sam's age." He chuckled at Nat's disheartened expression. "I take your point," he said, turning back to Berkeley. She was looking at him oddly. His grin disappeared. "What is it? What did I do?"

"You know how old you are," she said. "How can that be? Or was it a guess on your part?"

Grey sat back himself, struck by what he had said now that it was pointed out to him. "It wasn't a guess," he said slowly. "I'm thirty years old. My birthday was in May. The eleventh. I was born in 1820."

"Sam is fifty-five," Nat said helpfully, showing his slate work. When both adults merely nodded absently in his direction he checked his addition.

"Grey." Berkeley said his name softly, her voice awed. "You've remembered something." She came out of her chair and around the gaming table. She brushed his temple with her fingertips and examined his features for some sign that he was suffering. "Is there pain? Does your head hurt at all?"

Nat slid his slate onto the table. "I'm feeling a bit peculiar," he said, looking hopefully from Berkeley to Grey.

Berkeley's attention shifted briefly. "You may be excused, Nat. Find Sam and tell him to keep you out of trouble."

"Yes, ma'am," Nat said cheerfully. He almost tipped his chair over in his eagerness to be gone from the table.

Berkeley was pulled onto Grey's lap as soon as they were alone. "Are you quite all right?"

He nodded. "How did that happen? How can I know beyond any doubt that it's true?"

She shrugged helplessly, wishing she could explain it. It would have reassured them both. She could admit to herself that she was a little frightened by what had just happened. What if recalling his past meant forgetting the present? Was it possible that he would forget what had taken place these last five years? Berkeley felt small and selfish for wondering if he would no longer remember her. "Perhaps you shouldn't try to force your recollections," she said, swallowing her guilt. "It's never been helpful before."

"You're right," he said. His arms circled her waist easily, and the crease between his brows disappeared. "There's no point in rushing it or even in expecting that my memory can be rushed. Not after all this time. Another five years may go by before I remember something else as trivial as my birthday."

"I don't think that's so trivial. Trivial would be if you recalled the name of the first pony you rode or the first girl you kissed."

Grey answered before he realized what he was going to say. "Barbara O'Dare."

"What?"

"The pony's name was Barbara O'Dare," he said softly, his voice touched by awe. "I was four, I think. No more than five. Someone set me in the saddle and led me around the paddock before we went through the garden and up to the house." The vision in his mind's eye abruptly ended. Grey had no sense of who led the pony or what the grounds and house looked like. The occasion of the event had been his birthday. He was certain of that.

Berkeley watched him shake his head slowly as if to clear it. His blue-gray eyes recaptured their sharpness, and she became his focal point again. "Who was the girl?" she asked. "The one who shared your first kiss."

Grey didn't hesitate to answer though he didn't remember a thing about it. In spite of the ache forming behind his eyes, he said cheekily, "My mother."

"That isn't what I meant, and you know it."

"But it's all *I* know."

Berkeley was sensitive to the tightening of his fingers on her waist. "Your headache's returned, hasn't it?"

He nodded. "It will pass." Grey didn't release Berkeley from his lap. "No, stay right here. Tell me what you want to write to the Thornes."

She allowed him to change the subject though her own anxiety wasn't lessened by this topic. "I want to tell Captain Thorne

that I believe I've found Graham Denison and that if he wants
assurances, he will have to come to San Francisco. I'll explain
about your memory loss and that you may be of little help
in—''

"No help," Grey interjected. "Explain that it's likely I will
be of *no* help. There's nothing to be gained by raising the man's
hopes.''

"All right. I'll be very clear on that count. I will further
explain that I can give him no assurances that Graham Denison
is in fact Greydon Thorne. It's not something I've ever felt
when I've touched you. But that's perfectly reasonable when
one considers that Greydon was only an infant when he was
separated from his brothers. If you were never told that you
weren't a Denison by blood and birth, then you have no means
to communicate that knowledge to me. When I held your hand,
I've only ever sensed that Graham Denison was dead and
Greydon Thorne never existed.''

"Neither of which is true," Grey said. He paused, considering Berkeley's choice of words. As always, her careful expression of what she felt was open to interpretation. "And yet
there's a kind of truth in both those elements.''

Berkeley's gentle smile gave him full marks for understanding the subtleties. "I should also tell Captain Thorne that if he
desires more information about Graham Denison's birth, he
should make inquiries of the Denisons.''

"No!''

Grey's vehemence gave Berkeley a start. She was almost
unseated from his lap. Her smile faded as she regarded him
worriedly. "I only thought I should encourage him to try
again.''

"Try again? You mean they looked in that direction for
information before?''

"Well, yes. It was a natural place to begin their search for
Graham . . . for you.'' This time when she placed her hands
on his forearms and pressed, she was released. Berkeley stood.
Uncertain suddenly, she smoothed the material of her hunter

green gown across her midriff. ''I can hardly stop them from
contacting the Denisons again.''

''You can discourage them.''

''I suppose . . .'' Her hands fell to her sides.

''I thought you understood last night, Berkeley. I don't want
my family, if indeed they are my family, to know where I am
or who I am or what's become of me. It's clear to me that's
the way they've wanted it these past five years, and I heard
nothing yesterday that changes what I've thought all along.''

Without conscious thought, one of Berkeley's hands went
to her throat. Below the high neckline of her gown Berkeley
could make out the shape of the delicate gold chain and pendant
lying against her skin. ''But you can't identify the earring,''
she said. ''You can't explain how the genuine heirloom came
to be in your possession. It's something one of the Denisons
might be able to tell the Thornes.''

''They didn't cooperate before, did they?''

''No, but I have no idea what sort of questions were asked.
There may have been no mention of the earring. In fact, I would
find that likely. I can't imagine that Decker Thorne would have
been eager to let anyone know of its existence. The very last
thing he wants is a parade of strangers presenting themselves
as his missing brother. This earring represents the only link to
Greydon. The fewer people who know about it, the better it is
for Decker and Colin.''

''And I don't want either of them or their meddling wives
raising questions with the Denisons. In fact, I've changed my
mind. I don't want you to write to the Thornes at all.''

Berkeley bristled a bit at Grey's harsh description of Jonna
and Mercedes Thorne. ''It is beyond my comprehension that
you don't want to know the truth of this yourself. You are so
bent on sparing the Denisons, who haven't made any effort to
find you in five years, that you would turn your back on the
Thornes, who have only made it their entire life's work to be
reunited with their brother. *You* may be that brother.''

Grey reached for her hand, but Berkeley avoided him. He
was actually hurt by her withdrawal. Anger simmered while

she skirted the edge of the gaming table and returned to her seat opposite him. Pandora appeared from nowhere and jumped lightly onto his lap. He brushed the cat away, and she sought refuge in Berkeley's arms. It didn't matter that he hadn't wanted Pandora. Her leaving him was somehow traitorous now, an act of feline defection.

Grey's chair scraped hard against the floor as he pushed away from the table and stood abruptly. "I'm going out," he said shortly. "You can expect me back before the doors open."

Berkeley's leaf green eyes darkened with bewilderment and more than a little hurt of her own. A half dozen questions occurred to her, but all of them were left unasked. She merely nodded, unable to find her voice as he strode away.

The drizzle that persisted throughout the afternoon was a perfect accompaniment to Berkeley's mood. The sky held no sun that she could see. It was as if an old blanket, its color dulled by wear and washing, had been unfolded over all of San Francisco. It extended out from the shore and across the bay. In the distance the water fused with the skyline and the horizon became a seamless monochromatic shade of gray.

Berkeley turned away from the window in her own suite. The droplets of rain that struck the glass were thin and cold. They hit each pane with a familiar pinging sound and left behind etchings that could have been made with a spray of acid.

She folded the petticoat she was holding and laid it beside another on her bed. Had she been more enthusiastic about her task, her belongings would have already been moved to Grey's apartment. Instead, by her own reckoning, she was less than half-finished.

She sighed heavily. The melancholy and self-pitying sound of it actually lifted her mouth in a faint smile. How ridiculous it was, she thought, to allow Grey's mood to dictate her own. She realized she was twisting the ring he had put on her finger only the day before. Removing it would have made even less difference than it would have made sense. Berkeley stopped fiddling with it. She wasn't desirous of change, only of understanding.

She doubted now that Grey wanted anything so very different.

Shaking her head, her posture one of self-reproach, Berkeley applied herself to emptying her armoire. She was carrying two gowns in the direction of her sitting room when someone knocked at the door. She hesitated, surprised by the interruption, then laid the gowns over the back of the settee. She opened the door with no other thought than the face in the hallway would be a familiar one.

It was, but not in any way one she could have anticipated seeing.

"May I come in?" Anderson Shaw asked. His manner was flawlessly polite. He stood rather formally on the threshold of her suite, tall, handsomely distinguished, and very much alive.

Berkeley couldn't speak. She didn't feel faint, and her knees held her steady, but her voice was locked in her throat. Her eyes shifted from Anderson to the stranger at his side. Her glance was swift in its assessment. It only took a moment to understand that this man was one of the two that Nat had tried to describe earlier. Anderson himself was the other. She hadn't understood it then. In hindsight it was so patently obvious that she wondered if she had any gift for prescience at all.

Nat stood between the two gentlemen, his face turned upward, more misery etched in his features than any child should ever experience. A hand on either of his shoulders, one from Anderson, the other the stranger's, kept him firmly in place.

Berkeley's heart hammered in her breast. She opened the door wider and ushered the trio inside. Nat twisted away as the grips on his shoulders relaxed. He didn't try to run. He launched himself at Berkeley and wrapped his arms around her waist. The gesture was more indicative of his desire to protect Berkeley than it was of seeking shelter for himself.

Berkeley's fingers ruffled Nat's bright helmet of hair. "It's all right. I know one of these gentlemen. You haven't done anything wrong.''

"They've been here," Nat said. "Hiding in plain sight. They're registered guests of the Phoenix.''

"Only a short while ago," Anderson said calmly. He looked around Berkeley's suite with an interest that was at once genuine and somehow detached. When he had completed his inspection his polished chestnut gaze came to rest once more on Berkeley. "Please close the door. I prefer to have this discussion in private. Come here, my dear. I want to show the boy something.''

With some difficulty Berkeley removed Nat's limpetlike attachment. She forced herself to show no fear as she approached Anderson. Out of the corner of her eye she saw the stranger following her movements. She wondered if he knew what to expect. When she was standing directly in front of Anderson she stopped.

The force of the blow knocked her sideways. It was so quick, like a cobra striking, that Berkeley only felt it as she was being steadied in the arms of the stranger. Nat's cry of alarm came to her as if from a great distance. Her ears rang, and her vision blurred. One side of her face was unbearably hot, but Berkeley knew there would be no lasting mark. It seemed that Anderson Shaw was born knowing how to inflict pain without leaving evidence of it.

"For God's sake, Shaw," the stranger said. "That can't have been necessary.''

Berkeley thought his concern seemed real. He put her behind him, but she had no illusions that he was resolved to protect her. If Anderson insisted, he could be forced to let her go.

"I wouldn't have done it if it weren't necessary," Anderson said without remorse. He pointed in Nat's direction. "The boy needed to see what I would do and what I'm willing to do again." His attention moved to Nat. "Do you understand? You will not speak to Mr. Janeway about this. It can only go badly for Berkeley if you do. You may think you're helping her, but the effect will be just the opposite." When Nat simply stared at him, his blue-gray eyes more defiant than afraid, Anderson applied to Berkeley for assistance in explaining the matter.

"Nat, I don't want you to say anything about this to Mr. Janeway," Berkeley said. "I know it's confusing to you, but it's very important that you keep this secret." She was sufficiently recovered that she could walk steadily toward Nat. Bending so that she was at his eye level, Berkeley grasped him by his thin upper arms. There was no pleading in her voice—she would not give Anderson that satisfaction—but it was there for Nat to see in her eyes. "You must not speak of it. That is for me to do, and it is as much for my sake as his that I ask you to keep silent. I will tell Mr. Janeway when the time is right. You can depend on it, Nat. May I have your word?"

Nat was not immediately agreeable. "I didn't escort them here," he whispered. It was important to him that she knew that. "They knew where to find you."

"I understand. They only brought you with them to assure your silence. They don't want you to point them out if you see them about in the hotel. I don't want you to do that either."

"But this morning . . . you and Mr. Janeway were asking after them." Nat fell silent, realizing belatedly that he had already said too much. He'd been too slow responding to the small negative shake of Berkeley's head. "Very well," he said stiffly. He searched her face, regretting his promise as soon as it was given. If he were braver, he thought, he would throw himself at the man who had struck Berkeley and smash his face.

Berkeley stood. "You have his word," she said to Anderson. "May I see him out?"

"You may open the door for him. I would advise you not to step beyond it yourself."

Once Nat was gone Berkeley turned slowly to face Anderson. Her features were without expression. She had learned that to the extent she was able, it served her interests not to allow Anderson to see her vulnerability. "I understood you were dead," she said without inflection. "I visited your grave."

"Danced on it, I'll wager," he said.

"You were never an accomplished gambler. You would lose . . . again." The dry, appreciative chuckle this drew from Anderson's companion caused Berkeley to look in his direction. "And you, sir? Have you thrown in your lot with Anderson?"

"I have," he said. "But then I did not have the benefit of your wise counsel."

Berkeley acknowledged his slight bow by inclining her head. His resemblance to Grey was unexpected. He was of a similar build, though slender was more descriptive of his frame rather than lean. He did not project Grey's leashed power but had more than his share of the aristocratic, even arrogant stamp. His hair was dark brown, and he raked it back in a gesture that was familiar to her. It did not retain the wind-ruffled look of Grey's. His fingers had tamed the wayward strands. Grey's tampering would have lent him a vaguely rakish, disreputable air.

The mustache was an obvious distinguishing feature, the color of the eyes a more subtle one. Their singular blue reminded Berkeley of warm Pacific waters. They softened his features, blunted the smile that could have easily been derisive. In spite of his interference with Anderson on her behalf, Berkeley knew she was right to be wary. She was glad he had only bowed in her direction. She had no desire to take his hand.

"You're Garret Denison," she said.

Surprise was evident in the lift of his brows but his smile remained smoothly in place. "You *do* have a special gift," he drawled softly. "Anderson did not overrate your talent . . . or your beauty." Garret saw that Berkeley was unmoved by his flattery. She merely stared at him, waiting for a more deliberate acknowledgment of her statement.

Anderson Shaw observed Berkeley's raised chin and the faintly belligerent posture of her body, and his eyes narrowed darkly. This newfound confidence was as unexpected as it was unwelcome. Obviously he had allowed her too long a time on her own. He had anticipated that she would survive, but not that she would manage the thing quite so well. The fey charms that had captivated so many of their previous clients were not easily evident now. Berkeley had a more direct expression, still patient but with a hint of a challenge that Anderson thought did not suit her.

It certainly did not suit him. He took a step toward her and was gratified when her attention shifted to him, and she flinched. Her slender frame lost some of its militant rigidity. Her lashes lowered quickly, shuttering the defiance that had crept into her beautiful eyes. At her sides he saw that her hands remained clenched, but in a few moments even they relaxed.

"You're right, of course," Anderson said, staying his ground. "This is indeed Garret Denison."

"Ma'am," he said. "It's a great pleasure."

"My wife," Anderson continued. "Mrs. Shaw."

Berkeley's head jerked up.

One of Anderson's brows arched, and he regarded her consideringly. "Never say you thought our perfectly legal union had somehow been dissolved." His eyes dropped purposefully to her left hand and the gold band on her ring finger. "Yes, you must have thought that. I can't imagine that you would have agreed to marry Mr. Janeway otherwise."

"You know I thought you were dead."

He nodded. "Oh, I don't hold you in contempt for desiring to secure your future. Quite the opposite, in fact. It is gratifying to see that you've landed so nimbly. Rather like that cat I've seen trailing in your wake."

Anderson's words reminded Berkeley that he had been a registered guest of the Phoenix. "You knew about the wedding," she accused.

He did not deny it. "A rather lavish affair, we thought. Isn't that right, Garret?"

Garret Denison held up both hands. "I have no wish to be included in this discussion." He glanced over his shoulder and took note of the chair behind him. He sat down and crossed his legs. While he professed not to desire a speaking role, he clearly gave indication that he was interested in the proceedings. His cerulean eyes were raised expectantly in Berkeley's direction. "Please, continue."

Berkeley did not respond.

Anderson filled the silence. "You're thinking perhaps that I could have stopped the wedding. It occurred to me. Indeed, it occurred to both of us, though Garret seems unwilling to claim any particular responsibility. We certainly arrived at the Phoenix in time. As that boy said, hiding in plain sight."

"You didn't register in your own names."

"Certainly not. That would have rather defeated the purpose, would it not? I held a rather strong belief that your wedding should proceed as planned. It seemed uncharitable of me to deny you all the niceties of the occasion as I had before. Where was the harm in permitting you a splendid gown or a wedding banquet? I regretted, of course, that I could not be in attendance. Garret shared some of the same sentiments, but we endeavored to enjoy ourselves in a private celebration in our rooms."

"I can't imagine what you thought there was to celebrate," she said.

"Can you not?" Anderson asked skeptically. "Haven't you yet divined the purpose of our visit?"

Berkeley fell silent. It was difficult to keep her hands at her side when what she wanted to do was secure the earring pendant at her throat. It was the knowledge that it was hidden beneath the high collar of her gown that kept her still.

"Your patience does you credit, Berkeley," said Anderson. "If I thought it was stubbornness that kept you mute, I would not be complimentary." He lowered himself into a half-reclining position on the arm of the settee, one leg stretched out to the side for balance. "Naturally I believed there was something to be gained by permitting you to marry. Something beyond finally offering you the wedding night you'd been previously denied."

Berkeley could not help the faint wash of color that touched her cheeks. She felt Garret Denison's keen interest on her. Obviously there were things about her marriage to Anderson that had not been explained to him.

Anderson noted the tinge of rose in Berkeley's complexion. He was satisfied that the intimacies of marriage had not made her coarse or jaded. He had never desired her as he had other women, but she was endlessly fascinating to him. It had been the source of some surprise that he was able to share her with Grey Janeway. He had not expected it of himself.

"I was under the impression," Anderson said, "that you may not have been entirely honest with your husband."

"I don't know what you mean."

"Come, Berkeley. Don't dissemble now. What does Janeway know of me?"

"That you're supposed to be dead."

He smiled, his amusement genuine. "Do you believe saying it often enough will make it so? Yes, I know, you visited my grave. You've said that already, but you can see that I'm not buried in it. And I'm certainly no specter, though I suspect you wish that were true. What I meant by my question, since you pretend not to understand, is this: Does Grey Janeway think of you as a widow?"

Berkeley's hesitation gave away the answer.

"He doesn't know you were married," Anderson said. "I suppose that answers a question I had. I confess to wondering if you entered into your marriage a virgin or whether in my absence you had resorted to the whoring ways of your mother."

Berkeley's flush deepened. Her lips moved, but there was no sound.

"What? I don't believe I could have interpreted you correctly. Did you just tell me to go to hell?" He looked at Garret Denison as if for confirmation. Getting no response, he returned to studying Berkeley. "Well?" he asked.

"I told him you were my stepfather."

"Clever girl. Not a lie, but no longer the entire truth."

Garret Denison's mouth thinned, his distaste evident. He'd heard enough. "I want the earring," he said. "The boy led me to believe it was in your possession."

Berkeley frowned. "You've come all this way because of the earring? Aren't you going to make yourself known to your brother?"

"He appears to have carved out a new life for himself. By all accounts, it is a successful one. Why else would he let it be known that he killed Graham Denison? That's what the boy told us he'd heard. It's a good story." Garret straightened the sleeve of his jacket. "Graham can most politely be described as a disappointment at Beau Rivage. His penchant for gambling and whoring and drinking was not embraced by the family. Grandmother had some tolerance for my brother's dissolute behavior, but it was not shared by anyone else. Certainly not Grandaddy. He offered Graham the cane cure, but it didn't take." He heard Berkeley's sharp intake of breath and smiled faintly. "Frankly, I wouldn't seek him out at all if it were not for the earring. I want it back. It's rightfully mine."

Berkeley was aware of a vague weakness in her knees. There was nowhere for her to sit. The chair was taken, and she refused to share the settee with Anderson. "The earring is yours?" she asked. This revelation was rather too much to absorb. Was Garret Denison the brother Colin and Decker were seeking? She glanced at Anderson. "Have you always known this?"

He merely smiled.

It occurred to Berkeley to wonder if the Thornes could have ever correctly been called their clients. Anderson seemed to have had some previous arrangement with Garret Denison. "I don't understand," she said. "Captain Thorne said the earring was last in the possession of your brother."

"But not in his rightful possession," Garret said. "Did Graham tell you it was given to him?"

Berkeley's frown deepened, and a small crease appeared between her brows. Didn't they know Grey couldn't say one way or the other, that he had no memory of his past? She probed gingerly. "You call him Graham. He goes by Grey now."

"Gray was Grandmother's pet name for him. No one else used it. His disappearance killed her. He can't atone for that in my eyes. It's a bit of a conceit on his part to claim that name now. Just as it was for him to claim the earring. It's never been properly his. I want it back. It belongs with the family."

"I don't have it."

Anderson shook his head. "That's not worthy of you, Berkeley. The boy told us you did. He said he knew where you kept it.''

"Yes," she said. "I learned that much. Nat stole it from me and planned to give it to you. I can't believe that you offered anything close to its real value."

"I don't know," Anderson said, examining his nails with idle interest. "We offered the boy his life."

Berkeley felt her knees actually sag. Garret was on his feet immediately, offering first his support, then his chair. She accepted both numbly.

"Where is the earring?" Anderson asked.

Staring at her folded hands, Berkeley shook her head. "I don't know," she said quietly. "I never saw it again after Nat took it."

Garret swore but Anderson waved him off, unconcerned. "She's lying. I confess, I find it hard to believe that she would risk the boy's life, but she's lying to us nonetheless. She wouldn't let the earring out of her sight."

"I didn't," Berkeley said. "Not until Nat stole it from me. He did it at your request, don't forget that." She pointed to the intricately carved box lying open on the mantel. "I kept it there."

Anderson didn't look in the direction of the mantel, but Garret Denison moved there immediately. As Anderson had anticipated, Garret found it empty. "You can't really expect that she would lead you to it after denying she knows where it is."

Berkeley thought Anderson sounded almost bored. Clearly he did not believe her and in his own way was indicating his loss of patience. "It was at your request that Nat took it," she said. "I believe he meant to give it to you the same night he ran away. That he didn't can only mean that he sold it to someone else, perhaps someone representing themselves on your behalf. What I know with certainty is that when I found Nat that evening he no longer had the earring."

"You shouldn't have let the boy go," Garret said to Anderson. "You shouldn't have been so willing to believe him."

"I put more faith in the boy's tale than I do in Berkeley's."

"Nat was punished for his theft," Berkeley said, continuing the thread of her lie, pulling it gently through the fabric of truth. "The earring could not be returned. He couldn't name the persons who took it from him, and I had no reason to suspect you had any part in its disappearance. Indeed, the other night when you came upon Nat by the stables, he led me to believe you were Colin and Decker Thorne."

Anderson chuckled. "A touch of whimsy on my part, I'm afraid. I had to give the boy some names and those came to mind. Tell me, did you credit he was telling the truth?"

"I did . . . at first. Grey eventually convinced me otherwise. He believed you were Sydney Ducks."

"Much closer to the mark," Anderson agreed, taking no offense. "But I grow weary of this matter of the earring, especially when I have other business with you."

Before Berkeley could answer, Garret interrupted her. "Perhaps she has it on her person," he suggested. "A thorough search should uncover it."

Anderson saw Berkeley recoil. His own immediate reaction to her revulsion was anger. With some effort he kept it in check. "You would have to conduct such a search," Anderson told Garret. "Berkeley could never abide my hands on her. She said she found it painful, if you can believe that. I'm not talking about those times I meant to punish her and to elicit obedience in turn. I'm speaking of caresses which a husband may properly exchange with his wife. She can't bear my touch on her in that fashion. Shall I show you?"

Garret witnessed that Berkeley's face lost every trace of its color. He couldn't rightly say that he faulted her for sensibilities. Given a choice himself, Garret Denison would have had no dealings with Anderson Shaw. He imagined his reluctance stemmed from recognizing Shaw as a man of a similar moral, or perhaps, amoral code. He held the advantage, he thought, because Shaw did not seem to recognize the same in him.

"That won't be necessary," Garret said. "I'll do the search."

Berkeley's head swiveled in his direction. Did he really

believe she would permit him to touch her in that fashion? Her eyes widened fractionally as he took a step toward her.

Garret Denison paused. He spoke to her in his quiet, honeyed drawl and left no doubt as to his sincerity. "I assure you, I'm quite serious. It doesn't bother me at all that you're my brother's wife. Quite the opposite. There is a certain amount of satisfaction in doing this that Graham would understand. He's taken many more liberties with my wife than I intend to take with you. At least at this point in time." Garret placed his hand over Berkeley's shoulder as she would have vaulted to her feet. "If you will be so kind as to remove your gown," he said politely. "We can begin."

Chapter Thirteen

"No," Berkeley said. Her refusal was given quietly, without hysterics, without rancor. She did not give ground as Garret Denison approached.

"No?" he asked. "I do not believe you are in any position to deny me. I have your husband's permission." He extended one hand. His fingertips were raised mere inches from Berkeley's forearm. He noted the chill that swept her skin. Garret's kindly tempered voice was at odds with his words. "I'm afraid, Mrs. Shaw, I don't recognize your right to refuse."

Berkeley did not look to Anderson for help. "And I don't recognize your right to dictate to me. That puts us at something of an impasse, I believe, because I swear to you that if you touch me now, I will scream so loudly most of Portsmouth Square will empty into this room."

Garret's lowering hand was stayed. It hovered a moment, then he retracted it, letting it fall to his side. He glanced at Anderson Shaw. The slight suggestion of a smile around the other man's mouth led him to believe he could expect no real help from that quarter. "Do something with her, Shaw. I want that earring."

"And you shall have it, but really, Denison, your tactics are rather clumsy. My wife *will* scream, I assure you, and there are Sam Brannan's vigilantes to consider. You could render her unconscious and conduct a search of her person at your leisure, but I don't think one needs to go quite that far." His gaze swiveled coolly in Berkeley's direction. He knew her well enough to gauge her fear. She was not as calm as her brave, perhaps foolish, words would have him believe. "It's unlikely that she has the earring in her possession."

Garret Denison felt that pronouncement almost as a physical blow. "You can't possibly believe her," he snapped.

"You misunderstand. I meant that it's not in her physical possession. Berkeley's unusual gift makes that unlikely. She had a strong reaction to the earring when the Thornes gave it to her to examine. I believe I told you about that."

He had, Garret recalled now, but the real significance of it had eluded him. "You mean she could not tolerate to have it physically on her?"

"I mean precisely that. When I gave her the earring for safekeeping, she kept it in a small leather pouch attached to her belt. Even then there appeared to be some indications of discomfort." Anderson smiled encouragingly at Berkeley. "Come, my dear, remove your outer gown and show Mr. Denison that you no longer carry the earring with you. Nothing else will be needed. His curiosity will be satisfied, and we can move on."

Berkeley offered no reply and made no movement to indicate she intended to do as Anderson suggested.

"A compromise, then," Anderson said. "You will permit a rather modest search of your person." He saw she was about to deny him and went on, his tone approaching boredom. "Yes, yes, I know you'll threaten to scream, but how does that assist you? Mr. Janeway will certainly come, and you'll be left with some uncomfortable explanations. That is supposing, of course, that you're able to make them before his interference costs him his life. You take my meaning, do you not? Yes, I see that you do. Now, the choice of how to proceed is yours. Shall I conduct the search, or would you prefer Mr. Denison? There is no need to rush your response. I'll give you a moment to decide.''

Anderson's congenial smile chilled Berkeley's blood. She remained where she was because she simply could not move. Her eyes followed Anderson as he casually walked toward the window and looked out, his hands clasped behind him, his carriage confident and without visible strain.

There was a certain weariness in Berkeley's tone when she finally spoke. "If you will allow me to go to my suite, I will get the earring for you."

Anderson turned away from the window, his polished chestnut eyes hinting at his triumph. "You see, Denison, it's all in how the problem is approached." He studied Berkeley. "Though I confess, dearest, that I find this continued dislike of my touch insulting. I had hoped that Mr. Janeway had eased the way for me. You've been a proper wife to him, haven't you?"

Berkeley's pale cheeks filled with color. No reply occurred to her. She was too dazed to note that Anderson seemed disappointed he could not goad her into some intemperate remark.

Garret Denison filled the silence. "Whose bastard brat do you think she's carrying, Shaw?"

It was Anderson's stunned immobility that gave Berkeley her opportunity. She bolted for the door and grasped the handle. Even when Garret caught her she managed to twist it. The door opened several inches before it was slammed shut, blocked by Garret's body and secured by his weight. She wrenched free of his grip and stepped out of his reach. Her breathing came harshly, more from fear than exertion.

"Is it true?" Anderson demanded, his gaze dropping to her belly. "You're carrying his child?" He did not wait for a reply. Disregarding her earlier threats and his knowledge that she was revolted by his touch, Anderson closed the distance to Berkeley and used one arm to hook her roughly at the waist. He laid his free hand flat on her abdomen. "My God," he said under his breath. "You would bear him a child?"

Berkeley felt her stomach heave. There were no contents to

discharge, but the dry wretch was enough to make Anderson release her. She stumbled out of his reach, bent forward, hugging herself. A hand at the back of her neck forced her onto the ottoman and pressed her head between her knees. She stayed that way for more than a minute while the voice above her commanded her to take deep breaths and exhale slowly.

The weight of Garret's palm on her nape seemed enormous. Berkeley's slender throat was encircled by the high-banded collar of her day dress, hiding the gold chain of her earring pendant while pressing the links against her skin. She was so aware of its presence that she expected Garret Denison to feel it as well.

"Breathe," he ordered calmly, his voice near her ear as he stooped down beside her. He watched color come and go in her face. Her eyes remained closed. Garret glanced over his shoulder at Anderson. "I've seen quite enough," he said. "As soon as she's adequately recovered I will accompany her to retrieve my earring."

Anderson sat on the arm of one of the chairs. He ignored Garret and gave his complete attention to his wife. "I won't raise another man's bastard, Berkeley," he said softly. "I did it once because I had no choice. I won't do it again. You'll have to get rid of it."

"For God's sake, Shaw," Garret said. "Leave it for now."

"Shut up," Anderson said with mock civility. "Berkeley? You do understand, don't you? I will find someone in the city to handle the matter. San Francisco's full of abortionists. You need not trouble yourself with the details. Our reward for the return of the earring will be substantial. I will be able to arrange for a physician to treat you."

Berkeley shivered. She felt Garret's hand fall away, and she raised her head. Her eyes were dull but not defeated. "I thought you would be pleased," she said. "After all, upon my death you may decide you will want to marry this child, too."

He itched to slap her but thought perhaps Garret would not tolerate another assault. The man had peculiar scruples, and Anderson had yet to clearly define the limits of his patience.

Was it possible Garret had some feeling for his brother's bastard? His eyes strayed to Garret. "I don't seem to recall," he said casually. "You're blessed with children?"

Garret stood. He cleared his throat. "No, as a matter of fact, Alys and I have none."

"Then the bastard may be your heir. That is, if you have a wish to name one. He is, by both our reckonings, your dear brother's baby." It could come to pass, Anderson thought, that the child would prove more valuable than the earring. "That is if you should acknowledge him as such. Would that prove difficult for you? I recollect the Denisons have not been noted for laying claim to their bastards."

Garret's cerulean eyes momentarily lost their warmth. "Your meaning, Shaw? Speak plainly."

Anderson would not be goaded. He shrugged. "Perhaps I misunderstood something once told to me. It's of no account now. I beg your pardon if there's been offense given."

Garret studied him narrowly for several moments before he relaxed his stance. At his side he noted that Berkeley was somewhat recovered, her breathing light and even and her color returned. "The earring, ma'am. I'll trouble you to produce it, then I'll trouble you no longer."

Berkeley refused the hand he extended. She came to her feet of her own accord, though she knew herself to be somewhat distracted, her thoughts still centered on Anderson's odd aside. "Give me a moment. I'll return with it shortly."

Garret's smile held no warmth although it was pleasant enough. "I insist on escorting you."

"Do you think that's wise?" she asked, collecting the tattered threads of reason. "It's entirely likely that Grey is in our suite. Your presence would be difficult to explain."

"My brother left. We saw him go."

Anderson interrupted. "We've overstayed our welcome here. Berkeley's correct. Mr. Janeway may have returned. It would be better if I accompanied her. Janeway doesn't know me."

Garret hesitated. He had no wish to be seen by his brother,

yet he did not fully trust Anderson Shaw or his wife. "Very well. A few minutes. No longer."

Anderson followed Berkeley to the door. With a gallant gesture, he opened it for her and indicated she should precede him. He felt her hesitation the moment she stepped into the hallway, and his eyes shifted to the narrow opening at the hinges. What he saw made him allow Berkeley to close the door behind her, leaving him to cool his heels with Garret.

Berkeley's smile was fixed. "Grey!" She wondered at her own success at injecting a measure of warmth in her voice. "I was just coming to meet you. I saw you arrive."

He stared at her, puzzled, but made no comment. Instead he bent his head and kissed her cheek. "You've forgiven me, then?"

Had Grey known it, he could have asked forgiveness for any number of transgressions, real or imagined. At the moment Berkeley couldn't remember a single detail of their earlier argument. She turned her face so that her lips brushed his and raised herself on tiptoes. Her mouth sought his mouth, and she denied the desperation she felt in a hot and hungry and urgent kiss. Her arms lifted and circled his neck.

Grey returned the kiss, lifting her slightly against him, relishing the fullness of her response. It was with a large measure of reluctance that he slowly raised his head. His voice was husky and he made no attempt to hide his arousal. "This is a very public hallway," he whispered.

She nodded. In other circumstances she would have been embarrassed. "Take me to bed." It was all she could think to say.

Grey reached behind Berkeley to open the door of her old room.

"No!" She pressed herself against Grey, rocking him back on his heels. "Not here. Our bed."

He grinned, his eyes endearingly sheepish for a moment. "I was thinking any port in a storm," he said. "But if the wind's blowing in the other direction . . ." He let his voice trail off as Berkeley grabbed his hand and pulled him down the hallway.

* * *

It was sometime later that Grey rolled onto his side and raised himself on one elbow. Berkeley was curled against him, her body warm and still. The fragrance of lavender mingled with the musky scent of her sex. A quilt covered her naked shoulders, but he could make out the damp sheen of her skin along the length of her throat. Strands of pale hair curled at her nape. His fingers eased themselves lightly through the silky threads. She didn't stir although he knew she was awake.

He wondered at her silence and her distance. He had felt it all through their loving, this peculiar sense that she had retreated from him even while he was joined to her, *especially* while he was joined to her. Grey couldn't fathom her mood, yet he was coming to know her well enough to understand that something was wrong. She could deny it, probably would deny it, but he trusted the feeling of anxious restlessness in himself and realized she was its source.

He could have been satisfied to hold her and keep her close. He could have sheltered her in his arms and soothed her fears. She had wanted none of it. Almost as if she anticipated his consideration, her mouth had cut off his words, kissing him deeply until consideration was pushed to the back of his mind. And when he thought of them again her eyes had darkened with need, and he gave her what she seemed to want.

They had both been satisfied in the moment. Now Grey did not believe he was alone in feeling curiously empty.

"I know you're not sleeping," he said quietly. "It's no good pretending otherwise."

Berkeley didn't open her eyes, but when his hand slipped around her waist her fingers laced through his. She squeezed them gently.

"I thought you had forgiven me," Grey said. "But perhaps not."

"There is nothing to forgive." Berkeley fully recollected their earlier argument. She felt very young and foolish for having been so hurt when he walked out. It seemed so petty in comparison to what confronted her now. "It's certainly your right to decide what you want the Thornes to know. It's selfish of me to ask you to do more than you're prepared to. I'm quite sure they don't expect to hear another word from me. I'm afraid I've been insistent with you because I don't want the Thornes to think I've cheated them." She fell silent a moment. Her thumb brushed the heel of his hand. "Is that what you meant when you said good intentions often arise from selfish motives?"

"Did I say that?"

"Something like that."

"And you didn't call me a pompous ass?"

Her smile was watery as she felt his lips on the nape of her neck. His touch was profoundly tender. Berkeley's voice was trapped at the back of her throat, and she felt tears gather behind closed lashes.

Grey raised his head. "I walked for a while after I left here. Rather aimlessly at first. Or so I thought until I found myself at the harbor. Did you know there was a Remington ship making repairs?"

"I may have overheard it somewhere," she admitted.

Grey chuckled. "I wrote out a rather short and somewhat cryptic message for the captain to carry back to Boston. I have no idea what Decker Thorne will make of it, if anything. There may never be a response. I made no mention of you, not because I wanted to absolve you of anything, but because you've not done anything wrong. You never have."

Tears fell in earnest now. Berkeley wrested her hand away from Grey's and knuckled her eyes. "You can't imagine what I've done." The sentence was accomplished in fits and starts as her shoulders heaved and she left it to Grey to decipher. She was incapable of repeating it, not when he turned her over and pressed her face against his shoulder and held her in just that fashion until her sobs were silenced.

Grey released her long enough to take a handkerchief from the drawer in the bedside table. He handed it to her. Berkeley dried her eyes and heartily blew her nose. It was not a thing done prettily, but Grey found himself smiling anyway. He was thoroughly besotted, he thought, and not at all unhappy about it. He took the crumpled handkerchief from her and tossed it on the table. It unfolded slowly over the slender gold chain and pendant Berkeley had laid there earlier.

"Tell me what it is," Grey said. "I want to help."

She smiled a bit sadly. "That's your nature, isn't it? To help others."

"I'll deny it if you breathe a word." For a moment the hint of despair was banished. He held her eyes and willed her to talk to him. "Take my hand, Berkeley. Was it all a lie, the things you told me you sensed there? Can't you trust me to love you?"

"I'll hurt you."

"Your silence is hurting me."

Perhaps there was a way, Berkeley thought, to tell Grey something without telling him everything. If Garret Denison was only in San Francisco for the earring, he could have it. If Anderson needed to have his silence bought, she would pay him for it. They would have returned to their own rooms by then, knowing she wouldn't come back soon, frustrated a bit by her escape. It was a short reprieve at best. They had already learned how easily she could be cornered and how simple it was to command her silence. She didn't even know the names under which they were registered.

The earring and money. What else could they want from her that she wasn't prepared to give? Then she remembered what Anderson had said about her child. She suppressed a shiver.

"There's going to be a baby," she whispered, taking his hand.

Grey looked down at the palm she opened up. "I hope so," he said. "Four of them you said. Five, counting Nat."

Berkeley pulled his hand under the blanket and laid it across the faint swell of her belly.

"A baby."

She regarded him suspiciously. "You didn't know? You really didn't know?"

What to say? he wondered. Surely not knowing made him the most thickheaded man in all of San Francisco. On the other hand, admitting he had suspicions seemed wrong somehow. He took his cue from Berkeley and hoped for once that he'd got it right. "I really didn't know," he said. "A baby." This time his voice held more awe than surprise. "And this is what you didn't want to tell me?" *Don't lie to me, Berkeley.*

"Yes . . . no . . ." She squeezed his hand. "It's not so simple. Of course I wanted you to know but not before you asked me to marry you. I would have wondered if it were only about the baby, you see. You could have told me otherwise, but there would have remained a doubt. I did not want to doubt you. And then . . . afterward . . . I wondered if I had done the right thing, marrying you without telling. Perhaps you would think ill of me for it. Or perhaps you would think I married you because I was carrying your child."

"Did you?"

"No!"

"I believe you," he said simply.

She stared at him. "You do, don't you?" If this were her only secret, Berkeley knew the entire weight would have been eased from her shoulders. She raised her hands and held his face between them. "You honor me with your trust," she said softly.

If only you would do the same. But Grey only thought the words. They remained unspoken as Berkeley kissed him.

"You're pleased?" she asked shyly. "About the baby?"

"Pleased." He kissed her lightly to hide his growing fear that all was not as it should be. "Tell me. Am I the only one who didn't know? Annie? Sam? Someone must have suspected."

"Why? Is it so obvious?" It had been to Garret, she remembered.

"Only in hindsight. The meals you missed or left abruptly. There were mornings you lay abed. And you were uncommonly tired."

"You're so gallant to ignore the fact that I'm increasing."

"It's a very nice little swelling." He pushed the blanket

down a few inches and eyed her breasts consideringly. A blush fanned out across her skin, and her nipples hardened. Grey raised one brow. "Swelling and more swelling. I find all of it agreeable."

"So do I," she said. Beneath the blanket her hand closed around him in an intimate caress.

Anderson Shaw showed more patience than Berkeley would have credited. An entire week passed before he appeared in the gaming hall of the Phoenix. Berkeley was well aware the waiting had been purposeful on Anderson's part. His intention had been to put her on edge, and he had succeeded, perhaps beyond his own imaginings. Berkeley had been helpless in the face of it.

For seven days even the cat found ways to avoid her. She couldn't concentrate, could barely eat, and had little patience for conversation. As her pregnant state became more widely known it was offered as the reason for her prickly behavior. Outside of Berkeley's hearing it was generally agreed that the ninth month could not arrive too soon.

Berkeley's panic began the moment she thought she had lost the earring. While Grey slept she searched under the bed and between the sheets. She looked in the folds of her hastily discarded clothes and upended her shoes. Her hand flew to her throat a dozen times during her search in the unsupportable belief that she hadn't removed it all. It was as if she could feel the weight of it around her neck. Each time she was vaguely surprised when her hand came away empty.

Tears appeared in her eyes from the sheer frustration of her efforts. It was at that point that she picked up the handkerchief Grey had returned to the bedside table. Her blurred vision almost kept her from recognizing the very thing she had been seeking.

Berkeley had expected to feel a measure of relief as she took it into her hand. None was forthcoming. Not then and not a few minutes later when she left the bedchamber for the privacy of the dressing room and was sick in the basin. She disliked herself for being unaccountably angry at Grey, who continued to sleep. She did not want him with her and, perversely, she did. She would have resented any show of kindness in that moment, yet was resentful that he had not made the effort.

Berkeley understood she was not being fair. She did not want to be fair. She wanted to be angry.

It was still daylight when Berkeley arrived at the small jeweler's shop on Kearney Street. The jeweler protested when she explained that she wanted the earring separated from the necklace and returned to her in its original condition. A gold post would have to be attached to the pearl stud, she went on, and it must be done with the same exquisite care that marked all the work on the earring. They haggled a bit on the cost of resetting the pearl in a new gold crown, but Berkeley knew what the jeweler did not: She would have paid any amount. They both believed they each made the better bargain.

She worried throughout that evening that Anderson would approach her. Now her protests that she was not in possession of the earring would have been quite real and no more likely to have been believed. She occupied herself fabricating excuses, none of which turned out to be necessary. Berkeley reflected later that she should have spent more time on the excuses she offered her husband. There seemed to be no end to the questions he put to her.

"You're looking quite lovely this evening," Grey said. He had come to stand just to one side and a little behind Berkeley's chair at the gaming table where she was holding court. His gaze swept the faces of his wife's admirers and found all of them quite happily in her thrall. Grey had had occasion to observe this last week that while Berkeley's mood was often unsettled and unpredictable, the Phoenix's guests were none the wiser. She saved the tart edge of her tongue for those she loved.

At least he hoped that was so.

Grey bent his head and dropped a light kiss on her temple. He felt Berkeley stiffen, but he gave no outward sign. Inside it was as if his gut was being squeezed. He began to inquire after her health but stopped himself. Grey had noticed that she did not welcome questions in that regard. He did not want to give her an excuse to remind him. "I have something for you," he said instead.

Berkeley turned slightly in her chair and raised her face. She realized that Grey could not know it, but it was a relief to look on him alone for a moment. He made it possible for her to lower her guard and show some measure of her pain and panic. She wished she could explain it to him but believed she could not. For the Phoenix's guests she had a fixed smile, kindly eyes, gracious manners, and none of it was real. She doubted that Grey could appreciate these glimpses she allowed him. In his place she knew she would not be so patient.

"Yes?" Even to her own ears her voice was cool. She saw that Grey had heard it too, but only his eyes flinched.

Grey reached inside his jacket and withdrew a slender velvet-covered box. He held it out to Berkeley. "Go on," he urged quietly. "Open it." It was wrong, he thought, to give her this gift in front of others, but he required their presence to assure she would not reject it.

Berkeley's fingers trembled ever so slightly as she raised the lid. A string of diamonds captured the gaming hall's oil lamps, making it radiate brilliantly from each of the ice-blue facets. She stared at it, quite unable to believe what she was seeing.

Leaning forward, Grey gingerly removed the diamond choker from the box. The men at the table leaned in to admire the necklace and the neck it was about to embrace. "Mother of God," one of them said with rather more reverence than not. He spoke for all of them.

Grey watched Berkeley raise her chin. She offered her throat, but there was defiance in the gesture. She had seen through his gift, had known it was given because he had remarked that she was no longer wearing her pendant. She offered an excuse about a loose catch, but he realized she was lying, and she was aware that he knew. The diamond necklace was not strictly a gift. It was meant to rest against her throat and remind her of the truths that always seemed to stick there.

Berkeley ran her fingertips along the diamond settings while Grey finished securing the clasp. She stood and caught a glimpse of a woman she did not recognize in the mirror behind the bar. Pale and elegant, remote and without warmth, Berkeley almost turned to see who was standing behind her casting the cool and distant reflection. Here was a woman she did not think she wanted to know. It was then she understood she was staring at herself.

Berkeley took a step toward Grey, using him to block her view of the mirror. "Thank you," she said. For the benefit of the gathering crowd, she was careful not to shrink from his hands when they grasped her at the waist. She lifted her eyes and then her face. She gave him her mouth. For once she noted his lips were cooler than her own.

Soon it would not matter what Anderson had in mind to threaten her marriage. Berkeley was discovering she was capable of destroying it all by herself.

She heard Grey excuse himself and watched him go. At her waist her fingers tightened. She wanted to reach for him, draw him back to her side. She lowered her hand and rested it on the back of her chair, steadying herself. When she turned back to the table her smile was in place.

It didn't falter once, even when Anderson Shaw placed his hand in hers and asked for a reading.

Berkeley's fingertips grazed his palm lightly. She pretended to examine the lines and the mounts. "I believe some rather unusual business has brought you to San Francisco," she said. "You're not a miner. Or a merchant."

"True enough," Anderson agreed. He glanced around the table at the other men and let them see that he was suitably impressed by Berkeley's first revelation. "Can you tell me my business?"

She pretended to consider that. "I believe you are a performer," she said after a thoughtful pause. "You've come here to entertain."

He chuckled appreciatively. "And be vastly entertained in turn."

"Your voice suggests you may be a trained actor."

"I've made a study of it," he agreed. He took a calling card from inside his vest and asked for a pen. One was produced quickly, and Anderson scribbled a few lines, his free hand curled protectively around the card to hide his work. When he finished he clamped one hand over it and gave Berkeley the other. "Tell me my favorite play and speaking role and extinguish my remaining doubts about your talent."

There was a collective protest from the others. Not one among them had any desire to see Berkeley challenged in such a fashion. They enjoyed her company too much to appreciate any attempt to show up her talent as a fraud.

Berkeley laughed lightly at the grumblings around her. "Have you so little faith in me?" she scolded. "You've not made any friends here, Mr.—"

"Lerner."

Berkeley's heartbeat tripped over itself. Lerner was her mother's maiden name. It had been her own until she became Mrs. Shaw. He had used the name deliberately to see if he could make her stumble. Berkeley recalled her reflection in the mirror earlier and felt the weight of the diamonds at her throat. She continued flawlessly. "I think you have allowed me to misrepresent your business here," she said. "Acting may be a passion with you but I believe you've come here to expose me. Would that be accurate, Mr. Lerner?"

"And unwise for me to admit," Anderson said as he examined the glowering expressions turned in his direction. "Any one of these men may insist on calling me out if I agreed."

"I think you can depend upon it." Out of the corner of her eye Berkeley saw Donnel Kincaid leave the group that was standing nearby. He would have heard every word of the exchange between her and Anderson and understood the mood of the other men. Berkeley had no doubt he was going to bring Grey back to the table. "Why don't you give one of the others your card to hold?" she suggested. "Everyone then may be satisfied as to the absence of deceit.'' Berkeley had no idea if Anderson wanted her to succeed or fail. He could have written anything on the card. If he had not played fair, he would be lucky to leave the Phoenix with his life.

Anderson Shaw's subtle salute was for Berkeley alone. He made the gesture with his eyes. ''As you wish,'' he said, his tone grave and formal. Without a sideways glance he slid the card to the stranger on his right.

Berkeley's eyes shifted long enough to watch Joseph Allen decipher Anderson's scrawl. ''Very well,'' she said, returning her attention to the palm in her hand. She measured her words carefully, as if pondering her answer even as she spoke it. ''The play would be something of Shakespeare's.''

Joe Allen slapped his thigh. ''Damn me if she ain't got it right!'' He realized belatedly that perhaps he had spoken out of turn. He sheepishly held up the card to the men standing behind him for additional confirmation. ''Shakespeare wrote that, didn't he, fellas? Or was it the other gent? Something-Or-Other Jonson?''

''Aaah.'' Grey approached the table. ''A scholarly conundrum. You've raised an interesting point, Joe, and one that would be better entertained elsewhere.'' He laid one hand lightly on Berkeley's bare shoulder. ''Gentlemen, the Society for Literary Discourse and Enlightenment meets on Tuesday afternoons in Mrs. Richards's home on Powell Street. This establishment will continue to remain a gaming hall.''

There was appreciative laughter all around. Joe Allen's cheeks reddened, and he drew back the card he held before someone could snatch it from him.

''Dare I hope there's a wager on the table?'' Grey asked.

Art Madden raised his mug of beer to his lips. ''Seems the stranger in our midst doesn't think much of Mrs. Janeway's talent.''

Grey's eyes strayed to Anderson Shaw. ''Is that right, sir?''

''Nick Lerner,'' Anderson said. He removed his hand from Berkeley's, stood, and extended it to Grey. ''I'm afraid too much is being made of it. Didn't think I'd be stepping into a nest of hornets tonight. Your wife's talent is much respected here.''

"So is my wife," Grey said without inflection. Belatedly, he took the hand that was held out to him, shook it, then motioned Anderson to be seated again. "What was your challenge?''

"It's nothing," Berkeley said. To allay his fears, she reached up and patted the hand Grey still rested on her shoulder. The gesture appeared both absent and affectionate to others but she communicated her confidence to Grey. "Mr. Lerner is an actor. I'm to name his favorite play and role which he has been kind enough to write down and give to Joe. I've said I believe the play is one of Shakespeare's and Joe has confirmed it—more or less.'' Deep chuckles rumbled around the table as Joe Allen was put to another blush.

Grey did not join in the laughter. He was studying Anderson Shaw. "I have no gift for fortune-telling," he said. "But even I would have guessed Shakespeare. Isn't he every actor's favorite bard?''

Anderson nodded. "You would be in the right of it there. But he has a number of plays from which an actor can choose. Your wife has yet to choose mine.''

Grey fished out a gold coin from his pocket and placed it on the table. "I think she can do it.''

Anderson laughed. "The odds are always with the house, aren't they? Very well. I started this. I may as well be poorer for it.'' He extracted a matching gold piece from his vest and laid it beside Grey's. "You have your wager.'' He glanced at Joe Allen. "And you keep your silence.'' His gaze swiveled back to Berkeley. His polished chestnut eyes were expectant, mocking and daring her. "Mrs. Janeway?''

Berkeley took his hand again. She had no desire to draw out the drama. "The play is *The Taming of the Shrew*," she said. "But your favorite role is from one of the tragedies. I believe you fancy yourself a credible Shylock in *The Merchant of Venice*." Berkeley knew even before Joe Allen started whooping and pounding the table that she had got it right. She scooped both coins from the table and gave them to Grey. They were properly his winnings. What she had won was Anderson's surprise.

He asked her about it later when he was waiting for her on the way to her room. "You must have thought I had forgotten you," Anderson said.

"It never once occurred to me," Berkeley said. "In some ways you're very predictable, Anderson."

"Predictability had nothing to do with how you managed that trick this evening. You couldn't have known what I would write on the card."

"I didn't."

"Then how was it done? I have no particular fondness for *The Shrew*."

"And Richard III would be your role. Yes, I'm aware of that. But you gave the card to Joe Allen, and he moves his mouth when he reads."

In spite of himself Anderson Shaw laughed. "So simple as that, eh?"

Berkeley nodded. They had reached her suite. "I won't invite you inside," she said. "Say your piece, then go."

Anderson would not be hurried although he did look over his shoulder down the long hallway. "You have not inquired after Mr. Denison."

"I assumed he was in his room."

"He is. Pacing the floor, I'm certain. He hasn't half the patience I've shown." He thought Berkeley would comment, but she remained silent. "Do you have the earring?"

"Yes, but I'm not giving it to you. I'll put it in Mr. Denison's hand myself. What is his room number?"

"Three-oh-six. But not here. He's at the Palace. We considered it the wisest course of action following our first meeting."

"Garret doesn't want his brother to know he's here."

"That's correct. I suppose he has his reasons. Can you leave?"

"Not now. But tomorrow. Is that soon enough?"

"You're very eager to give over the earring. I wonder at

your change of heart. Can you be so relieved to see the last of us?"

Berkeley ignored him. "And what is it you want, Anderson? You've spent this last week thinking about it. What will it take to be rid of you?"

"Clever girl. Haven't you guessed it by now?"

Her voice dropped to a harsh whisper. "None of your games now. Of course I want you gone. You deserted me at the claim and left me to make my own way. Well, I have. And if I hadn't stumbled across Graham Denison, you would have never revealed that you were quite alive. You would have stayed with the Ducks in Sydney Town, where I imagine you've made your fair share of friends."

Anderson's hand snaked out and caught Berkeley's wrist. He held it tightly and would have enjoyed it more if she had struggled. He intended to leave bruises she would be forced to explain. "Do you know that if you hadn't returned to telling fortunes, I might never have found you? I'd heard of Grey Janeway but had no occasion to see him. The Ducks seemed to think he was better left alone. I believe the ruffians rather liked him, or at least they respected his power to retaliate. It was only when the rumor began of a certain young woman in his care who could tell a man about his past and divine his future that I became curious. Seeing that you had landed on your feet was only half as surprising as my first glimpse of the man who called himself Grey Janeway. I knew the truth immediately. I was not entirely certain you did though. From what I could learn it didn't appear you had contacted the Thornes. I regretted leaving you with the earring nonetheless."

Berkeley's fingers were numb from the pressure of Anderson's hand. "You left it with me because you could have never realized its true worth. It would have sold for a paltry sum in this city. You would have been better staked at the gaming tables if you had owned an orchard. At five dollars an apple you could have made the fortune you want." She twisted her wrist and felt the skin rub harshly against Anderson's palm.

He gave her no quarter. "Name it," she said. "Tell me quickly before someone comes and sees you here."

"Twenty thousand dollars."

Berkeley actually gasped. "You can't possibly believe I can get that kind of money for you."

"Why not? You're wearing half that much around your neck right now." Before she knew what he was about he stripped her of the diamond choker. "Room three-oh-six. At ten. You shouldn't be late, and you shouldn't come without the earring and the money." Anderson released her hand and walked away, satisfied with this evening's work. He left the hotel by the back stairs, oblivious to Annie Jack's severe scolding for mistaking her kitchen for a thoroughfare.

Nat Corbett was yanked onto his tiptoes by the powerful hand at the scruff of his neck. He yelped once before his shirt collar caught him around the throat and silenced him. Half-carried, half-dragged, he was deposited in front of Grey in the main gaming hall. The crowd had thinned, but there were still more than a hundred gamblers left to witness his humiliation. Nat felt the stares of every one of them.

Annie Jack stood facing Grey, arms akimbo, a severe frown on her face. To all appearances she was unmoved by Nat's whipped puppy expression. "Annie caught him sneakin' in her kitchen from the outside no mo' than a minute ago. That suggests to Annie that he also sneaked himself right out of here." She slapped her large palms together twice in a brisk hand-washing gesture and declared herself free of further responsibility for young Nat's welfare.

Grey consulted his pocket watch. It was nearing one o'clock. His own frown was a less fearsome one than Annie's but clearly communicated that he was displeased. "We can't talk here," he said. "Come, we'll go upstairs. I don't have to carry you under my arm, do I?"

In answer, Nat hung his head and began to lead the way. At

the top of the stairs he turned toward his own room. Grey put a hand on his shoulder and stopped him.

"My suite," he said. Nat's stiffening and the fear that leaped into his eyes provided Grey with the information he sought. "This way." He turned Nat in the direction of his own quarters.

In the front room Grey indicated Nat should be seated. The boy chose the large chair by the fireplace and sat stiffly on the very edge. Grey felt his eyes on him as he moved about the room, first closing the door to the library, then while he poured himself a small drink at the sideboard. "Do you imagine I'm going to beat you?" Grey asked.

Of course it had occurred to him, but Nat wasn't certain it was a good idea to say so. "I'm hoping you won't, sir."

"Well, I won't. You can set that from your mind and concentrate on telling me the truth. And I *do* want to hear it from you, Nat."

Nat's eyes strayed involuntarily toward the door.

"She's another room away," Grey told him. "And sleeping. She retired more than an hour ago. You don't have to be worried that you'll be overheard." He paused, sipping his drink. "I take it your late-night excursion had something to do with her."

Nat squirmed in his seat but said nothing. His abject countenance spoke eloquently of his misery. He could not meet Grey's eyes.

Sighing, Grey sat on the settee opposite Nat. "Did she send you on some errand this evening? Is that it?"

"No!" Nat blurted. He sat back a little, surprising himself with the vehemence of his reply.

"But you slipped out of the hotel because of her." It was not strictly a question and Grey didn't expect an answer. He regarded Nat in silence for a moment, thinking back over the past week to things he had noticed but not really seen: how Nat kept Berkeley in his sights when even the most intrepid among them gave her a wide berth; how he often would appear at the door to their suite looking for Pandora; and how he sat in the shadows at the top of the stairs while the Phoenix filled with customers, his attention on the doors.

''We've all been watching her these days,'' Grey said at
last. ''But I think you've been the only one watching *out* for
her.''

Nat's small chest heaved with a shaky breath. His expression
became marginally more hopeful.

''Listen to me, Nat.'' Grey rolled the crystal tumbler between
his palms. ''Whatever it is you've seen or know, it can't be
your secret alone. Berkeley's in some sort of trouble, isn't
she?'' Grey watched Nat bite his lip. ''Is she aware you know?''

A spot of blood appeared on Nat's lower lip as he bit down
harder.

Grey swore softly. ''She does know, doesn't she? And she's
asked you not to say anything.'' And keeping the secret was
clearly an agony for the boy. How could Berkeley have done
that to him? Grey's mouth tightened as he felt his own anger
taking form. It was not only that she had placed Nat in this
untenable position but that she had refused to share any part
of what was troubling her with him. No, that wasn't entirely
true. She had shared all the emotion and none of the information.
There was no betrayal of trust. There was simply no trust.

Grey finished his drink and put the tumbler aside. He leaned
forward, resting his forearms on his knees, his fingers clasped
together. ''Look at me, Nat,'' he said. His tone brooked no
refusal. ''I respect your promise to honor Berkeley's wishes.
Only you can decide if your promise was extracted unfairly or
given rashly, against your better judgment. I'm not going to
conduct an inquisition. I am going to ask that you think carefully
about this secret you're carrying for Berkeley and if you should
be doing it at all.''

Nat rubbed his kneecaps nervously, but he didn't look away
from Grey's penetrating stare. He was remembering the blow
Berkeley had taken seven days earlier. If he closed his eyes,
he would have been able to see her stumbling backward from
the force of it. She had been given the slap to assure his silence.
His life had been threatened to make certain of hers. And now
there was the baby to consider.

"She wouldn't have to know?" Nat said at last. "That I said anything, I mean."

The knot in Grey's middle began to loosen a bit. "She wouldn't have to know. I won't betray your confidence."

"That's the promise I made." Tears welled in his eyes, but he blinked them back. His gaze strayed to the door again. He almost wished Berkeley would appear. He could have made his escape then and let her face Grey Janeway. When he turned back to Grey his expression was one of resignation. For a moment he looked far older than his eleven years. He took a deep breath and exhaled softly. "What do you want to know?"

Berkeley's eyes fluttered open as Grey slipped into bed beside her. "What time is it?" she murmured.

"The middle of the night. Go back to sleep."

She hadn't thought she could sleep at all, yet somehow she had. "You're late coming to bed." She placed the flat of her hand on Grey's back and rubbed along the length of his spine. His skin was warm but beneath it she could feel the corded tension of his muscles. Berkeley pressed herself closer and placed a kiss at the base of his neck.

"Don't." Reaching behind him, Grey removed Berkeley's hand from his back. "Go to sleep."

His words, his actions, had the opposite effect. Berkeley was wide-awake now and wounded. She put some distance between them but remained stiffly on her side.

Grey hadn't considered how difficult it would be to join Berkeley in bed and pretend he didn't know the things he did. Worse, he had learned less than he wanted to. Nat could only relate what he had observed firsthand because Berkeley hadn't really confided in him. What Nat could tell Grey raised more questions. The only satisfactory conclusion to the evening, as far as Grey was concerned, was that Nat had been relieved of the burden of his promise. That had been worth some peace of mind to both of them.

Grey turned over. Berkeley's head rested on top of the curve of her arm. She hadn't closed her eyes, and, from what he could make out of her features, she was as alert and on edge as he was. He had never wanted to make love to Berkeley to hurt her. He resisted the urge now. "I'm heartily weary of you blowing hot and cold with me," he whispered. "You seek me out with your eyes and when I'm near you push me away. You shrink from my touch. You scorn my gifts. You act as if you want nothing so much as to be rid of me. What am I to make of this latest overture? You place your hand at my back and your mouth on my neck . . . what does that mean, Berkeley?"

She said nothing for a long moment. Her mouth was dry, and the back of her throat ached. "Have I made you hate me?"

The curve of Grey's smile was faint and bittersweet. "No," he said softly. "You haven't done that. You can't."

Berkeley's hand crossed the distance between them. Her fingertips touched his cheek and the corner of his lips. They swept lightly along the underside of his chin. She leaned toward him and searched his still features. She imagined his beautiful eyes darkening at the centers. She would lose herself in those eyes, she thought. She would lose herself in him.

Her mouth remained only a hairbreadth removed from his. "Love me, then."

Chapter Fourteen

Grey understood better once Berkeley was sleeping again. Her cheek rested against his shoulder, and her soft breath warmed his skin. The faint rise and fall of her breasts was itself soothing.

It had been different earlier when she was stretched out beneath him, her nipples hard enough to scrape his chest as he moved over her. She had cried out when he took one into his mouth and sucked. The warmth and wetness of his mouth drew a shudder from her, and she had arched into him, wanting more from him, wanting to give him more.

He felt it then, as she curved her arms and legs around him and pressed her mouth against his neck. He felt it, and finally had a name for the emotion that had had her restlessly walking the edge of a precipice for seven days and nights: desperation. Grey recognized it in her because he recognized it in himself.

He did not want to lose her. He was driven by the same need to protect her as she was to protect him. Grey only wished he knew what secret she was guarding so carefully. Not revealing it was destroying Berkeley. Above all else, he did not want to lose her.

So he had held her tightly and matched the upward thrust of her body. Sweat-slick, their legs and arms tangled. Their mouths fused, parted, and collided again. They rocked together and twisted, and their positions changed in fits and starts until she was under him again, this time on her stomach. He cupped her bottom, lifting her hips while she raised herself on her forearms. Her pale hair spilled over her shoulder. He looked down at the elegant curve of her back and rise of her buttocks; he felt her shallow breathing as she anticipated his entry and heard the soft cry she couldn't quite contain when he took her.

She had fallen asleep almost the instant he had withdrawn. Her soft, languorous sigh had been as deeply satisfying to him as his name on her lips when she climaxed. Grey smiled in the darkness and stroked her hair. "You shouldn't be afraid," he said quietly. "You should never be afraid."

Ivory DuPree's attention strayed from her companion as the main doors to the Palace were pushed open. There was not much trade this early in the morning, so Ivory's curiosity was piqued. Her brows rose a full half inch when she saw who it was.

"What is it?" Paul Henley wanted to know. He turned and followed the direction of Ivory's gaze when she was too long in answering. He whistled softly. "I'll be damned. Why it's—"

"Why it's a bump on your head you'll be having if you mention this to anyone." As an afterthought she added sweetly, *"Chèr."* Ivory watched Berkeley Janeway hurry across the Palace's hardwood gaming floor toward the staircase. She looked neither right nor left, but kept her head bent and her eyes lowered. Her green satin bonnet was trimmed with black velvet and adorned on either side with a black-and-white feather. A broad emerald ribbon secured it. It did not hide her features as much as she might have hoped. When she had stood for a moment in the doorway, uncertain and hesitating, it merely framed her face, bringing her features into clear focus. Ivory had no difficulty recognizing her.

"Excuse me," she told Paul. Without waiting for a reply, she slid her chair away from the table and followed at a discreet distance in Berkeley's wake.

Berkeley looked up and down the hall before she knocked on the door of room three-oh-six. "Hurry," she said under her breath. "Please hurry." There was a soft tread on the stairs to her right. She looked in that direction nervously, her fingers flexing in agitation. When the door opened she ducked inside so quickly her bonnet was knocked askew by Anderson's imposing shoulder.

"My," he said, watching Berkeley make adjustments to the ribbons and brim. "Such an entrance. One might think you're eager to see us again."

Garret Denison moved away from the fireplace and offered to take Berkeley's cloak.

She shook her head and retreated a step, putting more distance between them. Her eyes darted around the room. The Palace did not offer the same spacious luxury as the Phoenix. An iron-rail bed occupied most of the space against the far wall. The rest was filled in by a pine washstand on one side and a small night table on the other. An overstuffed chair, its upholstery shiny with wear, sat near the fireplace. Two wooden chairs were also available for sitting. Berkeley ignored them both. "This does not have to take long. I would prefer that it didn't. No one knows I'm even gone from the Phoenix. Please, may we just conclude our business?"

Garret extended one hand, palm up. "I've only ever wanted the earring."

Lifting her wrist, Berkeley removed the beaded drawstring bag dangling from it. She opened it carefully and reached inside. Her gloved fingers closed around the earring. "Is it really yours?" she asked without removing it.

"It's rather late to be asking questions. But yes, it's mine. I hired your husband to find it for me after my brother was . . . well, after he disappeared."

"Then you didn't hire him to find your brother."

"God, no. Graham didn't have the earring the last time we

spoke. In fact he made a point of telling me he lost it. I guessed he had sold it.'' He looked at the beaded bag, his eyes narrowing slightly. ''May I?''

Still Berkeley hesitated. She turned to Anderson. Her brows were drawn together, a small crease appearing between them. ''You found the Thornes because he told you where to start your search. Am I right?''

Anderson shrugged. ''Something like that.''

Exactly like that, she thought. ''Does he know about the other earring?'' Berkeley asked. She felt her heart begin to pound. ''Did you tell him what we found in Boston?''

''Enough,'' Anderson snapped. ''Give him what he wants.''

Garret lowered his arm slowly. He looked from Berkeley to Anderson and back to Berkeley. ''What other earring?''

''There is a mate to this one,'' she said.

''That's impossible,'' Garret said. ''My mother lost the mate years ago.''

Anderson reached for Berkeley's reticule, but she held it away from him. ''Give him the earring,'' he said between gritted teeth.

Berkeley skirted a large wing chair and put it between herself and Anderson. ''Have you ever considered even once that *he* may be Greydon Thorne?''

''For God's sake,'' Garret interjected. ''What the hell is she talking about, Shaw? What is Decker Thorne except an acquaintance of my brother's?''

Anderson held his ground, but his lean cheeks were mottled with anger. ''I swear I will strike you so hard, Berkeley, you will not come to your feet easily. Give him the earring!''

Berkeley paled but did not shrink away. She pulled her hand out of the beaded bag and extended it to Garret. ''You should know that you may not have been told the truth about this earring,'' she said softly. She unfolded her fingers, and the earring dropped silently into Garret Denison's open palm.

Garret turned away, his shoulders hunched, and examined the earring closely. He moved to the window where he could see it in the sunlight and studied the delicate gold settings that held the pearl. He turned over the golden drop that hung from the pearl like a tear and saw the familiar and exquisite engraving. ER. Evaline Randolph. He whispered her name. His mother's name. There could be no doubt the earring was hers. He had seen it hundreds of times growing up, had gone into her bedroom and opened her jewelry case to look at it. All because she had promised it to him. It was something he would have someday that he would not have to share with his brother.

Garret turned around. "It's the earring. My mother's initials are here on the drop. She will be grateful to have it returned to her." His fingers closed over it. "She isn't well," he said quietly. "She never has been . . . for as long as I can remember. This will be important to her." He looked at Berkeley. "I don't pretend to understand what you were going on about, but I'm confident it has nothing to do with me. *This* is my heritage."

"As you wish," Berkeley said. Her gaze shifted to Anderson. "My business is concluded. You may apply my share of Mr. Denison's payment for the recovery of the earring to what you're extorting from me. You already have my necklace." She reached into her reticule again. "I've had a note drawn up from my account for another thousand. It's all the money I have, Anderson. If you give me an address, I will send payments as funds become available to me. You may be sure I will pay you."

"This is very disappointing, Berkeley," Anderson said. "I expected better from you."

Garret pocketed the earring and sat on the edge of the bed. Relaxed now, he stretched his legs in front of him and folded his arms across his chest. "How much does he want from you?" he asked Berkeley.

"Twenty thousand dollars."

One of Garret's dark brows kicked up. "And you have that kind of money?"

"No, of course not. He expects me to get it from Grey. Which is ludicrous because Grey will ask questions, and I'll be forced to tell him the truth at some point—which is precisely the thing I'm trying to keep from him." Her eyes implored

Anderson. "Don't you see? I may as well tell him everything now if you're going to force my hand."

"Has he asked after your necklace?" Anderson said.

"No. But he will."

"You'll have to say you lost it, won't you? Or that it was stolen. I'm sure if you think on it, you'll come up with some equally plausible explanations for its disappearance."

Berkeley closed her eyes briefly. When she opened them weariness and a certain resolve etched her features. "I'm sick of lying to my husband. That's what I'm trying to tell you. I don't want to think on it. I want you to take what you have and leave here. Leave the city. Leave the state. But leave."

A small, rather stiff smile raised the corners of Anderson's mouth. "Or what?" he asked. "I believe you're prepared to threaten me. Have a care, Berkeley. Only consider this: I am, in fact, your legal husband. That will become the least of your problems if you don't show a more temperate nature."

"What do you mean?"

He shrugged. "I'm a better gambler than you've given me credit for. I know when to show my cards and when to keep them close to my vest. I believe I'll hold them for now." His eyes dropped to her beaded bag. Berkeley's right hand was still inside. "What do you have there? A pocket pistol?"

She shook her head. The knife she held felt very solid in her hand. Berkeley told herself when she lifted it from Grey's boot that she would be able to use it. Her conscience had been easier to convince when she was not confronted by a flesh-and-blood target. She let the knife drop to the bottom of her reticule and removed her hand. "I won't let you provoke me, Anderson, but it doesn't mean I'm frightened of you. You will do what you will, and I will follow my own course. Right now, I am going to leave."

Anderson watched her come around the chair. "You're infinitely more interesting than you used to be. I wonder how much credit I may take for this transformation. Leaving you to fend for yourself has given you courage. A false sense, to be sure.

How I will enjoy making you understand you're only being reckless.''

Berkeley made no attempt to reply. She nodded once, coolly, in Garret's direction, then took several steps toward the door. She anticipated that Anderson would grab her arm as she passed and he acted true to form. Berkeley swung her reticule in a wide arc at his head and felt the hilt of the knife connect solidly with the back of his skull. She wrested her arm away from him as he staggered sideways, partly from the blow, but more from sheer surprise.

Berkeley reached for the door handle. It twisted in her hand but not because she had done anything to cause it. Someone was pushing on the door from the other side. Instinctively she stepped back and found herself being trapped between the wall and the door as it was thrust open.

Grey Janeway stepped into the room. He was followed closely by Ivory DuPree. His eyes darted to the two occupants and he recognized one of them immediately. ''Mr. Lerner,'' he said. Grey glanced over his shoulder at Ivory. ''It's all right. I'm certain we've found the right room this time.''

Standing on tiptoe, Ivory looked past Grey and searched the room. ''I don't see her. You must be mistaken. Come, we'll try another.'' She flashed an apologetic smile at the Palace's guests and tugged on the back of Grey's jacket. ''Hurry. Or we'll miss her altogether.''

Grey removed Ivory's hand. ''She's here.'' Indeed, he had known it even before he had felt the slight resistance on the door as he opened it. It was her fragrance, faint to be sure, but nonetheless unmistakable to his senses. He had buried his face in her cloud of corn silk hair last night. He was not wrong about the scent of lavender now. Grey took another step and gently pried the door a few more inches away from the wall. Any doubts that she was behind it faded when he felt her pulling from the other direction. The outcome of this tug-of-war was inevitable.

Berkeley looked up at Grey as her face was revealed in a

shaft of light. "Hello," she said softly, a shade guiltily. "I suppose you're wondering what I'm doing here."

Grey took her by the hand and brought her out from behind the door. "An understatement."

She noticed he did not seem at all angry with her. His hand squeezed hers. "You remember Mr. Lerner."

Grey nodded. "From yesterday evening. The challenge about plays and roles. Yes, of course." The actor, Grey saw, was rubbing the back of his head. Something about the movement suggested to Grey that it was not a gesture of pure puzzlement, but one rooted in pain relief. What had Berkeley done?

"And this is Garret Denison," Berkeley went on. "Graham Denison's brother."

Grey inclined his head, his eyes cool, his features implacable. "I know the name."

Garret had jumped to his feet the moment Grey had barged into the room. Alarm and apprehension mingled to keep him silenced. Now his eyes narrowed suspiciously on his brother's face. "What game is this, Graham? Do you think I wouldn't know you? My God, you're a piece of work."

Berkeley stepped closer to Grey as if she could shield him. "My husband doesn't recognize or remember you," she said. "You have nothing at all to fear from him."

One corner of Garret's mouth lifted derisively. "Fear? You're quite mistaken there. I've never feared my brother."

"Then there's no reason to raise the past, is there?" she asked. Berkeley looked up at Grey. Her husband showed no interest in Garret at all; he was watching her. "Mr. Denison's come all this way to claim the earring."

"He's identified it?"

She nodded. "Yes, and claimed it. I gave it to him only a few minutes ago. It's why I've come here, you see. To pass it on. You've never really cared about it, and I thought we'd be better rid of it. Do you understand, Grey? I didn't want to distress you."

Grey smiled faintly. "I think I understand." He held her lightly by the waist and regarded Garret again. "You don't seem as though you believe us," he said. "I can fully comprehend your mistrust. It's true your face means less than nothing to me, but Berkeley has given me some information about my past. I'm aware that I've brought shame to the family and that you consider yourselves well rid of me."

Berkeley gasped a little at that. "Grey, I've never said—"

"She's right," he interrupted her. "That would be *my* interpretation. Would you consider it accurate, Mr. Denison?"

Garret's head jerked a fraction at being so stiffly referred to as Mr. Denison. It was unexpected, this civil tone and grave formality. How surpassingly amusing it was that he had gone to such lengths to avoid his brother. He had set himself the problem of what to do about Graham at the moment he learned from Anderson Shaw that his brother was alive. Throughout his journey west to San Francisco he contemplated the necessity of arranging his brother's death a second time. The only way to circumvent that end was to conduct this business with the earring without Graham's knowledge. He had vowed to give his brother a small advantage this time. Now he realized his noble gesture had been unnecessary and would never be fully appreciated.

It seemed the beating in Charleston all those years ago had served to end Graham's life after all.

Garret shook his head slowly. Low laughter rumbled deeply in his chest. He sat back on the bed again and let himself enjoy the irony. He laughed hard, with real amusement, and regretted only that he would never share this moment with any family member save the brother whom he hated. It took him more than a minute to compose himself. His eyes were damp. "Forgive me," he said somewhat breathlessly. "That was quite unpardonable. I imagined another outcome entirely upon seeing my brother again. This meeting . . . well, it's difficult to take in." Garret took out a handkerchief and wiped his eyes. "It's true then? You really don't remember me?"

"At the risk of sending you into another paroxysm of laughter, it's true."

Garret grinned. "And Beau Rivage?"

"Not a thing."

"It's incredible. There are certain similarities between your hotel and my home. I remarked on them as soon as I saw the Phoenix." He paused. "You don't mind that I refer to Beau Rivage as *my* home, do you?"

"Only as long as you don't refer to the Phoenix as *your* hotel."

Garret was actually enjoying himself. His expression warmed as he silently saluted his brother with a brief tilt of his head. "Alys?"

Grey frowned. He glanced at Berkeley. She had never mentioned anyone by that name. "Nothing, I'm afraid," he told his brother.

"You were going to marry her," Garret said. "Instead, I did."

Berkeley had no liking for how Garret was amusing himself at Grey's expense. She wanted to leave. Anderson's role in this meeting had been sidestepped for now, but Grey would have questions. Berkeley wanted to be away from Anderson when she was forced to answer them. She had no faith that Anderson would allow her to spin her own tale.

"Then I wish you happy with her," Grey said politely. "I certainly have no regrets."

Anderson used to hold her like this, Berkeley thought. One hand at the small of her back. His fingertips grazing her waist. She felt an unpleasant knot form in her stomach as she anticipated feeling his knuckle dig harshly into her spine. She tore her eyes away from Anderson and reminded herself that she was with Grey. "May we leave?" she asked.

"Of course." Grey looked back at Ivory, who was still standing behind him, bobbing and weaving a bit to get the best view she could of the room's inhabitants. "Please take my wife downstairs. I'll join you both in a few minutes."

Berkeley started to protest. She did not want to leave without Grey.

"Come with me, Mrs. Janeway," Ivory said, looping her arm through Berkeley's. "Let the men have their say. There won't be room for us once they commence puffing their chests and strutting. This isn't a suite at the Phoenix, you know." More firmly than gently, Ivory tugged on Berkeley's arm.

Berkeley's feet gave way reluctantly. She suspected that Ivory would drag her from the room if she didn't move of her own accord. She felt the light caress of Grey's hand as she was parted from him. His smile gave no hint that he was the least concerned. It was the flinty, blue-gray cast to his eyes that gave her pause.

Grey waited until the footfalls of the two women were out of earshot before he spoke. Ivory had had the presence of mind not to close the door behind him. He had a clear escape route if one was needed. "Is the earring all you came for, Garret?" he asked. "Do you have what you want?"

As if struck by Grey's tone, Garret's head snapped up. "Unless you give me reason to want something else," he said slowly. *Your life, perhaps.* "You haven't suddenly found your memory?"

Grey pointed to his temple. "Tabula rasa," he said. "A genuine blank slate. I don't anticipate that changing."

Garret's eyes narrowed. What was his brother saying? That he did remember and was choosing to pretend otherwise? Or could he be taken at his word? "I have the earring," he said. He took it out of his pocket and showed it to Grey. "Your wife was instrumental in delivering it to me. It's been an exhaustive search. For the earring, that is. Not for you. I could have done without laying eyes on you again, Graham."

"I understand that. I suppose, in your eyes, what I did was unforgivable."

"She's told you about Falconer, then."

Grey nodded. "It doesn't seem real to me. It's as if the name should belong to someone else."

"Oh, it's yours. You earned it running your blackbirds along the Underground. I confess I was surprised to discover you hadn't taken up the abolitionist cause again. Apparently a leopard *can* change his spots." Garret wrapped his handkerchief around the earring and put it away. He lifted his chin in Anderson Shaw's direction. "You haven't asked after my companion. I'm entertaining some peculiar notions as to why that is."

"I only wanted to be certain you and I are finished," Grey said. "I'm satisfied we are."

Garret nodded. He folded his arms across his chest again and waited to see how Graham's other business would be concluded.

Grey turned to Anderson. "You're younger than I thought you would be."

One of Anderson's chestnut brows rose. "Oh?"

"I pictured my wife's stepfather as an older man."

"Aaahh." Anderson expelled a breath slowly. "So you know. She told you after all."

"About you, yes. That you were masquerading as Lerner, no. I've only realized the truth of the matter since I came here. Now you've confirmed it."

"Clever."

Grey shrugged. "Not really. I was thinking I've been slow to realize quite a bit. Weeks ago, when you and Garret tried to get the earring from Nat, I should have suspected you. I only considered that you'd told one of the Ducks about the earring before you were killed. It didn't occur to me then that you might be behind the thing yourself."

"Every man should attend his own wake," Anderson said. "It's a humbling experience."

"How could you abandon her?"

"Short-sightedness on my part, I assure you. I did not suspect that she could become such a lucrative asset. Our funds were short, and the earring, as valuable as it is to Garret, was essentially worthless here." He held up his hands in a mocking, helpless gesture. "In light of how well she's done, I don't think she regrets being left behind. She's managed to land on her feet . . . or at least on her back." Anderson did not miss the narrowing of Grey's flinty stare. He also observed the faint forward lean to his body, as if he were straining at the end of his leash. "You want to plant your fist in my face, I suppose," he said. "That would be a mistake, Mr. Janeway."

Grey gave Anderson Shaw full marks for his quietly threatening stance. It would be the Ducks, Grey thought, who would retaliate on Anderson's behalf. He almost didn't care. "Is the earring all you wanted from my wife?" he asked. "Are you leaving with Garret?"

"I haven't decided. I was thinking I should come to know my new son-in-law."

Grey's smile held no warmth. "You wouldn't like him."

"Perhaps not."

Making his point bluntly, Grey asked, "What will it take for you to leave us alone?"

Anderson did not pretend that he had been insulted. "I'm not greedy, Mr. Janeway. I expect to realize a tidy sum from the return of the earring." He glanced at Garret for confirmation.

"That's right," Garret said.

"So," Anderson went on. "I could be satisfied with as little as ten thousand dollars. I could be very happy with fifteen."

Grey did not blink and he didn't hesitate. "Will you take a draft? Or do you want it in gold?"

"Gold, I think. A draft payment can always be stopped."

"I'll make the arrangements with the Bank of California this afternoon. You will have your money and a passage back East by closing. I'll insist on seeing you off." His gaze swiveled to Garret. "Both of you."

Leaving nothing to negotiation, Grey turned on his heel and left.

Berkeley was pacing a path in front of the staircase. She looked up when she heard someone on the steps. "Grey!" Her eyes moved quickly over him as he made his descent. He appeared all of a piece.

"You look none the worse for that encounter," Ivory noted when Grey reached the bottom. "I told your wife not to worry. Poor thing. Back and forth. Back and forth. I'm spinning, I know that."

Grey grinned at Ivory as Berkeley launched herself at him. He was rocked back on his heels. "She never does anything by halves." One of his arms came around Berkeley. The other

he held out for Ivory. She grasped it and they shook hands
warmly. Behind Berkeley's back Ivory blew Grey a kiss. She
was vastly amused to see him blush.

Grey released Ivory's hand and set Berkeley from him.
"Thank you, Ivory. I didn't think Berkeley could get away
from us today. You did the right thing by sending for me."

She smiled. "Your wife doesn't share that sentiment." Ivory's eyes gleamed. "You're not going to beat her, are you? I
think she believes you're going to beat her."

Berkeley sucked in her breath. "I never said any—"

"It has merit though, doesn't it?" Grey interrupted. "Thank
you again, Miss DuPree. Berkeley, we have to go." He didn't
offer his arm or wait for her assent. He moved toward the door
and forced her to hurry to keep up with him. The pace he set
outside only slowed marginally, and she had difficulty matching
his long stride. Grey took pity on her only as they were crossing
Portsmouth Square and he heard her labored breathing. He
stopped in his tracks so suddenly that she bumped into him.

Berkeley looked up. "Do you wish to drag me the last fifty
yards?" She began to loosen the ribbons of her bonnet. "By
the hair?"

"I'm more tempted than amused," he said dryly. He watched
her sweep the bonnet off to one side and shake her head. The
same wind that whipped her skirts against her legs lifted the
gold-and-platinum banner of her hair. He was reminded that
she had made a similar gesture the first time they stood in front
of the Phoenix. He might even have fallen in love with her
then. His lips moved around a single word, spoken softly, more
to himself than to Berkeley. *Tempted.*

Grey lifted Berkeley inches off the ground. Her mouth parted
in surprise, and her hands grasped his shoulders to steady herself. The bonnet slipped from her fingers and was caught by
the wind. It rolled and bounced and was ignored by both of
them. She searched his face, and what she saw made her close
her eyes. His mouth covered hers, and if she hadn't already
been dangling above the ground, surely she would have floated
half again as high.

They were oblivious to the miners and merchants who paused on the perimeter of Portsmouth Square, caught in mid-stride by the exuberance of the lovers. They didn't hear the appreciative applause or enthusiastic whistles. They could have been alone in their own room.

Berkeley buried her face against Grey's shoulder as she steadied herself. She was catching her breath again, this time for a very different reason. Surreptitiously she lifted one hand to her mouth and touched the faintly swollen outline of her lips. She could still feel the pressure of his kiss, the taste and texture of him as he had drawn her out and into him.

She smiled a bit shakily as she stepped back.

"This doesn't change anything," Grey said.

"I know." She was beaming. Her eyes were radiant. "I *know*."

His brows came together. He spoke slowly, as if to a child. "I mean I'm still angry with you."

"Yes," she said. Her smile didn't fade at all. "But it doesn't change anything. You don't love me any less. I'm just understanding that part."

Grey shook his head, relief and exasperation tugging at his expression. "It's damn well about time." He grabbed her hand and pulled her along, stopping just once to scoop up the wayward bonnet.

Anderson Shaw stood at the window of his room. He didn't turn until Grey and Berkeley disappeared from his narrow view of the street. "I think I made the better bargain," he told Garret.

Garret Denison shrugged and dropped himself casually into the overstuffed arm chair. He leaned back his head and momentarily closed his eyes. "I got what I came for," he drawled softly.

"Are you certain?"

The question surprised Garret. What was its purpose? "What are you saying? That I'm wrong about the earring?" He sat up and looked behind him for Anderson's reply.

"No, only wondering if you're sure."

"Of course I'm sure. It's not easily mistaken. There's not another like it."

Anderson said nothing. Actually, he was thinking, there were two.

Berkeley disappeared into the dressing room as soon as she and Grey returned to their suite.

"Don't think you can hide in there!" Grey called from behind his desk in the library. He poured a cup of tea for each of them from the tray Annie Jack had prepared. To Berkeley's he added a dollop of honey. He held out the cup to her as she swept back into the room. She had removed her cloak and bonnet. The reticule and gloves were gone as well. His eyes dropped to her hands. They were empty. "I believe, ma'am, you have something that belongs to me."

Berkeley reached for her tea, but Grey drew it back suddenly. She frowned.

"My knife?" he asked.

Berkeley had the grace to blush. "You might have said something before I went to all the trouble to put it under the armoire."

"Why on earth would you put it there?"

"To make it appear it fell out of your boots when you dropped them there."

Grey said nothing. His look in response to this bit of misguided subterfuge told Berkeley quite clearly what he thought of it. "You'll be so kind as to get it for me."

"If you must have it." She sighed. A few moments later she was exchanging the knife for a cup of tea.

Extending his leg, Grey slipped the blade back into the sheath inside his boot. Out of the corner of his eye he saw Berkeley watching him with some consternation. "Did you think perhaps that I had another?"

"I thought you must," she offered lamely. "Somewhere.

Though I admit I was distressed when I couldn't find one. It would have been my first choice."

Grey could only shake his head with a vague sense of disbelief. He pointed to the chair opposite his desk. "Sit down, Berkeley."

She sat. It was not so very different than her first interview with him, she thought. He had not been complimentary regarding her intelligence on that occasion either. "I know you think I've acted unwisely . . ."

"Not in all things," he said quietly. He saw her head come up and rivet her attention on him. "But yes, it's difficult to act or think reasonably when one is as frightened as you were. I wish you could have trusted me with your fear, but I don't fault you for it. It was just last night that I finally understood the only thing that really frightened you was losing me. In your own way you were trying to protect me. Have I got it right?"

She nodded. Her cup rattled a bit against the saucer. She steadied her grip.

"Thinking back," Grey said, "I believe it's been about eight days since you discovered Garret was in San Francisco and Anderson was alive." He saw by the slight widening of her eyes that he had hit the time just about right. "That would make it the day after our wedding. You and I had had a disagreement, and I walked out. When I came back you weren't in the suite. Someone said they thought you were preparing to move your belongings from your room into ours. I went looking for you. Do you remember meeting me in the hallway?"

Berkeley's eyes dropped a fraction. She remembered throwing herself at him. She had been desperate to get him away from her room. "I remember," she said. Her voice was reedy, not like her own. She cleared her throat uncomfortably.

"Perhaps if you drank some tea," Grey suggested gently.

"Oh, yes. Yes, of course."

He covered his faint smile by drinking from his own cup. He watched her over the rim a moment before he set it down. "I have fond memories of that afternoon. You were rather insistent in your attentions, as I recall." Grey saw her cheeks pinken. "I'd like to think your desire was not solely to keep me from your room."

Berkeley bit down on her lip.

"Oh, then perhaps it was."

"No," she said quickly. "That was part of it, of course. A good measure, I should think. At least at first. But when we were alone, and I knew there wasn't any immediate danger, well, then it was . . . well, then it was just desire, I suppose."

Under the desk Grey crossed his legs at the ankles. He leaned back in the leather chair. "So they *were* in your room then."

"Yes." Berkeley looked at him oddly. "You just said . . . oh, I see, you weren't entirely certain. You flustered me into that admission."

Grey thought he shouldn't be feeling so smug. It was too early for that. Berkeley wasn't likely to be tricked so easily again. "Tell me what they wanted."

"Garret wanted the earring. I was wearing it around my neck but under my dress. I couldn't give it to him as a necklace. Anderson would have known immediately that it was the fake. He knew I couldn't have tolerated the real one next to my skin. I needed time, and I bargained for it. Your arrival was helpful. Anderson was going to escort me back to our suite for me to get the earring. I'm not sure how I would have managed if you hadn't appeared. Did you suspect then that I wasn't alone?"

"I merely suspected something was wrong. You said you had seen me arrive. I wondered at the lie. It was an odd thing to tell me when I came in the front of the hotel and your rooms face the rear."

Berkeley didn't recall saying anything of the kind. "I chatter sometimes when I'm nervous."

"Oh? I hadn't noticed."

She regarded him suspiciously. His eyes were not so cool as their flint color would have suggested. "Hhmmpf."

Grey suppressed a grin. "And Anderson? What was his game?"

"To torment me."

Grey waited, expecting some further revelation. When Berkeley remained silent he realized she was quite serious. "You mean it, don't you? That's all he wanted."

"And money. But that was part and parcel of his torment. As a boy Anderson was the sort who liked butterflies better without their wings."

"As a man, too," Grey said quietly. Berkeley had never lost the vaguely fey, otherworldly expression that focused beauty in her eyes. Anderson would have tried hard to steal that from her.

Berkeley shifted uncomfortably under his steady regard. "I'm hardly a butterfly."

"More like a woodland fairy."

One lightly feathered brow kicked up. She gave him a patently skeptical look. "I would rather be seen simply as a woman."

"That's never been lost on me," Grey said.

Berkeley smiled. She remembered the fish wagon and the Ducks and her sprint across the wharf to find protection with this man. He had seen through her disguise almost from the first.

Grey's own smile faded as he returned to the serious matter before them. "You and Anderson came to San Francisco carrying the earring," he said. "Is it your understanding that he was working more on the behalf of my brother than the Thornes?"

"That's my understanding now. I didn't have any idea until I met Garret here. Apparently Garret is the one who pointed Anderson in the direction of Boston and the Thornes. I was never clear on how he came by his initial information. Your brother must have supplied him with a starting point for the search."

"Do you think he *is* my brother?" Grey asked.

"You mean is he the brother of Colin and Decker Thorne?" Had she not been holding the teacup, she would have turned over her hands in a helpless gesture. "I don't know," she said softly. "I've wondered the same thing myself. But I don't think Anderson's really told him everything about the Thornes. Garret doesn't seem to know about their search for their youngest brother. I started to tell him some things, but Anderson was insistent that I not talk about it.'' Berkeley took another swallow of her tea. ''Garret has a strong attachment to the earring, but it was clear to me that he doesn't comprehend the origins of it.''

''You mean he couldn't spot that it was a fake.''

''No, I don't mean that at all. I think there must have been a story about the earring in the Denison family. Something to explain its presence. Garret believes the initials engraved on the gold drop are his mother's. Evaline Randolph. I don't think he meant Anderson or me to overhear. He has no idea the earring—if it were one of the original pair—would be more than three hundred years old.''

''He doesn't know he was adopted.''

''You and I don't know that either. It could be that you were the one plucked from Cunnington's London Workhouse.'' She sighed. ''The truth is that you and Garret look more like each other than either of you resemble the Thornes. Your smile, I think, is a little like Colin's. There's a certain edge to it.''

''He's Lord Fielding, you said. The Earl of Rosefield.''

''Yes, that's right. But you have very little in common with Decker.''

''The reformed thief.''

''Your friend,'' she emphasized. ''If you could but remember that. You *are* Graham Denison after all. That question has been settled if little else. Anyway, I was thinking of his appearance. His coloring is a shade darker than yours, and he's quick with a smile. He has a way of looking relaxed even when he's taut as a bowstring.'' She regarded Grey's current posture: the slope of his shoulders as he stretched out in the chair; the eyelids that were raised just a fraction above half-mast; the casual way his arms were folded across his chest. Berkeley bent to one side and looked under the desk. His ankles were crossed.

''Would you be feeling the slightest bit tense right now?'' she asked curiously.

''Taut as a bowstring.''

"Oh, my."

"Indeed," he said dryly. "I suppose the only people who can properly unravel the mystery are our parents."

"James and Evaline."

He nodded slowly, rolling the names over slowly in his mind. "It seems they've been able to keep a secret all these years." He raised one hand and absently touched his temple. He rubbed the spot with his fingertips, unaware of the gesture.

Berkeley watched Grey's brows draw together and tension creep into the line of his mouth. "Your head?"

He nodded. The small movement brought almost blinding pain to the backs of his eyes.

Jumping to her feet, Berkeley rounded the desk. "Lean forward. Put your head on your arms on the desk. Close your eyes." She gave him a gentle push, and it was enough to get him started. As soon as he was bent over she began massaging the back of his neck and shoulders. "Have you remembered something?"

"No." *Nothing that he could understand or explain.* He groaned softly as Berkeley's fingers kneaded his flesh. There was a measure of relief almost immediately. And still there was other business. "Why didn't Anderson deliver the earring to Garret after you left Boston?"

"I can't be certain," she said. "Two reasons occur to me. The obvious one is that the Thornes arranged our passage. The Remington Line. Jonna chose the ship herself and there were no scheduled stops until we reached Panama. It would have been difficult for Anderson to suggest that we needed to go to Charleston first. Especially Charleston. The Remington ships aren't necessarily welcomed there. There is still some suspicion that Jonna and Decker were intimately involved in the Falconer business."

"With me," Grey said dully.

"Yes. With you."

Grey considered that he had a great deal to answer for. He wondered about his first contact with Decker Thorne. Had he initiated it or had it been the other way around? Perhaps they had been introduced by a third party, and a friendship had been forged without any awareness of their deeper common bond. "And the other reason Anderson didn't give the earring to Garret?"

"He may have had some idea that he could extort more money from the Thornes for it. Remember, Anderson believes it's genuine. I made certain he couldn't doubt me by having the earring removed from the necklace and carrying it in my bag today. I also wore gloves so I wouldn't have to handle it directly."

"And if he had insisted you put it in your hand?"

"I would have given him the performance he expected." She ran her fingers across Grey's shoulder blades. "I think Anderson decided to inform Garret about the earring only after he saw you."

"Saw me? Why would that make him likely to contact Garret? It would have made more sense for him to write to Boston and tell the Thornes."

Berkeley's hands stilled momentarily.

Grey felt her hesitation. He turned his head and tried to look at her. "Berkeley? Don't dissemble now. What do you know?"

She gently turned his head and resumed kneading. "It's not what I know, but what I suspect. I don't think Anderson thought you *could* be found. I think he believed you were dead. More to the point, he knew that Garret believed you were dead." She pressed his head back when Grey would have turned again. "Garret said something this morning that has never sat quite right. He said you didn't have the earring the last time he spoke to you. He said you made a point of telling him you lost it. Those are almost his exact words. He believed you were lying, that you had actually sold it."

Berkeley waited for Grey to catch her point. Perhaps the headache was making it difficult for him to think. She went on. "It suggests to me at least that Garret saw you sometime after you left Boston. You'd had the earring until then. That means he may have seen you in Philadelphia where you left the *Siren* or, far more likely, in Charleston, where you traveled in secret to meet him.''

Grey's headache was powerful enough now to make him sick to his stomach. ''Why the hell would I do that?'' he asked through clenched teeth.

Taking him by the elbow, Berkeley helped Grey to his feet and led him into the bedroom. He dropped like a stone onto the bed while she dampened some cloths in the basin. She placed one across his eyes then blocked more light from the room by closing the drapes. ''Better?''

''Hmmm.'' He thumped the space beside him with his palm.

Berkeley sat down and took his hand. ''I imagine you went to Charleston to make your good-byes. Perhaps to make amends.''

He snorted. ''Doubtful.''

''You're probably right. There's nothing about your character that would lead me to believe you could have a thoughtful or considerate nature.''

Grey winced.

''Good,'' Berkeley said, satisfied her barb had found its target. ''That was meant to hurt.'' She dropped her lips softly to his mouth and sweetly extracted some of the sting.

''It's a great deal of supposition,'' Grey said quietly.

''I know. It may also be the truth.''

''I know.''

''Garret could have been responsible for the beating that almost killed you. He may have planned just that end.''

Grey lifted one corner of the damp cloth. He eyed her. ''I took your point.''

''Oh. I wasn't sure.''

He let the cloth fall back in place. ''If you're right, then I may have made a small error in judgment this morning. I probably shouldn't have hinted to Garret that I may have regained my memory.''

Berkeley's heart sank. ''You didn't.''

''Afraid so. Watching him, seeing him laugh, so obviously enjoying the fact that he was a stranger to me . . . well, after you were gone I got a little of my own back.''

"Do you think he believed you?"

"I think he's uncertain. That's all I wanted to achieve. I wanted him to wonder."

Berkeley groaned. "I knew I shouldn't have left you alone with them. What are we going to do?"

"I'm going to the bank in a few hours to meet with Anderson. I'm paying him to leave California. I'll need the diamond necklace back, I'm afraid. He's not leaving poor."

Now it was Berkeley who lifted the cloth from Grey's eyes. "You need it back? How much did you agree to pay?"

"Fifteen thousand in gold. I wouldn't require the necklace if so much of my money weren't tied up in the Phoenix. Those diamonds were an extravagance I couldn't properly afford."

"I knew that. It was an expensive lesson. For both of us as it turns out. It seems Anderson didn't tell you he's already in possession of the necklace. That's what he extorted from me. And I promised him even more."

"Dear God."

Berkeley leaned to one side and dropped the cloth in the basin. She began to wring it out, but Grey stayed her hand. He started to get up. "Where do you think you're going?"

"If I don't have the necklace, then I'm going to have to arrange for some funding from other sources. Bankers don't generally give loans that profit blackmailers. I'll need to think of some reason for requiring the money."

Bowing her head, Berkeley studied her hands for a moment. "Let's not pay him anything," she whispered.

"What?"

"Nothing," she repeated. "No money at all."

"I thought you wanted him out of your life."

"I do." Her voice was earnest. "But I realize I can get rid of him by telling you the truth. If he has nothing to hold over my head, then he has nothing. He'll leave when he sees that you know the truth and it doesn't matter to you."

Grey frowned slightly. "What truth is that, Berkeley?"

She took a short, shallow breath. "I thought he was dead when I married you. You know I did."

"Yes? What has that to—"

Berkeley held up her hand and cut him off. "Anderson Shaw *was* my stepfather. I never lied about that. But I didn't tell you everything." She hesitated the length of a heartbeat, then plunged ahead. "I didn't tell you that after my mother died he also became my husband."

Chapter Fifteen

The bank was not crowded when Grey arrived. He made an inquiry into his account at the teller's window and a small withdrawal, then he waited on a narrow bench in the lobby for Garret Denison and Anderson Shaw. He watched the clock and occasionally patted the inside pocket of his vest for the passage vouchers he had purchased for them. Grey wished he could derive more comfort from the gesture. Having the vouchers was not enough, not when there was no guarantee that a ship would be leaving San Francisco today. The best he was told he could hope for was that one would be sailing back East in forty-eight hours.

Grey stood. He leaned a shoulder against the wall and crossed his arms. His head was cocked to one side, and his eyes were cast downward. No observer of this casual posture would have known it was tension that had driven him to his feet. His hooded glance seemed more thoughtful than worried, and the slight curve of his mouth gave the impression of humor turned inward. For all intents and purposes he appeared quite at his ease if slightly aloof. Several times he responded to greetings that were made in passing but he didn't invite or engage in conversation. No one of his acquaintance pressed.

Anderson Shaw entered the bank alone. His head bent, eyes on the floor, Anderson walked directly past Grey without noticing him. He stopped suddenly and turned, aware of Grey for the first time. Surprise made him slow to mask the malice in his expression.

Grey pushed away from the wall. He did not move to close the distance between them. "Shaw," he said.

Anderson made a slight nod. His acknowledgment was equally curt. "Janeway."

"Not here," Grey said. "Outside."

One of Anderson's brows arched as he considered this. It was certainly not a request. Before he gave any indication that he was going to go along with it, Grey walked out. Anderson waited, his eyes darting toward the clock. He stood there a full minute before he determined that Grey Janeway was not going to return. Slowly, his mouth tightening, he left the bank.

Grey was waiting on the lip of the sidewalk beside his carriage. When he saw Anderson he untethered the horses, climbed in, and took up the reins. He did not issue an invitation to Anderson except to glance in his direction.

Anderson climbed aboard. He sat back in the stiff leather seat beside Grey. "Where are we going?" he asked as Grey snapped the reins.

"Nowhere in particular."

Anderson looked around. Grey's open carriage gave him an unobstructed view of the street ahead. Wagons filled with feed and hardware lumbered cautiously along the rutted avenue. The rough plank walks on either side were considerably crowded with people moving briskly from one place of business to the next. Behind him he saw a pair of miners jump off the walk as soon as the carriage passed and head for the saloon across the street. "But you want witnesses," Anderson said shrewdly.

"Something like that," said Grey.

"A public place where we wouldn't be overheard."

Grey nodded. "Where is Garret?"

"Following us, I believe." Anderson glanced over his shoulder again and saw Garret Denison a discreet distance behind them. "Yes, that's him on the cinnamon mare."

Grey didn't turn. "And how many Ducks trailing in his wake?"

Anderson shrugged. "You'll not get that from me," he said. "I assure you, their number will be revealed if you renege on our agreement."

Pulling up the reins, Grey held back his team to give a wagon stacked high with chicken crates a wide berth. "About our agreement," he said, waiting for the wagon to rattle past them. "I'm going to allow you to keep the necklace you took from Berkeley, but that will be the extent of our charitable contribution."

Anderson was jerked unexpectedly into the uncomfortable corner of the carriage as Grey urged the team forward again.

Grey glanced sideways. "Sorry. They got away from me that time."

Anderson made no comment. He didn't believe for a moment that the apology was sincere or that Grey's handling of the horses had been anything but deliberate. He sat up straight and braced one arm on the side of the carriage. "Tell me what you mean about the necklace," he said instead.

"I'm certain I was clear." Grey reached into his vest pocket and removed the pair of vouchers. "The earliest departure from the city will be in the next forty-eight hours. These will guarantee you passage on the *Albany* as soon as her repairs are completed. The captain assured me you and Garret can move into your cabin now while the work is being done. There will be no chance you'll be left behind."

Anderson took the tickets and examined them. Shaking his head slowly, he tucked them away. "I can't speak for Garret," he said, "but I suspect he'll leave without incident. He has what he came for. As for me, I admit to some disappointment. I was looking forward to the voyage east."

"You have everything you're going to get," Grey said. "There will be no more money."

Anderson's voice lost none of its confidence. "My arrangement is not solely with you. Berkeley's made promises of her own."

"I know what she's offered. We decided together there will be no more."

Anderson's mouth curled derisively. "I don't believe you've spoken to her at all."

"How would I know about the necklace?"

Anderson went on. "She would never agree to this."

Grey glanced sideways at his companion. "It was her idea." He watched those words take effect. Anderson's handsome features lost some of their color, and his eyes became less focused as his thoughts turned inward. "She's finished with you, Anderson. We both are."

"Really?" Anderson said after a moment. He had regained a measure of his composure, and his expression reflected mild amusement rather than concern. "I would like to hear that from Berkeley."

Grey shook his head. "I won't let you see her."

"I don't think you can stop me, Janeway. I have more rights than you do."

"Because she's your daughter, you mean."

"Because she's my wife."

Grey didn't blink. He had wondered all afternoon what it would be like when Berkeley's surprising confession was finally confirmed. He had actually hoped Anderson could be pressed into revealing the truth if only to have the last niggling doubts removed. He knew now how much he hadn't wanted to believe her. Grey held the reins in one hand and rubbed the back of his neck with the other. It was not his head that ached, though. Habit had made him raise his hand there. Massaging his neck did nothing for the raw wound around his heart.

Grey continued to stare straight ahead. The carriage slowed a fraction until he took the reins in both hands.

"You knew about it." Anderson's tone was almost accusing.

Shrugging, Grey said, "You pushed Berkeley too hard. She realized if she got out of the way, you couldn't push at all."

"So she told you."

"Yes," he said softly. "She told me." Grey wished now he had not been so quiet as Berkeley had unfolded her story. He wished he had offered his hand instead of giving her his back. He might have said something rather than leave their bedchamber without any kind word to console her. He wanted to be with her now. He wondered if she were still lying on the bed, her body turned on its side and curled like a child's. Was she still weeping? "It makes no difference to me," he said. It was what he should have said to Berkeley, he thought. Those were the words she had expected to hear, the ones she had *deserved* to hear. Instead he was saying them to Anderson Shaw.

Grey pulled back on the reins and stopped the carriage. His eyes strayed briefly to the gaming house on their right. He had brought Anderson back to the Palace. "Was there anything else?" he asked.

"She belongs with me."

"You don't want her. You never did. If you ever had any great feeling for Berkeley, it was fear, not love."

Anderson's mouth twisted. "Fear? You're mistaken there."

"I don't think so. You exploited her gift and—"

"As you did," Anderson interjected. "Just as you did."

"As I did," Grey agreed. "But you were afraid of her talent, too. The way she couldn't bear to have you touch her, the way she looked at you, as if she always could see more than you wanted her to. She must have been an odd and maddening child. Still, it was better to keep her close than let her stray beyond your influence, and when her mother died—your wife—you convinced a bereft and confused young woman that she would be nothing and have nothing if she didn't throw in her lot with you. I imagine you didn't have to try very hard to get her agreement."

"No," Anderson admitted. "Not hard."

Grey swore softly and gripped the reins tighter. The horses shuffled in place. "She was only sixteen. You took advantage of her. You used her grief."

"Perhaps. But I made certain she had shelter and clothing. Berkeley wanted for nothing."

"She earned everything."

"I never took advantage of *her*," Anderson said.

Grey didn't argue the point. He knew the marriage had never been consummated, but there were a host of things Anderson had done to keep Berkeley with him. She had only been discarded when he no longer considered her of any use. "Leave her be now," Grey said. "She's done nothing to earn your enmity. She's only tried to make a life for herself. Let her be happy."

Anderson considered the request. He could discern no threat from Grey Janeway's tone and wondered that the other man could be so generous. It was not something Anderson understood, and therefore it made him suspicious. "Do you want me to divorce her?" he asked.

"I can only imagine what that would cost me. I don't expect it."

"You'd prefer to make her a widow. Is that it?"

Grey's flint-colored eyes were frank in their assessment of Anderson Shaw. They moved over him slowly, taking measure of the man, only this time for his coffin. "It's a tempting thought, and the more it occurs to me, the easier it is to consider. Don't make too much of my reluctance, Anderson. I could do it." He turned in his seat and faced Anderson squarely. "But your leaving will accomplish enough. I can be satisfied with that."

Anderson stared back. He wondered what to make of this adversary. "Very well," he said finally. The carriage rocked as he stood. "There seems to be nothing I can say or do that will make me richer than I already am; therefore, I accept your gift of the necklace and the passage. I do, however, want to see Berkeley before I board the ship. There's no need for me to come to the Phoenix. Have her at the wharf before *Albany* sails. You both can see us off." He saw Grey hesitate. "Have her there, Janeway, or I won't get on the ship."

"You misunderstand," Grey said. "I don't know if she'll come, and I won't force her."

"She'll come." Anderson was a shade more than confident. Smugness crept into his voice. "Tell her it's about her father. You won't be able to keep her away."

Grey found Berkeley in the small library when he returned. Except for a single oil lamp on the table at her side there was no light. She had drawn the heavy drapes and not laid a fire. A shawl was wrapped around her shoulders, and Berkeley had pulled a blanket across her legs. The gloom was penetrating and rather dramatic and overdone for Grey's tastes. "Less is more," he told her as he opened the drapes.

A shaft of late-winter sunlight struck Berkeley full in the face. She raised her hand to shield her eyes. "I'm not speaking to you," she said. "And I liked it dark. I don't know that I want to see you either."

Grey went over to the chair where she was seated and hunkered down. He closed the book lying on her lap and removed it to the table.

"You've lost my place," she said.

"Berkeley. It was upside down."

Twisting slightly in the chair so the sunlight glanced off her hair, Berkeley lowered her hand. When Grey reached for it, she offered only faint resistance.

"I'm sorry," he said. "I didn't know what to say or do when you told me, so I said nothing, did nothing."

"You walked out on me," Berkeley said. Her chin came up a fraction. "That was not nothing."

"No, it wasn't."

"You *hurt* me."

"I know." He held her pained glance. Even now, hours later, he could make out the faintly red-rimmed line of her lower lashes. "I can't even say that I didn't want to hurt you."

The honesty inherent in that flat, unadorned admission let Berkeley know, in turn, how deeply she had hurt him. "I was ashamed that I agreed to marry him,'' she said quietly. ''There was no coercion involved. If I had been more confident, even a shade more willing to face life on my own, I wouldn't have married him. I suppose I could have told you the truth from the first, but it seemed rather too much to explain. Later, after I thought he was dead, it was merely a fact about my past that seemed to have no relevance to my present or my future.''

Grey nodded. ''I seem to recall someone taking me rather harshly to task for keeping some secrets about my own past.''

Berkeley sighed. ''I suppose it was too much to hope that you wouldn't remind me.''

He grinned faintly. ''Yes, that would have been too much to expect. I'm not above getting a little of my own back.'' Grey gave her a knowing look. ''And you? What about the closed drapes and meager lamplight? Sitting alone here in the cold and dark. What was that in aid of?''

Pale pink color washed Berkeley's cheeks. ''I was setting a mood.''

''Yours?'' he asked. ''Or were you trying to provoke mine?''

''Both, I think.'' She looked around, remembering the cavernlike darkness and chill. ''Was it too much?''

''A bit.'' He squeezed her hand. ''In any event, I couldn't have felt worse than I already did. In the future you may as well save yourself the effort.'' Grey stood, released Berkeley's hand, and went to the hearth to lay a fire. ''Anderson's agreed to leave. He accepted the passages and my terms.'' He stacked kindling and logs and lit them. He was conscious of Berkeley's silence behind him. He turned on her as the flames began to crawl along the kindling. ''What are you thinking?''

She shook her head quickly, as if to clear it, and came out of her reverie. ''What? Oh, nothing. It's . . . well, it's nothing.''

Grey's gaze fell to Berkeley's hands. She had slipped them beneath the blanket that covered her lap. Without seeming to realize it, she was stroking the gentle swell of her abdomen. ''It's not nothing,'' he said, using her earlier words for emphasis.

Worrying her lower lip, Berkeley's silent distress was palpable.

"Is it the baby?"

"No . . . no, not the baby . . . not the way you mean."

Then Grey understood. Somehow he *knew*. "Anderson threatened our child."

She nodded slowly. "He told me I would have to get rid of the baby. He said he would arrange it. He was . . . he was insistent. Even when I changed the subject I could see the idea never left him. I couldn't believe what he was suggesting. At first I thought it was jealousy, but then . . ." She shrugged helplessly. "But Anderson never expressed any desire to have children with me. Why would he want to deny me this child?"

"He'd deny you anything he thought would make you happy. He only values what others want."

"You're probably right." But she wasn't certain, and it was evident in her voice.

"I know I am." There was more conviction there than he felt. "He can't make you do something against your will."

"No," she said. "He never could. Anderson always found a way of making his ideas seem like mine. That was his talent."

Grey watched her a moment. One of her hands still lay protectively over her belly. "Can he do that this time? Is there really something he can do that would make you consider visiting an abortionist?"

Berkeley's head snapped up. "No! I want our baby. He can't make me not want it."

"If you're afraid, if you have any doubts, you don't have to meet him."

"Meet him? Has he suggested that?"

Nodding, Grey turned and poked at the fire. "He says it's the only way he'll agree to leave. He wants to see you."

"I won't do it," she said. "I knew he couldn't have accepted your terms without wanting something else. It's always been like that. He has to have the last word. He never settles for what someone else wants unless it's what he's wanted all along."

Grey leaned the poker against the jamb, then stepped aside

to let the warmth reach Berkeley. "He would like you to be at the wharf to see him off. You would be with me, not alone."

"You sound as if you want me to go."

"Do I? Believe me, I don't want you within a mile of him, but it's your choice. I want you to know what he told me."

She waited as Grey's focus shifted from her to the floor. His fingers raked his thick hair just once. He seemed to be considering his options. "Is that all?" she asked finally. She couldn't imagine that it was. Anderson Shaw always had a hook in one hand and bait in the other. He was a master fisherman.

Grey's gaze slid back to Berkeley. "I told him I didn't think you would come and that I wouldn't force you."

"And?" Berkeley found she was holding her breath.

"He said to tell you it was about your father. He said I wouldn't be able to keep you away."

Berkeley felt as if her heart was being squeezed. She bent her head, hiding her stricken expression from him. There was the slightest catch in her voice as she said, "He was right."

Nat carried the news that *Albany*'s repairs were completed and the ship was preparing to sail within the hour. He was breathless from his run to the hotel, and his report was offered in fits and starts, but no one had any difficulty understanding it. As one, Sam and Shawn and Donnel and a half dozen others who were working in the hall that afternoon all turned to Grey to gauge his response. They heard him thank Nat quietly, then ask the boy to get Berkeley in her room.

Grey waited until Nat had reached the top of the staircase. He stood and laid down the cards he had been absently shuffling. "I don't know what to expect when we get there," he told them. "It could be the Ducks. It could be Anderson only wants my wife's best wishes." There was a murmur of disbelief among the others, but Grey ignored it. "You know where to station yourselves and what to do. Keep in mind that we're not Brannan's vigilantes. It's not our place to start a war with the Ducks or retaliate for the past. Especially not for the past."

He paused and looked at every one of them in turn, knowing full well each man was remembering Mike and the beating he had received at the hands of the Sydney Town Ducks. "There's no reason for you to do anything unless Berkeley is placed in danger." Grey was satisfied when they nodded. "Very well. Go on. Get out of here. And don't let me see you at the wharf. If I do, Anderson Shaw certainly will."

The hall was almost entirely deserted when Berkeley came downstairs. Nat dogged her footsteps. "Where is everyone?" she asked when she reached Grey. Her abrupt stop brought Nat's nose in contact with her spine. Sighing, Berkeley groped behind her and pulled him to one side. "Stand here," she said. "Beside me. Stop trailing me like a bread crumb."

Grey quickly raised one hand to his mouth, cleared his throat, and successfully hid the smile that Berkeley's description and Nat's crestfallen expression had brought to the surface. He touched the boy's shoulder. "You did fine, Nat. Go on. Annie Jack has something for you in the kitchen."

Nat's eyes brightened. He ducked his head and hurried off.

"He was stalking you like an Apache," Grey told Berkeley. "There was honor in that. I don't think he liked being referred to as a bread crumb."

Grey's attempt to lighten her mood failed. Berkeley handed him her cloak and turned around so he could fit it properly across her shoulders. She fastened the clasp at her neck and raised the hood. Black ribbon trim framed her face. The velvet was only a few shades darker than her eyes. "You haven't told me where everyone is," she said. "I thought Donnel and Sam were playing cards with you."

"The game broke up a while ago. Sam was the big winner. I think he's squirreling away his markers now. Donnel went off to make a repair. I can't speak for the others." Grey went to the storeroom at the back for his own coat. When he returned Berkeley was waiting for him at the main entrance. Impatience defined her posture. He didn't ask her if she was prepared to go. It was clear that she was. "It might be better," he said gently, "if you did not give Anderson an advantage by appearing too anxious."

"I don't think I can help it."

"I understand. But you realize he may have nothing at all to say about your father. It could be a ruse simply to get you there."

"I know." Berkeley had thought of little else these past two days. She considered her own disappointment the most likely outcome of her meeting with Anderson. "I have to go, though. He made certain it wasn't a choice for me."

Grey nodded. He opened the door for Berkeley and slipped a hand under her elbow. He was surprised when she hesitated. "What is it?"

"I don't want there to be trouble, Grey. I don't want that on my conscience."

"Neither do I."

Berkeley lifted her face, studying Grey's. She wondered if they meant quite the same thing. "Your brother will be there."

"I haven't forgotten." He indicated the open doorway again. This time Berkeley went through it.

Garret Denison tossed his valise to a crew member of the scow that would take him out to the *Albany*. Next came his trunk. He pushed it forward with his foot and tipped it over the edge of the wharf. Two large hands grasped it at either end and hauled it aboard. Garret turned and waited for Anderson to follow suit.

"Do you really think she's coming?" Garret asked.

Anderson scanned the wharf one more time before he picked up his carpetbag and threw it on the scow's deck. "I can't leave with you if she doesn't."

Garret shrugged. "Suit yourself." He jumped down. "It doesn't appear the skipper's going to wait for you. I know the *Albany* won't."

"A few more minutes," Anderson said. In spite of the cold air lifting strands of hair at his nape, Anderson Shaw was sweating. He lifted his hat and dabbed at his forehead with a handkerchief. His eyes darted past crates stacked five deep and taller than a man. He looked beyond the pyramid of barrels and the wagon traffic. His gaze never lingered on the men he recognized moving in the crowd. Bent Eddie. Jolly Waterman. Bobby Burns. The Ducks were there in the event Grey Janeway was of a mind to have his necklace returned.

"You'd better come," Garret said. Behind him the skipper was barking orders to his crew.

Anderson had backed himself up to the very edge of the dock. When one of the scow's crew tried to remove a secure line from the piling, Anderson stopped him. "You've waited two days," he snapped. "You can wait two minutes."

It was Berkeley who saw Anderson first. He was standing on the lip of the wharf, one foot resting on a piling, his arms crossed in front of him. She could see that he was looking for her. His chin was lifted, and his head moved with the alert, almost startled movements of a bird.

Berkeley did not give him an opportunity to observe her. She was out of the carriage before Grey could help her down, but remembering what he'd said about not giving Anderson an advantage, she held herself back while he tethered the team. She knew the moment Anderson caught sight of them. The handkerchief he was holding in his hand was thrust into his pocket, and the stiffness went out of his shoulders and back. By the time they reached him Anderson appeared to be very much at his ease. For the first time in any encounter with Anderson, Berkeley felt as though the scales had tipped in her direction.

"Berkeley," Anderson said in greeting. "Janeway. Good of you to come and see me off."

Just as if it were their pleasure, Berkeley thought. Anderson Shaw was acting in the only way his nature allowed him. She looked past his shoulder and saw Garret talking to the skipper of the scow. "I don't know that Mr. Denison can hold the scow for long, Anderson. You'd better say what you will and leave."

Anderson glanced back, saw that she was probably right, and nodded. "Very well. But alone. This is for your ears only."

Grey shook his head. "My wife isn't going anywhere with you."

"Your wife?" Anderson asked. "Must we tramp all over that ground again? Berkeley, tell him to step away. It needn't be far. Just out of hearing. You'll thank me for keeping this between us."

Berkeley glanced at Grey. She wouldn't ask this of him, her eyes said. It would be his decision.

Grey touched Berkeley's elbow lightly, then stepped back some five feet. Almost immediately Anderson turned so Grey could not read his lips. "Don't put yourself between me and Berkeley," Grey warned him. "And keep your own distance."

Anderson moved a little to one side. "I don't want anything from you, Berkeley. This time I'm going to give you something."

Berkeley merely looked at him.

"I know I haven't given you much reason to trust me or—"

"You've never given me *any* reason to trust you."

His slight smile held no humor. "Very well. I'm telling you this because of the child you're carrying. It's the only reason I would break the promise I made in Virginia. Your mother wouldn't allow me to tell you anything about your father. She's responsible for you coming to this end. Remember that, Berkeley. It wasn't me."

Berkeley's hand had unerringly found the swell of her abdomen. Her palm lay across it protectively. "Say what you mean to say, Anderson. If there's blame in this, I'll be certain to lay it at the proper door."

His polished eyes narrowed a fraction. She could not be as certain of herself as she sounded. "First, you should know this: Garret, not Graham, is the brother of Colin and Decker Thorne. He doesn't know it, and he wouldn't thank either of us for telling him. He's arranged his entire life around being the sole heir to Beau Rivage."

Berkeley was suspicious. "How have you come by this conclusion?"

"You've never understood how integral you've been to all of this, have you? Your mother told me, of course. Graham was a sickly child, so ill in fact that Evaline and James Denison traveled to London with him to seek a cure. It was while they were there that they visited Cunnington's Workhouse and took Greydon Thorne away. James wanted an heir, and Evaline had been informed she would bear him no more children. They named their foundling baby Garret and claimed him as their own. By the time they returned to Beau Rivage there were two miracles to celebrate: Graham's recovery and the 'birth' of a second child."

Berkeley's suspicions had not lessened. It was the kind of tale Anderson took great delight in spinning as it was almost impossible to corroborate. "How would my mother be privy to that information?"

Anderson allowed his smile to widen. It was smug triumph that pushed the corners upward, not humor. He leveled Berkeley with an arch look. "Can't you guess? Use your gift, Berkeley. Why is it that you're always afraid to use it when it's about you?"

Berkeley's hand fell still then slowly dropped to her side. Her eyes widened fractionally and lost their fey, otherworldly appeal. Innocence was stripped from her as she opened herself to a new, horrifying possibility.

Watching the change in her expression, Anderson was satisfied that she understood what he had yet to say. "James Denison was your mother's lover," he told her.

"No."

"Graham Denison's father was also yours."

"No." This time she held up one hand, palm out, as if she could ward off Anderson's words.

"You married your half brother, Berkeley. Your child was conceived of incest."

No! I won't let you do this to me! Not again. Not ever again. Had she screamed the words? she wondered. She had wanted

to scream them. But when Anderson stood there, unmoved and
unrepentant, Berkeley knew she had not. Shame, fear, and
loathing drew her hand back toward her mouth. For a moment
she thought she would be sick. Then, almost without knowing
her own intention, she struck out furiously. The flat of her hand
connected solidly with Anderson's cheek. His head snapped.
The blow was hard enough to knock him sideways, and Berkeley stepped back, watching him, stunned, as he tried to gain
his balance and caught the secure line of the scow with his toe
instead. The rope strained against his boot as Anderson began
to fall and, finally, it was pulled free of the piling. Anderson's
arms flailed in Berkeley's direction, but now she was the one
unmoved and unrepentant. Crying out, he tipped over the edge
of the wharf and fell headfirst into the scow.

No one aboard went to his aid. The crew grabbed the freed
line, pulled it back, and pushed off from the dock. From his
vantage point on the scow, the skipper smartly saluted Berkeley
as if the blow she struck had been for his convenience.

Berkeley didn't see it. She was staring at Anderson's still
form and the odd angle of his left leg in relation to the rest of
his body. His eyes were closed, and she wasn't sure if the rise
and fall of his chest was from his breathing or the movement
of the scow.

Grey had come up behind Berkeley and caught her by the
waist as soon as Anderson started his fall. Now his fingers
tightened and he held her steady as she swayed forward to keep
Anderson in her line of sight. The scow was already fifteen yards
out. A stumble now would have dropped Berkeley headfirst in
the bay. Grey noted she remained oblivious to any danger.
"You may regret it later," he said, "but you didn't kill him."

Berkeley had no appreciation for Grey's dry humor. Her
stomach turned over.

"See?" Grey said, indicating the scow with a thrust of his
chin. "Garret's going to take care of him." He watched his
brother kneel beside Anderson and make a quick assessment
of the injuries. "He doesn't appear to be overly concerned."

"He doesn't care what happens to Anderson. There's a difference."

Grey pulled Berkeley back a few inches. "Do you care?"

"I ... I'm not ..." Her voice trailed off as her stomach heaved again. "I think I'm going to be ill." She let Grey help her down to her knees. He held her shoulders while she leaned over the dock and emptied her breakfast into the bay.

Grey pressed a handkerchief into her hand when she was finished. Sam Hartford appeared from behind the pyramid of barrels and offered a silver flask. Grey took it, unscrewed the cap, and held it to Berkeley's lips. "Just a few sips." He looked over his shoulder at Sam. "The Ducks?"

"They're here," said Sam. "Saw it all. The same as we did."

Nodding, Grey removed the flask and gave it back to Sam. "Let's get her out of here before they make a move against us." He looked at Berkeley's pale profile. "Shall I carry you?"

"I can walk." To prove herself able she rose unassisted. Belatedly she became aware of Sam's presence. "What are you doing here?"

Sam rubbed the underside of his chin and wondered how well lying through his teeth would be received. Judging by Berkeley's shrewd glance, not well. "Thought I'd come along to protect your back, ma'am. Though, from what I could see, you can take care of yourself."

Berkeley did not thank Sam for his compliment. Her eyes darted along the wharf. She picked out Donnel Kincaid as he tried to slip behind a stack of crates. Shawn was walking casually toward them carrying a fishing pole over his shoulder. It did not take her long to identify several other of Grey's employees from the Phoenix. She also saw the Ducks. "Bobby Burns is here," she told Grey. "And that Jolly fellow. Remember them?"

"I couldn't forget. Let's go, Berkeley."

He did not have to repeat himself. Fully aware of the threat the Ducks posed, she hurried in the direction of the carriage. When he would have snapped the reins she stopped him. "No," she said. "A moment longer. I want to see the *Albany* leave. I want to be certain he's not coming back."

Grey pretended to indulge her because he was curious himself. "Would you like to see through the scope?"

"You brought it?"

He nodded. Taking it from his jacket, Grey extended the sight and offered it to Berkeley first.

Berkeley raised it to her eye and made a small adjustment. The scow was clearly visible. Anderson was sitting up now, a grimace of pain twisting his mouth. No effort had been made yet to splint his leg. They would leave that to the *Albany*'s surgeon. As soon as the scow drew alongside the clipper a canvas sling was lowered. Berkeley watched Garret and one of the crew help Anderson into the sling. She cringed as his features contorted into something unrecognizable to her, yet she didn't look away and felt no remorse. As they raised the sling Berkeley returned the scope to Grey. "You watch them put him aboard. I've seen enough."

"We've both seen enough." He collapsed the scope and put it away. "Good riddance," he said softly.

"Yes," she agreed. "Good riddance."

Grey signaled the team, and the carriage rolled forward slowly. Out of the corner of his eye he saw Berkeley dart a glance back toward the ship. "Are you ready to leave?" he asked. "We can stay until the *Albany*'s out of sight."

"What? Oh, no. We should go. I'm happy to see the last of him."

He turned his head and regarded her. "Berkeley," he said gently, "you're not happy. Just the opposite, I should think."

She forced a smile, which merely underscored Grey's point.

"Are you going to tell me what he said to you?" asked Grey. Beside him, he sensed Berkeley's withdrawal. Disappointment in her reaction turned quickly to anger. His fingers tightened on the reins. The horses responded almost immediately to his agitation by picking up their pace. It was Berkeley who remained unmoved.

More than a minute passed in silence while Berkeley stared off to the side. At first she was hardly aware that storefronts and gaming halls were passing with ever-increasing speed. Lost in thought, she didn't observe that pedestrians stepped back onto the sidewalks. It wasn't until her attention was caught by one miner tackling his drunken friend to keep him back that she realized the danger their speed was posing. "Please, Grey," she said. "Slow down. We almost hit that man back—" She stopped because of the look he turned on her. His flinty stare pinned her back in her seat, and the carriage ride continued without any reduction in its speed.

When they reached the Phoenix, Berkeley went inside without waiting for Grey's escort. He caught up to her as she was letting herself into their suite. He held the door open for her and followed her in. She rounded on him almost at once.

"That was childish," she said. "You might have hurt someone back there. You might have hurt *us*."

Grey made no move to approach her. His sigh was somewhere between exasperation and weariness as he leaned back against the door. "You're right," he said finally, quietly.

She had expected some argument from him, excuses that she would see through and counter. There was no apology and none was required, not when he was able to admit so simply and easily that she was right. She knew then that she had been spoiling for a fight, and he had purposely removed all reason for one.

Berkeley eliminated the distance between them. Lightly touching his hand, she raised her eyes and searched his face. "Have I complicated your life beyond bearing?"

Grey's mouth curved in a faint smile. "Not beyond bearing," he said.

She leaned into him, pressing her forehead against the crook of his shoulder. Her arms loosely circled his waist. "I didn't know what to say," she told him.

At first Grey didn't understand, then he realized she was referring to the question he had asked her almost half an hour earlier. "It shouldn't have required thought," he said. "I only wanted to know what Anderson told you. You merely had to repeat it."

She was glad he couldn't see her own humorless smile. "It's not so easy as that. Anderson lied to me. Everything he said was lies."

"They must have been particularly ugly ones. Is that why you slapped him?"

"Yes."

"And why you don't want to tell me?"

This time she only nodded.

Grey caught her by the chin and lifted her face. "Are you afraid I'll believe them?"

Berkeley understood that Grey's gesture had been deliberate. Unguarded for a moment, her eyes revealed the truth.

"You half believe them yourself," he said. "That's what has you so frightened."

"No." But there was no conviction in her voice.

"Let me decide for myself, Berkeley. Were they lies about me?"

Berkeley led Grey to the settee. She offered him a drink, and when he declined she prepared one for him anyway. By the end of her recitation Grey was staring at an empty glass in his hands. He didn't remember drinking it but the taste of whiskey was on his tongue. It did not mix well with the bile rising in his throat.

"It *is* a lie," he said. "All of it."

"I know." She noticed he sounded no more convincing than she had.

"You're not my sister."

"Half sister."

Grey waved that distinction aside. "We do *not* have the same father."

"I'm sure you're right."

"Anderson said it to torment you. He thinks he can make you get rid of our baby."

"That's what I thought."

But that night in bed, though no word was spoken between them, they didn't reach for each other, not even for comfort, and the distance that separated them was, at the same time, too much and yet not enough.

For a while they slept.

When Grey woke he was alone. There was a moment's panic until he touched the space Berkeley had vacated and found it was still warm. He realized she couldn't have been gone long. He was struck that in spite of their self-imposed isolation, he had missed Berkeley almost as soon as she left the bed.

Grey sat up and hooked his heels on the edge of the bed frame. Frustrated and tired, he raked his hair back and squinted at the mantel clock. It was just after four. He sat there a moment longer, expecting to hear some movement from Berkeley in the adjoining dressing room. When silence remained his only companion, he got up and padded quietly next door to investigate.

The dressing room was empty. The library and sitting room were also deserted. Returning to the dressing room, Grey pulled on a pair of trousers and shrugged into a shirt. The clothes smelled of stale smoke and whiskey from the hours he'd spent earlier at the gaming tables, encouraging the Phoenix's patrons to spend their money unwisely. All evening he had watched Berkeley go through the same motions, greeting customers, appreciating their stories, and pretending attention when she had none to give.

"Goddamn you, Anderson." The sound of his own quiet voice, the anger and pain, not just in the words, but in *him*, brought Grey up short. He pressed one hand to the back of his neck and rubbed. *I should have killed you.* This time he did not give sound to his thoughts. Neither was he sorry for them.

Grey slipped on his boots, feeling the familiar outline of his knife now as a mere annoyance. He hadn't used it when he should have. That was his regret now. He swore again, more softly this time.

Believing that Berkeley had gone to Nat's room, Grey was on the point of leaving their suite when a movement on the balcony caught his eye. Berkeley had just stepped back from the balustrade and was crossing her arms in front of her to keep warm. Apparently putting on her cloak or dressing in something warmer than her nightshift had not occurred to her. She was not even wearing shoes or stockings.

She didn't turn around when he joined her or affect any surprise. It was as if she had been expecting him. He stood behind her but didn't touch her.

"They're out tonight," Berkeley said without looking at him. "There's going to be trouble."

He didn't ask who *they* were. He had seen several Ducks mingling with the Phoenix's guests this evening. He hadn't suspected that Berkeley had known. Bobbie Burns and Jolly were not among the faces he recognized, and he didn't believe she knew any others. "Do you know what sort of trouble?"

Berkeley shook her head. "Do you suppose Anderson put them up to it?"

"Perhaps. But Berkeley, it's nothing you did. Anything that's going to happen is not because of you."

She realized then that he wasn't questioning her. He might have wondered *how* she knew but not *that* she knew. "There were Ducks in the Phoenix tonight," she said. "Did you notice them?"

"Yes, but I didn't know you did."

"One of them gave me his palm to read. I didn't suspect until I held his hand. It was too late then. I thought I was going to be sick." Berkeley shivered slightly, but it wasn't from the cool air eddying around her. The wind was nothing compared to the chill she felt in her marrow. "They don't go anywhere alone. Where there was one there was probably a half dozen."

"I recognized three," Grey said. But he hadn't known the man whose fortune she'd told was a Duck. That put the number conservatively at four. Berkeley was most likely closer to the mark with six. "Will it be tonight?"

"Yes, I think so. I didn't know that earlier, but when I woke I felt so certain of it I came out here. I thought I might catch a glimpse of them."

"They don't typically keep their presence a secret," he said. "Intimidation is one of their weapons. They do that in numbers, never alone. It would be more like them to march into Portsmouth Square with torches blazing than to skulk in the shadows making mischief.''

Berkeley turned on Grey. Her features were starkly etched by fear. "It isn't mischief they have in mind this night. They mean for people to die.''

Grey did not require convincing. He reached behind him for the door and opened it. "Come inside and get dressed. I'm going to get Donnel and Sam. We'll empty the hotel into the square. Wake Nat and take yourselves out. That's your only job, Berkeley. I want to know that you'll be outside waiting for me.''

She nodded. "Yes, of course.'' Before she thought better of it, Berkeley stood on tiptoe and brushed his mouth with her own. She hurried past him before he could catch her or comment.

There was grumbling and protests as guests were roused from their beds. Some had only left the tables an hour earlier and were groggy with drink and lack of sleep. Others had been in a deep sleep and required considerable convincing to leave their rooms.

The fact that Grey couldn't tell them what the danger was made them more suspicious than cooperative. Some made no secret that they thought it was all a ruse to separate them from their belongings. Many people took time to gather valuables and pack a valise. The gamers still at the tables on the main floor were even more difficult to remove from their cards and dice. Those in the middle of a lucky streak were especially physical in their opposition.

Up until the very last Grey thought he and Donnel would have to carry Annie Jack out of her precious kitchen. It didn't come to that. When he finally told her that he was acting on Berkeley's intuition that there would be trouble, she barreled right past him.

The oddity of the throng of displaced guests gathered in Portsmouth Square soon brought out the curious from the El

Dorado. They were joined shortly by men from other saloons and gaming houses bordering the square. The rising noise woke up whores and their customers and brought them to their windows. In a little more than the hour since Grey had risen from his bed, it seemed that no one was left resting comfortably in their own.

Berkeley laid one hand on Nat's shoulder to keep him close. His eyes were darting around the crowd at boot level looking for some sign of Pandora. Berkeley was more than a little afraid he would slink off when she wasn't looking to find the cat.

"There!" Berkeley said. "Over there!"

Nat looked up hopefully and saw Berkeley had spotted Grey. He raised his hand to join hers. Grey caught sight of their waving arms and ignored all those demanding an explanation from him to reach Berkeley and Nat.

"Have you seen Pandora?" Nat asked in the way of a greeting.

Grey tousled Nat's hair affectionately. "She was under my feet most of the time I was trying to get everyone out. I nearly stepped on her twice." He noticed that seemed to calm Nat rather than alarm him. Grey decided not to tell Nat he'd been close to pitching Pandora off the balcony at that point. "I'm certain she followed me out."

"Probably has." His eyes went back to the crowd.

Grey smiled a little guiltily at Berkeley. "I suppose I should have taken the cat in hand."

"No," she said, taking his instead. "She'll be fine." Berkeley looked around her. There were not many patient, understanding faces from what she could see. "Do you think they'll lynch me for provoking this?"

Grey could tell the question was asked only partially in jest. "I think you'll be this night's real hero," he said.

Looking at each other the way they were, Grey and Berkeley were not the first to see flames shooting from the roof of Peterman's hardware store on the southwest corner of Portsmouth Square. That sighting was left to a whore leaning out of her room at the El Dorado. Her shrill cry was lost on the crowd below her. What they all heard instead was the shattering of the store's large plate-glass window as it was blown outward by exploding cans of paint and turpentine.

Grey thrust Berkeley away from him. Donnel was already shouting for a brigade to form, and Grey took up the call. The crowd organized itself quickly, finding purpose where there had been chaos. Buckets were gleaned from every available source, and the pumps were manned. Even men who minutes before had staggered away from the bars were able to manage themselves well in the crisis.

Their first target was not Peterman's hardware. These men had enough experience fighting fires in San Francisco to recognize that the store could not be saved. The plan, the only one that made sense and had some hope of succeeding, was to keep the fire from spreading. They accurately judged the wind to be coming from the north and east, and while they approached their task with a single-minded grimness, knowing full well it was the worst condition they could face to fight the fire, it was the Gandy Dancer saloon that received the first shower of water.

The pumper trucks arrived pulled by men, not horses. Taking aim at the roof, water was unleashed on the saloon. The brigades, less effective but still so necessary, never stopped passing their buckets hand to hand.

"Fine work of the Ducks this night," someone shouted.

There was a general chorus of agreement, though no man among them thought it would ever be proved. "We'll be lucky if we don't lose the city," another observed.

Standing on the opposite side of the square, Berkeley couldn't hear the comments, but she was thinking much the same herself. The wind had already randomly lifted tongues of flame from Peterman's and set them licking at a storefront three buildings away. Without a miracle, the fire was going to get away from them.

"I feel as if we should be doing something, Nat," she said. "In addition to praying, I mean. Do you have—" Berkeley stopped because she was suddenly aware that Nat was no longer beside her. Worse, she couldn't recall how long ago she had

last noticed him. Had he taken it upon himself to help Grey
fight the fire? Her heartbeat quickened as she imagined him
among the crush of men, staggering under the weight of bucket
after bucket of water passing through his hands. Nat would
drop over before he would give up.

She started forward to search him out when his youthful,
anguished cry behind her stopped her in her tracks. The next
one raised gooseflesh on her arms. Berkeley whirled around
and faced the Phoenix. Her pale complexion reflected the
orange-and-yellow flames leaping through the open French
doors off Grey's balcony. They reached out toward Nat, twisting
and curling, trapping him in one corner.

Watching from below, her heart in her throat, Berkeley held
her breath while Nat climbed on the balustrade. He teetered
there a moment until he threw one thin arm around the Phoenix's
figurehead. Two arms would have been better, but in the other
he held Pandora.

The fire that was leaping from the Phoenix's windows was
still confined to the upper floors. Berkeley started to cross the
street for the main doors, but she was hauled back roughly.

Grey planted her. "Don't you move." His face was streaked
with soot and sweat. Beneath it his complexion had taken on
a ruddy hue from the heat of the fire. His eyes were like beacons,
and they held Berkeley in place after he let her go. "I'll get
him." He looked over her shoulder at Donnel and Sam, who
were just catching up with him. "Get a pumper here! Hose
down the hall!"

Having every expectation his orders would be followed, Grey
turned and sprinted into the Phoenix.

The stairwell was clear at the bottom, but by the time he
reached the first landing the smoke was thick. Grey took out
a handkerchief and covered his mouth and nose. He crouched
low so there was a little more visibility. After less than ten
yards he was feeling his way to the door of his suite. He held
his breath until he felt unsteady. The next full gulp of air seared
his lungs and caused a paroxysm of coughing. Stinging tears
blinded him.

When Grey finally found the door there was nothing he could do. It was hot to the touch and beyond it he could hear the fierce crackle and spit of the fire. In the few moments he stood there weighing his options, a thin sheet of flame began to creep out from under the door. He backed away, dropping to his hands and knees again, and headed for the stairs.

Shawn met him halfway and helped him out of the hall. "No good, was it?" asked Shawn. "We were worried. The boy's still out there. We think we might catch him with a blanket if he drops."

Grey shook his head. Now that he could see Nat again it was clear the boy wasn't going to let go of the figurehead any more than he would let go of Pandora. Berkeley was straining against the arm Sam had around her shoulders. Grey realized if he didn't think of something soon he was going to have to fight her as well.

He looked at the distance to the balcony from the ground, then at the flames that were flickering up the side of the building. "Give me a lift, Shawn." There wasn't time for something elegant. Brute strength was called for.

Shawn positioned himself under the balcony and hunkered down, making a firm step with his work-hardened hands. Grey stood back, measured his leap, and signaled Shawn he was ready. His first step put him in Shawn's callused palms. The boost Shawn gave him sent him up to the laborer's broad shoulders. Grey grasped the bottom of the balcony rail and began pulling himself upright.

Berkeley did not want to look, yet she couldn't look anywhere else. All around her she was aware that men were working tirelessly to save the Phoenix. The crowd in Portsmouth Square had swelled as miners, merchants, whores, and johns came from everywhere to fight the fire. No one wanted to lose another building. Sam Brannan's Vigilance Committee did not want to lose a chance at the Ducks.

Berkeley sucked in her lower lip, biting down hard, as Grey hauled himself awkwardly onto the outside edge of the balcony. She tasted blood in her mouth. Her eyes followed his progress, willing him over the balustrade. She pressed her hands together in an attitude of prayer and murmured her thanks as he landed safely on the balcony.

Heat kept Grey against the rail. He worked his way carefully toward Nat, keeping his eyes on the flames as they spiraled out of the sitting room and were whipped into a frenzy by the wind. He climbed on the balustrade when he reached Nat and used his body to protect the boy from the heat and fire.

"Give me your hands," he said. "I'm going to lower you over the side."

Nat's eyes were glassy with fear. He shook his head. His lips moved but there was no sound.

Grey made out a single word: Pandora. Apparently he would have to save the cat to save them. He didn't wait for Nat to come across with the feline. He tore Pandora out of the boy's arm and felt her claws sink into him. He grimaced but managed to keep his balance. Grey let Pandora perch on his shoulder like a parrot and began prying Nat's arm away from the figurehead.

He dropped back to the balcony and felt it begin to give. Nat felt it, too. He clutched Grey's arms, almost unseating Pandora. Grey leaned over the balustrade and saw Shawn in position below him. "We can't go together," he whispered in Nat's ear. "Shawn will catch you."

"Who will catch you?"

Grey smiled. *Who indeed?* he wondered. He hadn't thought that far ahead. "I'll get down. You'll see." Grasping Nat by the wrists, Grey swung him over the balcony and lowered him as far as he could. Pandora, seeing a path to freedom open up, jumped from Grey's back to Nat's shoulder and finally to Shawn. "Traitor," Grey said under his breath, watching the cat leap to the ground. "You have him, Shawn?"

"Close enough. Let him go."

Nat gave a little yelp as the sensation of falling filled his senses. He was pulled up short of the ground and immediately pounced on by the cat and Berkeley. Shawn moved them out of the way of the balcony. He realized he wasn't imagining the cant in its floor. He could hear it giving way now.

Shawn cupped his hands over his mouth and called up to Grey. "Jump! You've got to jump!"

Berkeley's head shot up, and Nat twisted in her arms to see the building. "Jump!" she called. "Dear God, Grey! Jump!"

Grey *did* leap as the balcony collapsed under him. He threw himself toward the face of the building and the figurehead from the *Lady Jane Grey*. She held him there, supporting him against her polished bosom while his fingers found purchase in her intricately carved hair. She held him there for twenty long seconds while scenes from his life played out in his mind's eye.

Scenes from *all* his life.

Then Rhea came away from her mountings and carried him with her as she fell, cradling him at first, crushing him in the end.

Spean cupped his hands over his mouth and called. "Hey Clou! Champ! Star! Let's go to town."

Barnaby's head shot up, and her twisted jutting wings at the building caught the caller. "What Clou?" he gasped.

Chapter Sixteen

August 1851

They came for the baby first. Colin Thorne found the phrase intruding on all his other thoughts. *They came for the baby first.* He had always imagined he could taste it on his tongue. It was a fanciful notion, perhaps, for a man who was no stranger to life's harsher realities, but these words had been formed in his mind as a child, and when he thought of them he could not help being that child again, with all the same bewilderment and hurt and desperate resolve. Yet something was different now, and Colin was finally struck by the contrast. *They came for the baby first.* At last the flavor of it was more sweet than bitter.

Colin didn't know what to expect. When the carriage stopped in front of the Phoenix he didn't move immediately to get out. Instead he glanced questioningly at his brother, and for once Decker could not summon up his casual, careless smile.

They both looked simultaneously toward the Phoenix. The red fireball that was the late-afternoon sun lent a pinkish hue to the brick. The windows were tinted rose. They had heard about the Portsmouth Square fire from their driver as soon as they gave him their destination. Now they looked for some evidence that his story was accurate and found only a subtle change in the shading of the brick to support it.

Decker got out of the carriage slowly, his eyes lifted upward to the polished wooden figurehead. He raised one hand to shield his eyes, squinting slightly for a better look. Where the figurehead was fixed to the wall there were thick black streaks among the strands of her hair, just as if she'd had her beautiful tresses dipped in an inkwell. Decker pointed it out to Colin.

Neither of the brothers were certain how he felt about a ship's figurehead adorning a gaming house. Their shared passion for sailing and respect for the sea made them wonder if this unusual mounting for Rhea, mother of the god of all the seas, wasn't somehow sacrilegious. They passed under it and into the Phoenix without any comment.

It was still too early for the grand hall to be crowded, but there was activity at many of the tables. Drinks were being set up at the long bar. The deep laughter of gamers enjoying a good story mingled pleasantly with the deeper groans of men disappointed in the turn in their fortunes. Gold coins were gathered in grateful arms, and always there was the sound of shuffling cards and rolling dice.

As soon as Colin and Decker were identified as hotel guests and not transient gamblers, they were ushered to the registry. Sam abandoned his duties at the bar and brought out the book. He opened it so that it was facing them, then slid a pen and inkwell in their direction. "We have one room available on the second and third floors or you can share a suite on the second." He glanced down at the names Colin had recorded in the register. "Mr. Pine and Mr. Pine." Sam rubbed the underside of his chin thoughtfully and regarded his guests with interest. "You brothers?"

"That's right," Decker said.

"Guess you'll be wanting the suite then." Sam started to make a note of it.

Colin placed his hand over Sam's bony one. "Separate rooms. Different floors will suit us admirably."

Decker laughed. "I'm weary of sharing a cabin with you, too."

"You come a ways, have you?" Sam asked, chuckling.

"Boston," Decker said. "My brother's come farther. He started out in London."

Sam was visibly impressed. "Thought I heard something out of the ordinary there. You fellas should make a point of taking in a palm reading while you're at the Phoenix. Mrs. Janeway's a good one for pickin' out where a man's from. Reckon that London might stump her, though."

"Mrs. Janeway?" asked Colin.

"Hmmm." Sam took the book back and closed it. "She more or less runs the Phoenix these days. Mostly more. Ain't much that gets by her." He glanced toward the stairs, then at his pocket watch. "Won't be much longer, and she'll be coming down for the evening. You don't want to miss her. She doesn't stay down as long as she used to. Doesn't have time. Not with the baby."

One of Colin's dark brows lifted. He looked at his brother but said nothing.

Decker shrugged. "I showed you the correspondence I received. There was never any mention of Janeway." But he shared his brother's suspicions. Reading palms was something Berkeley Shaw might do to exercise her talent. Decker felt the faint tug of hope again. They could be getting close. He leaned forward, bracing his arms stiffly on the registry, and gave Sam a level look. "I'd like to look through the registry," he said. "May I?"

Sam blinked but his expression remained friendly. "I don't suppose that's a problem. Someone in particular you're looking for?"

Decker didn't answer. He leafed backward through the registry, running his finger down one column of names and up another. "Nothing," he said when he finally reached the very first entry. "Not a thing."

Colin placed his hand on Decker's forearm and drew his brother back with the gentle, cautioning gesture. "Perhaps he'll come to us." He turned to Sam. "What about our things?"

"Gotcha taken care of there." Sam glanced around and spied Nat coming out of Annie's kitchen. From the look of the boy's distorted features and furtive expression, Sam guessed Nat had some of Annie's best pastry pouched in his cheeks. Sam raised his hand and waved him over. Nat's response was to hang his head guiltily and pretend he hadn't seen anything. Sam called to him. This time there was no ignoring, not with several of the house's regular customers echoing the message as well. "Nat here will see to your bags," Sam said. "You take a carriage from your ship?"

Decker nodded. "The driver was unloading as we came in." He eyed the boy and wondered if offering to assist with the trunks would be an insult or a welcomed gesture. He didn't have time to offer anything. Nat gulped down whatever he had in his cheeks and was hurrying outside.

"Nat'll show you to your rooms," Sam told them. "He'll take what he can carry in. I'll get someone else to bring the heavy things. Nat's a good one, but he hasn't figured out that he can't lift the trunks. He likes to help, though. A Janeway through and through."

"Janeway?" asked Colin. "But isn't that—"

"His mother," Sam interrupted. "That's what you were going to ask, wasn't it?"

Colin nodded. He exchanged another questioning glance with his brother. Decker's response was to shrug, a sure indication that he had no better understanding than Colin. It wasn't possible for Berkeley Shaw to have a child so old. They had to be mistaken that she and her husband had assumed the name Janeway. "We heard from the driver there was a fire here some months back." He made a point of looking critically around the hall. "That's hard to believe."

"Ain't it?" Sam said proudly. "I've seen eleven fires since I came here. Four of them took out most of the city. Never can tell a month or so later. That's San Francisco for you. The

Portsmouth Square fire was the last one. Some say it wasn't much of one, but that's because they weren't here that night and didn't see the fight it took to contain it. The fire gutted both of the upper floors of the Phoenix. Except for some water damage we saved most of what was down here. Your rooms, though, that was different. Everything there had to be brought in new.''

That caught Decker's interest. "Did you ship goods with the Remington Line?''

"Mostly. Always have done more business with them." Sam was struck by a thought. "You say you're from Boston? You must be familiar with the line.''

Decker's easy smile came to the forefront. "Just in passing,'' he said modestly.

Colin gave his brother an arch look. "Jonna would say that about sums up your knowledge of what goes on.''

Far from being offended by Colin's dry humor, Decker laughed appreciatively. "She would, too. God, I miss her.''

Colin glanced at the door. Not seeing Nat return, he addressed Sam again. "So the fire was confined to the Phoenix?''

"No. Not at all. It took out everything on the other side of the square.''

"Just on the other side? That's quite a distance for a fire to leap.''

Sam nodded. "I've seen it happen though. But not that night. You're right about that. There were actually two fires. The first was a diversion, but then I expect the driver told you some of that. Seems folks around here like to talk about that night, even if they weren't in the square to see it." His attention shifted to the doors as they were pushed open. "Here's Nat with your bags. He could tell you a thing or two. He saw more than most that night." Sam grinned widely at the bewildered boy. "Didn't you, Nat?''

"What's that, Sam?''

"The Portsmouth Square fire. These gents are interested.''

Nat looked Colin and Decker over. Fancy men, he thought. Probably kept a pistol up their sleeves and a lace handkerchief

in their vest pockets. "This way," Nat said, hefting the bags
"Set you up right and tight, we will. There's no better plac
to stay in Frisco than the Phoenix."

Sam grinned as Nat marched away. As an afterthought h
called out the room numbers. To Colin and Decker he said
"You'd better not let him get too far ahead of you. Your bag
won't be in the rooms you wanted."

Nat felt them on his heels at the halfway point on the stair
"Seems like you fellas plan to stay a while. I'm saying tha
because of the bags and trunks your driver's still unloading."

Decker chuckled. "Most of that belongs to his nibs here."

"His nibs?" asked Nat. He glanced at Colin. "Are you on
of those titled gents?"

"Afraid so."

Nat's brows went up. He reached the landing and turned
walking down the hallway backwards so he could see the broth
ers better. "Does that mean you're a lord, too?" he asked
Decker.

"Not bloody likely," Decker said pleasantly, ignoring hi
brother's scowl.

Colin almost ran into Nat as the boy stopped abruptly. "D
you need some help?"

"No, sir . . . I mean, my lord. But this is your room. Or a
least it's someone's room. Did you decide who would hav
this one?"

Decker took a coin out of his pocket. "I'll flip you for it."

"Not bloody likely," Colin said.

Laughing, Decker tossed the coin in the air. With gracefu
sleight of hand he made it disappear.

Nat's jaw sagged, and he dropped all four of the valises
"Where'd it go?"

Decker shrugged, holding up both hands, palms out.

Rolling his eyes, Colin opened the door to Decker's room
and tossed one of the bags inside. "Check your pocket," h
told Nat. "Could be you've just been given a bit of the read
for your efforts."

Nat patted down his jacket and found the coin. "I want to learn how to do that," he said, awed. "I surely do."

"Perhaps," said Decker. "I'd like to hear about the fire that went through here. We were led to believe you have a story to tell." He picked up one of Colin's bags. "Show us to my brother's room. We can talk there."

When Nat hesitated, Colin added, "I wouldn't be at all surprised if there weren't more coins for your trouble."

Nat hefted the two remaining bags and headed for the stairs. 'This way, my lord. You too, sir."

Colin's room faced the square. After the crowded accommodations on board ship this room seemed spacious, and the appointments, just as Sam had informed them, were all recent acquisitions. Colin stretched out on the bed while Decker spun a chair away from the small writing desk and straddled it. Nat took up a stool.

"What's your particular interest?" Nat asked. "Most visitors don't really want to hear stories about the fires and quakes. Spooks them, I guess. Did me at first, too. You learn to live with them though."

"So it seems," said Colin. "I'm interested in the last fire. The one our driver called the Portsmouth Square fire. I had the impression it wasn't caused by a quake."

"No," Nat said. "Ducks." He saw their puzzled looks. 'Sydney Ducks. I don't know how they came by that name except the place they live in Frisco is called Sydney Town. Now that I think on it, you both talk a little like them." Suddenly worried, afraid he had once again fallen into a trap, Nat started to rise off his stool.

"Sit down," Decker said. "We're not Ducks, and we're not Duck hunters." He looked at Colin. "I imagine he's talking about felons from the British penal colony in Australia. From Van Dieman's Land."

"That's what I was thinking," said Colin. He was also thinking how narrow his own brother's escape had been from a transportation sentence to Van Dieman's Land. Colin counted himself as blessed for having found Decker before that had come to pass. He had spent a considerable amount of time on the voyage to San Francisco preparing himself for the fact that he might not be twice blessed. He had come to learn what he could about the fate of his youngest brother, not with any expectation that he would find Greydon. At least that was what he told himself. In spite of that, it was difficult not to hope.

"Go on about the fire," Colin said. "There were two that night, I believe."

There was no harm in talking about the fire, Nat thought, though he was not particularly comfortable with the subject. His eyes slid to Decker, who had taken out another coin and was deftly moving it between his fingers with no visible effort. That was another trick worth knowing. "There were two," he confirmed. "The Ducks set up the first one in Peterman's hardware. No one knew then that it was the Ducks though there was suspicion aplenty. Everyone got out of the Phoenix before the first flames were seen at Peterman's. That's because Mrs. Janeway had one of her intuitions that there was going to be trouble. Some of the other gaming halls were emptying, too, but that was because folks were just curious.

"I was curious just like everyone else, but I couldn't see much. Mostly I was looking for Pandora."

"Pandora?" Decker asked. "Let me guess. Your snake."

"Wouldn't I just love a snake," Nat said wistfully. "But no, Pandora's a cat. Not just mine, though she sleeps with me mostly. That's why I felt responsible. She was in my room when I had to leave, but I couldn't find her. I suppose she got scared and Mrs. Janeway wouldn't let me take the time to look for her. I figure she'd come out when the place emptied, so I was searching hard for her. No one paid me any mind. Now after the explosion at Peterman's. Everyone took to fighting the fire. I was concentrating on finding Pandora, so I was the only one who saw the pair of Ducks moving about the Phoenix. I couldn't tell Mrs. Janeway. She would have tried to do something on her own and she was—" Here Nat clasped his hands together and extended them away from his belly to exaggerate Berkeley's pregnant state.

"With child?" asked Colin.

Nat nodded. "That's it exactly. So I went in to see what tricks they were up to. I didn't see that I had much of a choice." He paused, hoping for some confirmation from his audience. Virtually everyone of his acquaintance told him in the aftermath that he had been remarkably foolish. These men remained silent, withholding judgment. "When I went into the gaming hall they were already upstairs. I didn't know that then. I had to look around the kitchen and storage rooms first. I was quick, but they had already torn through Mr. and Mrs. Janeway's rooms by the time I got there. Jolly—that's what one of the Ducks called his friend—was fanning a fire on Mr. Janeway's carpet. I would have run and gotten help, but that's when I saw Pandora. She must have been wandering around looking for someone and came upon them. I thought I could get her and get out. They weren't looking in my direction at all, but Pandora jumped when the fire blazed and they turned and saw me." Nat ducked his head a bit, uncomfortable with the showing he had made from that point on. "Bobby—he was the other fella—nabbed me by the collar and flung me across the room. It didn't take but a few seconds for the fire to catch and put a wall of flames between me and them."

Colin's dark eyes narrowed. "They got out and you didn't."

Nat nodded. He pointed to the window in Colin's room. "The Janeways' rooms face the front, same as yours. They have a balcony, though. That's where I went. Mrs. Janeway saw the fire and me and Pandora and got help. I was hanging on to Rhea. Did you see her when you came in?"

"The figurehead," said Decker. "Yes, we saw her."

"Well, she held me steady until Mr. Janeway got up to me. He lowered me over the side of the balcony." Nat shrugged. "And here I am. That's what Sam meant when he said I saw more than most others that night." He started to get up again. The glint from Decker's ice-blue eyes put him right back in his place. Nat's fingers tapped on his kneecaps. "I'd like to learn a trick or two now."

An easy smile edged Decker's mouth but didn't reach his

eyes. "I'm certain you would. But I think you're stopping shor of the whole. How was the fire put out, for instance?"

"A miracle, most folks say. Mrs. Janeway had been prayin; pretty hard for one, though she says she didn't have any intuitio that it was about to happen. The same northeast wind that wa causing so much trouble with the fire swept in a storm. The skie opened up and everyone standing in that square got drenched. I didn't take but another twenty minutes for the fire to fizzle out It could have been different without the rain. The entire city' been in flames before."

"That's what we heard," said Colin. "It seems as thoug the Ducks intended it to happen again."

"That's a fact," Nat told him. "They pick their times rea well. Wind from the north and east can do damage to ever part of the city except Sydney Town. They know how to sav themselves. Of course they hadn't counted on the rain. No on had. Not even Mrs. Janeway. Jolly and Bobby Burns got ou of the Phoenix through the kitchen and made it back to Sydne Town easy enough, but they weren't too hard to corral whe Sam Brannan's Vigilante Committee went after them. Th Ducks didn't think I'd be alive to point a finger at them."

Colin realized immediately what this child had risked b coming forward. "That showed a lot of courage."

Nat screwed his mouth to one side. "Everyone says that,' he said. "But here's what I don't get: How come it was brav for me to point them out so Brannan's men could hang the and foolish for me to follow them into the Phoenix in the firs place?"

"There's a conundrum," Decker said sympathetically. H flipped the coin he'd been manipulating in Nat's direction "Foolishness and courage. Could be they're two sides of th same coin."

Nat looked down at the gold piece in his hand. Heads. H turned it over carefully. Heads again. His eyes lifted in Decker' direction with frank awe.

Decker grinned. "Something to think about, isn't it?"

Colin sighed. "Now you've corrupted the boy."

"Oh, no, my lord," Nat said earnestly. "I was corrupted a ways back. Sam says it's not his damn fault, but Mrs. Janeway says she's not so sure."

Decker laughed outright. Colin's smile was more reserved. 'We were led to believe that you're a Janeway."

"Oh, I am," Nat said proudly. He jumped to his feet and jammed Decker's coin in his pocket. "Can't stay. Sam'll be wondering what's keeping me. Maybe you could show me those tricks later." He ducked his head quickly, avoiding the pair of eyes that had been able to keep him rooted before. Without waiting for Decker's reply or Colin's objections, Nat hurried out of the room.

Colin pushed himself up higher against the headboard. He raised one brow in his brother's direction. "What do you make of that?"

"Another conundrum."

Colin pulled the pillow from under his head and threw it hard.

There were triple the number of people in the gaming hall when Colin and Decker returned to it that evening. They had no particular plan as they descended the stairs. They had already traveled a great distance on the basis of a single letter sent to Decker months earlier. The author of the note did not identify himself or sign his name. He never mentioned Berkeley Shaw. What was clear, perhaps the only thing that was clear, was that he believed he needed to be cautious. If Decker or Colin Thorne wanted information about an heirloom earring, he wrote, one or both of them should come to San Francisco and register at the Phoenix. He thought he *might* be able to help them.

It was not the content that intrigued Decker when he received the missive, but the handwriting. He had only one example of Graham Denison's script: his signature in the ship's log when he had boarded the Remington *Siren*. There was enough of a match to raise Decker's hopes. He delayed his trip to wait for

Colin. He couldn't imagine making this last leg of a very long
journey without his brother.

No matter what the outcome of the search, the brothers shared
the understanding that it ended here.

They saw her simultaneously, their eyes drawn in her direction first by the circle of men standing at attention, then by the
reason for their attention. She was every bit the diamond in a
bed of black velvet. Although she stood only shoulder height
to most of the miners and gamblers, she stood out. It could
have been the corn silk brightness of her hair against their dark
clothes or the radiance of her complexion compared to their
ruddier hues, but Colin and Decker didn't think so. It was not
any one thing, but the whole of her, from the fey charm of her
leaf green eyes to the laughter that broadened her smile.

This woman was a revelation to them.

Berkeley's eyes lifted slowly to the staircase. For the span
of a heartbeat she could not think or feel or move. Darkness
pushed at the edges of her consciousness. She wished she could
faint, but her knees, locked in position, held her stiffly upright
and then she was breathing normally, just as if nothing were
different than it had been one moment earlier.

Except something *was* different. Perhaps everything. They
were here, in the hotel among the guests, and they were coming
toward her.

"Mrs. Shaw," Colin said politely. He and Decker had made
their way to the inner circle because Berkeley had been unable
to look away from them. Her rapt attention did not go unnoticed
by any of the men surrounding her. At first they were indecisive,
uncertain if they should move in to protect her or step out of
the way. In the end they chose the step backward.

Berkeley held out her hand. "It's Mrs. Janeway now," she
said.

Colin continued to lift her hand smoothly, but he did not
think she missed his surprise. He kissed her hand. "Mrs. Janeway," he repeated softly. "You remember my brother?"

"Of course." When Colin released her hand she extended
it to Decker. "Captain Thorne."

"Mrs. Janeway." He was as gallant in his attentions as is brother. "We've heard your praises sung almost from the moment we arrived. You can imagine that stories about a woman who seemed to be able to predict a disaster intrigued s."

Berkeley felt her smile faltering. "I imagine you would like n explanation."

"That comes to mind. Tell me, is there a Mr. Janeway?"

"We should go upstairs," she said. Her eyes darted to the men around her, and she smiled apologetically. "I doubt I'll e back down this evening." Berkeley ignored the murmur of disappointment. "This way."

Colin noticed that she seemed unaware of how the crowd parted for her. He and Decker were not. What was it Sam had old them earlier? *She more or less runs the Phoenix. Mostly more. Not much gets by her.* Behind her back Colin and Decker exchanged a look. Bankrolled by Thorne money, it appeared erkeley and Anderson Shaw had done very well for themselves.

Berkeley climbed the stairs ahead of them, very much aware f their eyes boring into her back. She did not fault them for their anger. It was the most natural reaction when they understood so very little. For the benefit of those in the crowd still watching er, she continued to smile. It was the best way to protect Colin nd Decker Thorne.

At the top of the stairs Berkeley paused and allowed them o flank her. "You must know that I was surprised to see you. No one told me that you were here. Are you registered guests f the Phoenix?"

"Mr. Pine and Mr. Pine," Decker said.

She nodded. "That explains it. Then you would be the one who impressed Nat with your sleight of hand. He was so excited rying to show me what he'd seen that I didn't stop him to iscover the details." Berkeley turned her head so she could ee Decker more clearly. "Why now? It's been more than six months since my husband wrote to you, Captain Thorne. Even

accounting for the length of the voyage, it's been longer tha
I would have expected.''

Decker's steps faltered. "Your husband wrote to me?''

Berkeley's brows drew together slightly as she sensed Deck
er's distress. "Yes, of course he did.''

"Are we talking about the same correspondence?'' he aske

They had reached the door to her suite. "I imagine that w
are. I never saw it, but he told me about it. I suspect he wa
too cautious and cryptic. Was that the reason for the delay
You weren't certain what to make of it?''

Colin twisted the handle and pushed open the door. "Tha
would sum it up nicely,'' he said. He gestured Berkeley insid
"After you, Mrs. Shaw.''

She hesitated. He had used her former name quite deliber
ately, Berkeley was sure of it. Had they somehow been i
contact with Anderson? She hadn't considered that the Thorne
would want to make trouble for her. "Janeway,'' she correcte
softly.

"Yes,'' Colin said humorlessly. "I hadn't forgotten.''

Berkeley was startled by his barely leashed anger. She wishe
his wife had accompanied him to temper it. It was difficult t
be mindful of her own manners. She ushered them into th
sitting room. "Please, won't you sit down?'' She gestured t
the cream-brocade settee and wing chairs. "Would either o
both of you like a drink? The Scotch is plentiful, but the bourbo
is almost gone.'' Berkeley raised one of the decanters on th
sideboard and held it up for their approval. "Whiskey? I ca
ring for tea or some other liquor if—''

"Sit down,'' Colin said.

Berkeley dropped like a stone into the rocker behind her. I
creaked once, then she held it still. The flush that had been i
her cheeks when they surprised her in the gaming hall wa
gone now. She felt as if all of her blood had pooled in her feet
They were leaden weights that kept her in place in spite of he
wish to be anywhere else. What was troubling with these men
They were acting as if she'd done something wrong.

Searching for patience, Colin raked back his hair. Thread

the color of sunshine fell forward over his brow, and this time he let them be. Now that he had her seated and quiet he had no idea where to begin. The explanations were clearly hers to make, yet he didn't think he wanted to hear anything she had to say just now. He swore softly as she continued to stare up at him. "Say something," he told his brother.

Decker's mouth twisted wryly. He had been looking around the sitting room, searching for some sign that a fire had swept through the suite. It wasn't apparent at first that his brother was talking to him. Decker pointed to the balcony. "Is that where Nat made his escape?" he asked.

Berkeley was bewildered by his interest but she answered. "You're talking about the fire?"

"Yes. Your *son* told us something of what happened here."

She didn't care at all for the way he spoke of Nat. "Yes, that's where he went," she said. Then, because they seemed to be expecting more from her she added, "You realize that Nat isn't my son by birth."

"Oh, Colin and I both came to that conclusion, having made your acquaintance in Boston, but we wonder that you've gone to the trouble of taking the boy in. Surely there were easier ways for you and your husband to hide than by assuming a ready-made family."

Berkeley's eyes widened at his tone. "We took him in because we love him, not because we're hiding behind him. Really, Captain Thorne, you and your brother would be the last ones from whom I would expect such a jaundiced view. Where would either of you be if no one had shown an interest in you as children?"

"Dead," Colin said bluntly. "We would have both died in Cunnington's Workhouse."

Decker didn't disagree with his brother. He couldn't. "Forgive me, Mrs. Janeway, but your husband never struck me as a particularly compassionate man."

"How can you say that?" she demanded. "You were the one who told me about his—" She stopped. From the bedroom she heard a familiar cry. The response in her was instantaneous.

Berkeley's breasts swelled and beneath her sapphire evening gown she felt sweet droplets of milk dampen her chemise. Colin and Decker would have to physically restrain her to keep her away from her child. She didn't think it would come to that. Berkeley got to her feet. "If you'll excuse me, that's Rhea's hungry wail. I have to attend to my daughter."

She brushed past them, sweeping grandly from the sitting room into the small library.

Decker looked at Colin. "Rhea?" he asked. "Did she say her daughter's name was Rhea?"

"That's what she said."

"Did *you* hear a baby cry?"

"No, but then Mercedes says I never did when our children were infants. She, on the other hand, could hear them crying in another county."

Decker ignored most of what Colin said. "I didn't hear a baby. And who names their child after Neptune's mother?" He was starting to move in the direction of the adjoining room. "She thinks quickly, Colin. I'll wager she has another way out of this suite."

Colin followed close on his brother's heels. They went through the library quickly and to the door of the adjoining room. Decker yanked it open and found himself standing on the threshold of Berkeley's bedchamber. As he suspected, neither Berkeley nor her baby were in it.

But it wasn't empty.

From his bed, Grey Janeway looked up slowly as the door was flung open. He arched one eyebrow in Decker's direction. The stunned expression on Decker's face raised his own sly smile. "Hello, Captain Thorne," he said quietly. Grey's eyes lifted just past Decker's head to where his brother was peering into the room over his shoulder. "And the Earl of Rosefield. Welcome."

Neither of the men moved. Framed by the doorway, their features as still and cold as marble, it was clear they could not take in what they were seeing.

Grey pushed himself a little more upright and rested his back against the headboard. Beneath the cotton coverlet the splint that kept his left leg immobile from knee to ankle was visible by its boxy outline. He raised his right leg and rested one forearm casually across the kneecap. "Forgive me if I don't get up. It's a damn inconvenient thing, this injury. I do all right with the crutches now, but that's going to change. The doctor tells me another two weeks with this splint, then I have learning to walk again to look forward to. I shouldn't be surprised if Rhea has it mastered before I do."

From behind the closed door to the adjoining dressing room there came a series of frantic whimpers and gentle reassurances. Finally there was silence. "Berkeley and Rhea," Grey said. Then he saw Colin and Decker glance in that direction. "Did you think she had gone?"

Decker hadn't yet found his voice, and Colin Thorne was unconcerned about Berkeley. Still, he could do no more himself than state the obvious. "You're not Anderson Shaw."

"No," Grey said, his grin deepening a fraction. "I'm not." He watched Colin's expression clear a little as the truth was borne home. "It doesn't appear my friend here is able to perform the introductions." Grey held out his hand. "Graham Denison," he said. "But I go by Grey Janeway now. I have for more than six years."

Colin slipped past his brother and reached for Grey's hand. The grip was firm, sure, and oddly familiar. "Your wife didn't tell us."

"Didn't she? That's odd. But then I don't know what's going on. Or not much of it. She marched through on her way to get Rhea and only told me that you and Decker were finally here and that there weren't brains or manners between the two of you. I gathered from that there was a problem."

"That would be understating it," Berkeley called in from the dressing room. "They've accused us of taking in Nat to hide behind, and they insist on calling me Mrs. Shaw. You'd better tell them how we lost the earring before they say we stole it. This reunion is not going at all as I thought it might!"

Rhea wailed loudly as Berkeley's nipple was dislodged from

her mouth. "Here, darling ... Mama's sorry. It's not your fault."

Grey grinned and pointed to Colin and Decker. "She's saying it's yours."

Decker finally found his voice. He pushed away from the doorframe and came to stand beside the bed. "What the hell's going on, Graham? Did you pen the note I got a while back or not?"

"Grey. Not Graham," he corrected. "You'll have to get used to it. No one here except Berkeley knows I once had that name. All things considered, it's a name best left in the past."

"Jesus," Decker said softly. It was not his usual way to let things rattle him, or at least let it show. This was different. Everything about this meeting was too important. "I can't make heads or tails of this."

Grey chuckled. He carefully reached over to the bedside table and opened the drawer. After rooting around a moment he pulled out one of the coins Decker had given Nat. "What about heads or heads?" he asked, holding it up. "I suspected you were here when Nat showed this to me."

"Are you talking about that coin?" Berkeley called in. "You might have told me. I wouldn't have made a complete cake of myself if I had been expecting them."

It was Colin who responded. "You have nothing to apologize for, Mrs. Janeway. As you correctly noted, Decker and I don't have a brain between us."

"Or manners," Decker added.

When Berkeley didn't rejoin, Grey chuckled. "She's blushing." He pointed to the chairs by the fireplace. "Bring those over here and sit down. Were you offered something to drink? You'll have to serve yourself now, I'm afraid."

"Get the chairs, Colin," Decker said. "I'm feeling a need for that drink after all." He disappeared into the sitting room and returned shortly with a decanter of whiskey under his arm and the tumblers skillfully balanced between his hands. He set it all down and poured a drink three fingers deep for each of them.

Decker sat back in the armchair Colin had pulled to the bed. He stared at Graham ... Grey, he reminded himself. There were not so many changes in the past six years. It was not so much that his friend had aged but that he had matured. There were fine lines at the corners of his mouth that deepened when he grinned, and his eyes, though their coloring had not changed, the flintlike hardness of them had. There was a slight softening of his features but not of his character. Resolve and purpose were still there, but there was a difference, too. In the past Decker would not have described Grey as either happy or content, now he seemed both. It was as if he had determined to risk happiness in exchange for the wry bitterness he used to embrace. This man was Graham Denison, and yet he wasn't.

Perhaps he had earned his new name and his new life.

Decker rolled the tumbler between his palms, warming the contents slightly. "So you're married now."

"Berkeley has my name," Grey said carefully. "We have a child together. And Nat, of course."

"What happened to Anderson?"

"Is that what you really want to know?" asked Grey. "We haven't laid eyes on each other for six years and you want to talk about Anderson Shaw?"

Decker chuckled shortly and pretended he didn't notice that Grey was holding something back. He shook his head slowly, looking Grey over from head to toe again. "My God," he said softly. "I can't believe we've found you."

"Berkeley found me."

"Yes, she did, didn't she?" It was almost too much to comprehend. "Where can you begin? I want to hear what's happened since you disappeared from the *Siren*."

"That will take some time."

It was Colin who looked pointedly at Grey's splinted leg. "You don't appear to be going anywhere soon." He leaned back in his chair and stretched his long legs, crossing them at the ankles. "As for me, I came halfway around the world to hear this story. I'm certainly not leaving without it."

Grey wondered if they could see that his eyes were no longer quite dry. He glanced quickly toward the dressing room as if he'd been distracted by a sound from there and swallowed with some difficulty. Berkeley's timing was impeccable. She opened the door, Rhea caught in the curve of one arm, and immediately sensed his distress. It required very little effort on her part to make Rhea the focal point and allow Grey a moment longer to compose himself.

"Would you like to hold her?" she asked Colin. He had come to his feet as soon as she entered the room. "She's a good baby. Rarely cries except when she's hungry; then she carries on as if she has three stomachs to fill."

Colin came around the foot of the bed and held out his arms. He was unprepared when the words were raised in his mind again: *They came for the baby first.*

Rhea's dark sable hair was ruffled by her mother's affectionate touch. She had a round face and a quick, engaging smile. Her chubby limbs flailed at him, and she laughed at her play. Without effort or conscience, she charmed him, and it came to her as naturally as drawing a breath. It made Colin realize he was holding his. "Come here, Decker," he said quietly. "Look at her."

Decker moved to his brother's side, prepared to make amends with Berkeley by cooing over her baby. He said nothing, however. No words, however silly and meaningless, could make it past the hard aching lump in his throat.

Colin and Decker looked at each other first, and, without a word passing between them, they each turned to Grey. "She looks just like you," Colin said.

"Do you think so?" he asked. He tried to raise himself up to get a better look at his daughter's face. "Everyone here says she looks like Berkeley. Her hair's not the right color, of course, but that smile—"

"Is yours," Decker said. "The shape of her face . . . her hair . . . even her eyes."

"She *is* my daughter."

"Grey," Berkeley said gently. "I think they're trying to tell you something else."

"She's *you*," Colin said. "Or she could be. My memory can't be playing me so false."

"The thing of it is, *Greydon*," said Decker, "you should have been a girl. You were the prettiest baby. Mama and Papa both thought so. They remarked on it often enough."

Berkeley laughed as Grey flushed deeply. "I think you'll have to get used to your brother teasing you," she said. "I imagine he intends to do quite a lot of it during his stay." She reached for Rhea, but Colin shook his head and held the baby closer. He couldn't look away, and he couldn't release her. It could have been Greydon in his arms.

"No," he said. "Let me have her just a bit longer. You can't know what this—" He broke off before his voice broke. He bent his head and his face hovered about Rhea's. She stared up at him, her blue-gray eyes at once curious and trusting. When a single tear splashed her face she accepted it without a murmur.

Decker stared at the floor and blinked hard. Berkeley's own tears fell quite freely while her beatific smile never faltered. She went to Grey and took the hand he extended to her. She allowed herself to be pulled onto the bed beside him. His arm slipped around her shoulder and he gave her one corner of the coverlet to dry her eyes. Her watery smile deepened because he made no effort to do the same to his own.

The solemn silence was itself distracting to Rhea. She filled it with an abandoned little gurgle that was not meant to be ignored. Colin smiled as the vibration of the tiny bundle in his arms tickled him. Rhea squealed with delight and punctuated it with a hiccup. Decker chuckled at the abrupt quiet and surprise on her face. In turn that brought another peal of Rhea's infectious and bright baby laughter.

In the end they all succumbed. This time the tears had a different flavor.

Colin caught his breath first. He carried Rhea to her mother and passed her over, then he picked up his glass and raised it toward his brothers. Grey and Decker extended their tumblers in a silent toast.

Berkeley touched the tip of her daughter's nose. "They're going to get pie-faced," she said. "All three of them. Your father and your uncles. And they'll be no closer to sorting things out by morning. Just see if I'm not right."

It more or less turned out that she was.

Epilogue

Berkeley slipped into bed beside her husband, careful not to jostle the splint that protected his leg. She laid her hand lightly on his naked chest. His skin was warm. Berkeley snuggled closer, resting her head in the crook of his shoulder. She yawned hugely.

Grey chuckled.

"You're awake," she said, startled. "I vaguely recall your brothers sneaking out through the sitting room sometime ago. I tried to come back here, but I couldn't lift my head then."

"And not now either," Grey said, judging by the weight of it against him. "I think there are times that you're not at all sorry I'm virtually bedbound."

She raised herself up, kissed him on the mouth, and immediately resumed her position. "That's an awful thing to say. And why does your mouth taste like peppermint? I expected to be pie-faced myself just from kissing you good night."

"Colin gave me a handful of mints. He said you'd be appreciative."

Berkeley pressed another kiss against his skin. "He was

right. Perhaps you have a smart brother after all. Did Decker give you anything?"

"As a matter of fact . . ." Grey eased Berkeley up so he could reach across to the bedside table. He felt around on the top until he had what he wanted. "These are for you. Hold out your hand."

Berkeley's first reaction was to obey blindly but at the last moment she realized what he might be ready to drop into her hand. Her fingers folded convulsively, and the heirloom earrings glanced off her knuckles and fell harmlessly on the coverlet. Moonlight turned the gold to silver and made the pearls appear translucent. "Oh, Grey," she said, touched and saddened at the same time. "I thought Decker would know I can never wear them."

"He remembered, but when I wouldn't accept Rosefield, he said I should take these."

Berkeley peered closer into Grey's face. She searched his eyes. As far as she could make out they appeared quite clear. His speech wasn't slurred, even if he didn't make any sense. "I don't understand," she said. "Rosefield is Colin's property. He's the earl."

"He has the title and a portion of the estate, but the manor itself he arranged for Decker to take. It seems Decker's been waiting to hand it over to me. He has no use for it living in Boston with Jonna. I'm not certain I understand his reasoning, but then things got a little muddled after midnight."

Berkeley cocked one eyebrow and gave him a knowing look. "The earrings are the only inheritance he's ever cared about," she said. "Give them back to him and accept Rosefield graciously."

"You want to live in England?"

"No. Or at least I've never thought about it. But it's your heritage, Grey. Your true heritage. And Rhea's. You've built something here for Nat, for all of us. But don't deny Rhea a glimpse of your past, even if you would deny yourself."

Grey was quiet. He picked up the earrings and turned them over in his palm. "I hadn't thought of that," he said at last.

"As you said, things got a little muddled." She watched him put the earrings aside and was grateful for the arm he slipped around her again.

"You should have made them leave instead of falling asleep on the settee with Rhea. They felt very bad about that."

"I wanted you to have time together." She stifled a yawn. "It's odd how it turned out, isn't it? You've been afraid you could never convince them you were their brother, and they recognized it before you told them anything at all."

Grey pressed his lips to the pale crown of Berkeley's hair. "That's because you had the foresight to give me a daughter who apparently looks just like I did."

Berkeley smiled. Beneath the covers she found his palm and absently ran her thumb across the base of it. "Grey?"

"Hmmm?"

"Was it your letter that brought them here? It's been so long . . . I wondered if they might have heard from—"

"It was the letter. Not Anderson or Garret." He turned carefully on his side and propped his head in one hand. He let Berkeley keep the other. "You need to know, Berkeley. They're both dead."

"What?"

Grey waited for her to absorb the truth of what he said before he went on. "I was telling them about Anderson and Garret. They told me about the *Albany*. It went down in a storm near Tierra del Fuego. Word of the wreck reached Boston before Decker and Colin left. They didn't realize then that they knew anyone aboard. The ship was splintered between twenty-five-foot waves and the rocky coast. There were no survivors, Berkeley."

"Oh, God." She closed her eyes, squeezed them shut really, and tried to block out her last vision of the *Albany* in San Francisco Bay. Dizzying sparks of color replaced the outline of the ship against the sky and its reflection in the water. She felt a passing sadness for the souls lost, save two. For the man who had been both stepfather and husband, and the one who had been her half brother, there was no sense of loss. Word of their deaths brought a measure of relief, and for that she felt guilty. "Then Anderson was never able to spread his lies."

"No," Grey said. "They died with him and with anyone he told on board."

It struck her then that Grey had been as worried about Anderson's next move as she. "You thought he would tell Decker and Jonna about us, didn't you?"

"Yes."

"You never said anything to me."

"Neither did you."

Berkeley opened her eyes and tilted her head up at him. "I can't be sorry that he's gone," she said in a rush. "I can't feel anything for Garret's passing either."

"It's all right." He ran his fingers through her silky hair. The gesture slowly calmed her. "It's not so different for me. Anderson was determined to separate us. Garret, too, in his own way. They both meant us harm. I'm not sorry they can't try any longer."

"It's ironic, don't you think? Anderson wasn't satisfied that what he told me on the dock would hurt us enough, so he paid the Ducks to ruin us. The fire—"

"Ruin us?" Grey interrupted. "He meant for us to die in that fire."

"But it gave you back your life instead . . . and mine."

As he dangled above Portsmouth Square, holding on to Rhea's smoldering wooden tresses, Grey's memories broke through to his consciousness. Before he hit the ground and darkness overtook him again, he knew that most of what Anderson Shaw told Berkeley was a carefully constructed lie. Grey said, "I'm sure Anderson died perfectly satisfied that he had succeeded in all things."

"Well, I hope someone tells him how it turned out. That *will* be hell for him."

Laughter rumbled low at the back of Grey's throat. "I had no idea you could be so vengeful. I'll keep that in mind."

She wondered if her arch look was lost in the shadows. "You

should," she added for emphasis. Her features took on a more solemn cast. "What did you tell your brothers about him?"

Grey squeezed her hand. "Only what they needed to know. Nothing at all that he said the day he left on the *Albany*. I told them instead what I had come to remember and knew to be the truth: that I was the adopted son of James and Evaline Denison."

He could say the words now without the depth of hurt he had known when he had first heard them some eleven years earlier. At twenty they had felled him with the force of a physical blow. It no longer seemed that he knew himself, knew his parents, or his brother. Even his dear grandmother was suddenly a stranger to him.

Perhaps if he had been older or younger when he had learned the truth, he told himself. Perhaps that would have made a difference. All he knew now was that at twenty he wasn't prepared.

Over time he had shared all of it with Berkeley. Long days and nights spent in bed were good for reflecting on the past. His crushed leg, only in a splint now, had once been fastened to weights and pulleys to keep it from knitting shorter than the one that had only a simple fracture. His arm had been released from its splint and sling two months ago, and his ribs had slowly healed so that he could draw a breath without cursing the pain. Then there were daily exercises and sometimes unendurable massages to make certain his muscles stayed toned and supple. Grey was the first one to admit that at no time was he a good or grateful patient.

Berkeley was his eyes and ears and legs, running the hotel and supervising his interests, yet it seemed to Grey that she rarely left his side. When her time came she gave birth to Rhea in the adjoining dressing room, and when it was over she insisted on being carried into their bedchamber. It was only then that Grey was glad he was confined to the bed. The doctor wouldn't have allowed him to share it with Berkeley in any other circumstance. She put their beautiful, red-faced and wrinkled baby girl on his chest, and he cradled Rhea against his sling, just as if it were there for only that purpose.

At night, lying so carefully beside him, Berkeley would listen as he talked about his youth and recovered some new piece of his past at Beau Rivage.

He had never had any suspicion that he did not properly belong to Beau Rivage, but he had always known he didn't quite fit in. Of course there were times when he believed his younger brother was given special consideration or privilege, but he recognized the roots of these uncharitable thoughts as his own jealousy and tried to put them aside. Garret received more because he asked for it. He never questioned, as Grey did, if he was deserving. Almost from the moment of his birth, Garret proved himself to be the charming, amiable brother, and it was generally accepted that while the two boys looked a great deal alike, their temperaments could not have been more different.

It was the summer Grey returned to Beau Rivage from Harvard that he learned more about the differences between himself and Garret. He had not intended to listen to the argument between his mother and father, but when he heard his name he stood rooted to the floor outside his mother's room, knowing somehow that he had already heard too much.

His mother was having one of her spells. That was the polite term the family used to describe Evaline's bouts of melancholy and subsequent confinement to her room. Grey had been home three days, and, except for a brief audience upon his arrival, he had yet to spend any time with her. Armed with a book and a cup of tea he had gone to her room, determined to break through her self-imposed isolation.

Standing in the hall outside her door, listening to the raised voices, Grey remembered that when he was quite young he had known with certainty that his father loved his mother. That feeling had long since passed. What his father had once indulged, he now only tolerated.

The argument could have started about anything. With no parameters for the participants, with no subjects placed off-limits, it had rapidly deteriorated into an argument about past slights and hurtful actions that had never been resolved. Hadn't he tried every method at his disposal to please her? his father was asking. Had she forgotten it was her fear of humiliation that he had responded to when it seemed she could not conceive? Hadn't he arranged their trip to London for one purpose alone? *To find a child they could present at Beau Rivage as their own.*

There was a great deal more said about it then, but Grey only heard disjointed bits though he never left his place by the door. It was over that entire summer that he pieced together the whole of the story. What he discovered was that he was the last in his own family to know.

When Evaline, against all expectations, found herself pregnant after the visit to London, she felt compelled to apologize to her in-laws for her deception. Although not eager to do so, James was forced to admit to his parents that the child he presented as his own was, in fact, a foundling plucked from a London workhouse. Even Garret had been eventually made privy to the truth some years earlier.

Grey came to realize the Denisons had a family secret, and the most damning evidence that he was not part of the family was that they kept it from him. Just as hurtful was Grey's realization that they maintained the secret not to spare his feelings, but to spare their own. With the sole exception of his grandmother, Grey sensed his family was embarrassed by his existence. His grandfather hated the idea that Beau Rivage would pass to someone not of his own blood. To his mother he was a reminder of the panic and humiliation she experienced when she had not been able to conceive. His presence reinforced his father's decision not to indulge Evaline's every whim, and, as she withdrew, so did he. A succession of mistresses—Berkeley's mother among them—kept him away. Somehow, even the responsibility for those infidelities was laid at Grey's door.

It was no different to Garret. To Garret he was not a brother, but an obstacle.

The secret of Grey's birth could not be properly kept from

society if he did not inherit Beau Rivage, but if he was to be disowned, there would have to be a reason.

Grey decided to give them one. It only took some time for the plan to unfold.

He had never given a great deal of thought about the slaves that his family owned. They had always been there, field hands and house servants, quartered in a row of shanties that could be seen from his bedroom if he cared to notice. He didn't, not often anyway. He grew up alongside black children, played with them and worked with them, and had never once questioned the premises that mandated that one of them would be the owner and the others would be owned.

Education north of the Mason-Dixon Line opened his eyes to another way of life. The ideas that accompanied it were revolutionary. In his first year at Harvard Grey did not embrace what the abolitionist movement in Boston was preaching. He needed the summer away from the fanatics at Faneuil Hall to think more about it. When he returned to classes in the fall he was still uncertain what he thought about slavery, but he was absolutely certain what his family thought.

There was no better way to disgrace himself with the Denisons than to get involved with the Underground Railroad.

First he made himself a scapegrace. He rebelled in small ways. He quietly voiced unpopular opinions at the dinner table. He drank more than he could properly tolerate. He visited brothels in Charleston and lost money at the gaming tables. His three-year engagement to Alys was abruptly ended, and he accepted the blame for its dissolution. He never revealed to anyone that she hadn't left him because of the change in his behavior, but because he had explained the change to her. She left him because he had confided in the woman he loved. She left him because she wanted to marry a Denison.

Alys Franklin made it clear that she could accept his drinking and gaming and whoring, that she, like so many of her friends, had been raised to accept those intemperate and self-indulgent traits in their husbands. What she could not accept was that she would not be getting a Denison in exchange for her sacrifice.

The pain of that betrayal left Grey numb. His only solace was that he had not confided the whole of his plan to her. Alys became as much the focus of his revenge as his own family. The first slave he freed came from Alys's plantation at Westerly. Her name was Cristobel, and she was Alys's personal maid.

Grey was suddenly aware that Berkeley was watching him. In the shaft of moonlight that glanced off her hair, her eyes were very nearly black. Their focus was intense. He smiled a shade guiltily.

"Tell me," she said.

He shook his head. "You've heard it before."

"I don't mind. I like the sound of your voice. Tell me where you went just then, what you were thinking."

Grey sighed, but he was relieved not to be able to refuse her. He wanted, no, he *needed* to talk about it. "Did you mind very much discovering I was not Falconer?"

"No." Berkeley ran her fingers back and forth lightly along his collarbone. She remembered that Grey had never accepted that the name had belonged to him. Even before his memory was returned he had somehow sensed his connection to Falconer wasn't what others thought. "You took the name and the credit—and the damnation in some quarters—to protect Decker's secret. He and Jonna couldn't have continued their work on the Underground if you hadn't identified yourself as Falconer. And it's not as though you hadn't been engaged in the very same work for years. You might never have met Decker if you hadn't been a conductor with the Railroad. Why should I think less of you because you're not the one they called Falconer?" Her fingers stopped their tracing motion. "Do you think less of yourself?"

"It's not that precisely. I suppose it's more of a regret that my involvement wasn't because of an ideal. I remember that Jonna once characterized my actions as noble. It made me uncomfortable, knowing as I did that my behavior was motivated by revenge."

"Someone told me that great change is not always prompted

by a high-minded, heroic code. Sometimes it only takes a profound act of selfishness.''

Grey's smile was wry. *''I* told you that.''

"So you did.'' Berkeley raised her hand and touched his mouth, silencing him gently. "And I say it's not so simple as that. It began one way for you and finished another. In the end you embraced an idea that you hadn't always believed in. If that weren't true, you wouldn't have hidden your activities from your family as long as you did. You let them believe you were a self-indulgent wastrel, that you were no better than your own bad blood would allow you to be. You encouraged them not to bear any responsibility for raising you badly, only for *choosing* badly. You could have allowed them to see through your charade at any time, and yet you didn't. Not after the first slave you led out, not after the first score. One wonders if you would have ever told them if you had not been moved to help Decker.''

Berkeley removed her hand and raised her face. She kissed Grey lightly on the mouth. "I don't know if you understand the true nature of revenge. In order to make it felt, you have to make it known. That you finally did was more by accident than design.''

"So I can start posing for my statue?'' he asked dryly.

She laughed and tapped his chest with her forefinger to drive home her point. "You can take comfort in the fact that you're wonderfully human: complicated, simple, wise, foolish, enigmatic, and transparent. You can embrace the contradictions in your nature or you can spend the rest of your life trying to make sense of them.''

Grey didn't have to think about it. He grabbed her hand before she withdrew it. "I'd rather spend the rest of my life embracing you.''

That should have deepened her smile. She knew he meant it to. Instead it was marked with a hint of sadness. Her expression had become grave. "The revenge you meant to take on your family never involved killing one of them. Don't forget that, Grey, when you look back on what you did. Garret planned for you to die.''

"Because I dishonored the family."

"Because he couldn't be satisfied with the family's disowning you. In his mind you had tainted everything he stood to inherit. Beau Rivage. Alys. His way of life. Your mother's prized piece of jewelry that rightfully had always been yours. Your actions gave him what he wanted and in the same stroke made it all seem so much less than it was.'' She searched his face. "I've given it a lot of thought, Grey, and I really believe Garret had come to learn I was his half sister. Anderson said I never understood how integral I was to everything that happened. I think that well may be one of the few truths he told me that day. We've found it so easy to blame Anderson that we don't often consider the role Garret played. Perhaps he was afraid that I would want something from him—or from the father who never showed me the least attention. He couldn't know that I want only what I have. More is never enough for someone like Garret, and he didn't have the capacity to understand someone like me. He needed to have everything for himself.''

Grey stared at Berkeley for a long moment. When she looked away, made self-conscious by his scrutiny, he touched her chin and brought her back to him. His voice was softly intent. "You're a marvel."

This time her smile revealed a glad heart. "Yes," she said simply, "I am."

His deep, throaty response was part laughter, part growl. Before she could suspect what he would do, or even that he could do it, Grey raised his injured leg over both of hers and trapped her under the wooden splints.

Berkeley looked up at him, her eyes wide as a startled fawn's. "What do you think—"

"Does it hurt?" he asked. "Have I hurt you?"

She felt the extra weight the splints lent his leg, but they were wrapped in thick bandages, and while heavy, were not uncomfortable against her. "No, but—"

''Because it doesn't hurt me,'' he said. ''And I find I very much want to make love to my wife.''

Berkeley frowned. It was not that they hadn't been intimate in the weeks following Rhea's birth and Grey's slow mending. It was just that there were limitations. Berkeley's hand slipped between their bodies and found the edge of the towel that was wrapped around his waist. Her fingers began to tug on the knot that secured it in place. ''Grey, you know I'll—''

''In the more traditional way,'' he said. ''I want you all around me.'' His breath caught as her hand went under the towel. She circled his penis with her fingers. Grey lowered his head until his mouth hovered just above hers. ''I want to be inside you.''

Her mouth opened. ''Yes,'' she said. Just that. *Yes.*

He kissed her deeply then, and she lifted her arms around his shoulders. His skin was warm and smelled faintly of soap. At the nape of his neck there were still some damp strands mingled among the dry ones. His jaw was clean-shaven. Berkeley smiled, tasting peppermint on his tongue.

His brothers had helped him, of course. While she slept in the sitting room they talked and drank and laughed. They had probably cried again, the three of them, separately and together, and laughed some more. They shared their pasts, their secrets, and their hopes for the future. It was then that Grey must have been moved to tell them that he hoped to seduce his wife.

She imagined Colin and Decker had made it their mission for baby brother to succeed. They sobered him, washed him, buffed and polished him, and fed him peppermint for good measure. She would have to find a way to thank them for their efforts without being obvious or coarse, but they really needn't have gone to so much trouble.

The truth was, she was easy.

Grey felt the outline of Berkeley's smile against his skin. ''What is it?''

The closeness of his mouth tickled hers. ''Hmmm. I'll tell you later. Lie on your back.''

He was easy, too. When he rolled over she followed him.

Grey watched her, fascinated and aroused by her lithe, graceful movements. She sat up and straddled his thighs. Leaning forward, she placed her palms flat on his chest and gradually drew them downward. He sucked in his breath when she removed the towel and then let it out slowly as she raised her nightshift. She placed his hands on her hips and felt his fingers press into the taut flesh of her bottom. She was lifted, partly by his efforts, partly by hers, and then she drew him into her.

It was sometime later that they slept and much later when Grey finally woke. Beside him, Berkeley didn't stir. Pale sunlight had replaced moonshine in slanted beams across the bed, and the brightest of these glanced off her shoulder. Another beam caught the pair of earrings lying on the bedside table. The gold crowns glinted, and the delicate engraving was visible on one.

From the dressing room he heard the small snuffling sounds that Rhea made as she rooted through her covers. Usually this preceded a wild bansheelike cry which she had perfected to announce her hunger. Grey prepared himself not to start when it came.

What came instead was blessed silence. After a minute he dared believe that she had fallen back to sleep. Grey's eyes traveled over Berkeley, imagining his daughter was slumbering very much like her mother, her face turned to one side, long lashes shadowing her cheeks, one arm slightly under her body, the other flung awkwardly toward the center of the bed with her palm up and her fingers lightly curved as if around an invisible object.

Grey folded his hand over Berkeley's fingers and closed them with great care. There was a corresponding pressure in his own chest. His faint smile deepened. It required no special sighted gift to see that she held his heart.

Dear Reader,

The publication of *With All My Heart* represents the end of the Thorne trilogy. Colin, Decker, and Grey have amused and frustrated, and in some ways, enriched me. It has been through the Thorne brothers that I have been privileged to hear from new readers as well as had the opportunity to thank some old ones. It was a reader from Washington who helped me recognize that Colin's search for his brothers had a parallel in my own family. It was a subconscious influence that I only understood as I responded to her letter. It allows me to correct an oversight by honoring the memory of my brother Olaf and his courage for searching out the father (and the family) he never knew. *My Steadfast Heart* should have been dedicated to him.

September, 1999 will bring the reissue of *Crystal Passion,* originally published in 1985, the first of three books about the McClellan family. The adventures and fortunes of the McClellans closely follow the twists and turns of the American Revolution through the writing of the US Constitution. It will be followed by *Seaswept Abandon* in September, 2000.

Readers can also expect *More Than You Know* in March, 2000. At this time I'm only thinking of a brother and sister but families have a way of growing once I get started. That's all I can tell you. Anything else is, I'm afraid, *More Than I Know*.

Readers who wish to write me should send their letters with an SASE care of the publisher or e-mail me at jdobrzan@weir.net. As always I look forward to hearing from you.

Happy Reading!

Jo Goodman

ABOUT THE AUTHOR

Jo Goodman lives with her family in Colliers, West Virginia. She is the author of eighteen historical romances (all published by Zebra Books) including her beloved Dennehy sisters series: *Wild Sweet Ecstasy* (Mary Michael's story), *Rogue's Mistress* (Rennie's story), *Forever in My Heart* (Maggie's story), *Always in My Dreams* (Skye's story) and *Only in My Arms* (Mary's story), as well as her Thorne Brothers trilogy: *My Steadfast Heart* (Colin's story), *My Reckless Heart* (Decker's story) and *With All My Heart* (Grey's story). In September, 1999, Zebra books will be repackaging and reissuing *Crystal Passion*, Jo's second historical romance (originally published in 1985), which is the first book in her three-book McClellan family series. Jo is currently working on her newest Zebra historical romance, which will be published in March, 2000. Jo loves hearing from readers, and you may write to her c/o Zebra Books. Please include a self-addressed stamped envelope if you wish a response. Or you can contact her via e-mail at jdobrzan@weir.net